TALES OF THE LAST FRONTIER

FIVE TRAILS WEST, BOOK 4

TALES OF THE LAST FRONTIER

ONE FAMILY'S WESTERN ODYSSEY

JAMES D. CROWNOVER

FIVE STAR

A part of Gale, Cengage Learning

GALE
CENGAGE Learning·

Farmington Hills, Mich • San Francisco • New York • Waterville, Maine
Meriden, Conn • Mason, Ohio • Chicago

GALE
CENGAGE Learning·

LIBRARY OF CONGRESS CATALOGING-IN-PUBLICATION DATA

Names: Crownover, James D., author.
Title: Tales of the last frontier : one family's western odyssey / James D. Crownover.
Description: First edition. | Waterville, Maine : Five Star, a part of Gale, Cengage Learning, 2017. | Series: Five trails west ; book 4
Identifiers: LCCN 2016057784 (print) | LCCN 2017004790 (ebook) | ISBN 9781432834166 (hardcover) | ISBN 1432834169 (hardcover) | ISBN 9781432836986 (ebook) | ISBN 1432836986 (ebook) | ISBN 9781432834111 (ebook) | ISBN 1432834118 (ebook)
Subjects: LCSH: Families—Fiction. | Frontier and pioneer life—Fiction. | BISAC: FICTION / Historical. | FICTION / Westerns. | GSAFD: Western fiction. | Historical fiction.
Classification: LCC PS3603.R765 T35 2017 (print) | LCC PS3603.R765 (ebook) | DDC 813/.6—dc23
LC record available at https://lccn.loc.gov/2016057784

First Edition. First Printing: May 2017
Find us on Facebook– https://www.facebook.com/FiveStarCengage
Visit our website– http://www.gale.cengage.com/fivestar/
Contact Five Star™ Publishing at FiveStar@cengage.com

Printed in the United States of America
1 2 3 4 5 6 7 21 20 19 18 17

To Megan, who can keep a secret
And to JD, who likes the West

PROLOGUE

I have been sitting here laughing at myself because looking over the contents of this volume, I realized that this is just the place where I thought we were beginning so many months ago when I sat down and began writing the story of Zenas Meeker's life. His little joke back then looms large now.

Not that I would have it any other way. After all, we, you and I, would have never heard about the river pirates or the events of the earthquake or the Fallen Ash Trail. Flee's Settlement and the Cherokee and Osage villages would be buried still. *The Battle of Half Moon Mountain,* Cherokee ponies, the California Road, and the Cherokee Trail would not be stored in our memory where we can bring them up and think about those events of not-so-long-ago.

We got a taste of things to come in the stories of Stuttering Stan, Asa Willis's meeting with the washerwomen, and Silver Buttons in *Picketwire Vaquero.*

Comes now *Tales of the Last Frontier* with its cattle drives, Black Cattle who behave so differently from the Longhorn, the Red River War, the Gunman. They all have their Possibil-ities.

As they have been since time began, the old-timers are passing away until one day we will be so viewed. I have been very privileged to have shaken the hands and listened to some of these who lived through those early times, and I hope I have done them justice by putting their stories down in print.

Zenas Leonard Meeker was three-quarters Indian. Yet he

embraced the civilization of the white man and, taking with him the best of the red man's world, he succeeded in the white man's world, as have many a red man. In one or two generations they had stepped from essentially Stone Age civilization to the verge of the twentieth century. No longer did they have to rely on the whims of nature for their well-being. No longer was there the Starving Time when the provisions of the winter ran out in the spring. By raising and carefully storing their bounty *and living in a society that respected the individual's property,* they could get by.

Looking at the white man of that time, it might not have been so great a leap from one civilization to the other as we sometimes think. Certainly, it wasn't so great a step for the white men to live in the red man's world. Not to say that is bad nor that one world was better than the other. We are a society of mixed blood and much of the red man can be seen in us in our love for the unspoiled, the simple, the wilderness and the life that inhabits it.

But I have digressed far from our present subject. Here among all the notable things of that region and time—the Lincoln County War, the Santa Fe Ring, the Falls and Fountains and Lees and Bacas—is a man who lived his own life doing the things he loved and telling us about them. I hope you enjoy his stories.

James Daniels

Chapter 1
The Dry Run
1871

You may recall that at the end of Picketwire Vaquero *we left Zenas and Bob Green in a Tularosa saloon admiring John Jones's new leather vest with the silver buttons. We will pick up there to begin this, the last of Zenas's story:*

We stayed in town a couple of days and about midmorning of th' third day gathered our horses and headed south, picking up Lon and Van below La Luz. Manuel had gone on ahead and was camped at th' mouth of Dog Canyon.

"I swear, Señor Bob, I would not spend 'nother night heer alone. Many noises in thee night keep you awake an' I feel my hair tingle all thee time."

"It's a reg'lar 'Pache highway, I know, but th' only water for a ways. I wouldn't want t' spend nights here by myself, either."

It was quiet that night, though we kept watch.

"Usually don't have much trouble from Injuns, 'cept when they're comin' er goin' . . ." Ol' Van explained.

". . . which is all the time," Lon added.

A little south of Dog Canyon we turned up a draw and climbed over a divide into th' Sacramento Valley. It sure was, and still is, a pretty place. Ranch headquarters was a nice place, fixed up and neat to a woman's taste. Bob introduced me to John Dearing, th' owner and his wife, Mrs. Virginia Dearing. They were very nice and made me welcome. I never heard either of them referred to by their first names, it was always Mr. Dearing and Mrs. Dearing. She even called her husband "Mister."

We might call Mr. Dearing "Boss" or "Old Man" but never in his or Mrs. Dearing's presence.

The morning after we arrived, Mr. Dearing took breakfast with us. After he left, Bob paid off th' boys an' said they would be hiring in th' spring for roundup and summer work. Bob and Manuel were th' only ones kept on year 'round.

Soon th' boys were packed up an' ready t' go, most o' their baggage fitting in their bedrolls. Lon, Van, and Jones headed back over th' trail we had come in on an' Tom hollered, "Tell th' girls at La Luz howdy fer us!" He had invited me t' join him in his trapper cabin and I accepted, knowin' if it wasn't to my satisfaction, I could move on. He rummaged some time in th' barn an' when he came out he led a horse packed with traps, plews, gear, and enough canned goods t' last an army a month.

"Ready at last, Zee," and we were off.

I had thought we would go further up into th' mountains but to my surprise we took that back trail too. On th' divide, we turned north, past Sacramento Peak, then dropped down into th' Tularosa Basin watershed. Tom explained that animals moved down with th' snows and the foothills were full of game all winter. He had a little half dugout cabin by a branch that supplied him water and ran traps and hunted deer and elk up and down those mountain draws. It snowed off and on. Once in February we were snowed in a couple of days.

That inaction made me restless an' after it melted, I determined to ride down to see th' sights in the valley. Tom pointed me down th' right draw an' said he would meet me at La Luz come spring. I explored up and down th' basin, keeping close to foothills and water. Once I rode out on th' White Sands and looked around. It was all new and interesting to me.

Toward spring, the boys started gatherin' 'round town anticipatin' the Boss sendin' for us to start spring roundup. When we run out of money, we camped down by th' creek where the horses could graze some and we could be out of the way of folks with money to spend. They was five or six of us layin' 'round wishin' we had the word to go and something to go on 'sides beans and watery coffee.

"I swear," says Les looking up from patching th' patch in his boot sole, "if I don't get some meat in me 'fore long, I'm gonna bile this boot 'til it's soft enough to eat."

"If'n you do that, be sure you scrape the manure off first and boil it a lo-o-ong time," observed Tom as he thoughtfully contemplated his own perforated boot sole. "If I had a bullet, I could get us a 'lope for supper."

Now, after sellin' his furs, Tom wasn't really broke, but he did without along with th' rest of us. I'll tell you more about him an' where his money went later.

"The only 'lope you ever shot with one bullit was a cant-i-lope, and it wasn't too far away, then," came a lazy voice from under a much-worn sombrero. "How can a soul git a little rest and sleep around here with all that yammerin' 'bout boot leather and meat? Come May, you'll be wishin' you had stored up more sleep."

"Looky there, we done woke up ol' Rip Van Winkle," chuckled Les. "You can't store up sleep for the future, all you can do is catch up on what you lost playin' faro down at that Mex cantina. 'Course, you can't dream up the money you lost—an' dreamin' won't fill your belly, nuther."

We had all been eyeing a buckboard kicking up dust from the direction of town. "Looks like the Boss's rig with a passenger," observed Jones. "Maybe he's ready to go to rounding up those mossy-horns of his." He squinted a little, "That's ol' Lon riding with him, wonder where he dug him up?"

"Probly from the wood yard behind Ma Thompson's board-in' house. He's been splittin' wood for his supper an' sleepin' ahind the woodpile," Rip said as he beat the dust out of his jeans with his hat.

We all stood up and said our "howdys" as the buckboard rolled up. The Old Man must have been all of forty-five or fifty years old then, he was still lean and hard muscled, though a little gray was showing here and there in his hair. He walked with a limp from a broken leg he got when his horse found the bottom of a prairie dog hole with his hoof. Th' Old Man always said they should have shot him along with the horse, as much trouble as that bum leg cost him. Anyway, riding a horse pained him some, so he mostly rode the buckboard. Lon hopped down, took his roll from the back and threw it under an unoccupied mesquite.

"Looks like you boys got a pretty good camp goin' here," the Boss observed. "I'd light and set a spell, but I'm under orders to hurry back to town and get the wife home 'fore dark. She's stockin' up before we start the roundup—said something about a big bait of bear sign for you the first day."

There was grins all around at that. Not a one of us but wouldn't ride fifty miles for a good bait of bear sign, and the boys said Old Man's wife was one of the best cooks around.

"When you anticipate needin' us?" queried Les. "We was all hopin' sooner than later."

"I'm sending Manuel in tomorrow to get the chuck stocked. He has Bob helpin' him fix up the chuck wagon for loading. Looks like the end of next week or the week after, depending on weather. We need a shower and some warm to green up the grass, then we would be in shape to go." He picked up the reins to go, "By the way, I saw a yearling on the way in with a gimped leg. Looked like he got in a quarrel with something and come out second. Anyway, he wa'nt branded and wouldn't do for the roundup. Think one of you boys could go by and put him out of his misery? Skin him out so's we can show that we didn't know whose he was. I don't think he was mine."

He could have saved that calf for himself, but I guess he knew we was down to boot soles and beans for chuck. We all nodded, trying not to show too much enthusiasm.

"He was just where Dog Canyon comes out on the flat—don't think he could get far on three legs. I would appreciate it if you could do that."

He clucked to the horse and wheeled around toward town. He hadn't gone far enough to raise a dust before two horses was caught up and saddled and Tom and Jones was on their way to Dog Canyon.

"Stoke up the fire, boys, we'll be back in no time," called Tom as they rode off.

"You better be," I called back, "and with a *whole* calf too!"

Leapin' Lon just grinned and rubbed his full belly. I kicked him in the boot leg, ducked his swing, and headed for the trees to gather wood. Les was already there getting an armload and Rip was down by the water scrubbin' out a big pot with sand. When we got back to the fire with the wood, Rip had the pot full of water and on to boil. We just piled up the wood and sat and watched for the water to boil and wait on supper.

Lon filled us in on the latest news from town. It had been a few days since anyone had been in, there being no need to go without any cash.

"Gene Little came through from the Jornada yesterday, said he heard from a prospector that they had hit placer gold in the gulch behind Big Rock. He didn't put much store in it, said them prospectors was always hittin' gold somewheres unlikely. He said the water was gettin' scarce across the basin with no rain and scarce snow on the mountains."

"Hope this ain't a dry one like last year," said Les. "I ate so much alkali dust my blood turned pale."

It seemed like a long time before we saw them coming, but I guess it wasn't that long. Les made a big deal about seeing that the calf was all there. There wasn't much fat on that carcass and from the looks of the hide, that leg had been mangled awhile. Rip took the liver and sliced it up and fried it in the skillet with what fat he could carve off. The meat looked to be tough, but it was still meat and that was enough for us. I dug up some wild onions down by the river and threw them in with the liver. It wouldn't be like homemade, but it would have to do.

Everyone carved off a good-sized steak and soon had it sizzling over the fire. We was so hungry we would chew the done off to the red meat and cook some more until it was all gone.

Leapin' Lon just laughed at us and cooked his whole steak to a turn before he plopped it in his plate and dug in.

"You boys act like you haven't et or seen meat since Noah's flood!"

"We ain't been sleepin' in a woodpile and cozyin' up to Ma Thompson and her table board, either," shot Jones. "When we git on the range, I want you to show us how to chop wood for Cookie's fire. I bet you could really make the chips fly—got your own axe in the roll, I see, an' that handle don't look too worn t' me."

"Reckon he got a cord a day, Jones?" asked Tom between bites.

"He'd have to get two cord a day just to pay for his board, judging from the way he's fatted out, but I doubt he made over half a cord. He must have done more cozyin' than choppin' to stay around as long as he did," rejoined Jones.

"Don't cast no 'spersions on Ma Thompson," Lon said without smiling. "She's a good woman and we're all better off for her being around here." They all nodded and agreed, Jones included. It was all said in jest to Lon and not to hurt Ma. Besides, she was old enough to be Lon's mom—or any of the rest of us.

"Say, ol' Lon says they struck gold behind Big Rock," I said.

"I didn't exactly say *that,* what I *said* was that Gene Little passed through and said a *prospector* said they hit placer. He didn't give it too much weight, though, and I agree with him."

That tough yearling steak wouldn't have tasted half so good if I hadn't been half starved. In good times on the range, Cookie would have thrown it to the wolves and cussed us for bringin' it in, but when you have gone as long as some of us had without a good meal, it was fit for a king—and us too. We downed the liver and onions, such as they were, then sat around feeling a little green from all the bounty we were not used to.

"I swear, my stomach must have shrunk to th' size of a thimble, th' way I feel now," Tom allowed.

"I felt my stomach pull away from my backbone when I stood up," replied Rip. "If I had gone another day without good food, I reckon it would have growed there. We're going to have to be careful with this meat if it will last us one or two more weeks."

"Maybe th' Old Man will find us another cripple 'fore then," Tom said. He was stretched out on his roll feeling full and not lookin' too comfortable.

"Don't count on it!" Les said, "He wouldn't have told us about this one if it had his brand on its hide."

"You only half believe that," Ol' Van said, "the Boss is pretty good to us. When things got tough, he stuck with us as much as we would stick with him in the same situation."

"That carcass won't last us a week, even if we biled the bones and gnawed on 'em," observed Lon. He was in the same shape as us, since he had split enough wood to last Ma Thompson the whole summer.

"It might last long enough for us to go 'round to th' Jornada and pick up some of that gold out of Big Rock Canyon," Tom mused.

"I doubt there's any there," said Lon and Rip almost in unison.

"Yeah, but it would be fun just to see the pilgrims that'll flock to it, and there's always something goin' on around those boom camps," Jones said.

"Prob'ly be some wimmin jinin' in the rush. We haven't seen many of that species 'round here," Van drawled.

"You bet not 'round here, no Soiled Doves could live long on cow country money, and it's a good thing too, Mr. Tight Britches, you might come home with more than you bargained for from them."

Rip always shied away from the loose women we occasionally met.

Les sat up on his roll and said, "It would be fun to see the doin's over there and we're just rustin' away laying around here. Who knows, we might find somethin' t' tide us over 'til the Old Man is ready for us."

"I wouldn't mind taking a ride that way, but I wouldn't plan on pickin' up any gold," said Lon.

"What you gone ride, seein' as you done et your horses and don't have wheels on your feet?" asked Jones.

"I ain't et my hosses, I left them in the horse lot at the ranch. I shore ain't goin' t' start out walkin' the Sands, though. Maybe I could borry Rip's mule for th' trip."

"You'd be walkin' the Sands and Pet would be trotting back to camp before half a day passed!" Rip vowed. "That ol' fool don't hardly allow me to get on her back, much less some stranger fattened up like you; but you can borry Buck if you ride easy and don't wear him out. I think I'll stay here and watch camp and rest up some."

"I wouldn't want to borrow your horse for a lark, Rip, 'sides, it ain't been decided if we will go or not. What about it, boys, is it a go?"

"I'm for it if you are and we don't stay too long—shore would hate t' miss the startin' gun for the roundup and that tub o' bear sign Mrs. Boss is cookin' up for me," remarked Jones.

The rest of us allowed we would tag along if we weren't gone past time.

"That still leaves Lon afoot, unless we catch a cayuse loose sommers," said Les. "Then I would have to spend time gentilin' him down so's Lon could ride him."

"I break my own horses, you broke-down bronc buster," growled Lon. "I'll just stay here and keep camp and listen for the Ol' Man t' call."

"An' make so much talk an' fuss a feller wouldn't git a speck of rest? No, sir, mister. I'll call up ol' Buck and saddle him myself just to get rid o' you. 'Course, if you don't care for Buck, you can try to fork that mule."

It was a generous thing Rip did in offering Lon his favorite horse and Lon wasn't about t' insult Rip *or* Buck by choosing t' ride the mule. Rip had him cornered and he couldn't turn down his offer. Very few cowboys would loan out their horses like that and I doubt if any of th' rest of us would have gotten th' same offer. Lon and Rip were close buddies. None of us would have ever *asked* for the loan of another man's horse, and Lon hesitated to accept the offer—it just shows how they trusted each other and stuck with their pals.

With that settled, we all got busy preparing for th' trip. Since we were only going to be gone a few days, we would travel light and leave bedrolls in camp with Rip. A blanket was all we would need for sleeping. We filled our canteens and caught up the horses so we could get an early start in the morning. About dark, we all bedded down t' get some sleep.

It seemed like I had just closed my eyes when I heard things stirring in camp. Someone was stoking up th' fire and I smelled coffee. There was just a hint of gray behind the eastern range.

Rip was cutting steaks and acting grumpy, though it was his normal time to rise every morning.

"You boys make more noise than a covey of ducks gittin' up. If a body could sleep through that, he could sleep through a hurricane. I hope you practice bein' quiet 'fore we start night herdin' or we'll be up all night listenin' to you change shifts."

A well-done steak washed down with hot coffee served for a good breakfast. Les cut off a portion of the carcass for Rip, rolled up the rest of the meat in the skin, and looped it behind his saddle.

"You be sure to leave that skin at the livery in town. I don't want my neck stretched if someone finds me with this piece of meat and no means of provin' where it came from," hollered Rip as we rode off. "Ask Ma Thompson for a flower sack to put that meat in. She'll have a lot of them layin' 'round after fillin' up Lon like that."

There were several replies to that remark that would not do to repeat here, and we all rode off at a trot to get the kinks out of the horses. We left the hide at the livery stable where nearly everybody stopped off when they came to town. Killing th' calf on the Boss's say-so would carry a lot of weight with folks since they knew he was straight up about things. Tom talked Hank, the livery man, out of a bag of oats on the tab until payday and we headed out of town.

Now, travel in dry country was different than travel in more watered lands. There, you just struck out straight for where you were going—that was before fences, of course. In dry country, a direct path could get you in deep trouble if you was goin' far. Dependin' on the time of year an' abundance of rain, a smart traveler planned his route from water hole to water hole.

Nowadays, it's a lot easier to travel the basin, 'cause you can navigate from windmill to windmill. Of course, you want to pick the ones that are turnin' if possible, and you always steer for the ones with a house under 'em, 'specially if it's near supper. Back then, they wasn't any windmills.

On this trip, for example, Big Rock was somewhat north of west from camp, but we went south along the foot of the mountains to get around the White Sands and water at Wildy's Well before turning west across the flats. It seemed it was midmorning before the sun peeked at us over the Sacramentos and even on that early date, it got pretty warm on us by mid-afternoon when we got to Wildy's.

Wildy wasn't home, so we drawed water for the horses and refilled the canteens for the trip across the flats. While the horses rested, we filled the trough for the cows lowin' around the place.

"Wildy must have got the gold fever," opined Jones. "Judgin' from these thirsty cows, he's been gone awhile."

We had to fill the trough twice for them, then filled it again for those that would wander in after dark. From there, we headed a little south of west for the Jarilla Mountains. There wasn't any water there, but we could afford a dry camp at Monte Carlo Gap and get a good jump on th' long dry haul across the Tularosa Basin. We were feelin' good and with high spirits and joshin', th' afternoon passed quickly.

Twenty miles later and a half hour after sunset found us a couple of miles from th' gap. We tethered our horses on some bunch grass and cooked a little meat for supper. After it was full dark, we broke camp and moved off th' trail a mile or so to a draw where we slept.

The Apaches were active and we didn't care t' meet up with them in our present unammoed state. They was also some "White Injuns" about that you wouldn't want wanderin' into camp in th' night. Les held back some and watched th' back trail awhile to make sure we were not followed.

"I didn't see nothin' movin' afore I came in, but I thought I saw a little light on the top of the hill south of the gap once," he reported when he came in. "Might not have been, though,"

There wasn't any light in the east when we caught up and

saddled. We wanted a good jump on the day for th' long dry trip ahead. There was just a hint of gray in the east when we got t' th' top of the gap. Stopping t' give th' horses a blow after the climb, we looked over th' valley ahead. As dry and forbidding as it is, th' high desert holds a beauty that isn't found anywhere else. The dark purple of night still hung over th' flats, but even at this early hour, th' Organ Mountains across th' valley cast back a faint glow, looking much like hills of soft yellow.

"There's th' only gold we're likely to see on this trip," said Tom.

"Almost worth the trip to see that," Leapin' Lon observed.

He enjoyed the desert scenery more than all the rest of us. Many times he an' I'd be out working and he would stop atop some rise and seem to just drink in the air and the sights and the stillness of this land. It got so that I would enjoy it near as much as him. We used to ride together most of a day without so much as a word passin' b'tween us, just th' whisper of hooves in the sand and an occasional call of a hawk circling above to break the silence. Not that either one of us couldn't carry our end of any conversation, but there are times when talkin' breaks some spell nature casts up here and you have to listen to th' quiet. High country can be mighty intoxicatin'.

We could see Antelope Hill and Mineral Hill almost due west of us. They seemed close enough to spit on, but it's near twenty-five miles of dry trail to get there. Behind them rises San Augustine Peak and the pass of the same name through the Organ Mountains. Our next water was just over that pass near what is now the town of Organ. From there we would turn north along the western foot of the San Andres Mountains toward Big Rock Canyon.

Chapter 2
Organ Tank

We took it slow across the flats to save the horses and it was an all-day trip to th' pass. Easing down th' west side, our horses smelled water at Organ Tank. After over twenty-four hours without water, they picked up their pace anticipating a long drink. Buck lowered his head to drink at th' water's edge, then snorted and shied away. All other horses did th' same. In th' gloom, we could make out a carcass laying out in th' tank. It had tainted th' water so much those horses wouldn't drink.

Lon rode out into th' water a ways and threw a loop over a horn sticking up. Van also got a loop around that horn and together, they pulled a big steer up on th' bank and away from th' tank. Les walked over to shake their ropes loose for th' boys, lettin' out a long string of cussin' like you never heard.

"Who is the sorry low-down rotten skunk that would shoot a cow out in the middle of the only water in the country?" he bellered.

"Well, do you think steers grow feathers around here, or is them arrers stickin' out his side?" drawled Jones.

I had learned that the madder Jones got, the slower his speech got and if he ever stopped talking, you better duck for cover, 'cause things're goin' to git hot fast.

"Them sorry low-down rotten skunks are 'Paches, Jones, and I'll bet they are still sniggerin' 'bout it," growled Tom.

"This puts us in a fine fix," said Lon, "I guess the next nearest water would be back at Aguirre Springs. Dripping Springs ain't likely to have much after this dry spell."

"But that means we would have to backtrack over that pass again and then turn south," mused Tom. "What do you think th' chances are that there would be water in Bear Creek?"

"I don't know, but I shore don't envy draggin' these horses back up that pass. Chances are that those 'Paches either tainted the springs or are sittin' there waitin' for some thirsty pilgrims to show up unawares. My hair gets prickly jist thinking' 'bout it."

"We'd best stay off the beaten path if we want to avoid dodgin' arrers," said Jones. He was regainin' his temper. "I think I would go for Bear Creek and take my chances on hittin' water. We'll prob'ly have to dig fer it."

"If we don't hit water there, I guess we could hunt up the creek and head down Bear Canyon to San Juan Spring," put in Les. "If we don't hit nothin' there, it's just a skip to San Nicolas Spring. Barrin' that, there's always some moisture 'tween Lake Lucero and the mountains."

"That gyp water at the lake would kill us all. Those springs south of the lake would be our best bet—if Injuns hadn't got there first," Les said. "I for two would vote for our chances at Bear Creek."

No one asked for my opinion, knowing I didn't know this country like they did. I was at their mercy, but I had a lot of faith those boys would come to th' right conclusions, given an opportunity. We were in a spot where we needed all th' knowledge and experience we could muster—and a lot of luck! I tried to steer my pony back to th' water to get him to drink, but it was no use. Horses won't drink where they smell blood and death. By th' time I got back to th' crowd, they had decided that our best of bad options was to try Bear Creek. So we moved off from Organ Tank a ways north and made dry camp for a second night.

Without much water in our canteens, no one was hungry, so we just rolled up in our blankets and tried to sleep. 'Way in the night, I woke up thinkin' I heard rain, but it was just th' breeze through dry leaves. Those horses were restless all night, not grazing much for lack of water. I lay there a long time looking at stars and wonderin' if I would be seein' them tomorrow night or if my hide would be dryin' from the desert sun. More likely, some coyote would be gettin' a good meal. Jones was restless, too. I could hear him mutterin' and cursin' Indians and their like.

Finally, I sat up and looked around at th' others. "Not much use layin' around here drying up, with those horses restless, we might as well git along with starlight."

Jones and Lon were folding their blankets before I finished talkin' an' th' rest were not far behind. We saddled up, and started out, leadin' horses slowly. Les complained about walking in his boots and I was glad I still had my brogans and not those high heels. Jones pulled his moccasins out of his bag and tied his boots across the saddle.

The stars were so bright you could see your shadow, but you couldn't see very far ahead. Fortunately, th' land was fairly flat with only an occasional wash to navigate. We did pretty good until stars began to fade just before dawn and it got too dark to see. Stopping by a dried-up marshy place, we let our horses graze a little. They must have gotten a little moisture off th' grass, 'cause they did eat some.

No one talked much. I sat and laid my head on my knees and dozed. Pretty soon, th' sky lightened and we could see enough to travel. This time we mounted and rode, though our pace wasn't much faster than walkin'. The horses was gettin' weak, bein' without water more than thirty-six hours. No one said a word now. It was work enough to keep movin' and save moisture. I slipped a smooth pebble in my mouth to call up any moisture I could.

When we stopped after negotiating a wash, I used th' last of my water to wash out the mouth of my horse. He seemed to appreciate it, though I'm sure he would have preferred more. In a scrape like this, it's smarter to take care of your horse and suffer yourself, though most folks do just th' opposite. I always believed a horse had better instincts than I did when it came to findin' their way and gettin' to water. And most horses are faithful to their rider to death. Many's the time a horse has given his last breath to do his master's bidding.

We cut up th' gap between Quartzite Mountain and Bear Peak. I slipped off my horse when we started up th' rise and walked the rest of th' way. When we came in sight of Bear Creek wash, we spread out, each man heading for a spot along the creek so's we could search quicker.

Bearing to the right, I aimed for th' wash close to where it came out of the hills, thinking it would be more likely to have water in it upstream from the flats. It was midmorning and th' sun was already warming things up. The brush along th' creek didn't look very green and those horses didn't sense any moisture.

Dropping down in th' bed of the wash, I scratched around for any sign of moisture. It was pretty dry on top, but maybe if I dug a little, I might run into water. With a stout mesquite stick, I dug, pulling out rocks and gravel. I went down more than two feet and only hit a little moist sand. Grabbing a big rock, I pounded my stick down until it struck something solid and wouldn't go any further. If that was bedrock, there would be th' best chances for water. That stick went in about a foot, so I began to dig again. Sure enough, I had hit a sheet of solid rock, but there was little moisture there and no water flowed into th' hole.

Chapter 3
Injuns!

Just that little bit of work wore me out and I sat back and stared at th' bottom hopin' just a little water would seep in from somewhere. I don't know how long I had been sittin' there when I looked up and there were the rest of th' boys lookin' down at me from th' bank.

"Better crawl out of that hole, Daylight, starin' at it won't git you any water," rasped Van. "We're headin' over the pass to San Juan Spring."

My horse was on th' opposite side of the creek from them, and it seemed like it took me forever to climb out of that hole and up th' bank. I felt as weak as a kitten. Grabbin' at a root at th' top of the bank, my hand ran across a smooth-feelin' rock and I stuck it in my pocket without looking at it, thinking I would suck on it later.

As I was tightening th' cinch, I glimpsed a movement in th' brush and looked straight into th' eyes of a painted Indian! He ducked and turned back into th' brush. He was wearing a feather blanket across his shoulders as he disappeared. I stepped back a couple of steps and tumbled down th' bank into that wash. Usually when something like that happened, you could hear them hootin' a mile, but all th' boys could get out was a sort of raspy cough.

"You ok, kid, what skeered you?" rasped Tom.

"Injuns!" I whispered.

"Where?"

"In th' brush beyond my horse."

I could hardly talk. I don't know whether it was from lack of water or breath from fallin' or just plain fright.

"You're seein' things," Les whispered.

"No, I ain't," I tried to yell, but it just came out like a growl. "His face was smeared with black paint and he was wearin a feather blanket!"

Jones handed his reins to Lon and slid down th' far bank. "Better have a look, he may be right."

He crawled up th' bank with me beside him and I showed him where I saw that face. Jones crept over to th' spot, looking all around as he went. He stepped into th' brush and picked something off a thorny bush. Looking at th' ground, he pointed to a spot where a foot had spun around. A bare footprint showed where he took his first step. Then he was on a rock shelf and we could not see any more sign. Jones squatted on his haunches and stared across th' hillside for a long time. He opened his hand and there was a single white feather in his palm. After several minutes, he grunted and stood up headin' for th' creek.

"He saw someone alright, but that Injun was barefoot and I never knowed of them makin' a feather blanket with white feathers in it, did you?"

They all shook their heads and signaled to move on up th' pass. Jones walked with me and we kept our eyes out for anything that might be movin' around. Fortunately, th' west side of Bear Canyon pass is not very steep and we had been almost to th' top when we got to th' creek. Not far up the hill, th' boys found a crossing and came over to our side. We went close single file, mostly leading our horses. They were about played out. Turning north at th' bottom of th' east canyon, we headed across th' flats for San Juan Spring, about two miles away.

It seemed like it was hotter on th' east side of those

mountains, and I don't see how it could have been any drier anywhere in th' world. I had a sinkin' feelin' as we approached San Juan Spring. Our horses didn't show that they sensed water. Sure 'nough, that spring was just a muddy hole and not a drop of water.

"Rest up and we'll try San Nicolas Spring," Lon whispered.

"Probably dry too," Les growled through cracked lips. "I could drink gyp water now."

We squatted in th' shade of our horses. They just hung their heads and stood there. Things looked awful grim. I didn't know if that gyp water would kill horses, but I decided I would rather take my chances on it than to die by dryin' up. After a few minutes, Tom stood up and started toward th' next spring. No one else stirred. In a few minutes, he stumbled back.

"Someone's comin' from the lake!" he croaked.

We could see a horse 'way out on the flats and as we watched, we could see that someone was leadin' him and he was headin' our way. Tom climbed up th' slope a ways and waved his shirt so th' traveler could see us. We watched his progress, but there wasn't much hope he could help us without he was carryin' a bunch of water.

"Probly some old prospector headin' for his riches," Jones reckoned. "Won't do us much good."

The glare off them White Sands was so bright we couldn't see much more than a shadow movin' across the flats. He came at a slow steady gait—it seemed his horse was pretty heavily loaded.

As he neared, Les, squinting, said, "That's a mule and he looks awful familiar." After a few minutes, he said, "I think that mule's ol' Pet!"

Jones stood up and stared at th' figures trudging toward us. "That's ol' Pet or her twin. If it is, that's Rip or he won't be far behind, he'd never let that mule get away without him!"

Our curiosity roused, we watched th' figures approach. About a quarter mile north of us, they stopped and Rip tied his mule to th' brush and began unloadin' her. It looked like he had four or five small kegs of something heavy and he carefully set them down under th' brush. Then he reached for a large canteen, slung it over his shoulder, and headed our way. Lon rasped. "Shore hope that canteen is full."

He stood up and started toward him. Rip motioned him to stay where he was and Lon stopped and stood there watchin'.

"Howdy, boys!" Rip called in th' first clear voice we had heard in a couple of days. "Thought you might be a little lost out here by yoreselves and shore 'nough here you are a hundred miles off track, what you doin' over here?"

Les didn't speak, but drew his pistol and dry clicked it at Rip a couple of times.

"Anybody thirsty?" Rip asked.

Les pulled his trigger again. It made a loud click in that still air.

"Shore glad you ain't got any ammo, Les, here take a sip of this."

Rip handed him a cup of the sweetest water I have ever tasted. Les took a small sip and washed it around in his mouth a minute, then drank the cup dry. Taking th' cup back, Rip poured another cup and handed it to Lon, who had followed him back to the crowd.

We each got a cup in turn, Rip prattling away with wise cracks about our condition and the trouble we had caused him, then he corked th' canteen.

"That'll do you for a few minutes, don't want you to waste this stuff by drinkin' too much and pukin' it all over the place. I didn't come out here to water you boys, I was more worried 'bout Buck and the rest of th' horses. Looks like you failed to water them properly. Well, *I* brung them a drink over there and you jist set yourselves down and I will take one at a time and water 'em from those kegs Pet brung. Don't want to start a stampede."

He picked up th' reins of Les's horse and started for th' mule. "Don't want to antagonize Les any more'n necessary, no tellin' what he'll do if he ever gits a bullit or his strength back." He handed th' canteen to me. "When I finish waterin' this horse and start back, you can pass out another cup of water, Daylight. Don't cheat time on me and watch these boys don't grab too much of that stuff."

He led th' horse to where th' mule was tied. Shakin' out a leather bucket from his pack, he poured a couple of quarts into it. You should have seen that horse perk up when he saw water. He drank every drop and licked th' bottom of th' bucket. Rip had a little trouble gettin' him to leave. As he left the mule, I poured Les a cup of water. He drank it down, savorin' th' last swallow and grabbed th' reins of th' nearest horse and struck out to meet Rip. They exchanged horses and th' waterin' process started over.

"We've had enough water for a while, Daylight," said Lon. His voice was clearer. "Let's git these varmints took care of and we'll see to ourselves later."

We helped Rip with th' waterin' and after they had digested that first sip of water, they all got a bucketful. You should have seen them perk up when someone started them toward that water. Only a few steps was necessary and they went on their own. The hard part was holdin' back other horses so's one could drink. After that second drink, we staked them out in th' brush to rest up and sat down to help ourselves to another cup.

"I swear, I'm gonna have to teach you boys how to take care of animals," railed Rip in spite of th' mean looks he was gittin'. "When you go out in the basin or Jornada, you have to see that they git proper waterin'. I thought you knew that!"

Jones threw a rock at him. "How'd you git 'way out here, you old broke-down nag, I thought you was stockin' up on sleep?"

"I was 'til a squad of Buffalo Soldiers come to the creek lookin' for water. They had chased a bunch of renegade Mescaleros across the flats, said those skunks had fouled the Organ Tank an' water was mighty scarce ever'where. They saw your trail headin' north. I figgered right then you was gittin' in a scrape and loaded ole Pet with a bunch of kegs I borryed from the saloon. We walked across south of the Sands overnight. I figgered to cut your trail on the other side of Bear Canyon pass. Lucky you got this far, we're that much closer to camp and I can recover some of my sleep I'm losin' nurse-maidin' you scalawags."

"Since you're here, you can go on with us up to Big Rock," I offered.

"No use goin', no one's there. It was all a hoax some feller cooked up to sell some worthless claims he had. The others got wind of it and tarred and feathered the bugger and rode him out of camp on a rail."

It took us a minute to soak that in and Rip looked awful surprised when we all roared with laughter, 'til I told him about th' creature I had seen.

"That musta been him," he said, "they headed him south alright. Guess he'll enjoy drinkin' tainted water at Organ. It ain't far on to Las Cruses if you've had a drink and that feather blanket ought to keep him warm nights. Another minute or two and he may have run off with your horse, Zee. Shore would have been the end of him to go back to the tank."

"Well, Mr. Smarty, you got us water, but there ain't enough to git us back 'cross the Sands, what you propose us to do, sprout wings?" asked Ol' Van.

"Them horses'll come nearer sproutin' wings than you," he retorted, "Bob come by when I was catchin' up that ole mule and said Mrs. Dearing wanted us to come in next Sunday for dinner and bear sign. The Ole Man wants to start gittin' ready for roundup Monday. Thinks we will hit the range sometime Wednesday, if you boys ain't too slow. Anyways, when Bob heard the predicament you had gotten yourselves into, he was some put out. He guessed he would have to send word back to the ranch and come rescue you. He went to load the wagon in town with provisions and meet us at the south end of the Sands. I'm countin' on him bein' there by some time today."

That sounded good to us, but our horses were still too fagged to travel. We spent th' afternoon laying around and waterinn' horses occasionally—and ourselves too. After Ol' Sol had dipped down below th' mountains, we lit a fire and cooked th' last of the beef. It shore tasted good after our fast and that coffee we washed it down with was better. 'Way out on th' basin southwest of Point of Sands, we saw a little flicker of light. It must have been Bob with th' wagon. I think I slept without moving all night. Some time toward morning I heard someone watering those horses with th' last barrel. There was just a hint of gray over th' San Andres when we rolled out.

"Saddle up, boys," sang out Rip, "you can gnaw the last of that steer while we ride, it's a long way to that wagon."

We saddled horses and headed out, Rip leading th' way with Pet close behind carrying empty barrels. Our horses were much better, but they would need a good rest when we got back to be up to full speed. Th' chill air warmed quickly when that sun peeked over th' mountains and everyone seemed to regain their good spirits. There was a lot of joshin' and Rip took a good portion of it. He knew we all were grateful for his rescuing us, though it wasn't spoken outright. About midmorning, Lon made Rip mount Buck and he led Pet 'til near noon when Pet nipped his elbow, needin' a rest. We pulled up under a cut bank to git as much shade as possible, and let th' horses rest.

"Fine tribe this is to let a mule tell us when to stop and when to travel," groused Tom.

"So long's it's *that* mule, I won't mind," I said.

"That mule's been bossin' me a long time," said Rip, "and I don't think she's been wrong yet, but it wouldn't do to let her know that—might go to her head."

"That head's big enough a'ready," observed Les. "Next thing you know, she'll be tryin' to run the ranch."

Even though th' sun was still a ways south, that cut bank didn't give much shade at midday. I leaned back against th' bank and looked up at that sky. The deep blue of a high country sky has always attracted me. I don't know of a bluer sky anywhere else, and I've always gotten a lift just bein' under it. A good horse and a blanket to lay on are all you need with that sky for a roof.

We were restless and it wasn't long before we were readyin' to go on. I tightened th' girt, but walked a ways to stretch my legs. It would be good to get to Bob's wagon where water was more plentiful. Maybe he would have some grub, too. It was about twenty-five miles from San Juan Spring to west of Point of Sands where we estimated Bob had set up camp. Likely, we would make it by late afternoon, and we did.

Bob had made a shade from th' wagon sheet and was restin' under it. His hobbled stock had their heads stuck under its shade and he was keepin' them from creepin' all the way into the shelter and crowdin' him out. When we neared, he walked out to greet us.

"Howdy, boys, how'er yuh makin' it?" he called.

"We're doin' as fine as we can with this yahoo you sent to harass us," Les called back.

Bob grinned, "Well, if it had been up to me, you would still be out there scratchin' for water and me an' Rip would be wonderin' how we was goin' to round up all those cattle on our own. 'Course, the pay would have been good if we could have made it, not havin' to divide it up with you mavericks and all. Light down and rest a spell. Manuel rode out jist to dance on your graves and he's been grouchy ever since we saw your fire on the hillside last night. May be if he's gotten over his disappointment a bit, he'll cook us some supper."

The first thing we did was unsaddle and water our horses, then we turned them out to roll and shake off dust while we got a long drink ourselves. Manuel was all grins and nods when we came in. He seemed as glad to see us as we were to see him. He had been the ranch cook since the Boss had first settled in this country, came with the ranch, he always said. When the ranch got enough cattle to need a big roundup, Manuel was roped into the cooking chore. The boys say he wasn't too good at first, but by the time I came along, the chow was pretty good. He sure could make a decent dried fruit pie.

"Meester John, he plenty worried you boys lost, sent me down here to help Meester Bob find you. I have supper-r soon, you seet down and rest some. Wash pan is on thee side."

It was quite a luxury to have enough water to wash in and we wasted no time in gettin' head, arms, and hands free of alkali dust. We hobbled th' horses, then sat around and talked, waiting on supper.

After a while, Manuel sang out, "Come and geet eet," and we all grabbed our plates and headed for supper. This wasn't the chuck wagon, but Manuel had made th' tailgate as much like one as possible. Imagine our surprise when he opened a Dutch oven and pulled out hot biscuits! There was biscuits and molasses and fried chicken and scaldin' hot coffee.

"Mees Ma Thompson geeve me a start of sourdough and thee 'lasses. I no have beef, so we buy cheekens from Ismael Orteez. Won't not hurt you some to eat it," Manuel grinned. No one disagreed with that!

Now, meal time is serious eatin' time in a cow camp and no time for usin' your jaw for anything like talkin'. We took our plates and hunkered down in th' shade of that wagon sheet and tended to business. That sure was a memorable meal, even if it was chicken and not beef. Ever' once in a while someone would groan an "unhuh" or you would hear "mmmmhum."

By the time we were full, those biscuits were gone and there wasn't nothin' but bones left of that chicken. We was all so grateful we pitched in and helped Manuel wash up. That's th' only time in over fifty years of range life that I saw that happen. Cowmen don't get dishwater hands often and most cooks would shoot any one of them that messed with their kitchen tools. With this outfit, th' horse wrangler was expected to run the wreck pan—dish washin'—under the cook's close eye.

CHAPTER 4
A SILVER CUP AND APPLE PIE

I woke th' next morning to th' aroma of coffee boilin' and stamping of horses eager to get th' day going. After breakfast we harnessed Manuel's mules to th' wagon and saddled up for our ride to th' ranch. Rip threw those barrels into th' back of th' wagon and pulled a saddle out to put on Pet. While he was seein' to some chore, Lon sneaked over to mount Pet so Rip could ride Buck. When he started checkin' th' rigging, Pet looked around with a rolling eye, whirled, and nipped Lon on th' rear.

"*Yow,* you onery sack of bones, it wouldn't hurt you at all to let me ride you and let Rip mount a real critter for a while," yelled Leapin'. "If I had a pole, I'd git your attention, shore!"

It was th' funniest thing watching Lon rubbing his rear and blessing out that mule. She had turned to face him head-on and watched him with a baleful eye. It was plain that Lon wasn't ridin' her. We roared with laughter. Rip took Pet's reins and she nodded her head at Lon as if to say, "That'll teach you to mess with me!"

Manuel headed th' wagon due east, aiming just north of Twin Buttes, so as to get to solid footing as soon as possible. Even as lightly loaded as that wagon was, it was hard pullin' through that sand. We trailed along beside and behind th' wagon, taking it easy. Before midmorning, we hit th' La Luz to Las Cruces trail and followed it northeast. Travel wasn't much easier and we soon came to Luna's place. He had built a jacal

35

beside th' trail and there were a half-dozen kids playin' around th' door. A winch was erected over a well he was digging in th' yard.

"Buenos dios, amigos," Luna called from th' lip of th' well. He looked down into th' well and called something in Spanish. Shortly th' head of a teenager appeared and he climbed out of th' hole, grinnin' and wiping dirt off his raggedy clothes. "We deeg well for r-r-ranch and travelers on r-r-road." Luna rolled his r's in the Spanish fashion. "All r-r-ready, the hole is damp, no, Juan?" he looked at the boy questioningly. "Sí," nodded Juan, grinnin' and flicking mud from his pants legs and from between his bare toes.

"If you hit good water here, it sure would be a boon for travelin' the basin," observed Bob. "Shore would make a dry trip easier."

"Sí, Señor Bob, and make Lunas r-reech!" Luna grinned. "I see you find your str-r-ray honchos!"

"Yep, Rip found them at San Juan Spring scratchin' for water. San Juan and San Nicolas are both dry."

"I theenk mebby so, with leetle snow een mountains theese winter," replied Luna, "Mebby dig wells an' have good water an' we no need spreengs so much."

"If you find water here, there sure will be a lot of well diggin' 'cross this basin," observed Les. "Ranchin' would take in a whole lot of new territory!"

"Wee weel see, Señor Les, theen no need for you to go thirsty wheen you str-r-ray away from r-r-ranch," grinned Luna.

Les grinned a little sheepishly, "An' maybe I clean your plow next time we play a little faro in town."

Luna glanced anxiously toward the house, "I no play faro, Señor Les, too many bambinos at my door!" He raised his voice slightly in case there were other ears listening.

"Well, Luna, we need to get movin' along," Bob said, "got to get these strays to the ranch to start roundup next week. Hope you have good luck with the well. Adios." He touched his horse with spurs and we started on our way. At Point of Sands, Manuel turned east again for th' foothills.

"Durned if I'm gonna be called a stray the rest of my life," grumbled Jones as we brought up th' drag. We rode upwind of th' trail to avoid dust kicked up. "There must be some way we can scotch that wagon before it gets rollin' too fast t' stop."

I could tell he was quite serious about it. There sure would be a lot of ribbin' in store when word got around that we had to be rescued from the basin.

"We'll have to think up somethin' afore we hit town or we'll be in for it rest of the summer, 'specially if them C-B's git wind of it." He was talkin' low to me, but mostly thinking out loud.

I was used to a lot of ribbing, but I shore didn't look forward to the kind of ribbing we were in for from other outfits. After a while, he turned to me and said, "Put your thinkin' hat on, Zee, we got to figger this out b'fore we hit town." Jones rode along deep in thought and I didn't interfere with his ruminations. After a while, he raised his head and waved to Les when he happened to glance our way.

Les pulled up and Tom stopped beside him and pulled off his hat and wiped his face. "Gets hot on these flats this time of day," he said as we rode up.

"You rannies cotton to bein' called 'strays' the rest of the year?" queried Jones.

"Not me," said Tom, "but I don't see a way out of it, do you?"

"Not yet, but I'm gonna be thinkin' on it," replied Jones.

We rode along not sayin' much, thinkin' about how we could get out of this mess, when Leapin' Lon motioned for us to follow him and peeled off into th' brush. He was waiting for us just out of sight.

"You boys can go on into town and face the hooraws if you want to, but I'm gonna bypass that little meetin'," he said as we rode up. "Rip and Bob are so far ahead of the wagon they won't miss us till they get to town. Let's us hotfoot it around and meet them on the other side."

"Yeah, we can pretend we stopped by the creek to git our gear," said Les, "that should throw some of those barflies off our trail, maybe we can throw enough doubt into it so that they won't be so sure it was us that got rescued."

"Beats anything I can come up with," nodded Jones, "let's go."

We beat through th' brush to bypass town and steered toward our camp on th' creek. Just as we broke out of brush on th' south road, we ran pell-mell into a kid on a black horse flying down th' road at a gallop. All was confusion and tumult with horses and men flying every direction. I almost lost my seat and Tom's horse went crow-hoppin' back into th' brush. It took us a few seconds to regain control and settle the horses down.

"Who was that?" asked Leapin'.

"I don't know, but he was sure in a hurry to git somewhere else," observed Tom. "Lost his cargo," he said, nodding toward a flour sack layin' in th' dust. He leaned over from th' saddle and picked it up. It clanked with th' sound of silver. Tom's eyebrows raised a little at us and he untied th' string around th' top of th' sack.

"Must be twenty dollars in silver in here—say, ain't this the silver cup Ma Thompson keeps full of spoons on her table? Shore 'nough, and there's a spoon or two."

He had his head in th' sack so far, we could only see his hat. His head popped out and he reached down into th' bottom of th' sack fishing around and rattling its contents. His bony fingers came out clutching th' barrel of a pistol.

"Hey, that's my gun I hocked at the store for grub!" Jones

exclaimed. It was his spare .44 he kept in his bedroll. "I'll bet our friend there has been up to some mischief in town," he said, looking at th' fast-fading trail of dust far down th' road.

"Got too much of a jump on us to ever catch up to him with these horses," observed Lon, "guess we'd better mosey into town and return Ma's spoons and cup."

We turned up th' road toward town, forgetting about th' "Strays" song that would greet us. As we approached th' store, we could see old man Johnson standing on th' loading dock out front and waving his arms angrily and talking loudly to Rip and Bob who had just rode up and hadn't even dismounted. Ma Thompson was standing on her porch across th' street wringing her hands nervously in her apron and listening to th' one-way conversation. Manuel was just pulling up to th' store as we rode into town.

". . . was looking at that gun to buy, then grabbed a hand full of money when my back was turned and ran out and jumped on little Libby's horse I had tied at the rail." He was fairly shouting the story for the third time since we had come into hearing range. "Ma gave him a meal, which he paid for by stealing her silver cup and some money right off the table!"

Meanwhile, Tom had quietly ridden up to Ma's porch, removed his sombrero, and fished in the sack for th' cup. When he produced it, Ma's eyes lit up.

"Oh, Tom, you got my cup back!" she exclaimed. "Thank you so much! I was afraid I had seen the last of it, and it was a gift from Mr. Thompson on our wedding day!" She wiped th' corner of her eyes with her apron tail as she clutched th' cup. Tom hid his face in th' sack and came up with three or four spoons in his hand.

"Yes, ma'am, and here's all th' spoons I could find," he said, with a hint of a blush under his dark skin. "I don't know about th' money in here, guess you and Mr. Johnson will have to work out how much belongs where." He handed th' sack over to Ma.

"He got his dirty hand into my dollar tray." Ol' man Johnson had calmed down some when he saw what was going on at Ma's place.

"And not one of my boarders had a dollar to their names when they ate lunch," laughed Ma. "So if it's all right with you, Mr. Johnson, I'll keep the small change and you can have your dollars back—oh my, there's a gun in here!" Ma called, peeking into th' sack.

Mr. Johnson had jumped down and joined Ma on th' porch. "That's th' gun that thief was looking at when he bolted." Mr. Johnson tucked it into his waistband behind th' apron he had folded bib down and tied around his waist.

"I thought you were holding that for me to redeem when I got paid!" Jones almost growled.

"He was just admirin' it, John," Old man Johnson said. "I wasn't goin' to sell it to him. From now on, I'll keep it out of sight."

Mr. Johnson always referred to Jones by his first name, but he was the only one I ever heard use it. Everyone else just used the "Jones" handle.

"How'd you boys come by this, and where's the scoundrel that was holdin' it the last time I saw it?"

"He nearly ran over us on th' south road and dropped th' sack as he was running through. He was just a dot on th' horizon and disappearin' fast when we discovered what he had been up to," I explained. "Our horses are too tired to chase him."

Old man Johnson's eyes widened in remembrance. "That's right, you fellers was lost in the basin, last time I heard!"

He was grinning, but thought better than to say more at the moment. He was real pleased to get his plunder back. The teasing would come later.

"My goodness, I had plumb forgot," exclaimed Ma Thompson, "you poor boys must be half starved and dried to parchment! I've got fresh apple pies baked and good cold milk to wash it down with. You boys wash up and get to the table and I'll have a glass and slice of pie for all of you!"

She waved impatiently at our protests as she disappeared through the doorway. "Hush! And wash up and it'll be on the table before you're ready."

I was already heading for th' washstand, not thinkin' beyond that piece of pie. Th' others followed somewhat reluctantly. They didn't want any special treatment, especially at Ma's expense.

While I was waiting on th' others to get washed up, I felt that pebble in my pocket I had picked up on Bear Creek. Looking at it for th' first time, I nearly dropped it in surprise. It was a gold nugget! Most nuggets I have seen have been very rough and irregular, but this one was as smooth a nugget of gold as I ever saw, almost like it had been melted into a ball. As quickly as I could, I dropped it back in my pocket. If there were any more where that came from, I wanted to be th' one to find them. Maybe that trip across the basin to Bear Creek would pay off after all.

We filed in to Ma's dining room, dusted off, washed, hats hangin' on pegs over th' washstand. I hadn't been in a reg'lar house since last fall, and for some of those boys it had been longer than that. We were standing around kind of awkward like, not knowing what to do next when Ma bustled in from th' kitchen with a pitcher of milk.

"Well, don't be shy, boys, take a seat. Tom, you sit at the head there. Zenas, sit here by me; and Van, you and Lon and Rip on this side. Les, you and Bob and Jones take the other side of the table."

We sat in our designated places to th' unfamiliar tune of scraping chairs and boots on polished floors. There was a big slice of apple pie at each place and Ma busied pouring each of us a cup of milk. Already in th' middle of the table was that silver cup, brimming with bright spoons.

"Mr. Thompson insisted that I use that cup every day," Ma explained. "He said it would remind us of our wedding day. It's gotten banged up some, but it is a nice reminder of our times together, and I just couldn't set it on a shelf, forgotten. Now dig in, boys, if you expect to make time getting to the ranch, you will need the nourishment. I'm so glad to get the cup back. The money didn't mean near so much as that old cup."

Well, she didn't have to say "dig in" twice before Les had reached for th' spoon cup and passed it around th' table like he was a New York dude. That was th' best pie I ever ate—until I got married, that is. The crust was golden brown and flaky and apples fairly melted in your mouth. The milk really was cold for them days. Mine had a little skim of cream on top.

Now don't tell me real cowboys don't drink milk, I've seen too many of them relish it. I once watched two boys rope a fresh cow on th' range and fight until they had a bucketful. They sat right down and finished off th' whole gallon before it had time to cool. Luxuries like milk and pie and cloth-topped tables were few and far between for us in those days—and we didn't object to hearin' Ma talk on like that, either. A woman's voice got mighty rare on th' range. I might have enjoyed it more than th' others, bein' long from home. I still got homesick at times.

We ate slow, savorin' every bite. I got to thinkin' how grateful we all were for Ma's hospitality and how we all didn't have a way to show our appreciation. Then I thought of that nugget. It would be a little something besides th' "thank yous" we would hand out. I slipped it into my hand without bein' seen and when Ma got up to pour more milk, I dropped it into her spoon cup and shook it to th' bottom, pretending that I was just moving it back to its place in th' middle of th' table.

It seemed that th' pie was gone and milk drunk all too soon, and Bob rose, clearing his throat, to catch our attention so we would rise also. "God bless you, Ma. That was the best pie I ever et," he said, bowing a little, "but I got to get these rannies moving or we'll never git to the ranch before Sunday, and Miz Dearing would be awful disappointed if we missed the bear si— doughnut party. I hope your boarders ain't too put out we ate their pie."

"Don't you worry about those boarders, they're so hungry they hardly notice what's set before them. I'll have crust baking in no time and they love a good buttermilk pie mostly as much as apple. Too much apple pie would spoil them and they had it last week, anyway. I am so glad you got the cup back, I'm tempted to feed you the whole meal!"

We grinned at the thought of those hungry boarders trooping in for supper just as we got up from consuming it, but that pie was enough for us and we had to be moving on.

"Thank you very much for the pie and milk, Mrs. Thompson," I said as I passed her at th' door. She gave me a big hug and said, "You're welcome, Zenas, now you come by to see me next time you're in town, might be I would have more pie to slice." She was always motherin' us all.

CHAPTER 5
DOG CANYON CAMP

Manuel had stayed at th' store to restock his wagon and pick up some other things he needed and then headed out of town toward th' ranch. We picked up our bedrolls and caught up with him where he stopped a little ways from th' mouth of Dog Canyon late that afternoon.

There was some grass on th' hillsides for our stock and it was still a day's ride to ranch headquarters. The horses could get a good rest and have an easy day of it tomorrow. Th' spring branch coming out of th' canyon had a trickle of water in it and someone had dug out a hole for it to fill.

I guess th' Apaches have used that canyon trail forever to go back and forth from basin to mountain. A little later on after this, Frenchie would settle there. They say he traded with th' Indians and th' 'Paches let him be. Not long after that, Oliver Lee set up his ranch on th' flats. They ran water from th' canyon down to th' ranch house.

Frenchie got shot in his own house, probably by one of those outlaws that run out of room in Texas and infested this country for a while. Never found out who or why. He was a good man and a good carpenter. Helped Lee build his house. You can still see ruins of his cabin and those rock walls he built clearin' his fields. There wasn't anything there except th' trails when we camped there that night.

Before dark, we brought our horses in and tethered them close in around th' wagon. Bein' so close to th' trail, Bob set a watch and th' rest of us would sleep light. I got first watch for two hours. Some of th' others would still be up during my time. All was quiet when I woke Rip to take his turn. I rolled up in my bed and slept.

Just like we were on th' range, Cookie woke up at 4 a.m. and stirred up his fire for breakfast. He was th' only one in camp with a clock. I could hear him stirring around with pots and kettles and soon smelled coffee boiling. Just as I threw back my blanket to get up, I heard him exclaim in Spanish.

"What is it, Manuel?" I asked. "Was there a snake in that firewood again?"

"No, amigo, but there's an antelope hide on the tailgate!" Heads popped up out of bedrolls like corn on a griddle.

"What antelope hide?"

"No one had any hide with them."

"Are th' horses all here?"

"You shore know how to stir up camp, Manuel," this last from under Rip's sombrero.

"Don't nobody move, 'til we look around," said Tom as he pulled on his boots. He stood up and tiptoed to th' wagon for th' lantern Cookie had lit.

"Ow, there's a thorn in my boot!" he exclaimed, sitting down and pulling off his right boot. Shaking it, several sand spurs fell out. With a funny look that made us laugh, he wiggled his left foot in the boot.

"Some yahoo's put spurs in my boots!"

Sure enough, both boots had a few sand spurs in them. Making a few choice remarks directed at an anonymous jokester, he resumed his survey of th' area. Stooping low, he swung th' lantern along just above ground.

With a grunt, he said, "Moccasin tracks, toe in like Injuns. Here's another one, looks like th' same person; reckon we had a visitor in th' night, boys, Manuel, better check and see what that Injun traded that hide for, we might have to run back to town if he thought it was very valuable."

"There's a can of peaches gone from the box, and I don't see but one bag of salt," Manuel said, with his head deep in th' wagon box. He lost a lot of his accent when he was excited.

"All our stock is here," Les called as he strode back into th' circle of light.

"Must have been goin' *up* th' canyon," mused Tom, "else we'd be on shoe leather express if he was goin' into th' basin."

I grabbed a bucket and headed for th' spring branch. As I passed along th' path, I saw something white laying in th' way and picking it up, I caught the aroma of a bar of soap. The visitor must have dropped it on his way out of camp. I stuck it in my pocket. It didn't take me long to fill that bucket and get back to camp. Th' whole time I was out there, I felt a dozen eyes were watching me, though I knew in reason that any prowler or prowlers were long gone.

On th' way back, I noticed the soap wrapper where the "trader" had dropped it. Cookie was still rummaging through his plunder when I got to th' wagon. He stood up and held th' lantern high and looked around the wagon bed.

"Eet look lak he only got peeches and salt, Meester Bob, I guess that green hide not so valuable."

"That salt would be pretty valuable to him," replied Bob. "Those Mescaleros must be gettin' a taste for it and it will make a good tradin' item with the Comancheros. At least he didn't get anything we can't do without. There's enough salt at the ranch."

"He won't be as clean as he expected," I said, hoisting the bucket on to th' tailgate. "He dropped his soap on th' trail."

As I pulled the bar out of my pocket, I felt a roughness on one corner. Thinking it was grit from the path where it dropped, I held it up to the light. There on the bar was the perfect imprint of a set of teeth, upper and lower!

Bob looked at it and laughed, "Must not have been very good candy ol' snaggletooth just throwed it away!"

There was a gap in th' tooth pattern where that culprit must have a missing tooth.

"Too bad he didn't know how to use that soap, it would've made him easy to identify," Rip laughed.

"You ain't been too close to a bar of soap lately, yoreself," Leapin' grimaced. "I would appreciate it if you rode downwind from me the rest of the way in."

"I'll ride where I please, and you can adjust yoreself as you see fit, Mr. Pot. Soon's we find water in abundance, this kettle will smell like a clothesline on washday and you'll still be rubbin' on that rusty neck o' your'n!"

Rip pretended to be insulted, while the rest of us laughed. None of us were very clean after our adventure and it would be good to wash all over and change into pants that wouldn't stand on their on.

"That visitor was either a small person or a woman, judging from these tracks," Jones surmised. "Shore was quiet to git in here without makin' a sound and gittin' by the lookout, whoever *that* was. He came from the west and hit up the canyon trail when he left. I couldn't tell if he wuz alone or not."

"Wonder if he counted coup on anyone," Jones asked no one in particular. "Must have done it with a feather if he did on me, I didn't hear or feel a thing."

"Reckon he counted coup on Tom's feet with the sand spurs?" asked Les.

Everyone stopped what they were doing for a moment, then a chorus of voices denied complicity in the prank.

"I bet you're the victim of a 'Pache attack, Tom, never heard of counting coup with thorns before."

Tom couldn't suppress a grin, "They could probably have

carried me up th' canyon and I would have never knowed it as tired as I was."

Manuel had been busy with breakfast while we were bantering and we ate in a hurry, anxious to be on our way. It was good to be gettin' regular meals even if we weren't on th' payroll yet. We would more than make up for what we consumed when roundup started. No cowboy worth his salt ever had to back up to th' trough or his paycheck.

The rest of that trip was uneventful. We rode southeastward along th' foothills and up over th' pass into Sacramento Canyon. At th' river, we stopped and washed out our clothes. While they were drying on the rocks, we used up that bar of soap washing off th' grime of several days' accumulation. Our horses watered and stood hock deep in water and seemed to enjoy it as much as we did. It didn't take long for clothes to dry and we were soon back in th' saddle for th' last leg into th' ranch.

We rode into th' yard about sundown on that Saturday. Half of us tended to horses while th' rest helped Manuel unload th' wagon and stow supplies in his chuck wagon.

Mrs. Dearing came to th' porch and greeted each by name. She always made us feel like a part of th' family and took an interest in our doin's.

"You men be on your best tomorrow, I've got company coming and there may be a surprise for dinner."

'Course, we all knew that meant a bear sign feast and you can be sure no one would be rockin' that boat!

Chapter 6
Bear Sign

Sundays was generally a day of rest around th' ranch when we were not on th' range. It was th' only day we allowed ourselves to sleep late and not plan any chores to do. The boys said it wasn't much that way 'til the Boss brought Mrs. Dearing out, but I didn't hear any complainin' about it, either.

In later years a Methodist Episcopal circuit preacher would come by for a few days after roundup and hold services. We'd build a brush arbor and neighbors would come in from all around. The preachin' and visitin' was good, but us cowboys enjoyed fried chicken, potato salad, and pies most of all. Most likely there would be a horse race or two and of course some sparkin' of eligible girls if they was any.

This particular Sunday I'm talkin' about, we didn't sleep late anticipating th' activities of th' day. Knowin' there would be company aplenty coming, we set about cleanin' out th' bunkhouse, sweepin' th' yard, cleanin' out th' barn and spreadin' new hay in th' hallway, tossing down hay for th' horses we expected, and seeing there was plenty of water drawn in th' troughs.

Manuel was helpin' Mrs. Dearing in th' kitchen, and Lon set about splitting firewood for th' stove. We set th' bunkhouse cookstove up in th' yard so it would be cooler for th' cooks and have more working space around it. With two bunkhouse tables lined up beside that stove, we had a neat kitchen set up right there under the elms and cottonwoods.

By the time we were done with all our chores, it was past midmorning and we could see dust comin' our way from two directions. We just had time to freshen up and put on clean shirts before that first buckboard pulled into th' yard with a half-dozen cowboys trailin' behind. It was the C-B outfit from over on the Agua Chiquita. Charlie Austin's wife, Miz Jeanie, was sittin' on the seat by Charlie with a big bowl of dough covered with a cloth. Amidst all the howdys, Jones took th' bowl for her while Rip helped her step down and escorted her to th' ranch house where Mrs. Dearing had stepped out on th' porch to greet her visitors.

"Step down, boys, and rest awhile," called th' Boss from th' stoop. "Just turn the horses into the corral, there's plenty water and hay there for all of them. I swear, Charlie, if you aren't gettin' near as fat as me, that Miz Jeanie must be takin' good care of you!"

The Boss and Charlie came into this country together, driving one of th' first herds of mixed cattle after Charles Goodnight and Mr. Loving blazed their trail up from Texas. They worked together for several years, then split the herd after it had multiplied considerably and th' range was gettin' crowded. Charlie moved to th' Agua Chiquita range and Mr. Dearing kept his outfit on th' Rio Sacramento and registered his Rafter JD brand.

When I first got to th' ranch, it wasn't unusual to see an old cow with both brands on her hip, the Rafter JD above the C-B, indicating that she had been with the original C-B and split out for the Rafter JD. Boss was partial to them and I guess most of th' brood cows died of old age right there on th' range before he would let them go.

I wasn't too acquainted with th' C-B outfit, though I had seen a few of them around town and I knew Gene Little was wagon boss for them during roundup. They stepped down amidst a lot of banter and handshakes from th' boys. The two outfits were on friendly terms because of Boss and Mr. Austin. That's not to say there wasn't a lot of competition between th' two—and sometimes it got pretty heated.

"How's that nag of your'n doin, Tom?" Jones called to a rangy little cowboy stepping down from a fancy paint horse.

"Doin' fine, Mr. Jones," this Tom replied. "He shore was anxious to git some exercise when I caught him up this mornin' an' I could hardly hold him back when he saw the direction we taken. I don't know whether it was the prospect of a good race or bear sign he was thinkin' 'bout!"

Tom looked to be about my age, maybe a little older. He was as tall as I was but built slight and lighter by a few pounds. I knew then he was riding his paint because it was that outfit's racehorse, paints weren't used in herding cattle. We always preferred solid colors, th' plainer th' better around a herd, and th' nature of a paint didn't speak too well for his herdin' ability.

"Well, now, I bet six bits we can find some activity to take some of that bounce out of him—after dinner, of course. We'll get him settled down some so's you can have a gentle ride home."

Where Jones could get six bits, *I* didn't know, since he hadn't had two half-dimes to rub together for a month or more, but I knew there was a hot race brewin' and some tall braggin' rights was at stake. Bob, our foreman, had a little grulla mare that loved to run and had her best speed in short sprints. Buck was our best distance runner, so it would depend on the length of th' course which one we would put up. About that time two more outfits rode into th' yard and racing prospects were forgotten in the midst of another spate of greetings and howdys. I didn't know these cowboys or their brands, but I would get to know them well in the next few weeks on our roundup.

Elfuego Sanchez and his son, Mecio, rode in from th' lower

Sacramento. They had a little place in th' foothills just before th' river hit th' basin and sank. Not much water got that far except in th' rainy season and they didn't run many cattle there. We would find quite a number of them scattered over our range where they wandered up to feed. Mecio would rep with us on th' roundup. He was a good hand and carried his own weight and then some. When it was all over, he would have a little herd to trail back south.

Manuel had quite a fire goin' in his cookstove. It almost glowed red when he set four big kettles on it and started ladling lard into them. He kept stirring with a wooden paddle until all lard had melted and watched as it heated up. Mrs. Dearing and th' other ladies came out on th' veranda with trays loaded with food and shaped-up dough. They were met by a half-dozen cowboys offerin' to assist in carrying platters and trays to th' tables. The ladies fussed about settin' out food on one table while Manuel and Mrs. D. arranged th' stove and bear sign for cooking.

Rip nudged me from behind, "You ever see such a layout for a bunch of guys who were starvin' two days ago, Daylight? I'll watch you so's you don't eat too much an' founder."

"It'll take a lot of feedin' t' founder me," I replied. "If'n I need any help, I'll shore call for your advice, if you're still standin', that is."

It was a feast for sore eyes, all right. There was potato salad, snap beans canned last summer, a pile of fried chicken that must have emptied the henhouse, and someone had brought a cured ham big as a nail keg. Manuel had sliced it into big thick slices. There must have been ten gallons of coffee simmering on the stove, and the oven was full of Manuel's biscuits.

On a nod from Mrs. Dearing, the Boss sang out, "Come an' git it, boys," and we all lined up with our plates from th' chuck wagon. I finished my plate and was eyeing that table again in spite of th' smell of bear sign frying.

"You boys can't have any doughnuts until this food is all cleaned up," Mrs. Dearing called out.

That caused another rush on th' table. By th' time potatoes and beans were gone, there were piles of piping hot doughnuts sprinkled with sugar waiting to be devoured, which we all promptly did.

"That was so-o-ome satisfyin' feed," crooned Jones as he brushed sugar from his hands and shirt. "Makes me wish I could do it all over agin."

"I never been full of bear sign, but I got a might closer today." Leapin' almost groaned as he rose and headed for th' wash pan.

"You must have two stomachs, Lon," Tom called. "One Ma Thompson filled and a spare you filled up today. That's the only way to 'splain how you got around all that food on top of th' good grub you been gettin' at Ma's."

"Yeah, I can understand how young Sanchez and young Tom can put away all that grub, they're still growin', but you beat all, Lon." Rip was shaking his head in mock wonder.

"I *do* have two sides t' my stomach, a food side an' a dessert side an' now they're both filled t' my satisfaction, thank you. If I'm a pig, you-all are hogs of the first order," Lon shot back. "I could beat you all in a foot race and be back for more grub before you half finished the course."

"That would depend on whether you were running *from* or *towards* the food, Lon," laughed one of the C-B boys.

Old Tom rose from his seat against th' trunk of a cottonwood and, removing his sombrero and bowing to th' ladies, made a little speech: "That was about th' best feed this pore cowboy's had in a long time and we are sure beholdin' to you ladies for puttin' it out for us. If'n any of you would hire on as cook, we'd be pleased to have you and we'll put Manuel to night herdin'. Now, if you will jist direct us, this crew will gladly clean and straighten up this here outdoor kitchen afore them that kin still move git to racin' and playin' horseshoes and all that other foolishness they's liable to git into."

There was a general scrambling to get up and a chorus of "Yes, ma'ams" from the rest of us. The ladies blushed with pleasure, then bustled around directing us in a general cleanup. Mecio Sanchez and I helped Manuel wash up and dry dishes and store them in their proper places in th' wagon. Manuel was as fussy as a hen with chicks about gettin' everything stored in its rightful place, but then it had to be just so when that wagon got to moving over rough range.

The cleanup was soon finished and th' ladies retired to th' ranch house porch to sit and visit and watch any goin's-on below. Soon th' clink of horseshoes was heard as a hot game was started with Mr. Austin and the Boss partnering against all comers. The rest of us were content to watch and let our meals settle and squat in the shade for a smoke and talk with our visitors. It didn't take long for those two bosses to clean out the competition. They sure were sharp when it came to tossing horseshoes.

"I think we must have wiped out all the competition, John," Mr. Austin grinned as he wiped his face with his bandana. "That winter on the Pecos sure honed our tossin' skills. We must have wore out four sets of mule shoes waitin' for the spring green-up."

"Yeah, but Bill got better than any of us," Boss replied. "He could beat both of us together and laugh while he did it! Too bad he didn't ride over with you, he could have showed us all how it was done. Let's go see if the ladies might have some lemonade to sip and talk about the rodeo while these boys git some of the kinks shook out. I think I heard Lon challengin' someone to a footrace and young Tom is itchin' to see if that paint can run."

The Boss and other ranch owners wandered over to th' porch where they could talk business and organize our rodeo while visiting with th' ladies.

"How 'bout it, Lon," called one of th' boys, "you ready to put yore feet where yore mouth is, so to speak, and show us lubbers how to run?"

Lon yawned and streched lazily. "Why I could beat you boys barefooted in a cactus patch, what I'm wonderin' is if that C-B paint can run as fast as some of you boys think. He don't look like he has much bottom, probably not good for much more than a quarter, is he?"

"He'll do for a quarter, a half, or a mile," vowed Little Tom defensively.

"I don't know," spoke up one of the boys from an outfit over the divide, "my bay's never been beat in a quarter, but he'll fade in a mile."

"If ol' Buck is up to it, I think he can beat ever' horse here in a mile an' have time to rest up 'fore anyone else got to th' finish line," Rip allowed.

" 'Stead of standin' 'round braggin' how 'bout toein' the line and lettin' the horses do the braggin'?" shot back Little Tom.

"You tell 'em, Tom," someone called out and there was a chorus of agreement from the crowd gatherin' 'round.

"You choose how far that nag can run an' we'll match you and beat you," said Rip.

One of the C-B boys spoke up, "I don't think that outfit has a horse that can *run* a mile, much less beat that paint. Tom, let's go whole hog and let 'em eat our dust."

That brought a rumble from th' crowd. After a lot of jawing back and forth, it was decided that a mile course would be run. Lon hopped up on th' wagon and raised his arms and called out for attention.

"Fellers," he called, "it seems to me that there should be

more than just braggin' rights ridin' on this here race, but I 'magine if we had to ransom an ant this time of year, we couldn't raise a dime if the whole crowd chipped in." There was general agreement to that.

Someone called out from the back, "Ol' Boog still has the first dime he earned, but we'd have to kill an' skin 'im to git it!"

"Taint so!" called a red-faced cowboy in a worn outfit I took to be Boog.

The crowd roared at that. Someone slapped him on the back and Boog couldn't suppress a grin.

"Anyway," continued Lon, "I was thinkin' what we could wager on this here race an' the thought come to me that we're all going to be in this rodeo together, how 'bout somethin' to do with the roundup?"

"Yeah," called someone, "like who gits brandin' duty, an' what outfit gits to do all the cuttin'," (meaning castrating the he-cows, but he couldn't say it out loud for fear the ladies on the porch would hear).

"You ain't gonna git me doin' the ground work the whole time," someone called out.

There was general agreement to that. No cowboy relishes chores that can't be done from horseback and branding and cutting is a hot dusty job that wears you out quick.

"How 'bout ridin' night herd?" a lanky cowboy called out.

"You wouldn't be givin' up much there, J.O., since you sleep in the saddle an' yore horse does all the work!"

"Yeah," called out someone else, "I caught him the other day tryin' to teach his night horse to sing!"

"We're goin' to have a pretty big herd toward the end of the roundup and we will need everyone we can git on night herd," Mr. Austin called from the step. "How about bettin' for no night herdin' the first two weeks of the rodeo?"

There was general agreement to that, so it was decided that

th' winning outfit would get two weeks without night herding. There was some discussion about th' number two outfit getting some prize, but in the end, it was decided that th' winner took all.

Negotiating for terms and conditions now began in earnest. Some outfits had only long-distance runners and some only sprinters. With some maneuvering, the outfits joined up in teams so that each team had a sprinter and a long-distance bronc. We ended up with four teams and eight horses in th' race. Mecio Sanchez threw in with us since he didn't have a horse to race. It was decided that th' winner would be decided on a point basis with the winner of each quarter getting three points, two points to second, and one point to third place. Whoever got th' most points won.

A half-mile-long course was agreed on with a turn around a barrel set at th' end and a full half-mile race back to th' starting line for the finish. Some stepped off th' course by step and th' rest got their respective horses ready to race. Rip brought out Buck and Bob saddled up the grulla mare. They trotted their horses around th' course to get them familiar with th' track and warmed up. As they walked th' horses back to th' starting line, Jones looked up at Bob and said, "You look like you put on a few pounds layin' 'round the ranch this winter, Bob, how much you weigh now?"

"I weigh just enough to whip yore skinny butt," Bob shot back, but Jones ignored him.

"I was lookin' at young Sanchez there and thinkin' he might undershoot yore weight by fifteen or twenty pounds. That could make a difference in the outcome."

"If we're goin' on a weight-savin' program, I guess yore goin' t' say I'm bigger than Daylight," Rip glowered.

"Now that you mention it . . ." Jones rubbed his stubbled chin. "Anything we do that would git us out of that night herdin' would be good. What say we strip down the gear and put the lightest ones on those horses and see what happens."

"I 'low you could be right," mused Bob. "The mare is pretty gentle and Daylight could handle her better. Mecio has more experience ridin' and he could handle Buck ok."

So it was decided that Mecio and I would do th' jockeying. The boys set about stripping my saddle to bare minimums and I emptied my pockets and put on moccasins instead of my old brogans. It was decided that I pull Bob's mare out of th' race at the barrel since there wasn't a chance for her to win and no use in running her unnecessarily.

Meantime, Mecio mounted Buck and rode around feeling th' fit of the saddle and th' horse's responses. He rode back up to us and hopped off.

"Meester Reep how does Buck do bareback?" he asked.

"Why right well," Rip replied, "I used to ride him bareback a lot."

"Eef I could ride heem bareback, it might geeve us the edge een the race."

Rip nodded, "You think you could make the turn ok?"

"I could swing a little wide for the turn and be hokay, I theenk," he replied.

"Ok, cowboy," Rip began stripping th' saddle off, "just be careful in that herd of horses you don't fall off."

Les was busy shortening my stirrups. "This will help the horse in running some, when you start, lean forward as far as you're comfortable with and talk to her. Use this quirt sparing toward the end if you are pushed."

I got more advice on how to run a horse race in th' next five minutes than I have had in my whole life, before *and* after. Most of it I already knew, some of it was contrary to previous advice, and some of it was just plain useless. In th' end I determined to run my way using a few pointers I had been given. After a lot of discussion, it was decided that th' most trustworthy judges were th' ranchers, so two were set up at th' quarter/three-quarter mark and the barrel at the halfway point, and two judges were assigned to th' finish line. I remember that our boss was one of the judges at th' barrel, but I don't remember who or where those other judges were.

There was some jockying for starting places. I chose th' outside so I wouldn't interfere with other racers when I pulled up at th' halfway point. Mecio was about halfway down from th' post position.

The starter stood up on th' far barrel and held out a white flag. When he dropped th' flag, th' race began. We took off in a whirl of dust, yells, and cheers. That little grulla mare leaped off so fast when I touched the spurs to her it almost unseated me. She was out and away ahead of all others, and she held that lead all the way in the first quarter. Nearing the halfway mark, she began to flag out and a buckskin pony nosed her out.

There was quite a scramble at th' turn. Little Tom's paint had gotten th' inside track and turned th' barrel on a dime. All others were bunched up behind him and one horse got tangled up with th' barrel and tumbled. The rider, J.O. Pierce, bailed off and ended up astraddle th' overturned barrel. He never did live that down, went to his grave as th' one who tried to ride a barrel in a horse race.

By th' time I got my grulla turned and was trottin' her back toward th' finish, it looked like a three-way race between Buck, th' paint, and a rangy roan from another outfit. Mecio was almost on his knees on Buck's back and leaning flat against his neck. Young Tom was giving his paint th' quirt and that roan was stretched out so much it looked like his belly would drag any minute. There was a great yell at th' finish, but I couldn't tell from my position who had won.

"How did you do, Daylight?" Bob called as I rode up.

"I was first at th' quarter, but got nosed out by that buckskin at th' half," I replied.

"Well, that's a three at the quarter and a two at th' barrel." He had a pencil stub and a scrap of paper he was figuring on.

"Who finished first?" I asked.

"The paint won by a hair at the finish line," Jones said as he walked up. "How did you do?"

"I got a three and a two," I replied.

"That makes it awful close, wish you could have won both," Jones frowned. "Shore would hate for that C-B outfit t' win, never did like t' hear them crowin', 'specially after that White Sands ordeal."

The judges were all huddled up tallyin' scores and it took a few minutes for them to get th' totals. There was a laugh from them and th' Boss stepped up on th' porch and addressed the crowd.

"Here's the final scores, boys; C-B four points . . ." He was interrupted by a cheer from the C-B boys. ". . . Rafter JD four points," he continued, accompanied by groans from the C-B boys and grins from us. "Looks like you aren't through with this contest yet, boys. There can't be any ties in this contest, so figger out how to break it."

He grinned as he sat down lookin' over the hubbub in th' crowd. There was going to be more entertainment than they had anticipated.

"Well, ain't this a kettle of fish?" Les hollered. "We gonna hafta run that race agin?"

"Not with my horse," called Tom, "he wouldn't have enough left to git me home!"

He told me later that he knew that Buck had more bottom than th' paint and would beat him in a second race.

"I don't want to run my mare agin, nuther," Bob said. "Maybe we got other horses that can race."

There were groans from everyone at that. When it came to th' seconds in a horse race, no one could pick th' fastest ones, nor predict how they would run.

"Seems like Leapin' was bragging on his runnin' ability not long ago, maybe we could saddle him up for a race," someone called from th' back of the crowd.

"Who said dat?" Lon whirled around and craned toward th' back, to th' amusement of th' crowd. He never discovered who that yahoo was, but always suspected it was Rip or Les puttin' someone up to sayin' it. "I'll bet you want me to do it barefoot too, don't you?" He had that little grin that made me know he was up to some mischief.

"I'll run barefoot with you all day long and leave you eatin' dust the whole way." It was Little Tom of the C-B speaking.

That started it, there were challenges flung back and forth like hail in a storm. In a lull in th' noise, Gene Little spoke up, "I could beat Leapin' Lon myself, Tom, and we could save you for a race with real competition!"

The fuss started all over again. Folks on the porch were laughing at the goin's-on and th' rest of us were enjoyin' it too.

From somewhere in th' back, Old Tom called out, "You take Lon on, Gene, an' I'll beat Little Tom clear into tomorrer!"

You can imagine the hubbub *that* caused, th' idea that th' two Toms would race and Leapin' an' Gene would race caught on quick. It was decided that all four would race, winner takes all, then th' argument started again about how long and where th' race was to be run. Gene wanted to run on grass and Lon wanted dirt. The Toms didn't care.

"Why don't you run down the road, then you could choose grass or dirt as you please," someone suggested.

As to length of th' race, no one could agree. Being th' youngest and most fit, Little Tom wanted a mile. That was quickly vetoed by th' other three. After arguing back and forth for a while, they decided that th' Toms would run a half mile from barrel to finish line and Lon and Gene would start for th' finish line from the quarter mark. They would race first, since all bets were that th' two Toms would provide the closest and most interesting race. Lon sat down on th' porch steps and began removing his boots.

"Git those boots off, Gene, if you are goin' t' run this race like we agreed." He sat there in his socks waiting for Gene to unshod himself.

"*I* didin't agree to go barefoot, it was Little Tom's idee," Gene protested.

"Nevertheless, I was told I had to run barefoot, and if I do, so do you," replied Leapin'.

"I ain't runnin' barefoot," Gene asserted.

"You'll have to or forfeit," Leapin' shot back.

"I won't forfeit an' I won't run barefoot," Gene said heatedly.

That was where th' crowd got involved in th' argument, each side backing his runner. Finally, they agreed to flip a coin. Lon called "heads" and won. Among many a groan and protest, Gene sat down and began taking his boots off. While th' attention was on Gene, Lon slipped a pair of moccasins out of his hip pockets and strapped them on. You can imagine th' howl that went up when he was discovered.

"I never *agreed* to runnin' barefoot, it was Little Tom's idea," Leapin' calmly said.

More howls and laughs at that. Someone from the C-B produced a pair of moccasins for Gene and th' runners trotted off to take their places. Since there were no horses to spook in this race, th' starter stood at th' finish line, held his gun high, and fired. Gene was watching and when he saw smoke spout out of th' gun, he took off. Lon had his head down waiting for th' sound to reach him and got a late start. Pouring on th' coals, he made up th' jump Gene got and they were neck and neck th' rest of the way. It was quite a spectacle seeing those two older guys puffing down th' road and we alternated between cheerin' an' laughin' at their efforts. Just before th' finish line, Lon stumbled and fell headlong across the line. The race judge raised his arm and shouted, "Rafter JD by a nose!"

We raised a cheer over howls of protest from C-B partisans. The judge took so much jawin' he appealed his decision to th' porch gallery. They all agreed that Lon's head crossed th' finish line before Gene's knee. We were halfway there.

By Little Tom being several years younger than our Tom, we felt that he would have a big edge in th' second race. Jones allowed as how we would be happy with a tie in th' contest if our Tom lost and hope to win in another tiebreaker of some kind. Little Tom was slim and hard as a split rail, but our Tom was in tiptop shape, well muscled with strong legs and a deep chest. We still had a chance.

Th' gun start of th' first race wasn't good, so th' starter stood up on the porch, held th' white flag high, and dropped it. In a few steps, Little Tom had streched out and was taking long strides that ate up the distance. Our Tom was taking shorter but much faster strides and staying right with him. They were neck and neck all the way. When they got in th' last thirty yards, our Tom lengthened his stride to match Little Tom's. Th' din from th' crowd was deafening. They came on matching step for step across the finish line. Th' judges (there was one on each side) were almost on their knees watching the line. It was suddenly so quiet you could hear horses stomping in th' corral.

Those judges looked at each other and inched toward th' place both runners stepped on th' line. Th' crowd closed in all around. There in swept dirt, crossing that line were two footprints of our runners—and th' toes were exactly even with each other.

"Their feet hit the ground at the same time, didn't they, Joe?"

"Yeah," replied Joe, "it looked like one foot when they hit the ground."

"I'd say it was a dead tie, wouldn't you?" said th' first judge. There was a low groan from th' crowd.

"That was the most exact tie I have ever seen in my life," declared Mr. Joe.

One of the C-B boys pointed at th' two tracks. "But Little Tom's foot is smaller, his heel is closer to the line than Old Tom's."

Th' first judge looked disgustedly at th' speaker. "We ain't measurin' whut got over the line last, John, it's the toes up front that counts!" Straightening up, he declared, "This race is an exact tie!"

The Rafter JD boys yelled and the C-Bs groaned. We had won th' contest by a head, or a nose as th' judges said. We got our two weeks of no night ridin' but didn't boast too much about it. They put me in the roundup and hired a couple of young Mexican American boys to herd the horses. I guess I must have done ok.

The old man chuckled as he looked back over the years at those long-ago events. He shook his head and pushed his hat back a little further on his head. I could tell he was some tired so I didn't ask any questions. We just sat there on the porch gently rocking our chairs occasionally and watched the sun slide down behind the Organ Mountains and their shadows creep across the basin. Somewhere a coyote yipped and I roused from my chair to leave. Zenas rose from his chair and turning toward the door called through the screen, "Sophie, when's supper? I'm gettin' hungry."

CHAPTER 7
THE HUNGRY CAMP

Mrs. Sophie had scolded me the last time I had been to the Meekers'
because I had failed to mention previously that I had a birthday just
passed, so she insisted that I come to eat dinner with them on my
next visit (dinner being the noon meal for those of you who mistakenly
think otherwise). So, on the appointed day I arrived at the Meeker
place a little after 11. We sat on the porch and talked while Mrs.
Meeker put the finishing touches on the meal. We went in when she
called and my eyes almost popped looking at the spread she had.
There were five different dishes steaming on the table, any one of
which I would have considered a complete meal. She had made
hand-rolled beef tamales, a chicken and rice casserole with chunks of
chicken in it, a guacamole salad with fresh garden tomatoes and
onions,

It was without doubt the best birthday meal I ever had and I said
so to Mrs. Sophie over and over. I was overwhelmed and did my best
to do the meal justice. When Zenas and I retreated to the porch, he
said, "That meal reminded me of a time on th' trail when we didn't
have anything *to eat." He settled back in his rocker and thought a*
moment.

In th' spring of '70 th' Rafter JD and C-B outfits put two
thousand head of steers on th' trail to Dodge City. Things were
so bad both ranchers refused to deal with reservations and the
Santa Fe Gang an' chose to ship their cows north instead. We
had a mixed crew, half C-B and half Rafter JD boys. Preston

Dycus from the C-B was trail boss and the Rafter furnished the chuck wagon an' cook, bein' that Manuel was a much better cook than th' C-B cook.

Spring come early in th' mountains and snowmelt was heavy. We got across th' Pecos near where Anton Chico is an' went around th' head of Aguilar Creek. Rio Gallinas was bank full, but we got across an' up Cañon del Agua onto th' plains east of Las Vegas. Bein' grass was green and water plentiful, Pres decided to cut across well east of th' Santa Fe Trail, avoidin' trail traffic an' such "waterin holes" as Las Vegas, where he would undoubtedly have had his hands full keepin' or gettin' us out of trouble.

We took our time across th' plain lettin' cattle fatten on new grass. The ground was soft, but th' sod held so long as they didn't git into marshes. Only one or two got bogged down. From th' ridge, Cherry Valley Lake looked twice its size an' Mora River was backed halfway up th' draw to Shoemaker Crossing. There wasn't nothing t' do but mosey upriver to a spot we could cross, and we were near where Watrous is now when one of those March blizzards hit. This one wasn't as fierce as it could have been an' instead of driftin', our cows bedded down tight. Th' whole outfit spent a miserable day ridin' herd 'round them, but they stayed pat.

By night, th' storm had blowed by an' it was just plain cold. Pres says, "Boys, if it's this cold here, think how cold it must be up in them mountains. If we mosey back to Shoemaker Crossing, I'll bet it will be down enough t' cross." He chose Shoemaker instead of waiting an' crossin' where we was at on account o' steep hills north of the river at this place. Two draws come together on both sides of th' river at Shoemaker an' it was easier t' git across an' back up on th' prairie towards Wagon Mound.

We circled out on th' hills some to avoid backtrackin' an' give that herd fresh grass, takin' a day an' a half t' git back to Shoemaker. It's surprisin' how fast those rivers can go down when snowmelt stops an' when we got back to Shoemaker, that river was back in its banks but still flowin' fast. Some o' th' boys tested it an' could git across ok, but their horses were swimmin' most of th' way. Pres decided t' wait until mornin t' try t' cross, so we pulled back from th' river about a mile an' bedded th' herd. We ate breakfast in th' dark an' Pres come in from th' river while we ate. "It's a go, boys, th' river's down more—shouldn't swim more'n thirty-forty feet this mornin'." That put th' move on us. Cookie got his wagon loaded in no time an' struck out fer th' crossin' with four or five ridin' with him t' help.

We give them a half hour's start, then lined our herd out on th' trail, pushin' them hard. They funneled down th' south draw an' right across th' river. By th' time our drag got across, most of that herd was up th' north draw an' headed for prairie green.

For a while, we was in sight o' th' Santa Fe Trail, but there was little traffic on it this time o' year, just traders mostly headed north for Freeport in Missouri. A cavalry patrol out of Fort Union rode over an' visited with us—ate most of a pot of Manuel's frijoles—an' said Injuns was expected t' give trouble this year, which was about th' same expectation ever' year back then.

We stayed east of Wagon Mound an' Conjelon Mesa, anglin' for th' trail crossin' of th' Canadian River below Taylor Springs. All th' while, weather was warmin' an' we was keepin' our weather eyes out. The warmin' trend would come down from th' northwest, warmin' mountains an' all that snow b'fore it got to us an' that was bothersome.

The last day b'fore we got t' that Canadian crossin', Pres says at breakfast, "With a hard day's drive, we can cross th' river b'fore sunset. Manuel, go on ahead an' cross as soon as you can. We can camp on th' divide between th' river an' Chico Creek."

While we roused our herd, Manuel an' nighthawk struck out for th' crossin'. We didn't hardly stop for noonin', just long enough t' trade horses an' send a couple wranglers with th' cavyyard t' help git our horses across. It was just about a half hour b'fore dark when we pulled in sight of th' crossin'. Somethin' didn't look right from a distance. Pres rode ahead an' soon came trottin' back signallin' t' bed th' herd. We knowed that river had risen an' we wern't crossin' that night. Bad part was that wagon an' horses was on t'other side an' there would be no supper. Missin' supper wasn't all that bad—or unusual on th' trail—but ridin' night herd without our night horses an' with horses that was already tired *was* bad. But we made do, hobblin' our horses an' stakin' them out with our lariats, sleepin' on horse blankets.

Mornin' came and that river was higher. We let th' herd graze, spread out over a hundred acres an' us ridin' a loose circle 'round them. They wasn't a bite t' eat for us vaqueros an' no game in sight. Th' drag in this bunch was in purty good shape with nothin' bad enough t' kill, so we just pulled our belts up a notch an' gritted our teeth. Pres drove a couple of stakes at th' edge o' th' water. Next mornin' both stakes was in water an' those rags tied to them was a foot below water level. That night, we gathered 'round our fire for a third night without food.

"I swear, I'll go tie down a heifer an' milk her fer breakfast," Rip vowed.

"They's all *steers,* you idjit," Les growled, "now don't go talkin' 'bout food, it's bad 'nough hearin' my stomach growl."

"I seen a antelope a couple days back," said Tom, "Think I'll mosey back that way in th' mornin' if that river's still up."

"Thet wus a coyote an' he was near all th' way t' Wagon Mound," Leapin' drawled.

"Enyways, he'd have *some* meat on hisself, more'n I can say for you," Tom replied.

"I hope you wasn't considerin eatin' *me*! Jist so you'll know, I sleep with my gun in my hand."

Tom shuddered, "I'd druther eat a skunk, you'd be tough an' stringy an' pizzen from all that terbaccy juice you's swallowed."

"That Manuel an' nighthawk's over ther eatin' s.o.b. stew an' biscuits an' here we sit with nothin'," Pres allowed. He wasn't any better off than th' rest of us an' could complain as much as we could. "J.O., what'd yore mama fix fer you when you were hungry?" This was J.O. Pierce who rode th' barrel at that bear sign dinner.

J.O. leaned back on his saddle an' closed his eyes, "We-e-l-l-l, I s'pose she'd hev pork chops rolled in flour an' fried in a cast-iron skillit; turnip greens and poke salit with baby turnips"— Les groaned an' walked out into th' dark—"snap green beans; radishes cooled in spring water; sliced cucumbers in vinegar an' black pepper; new potaters boiled in a cream sauce with sweet peas; all washed down with milk with cream floatin' on th' top. For dessert, we might hev apple dumplin's an' sweet cream." There was quiet for a minit while we all digested that meal.

"I think my Ma'd hev crispy fried chicken an' chicken gravy from the same skillit; buttermilk biscuits; springhouse butter; black-eyed peas with hog jowl; fried okra; a wilted lettuce salit with bacon crumbles an' vinegar. She made the best white layer cake an' sometimes had chocklit icing on it. I'd drink 'bout a gallon o' sweet tea, 'long with it," Rip heaved a big sigh.

"Fer breakfast, my mammy 'ould hev fresh soft fried eggs an' grits with a big gob o' butter under it; hog sausage patties, all you could eat; milk so cold it wus 'most icy; biscuits an' slow molasses an' scuppernong jelly—thet's white muscadines fer you who don't know. Ef you got hungry b'fo dinner, there'd allus be a cold biscuit with a sausage pattie stuck in it." Wayback

Tom wiped his mouth an' closed his eyes. "Ye-e-s-s, sir!"

"After hog killin', we allus had breakfast with potaters sliced thin an' fried; eggs scrambled in head cheese; hot spicy sausages; hotcakes with butter meltin' on 'em with maple syrup; an' *hot* coffee with heavy cream. Sometimes, Ma'd whip cream an' put a dollop on top o' th' cups o' coffee."

"Leapin', by thet breakfast, I can tell you's frum th' nor'east," Pres allowed.

"Damnyankee, thet's whut I ur!" Leapin' mocked.

"Never hed much, but Pa an' Ma seed we didn't go hungry," Jones said. "Best eatin' I 'members wus brown beans an' pork belly with the buttons on; t'maters an' onions diced up an' stirred t'gether with salt an' pepper; okra, sliced an' fried and some steamed with the stems on so's it wouldn't be slimey— buttermilk biscuits. Ma'd steep tea overnight, cool it in the spring, an' put wild honey in it fer sweetenin'. But the meal I 'members most was supper when Ma baked cornbread in a square skillit with crispy corners an' I crumbled thet hot bread in a big ol' glass o' cold buttermilk an' ate it with a spoon. Wasn't fer cornbread an' buttermilk I would hev been stunted—or starved."

"My Ma allus said cornbread was Johnny Everyday an' biscuits Billy Seldom," I recalled.

"I shore hope you boys is enjoyin' yore meals," Les called from th' dark where he had been listenin'. "I don't s'pose enny uv you ever ate a *real* Pennsylvania Dutch meal like I uz reared on. We hed sweet potaters baked in the peel; chicken an' dumplins so white they hurt yore eyes t' look at em; 'sparagus sprouts steamed in butter, so tender they fairly melted in yore mouth; thick slices o' sugar-cured ham, cold or fried; green onions b'fore they bulbed; cabbage boiled an' sprinkled with cayenne pepper; hot loaf yeast bread browned with salt-water crust an' lots of sour cream butter; strawberry an' rhubarb pie. Sometimes there'd be punkin pie or shoofly pie in off seasons."

"Never heered o' shoofly pie, but I shore loved buttermilk pie," Tom said. There was a long quiet spell while some rolled another cigarette. "You been awful quiet while we wus eatin' so much, Daylight, what did you'uns eat in the Ozarks?" Rip asked.

"We allus ate well," I replied, "Don't 'member ever goin' hungry, an' we allus had a great variety to eat frum th' truck garden. I wus r'memberin' a meal I had when I wus a teenager on a trip into th' hills with my pa. He had some business up in th' hills west o' Village at th' Forks an' he said I could come along. Well, 'way back in th' hills we came to a small farmin' community an' passin' a house th' man haled us frum th' garden. He came over to th' fence with his hoe in his hand an' talked to Pa awhile. Pa introduced me to him, 'Zenas, this is Uncle George Clutts.'

" 'Glad to meet you, Zenas,' He had a big white mustache and though he seemed quite old to me, his hand was firm and rough from work an' I liked him right off. After they had talked awhile, Pa said we had to git on so's we could git home afore dark.

" 'You'll have t' be by here by noon to make it,' Uncle George said. 'We'll have dinner ready for you.'

" 'That won't be necessary, we brought some meat and bread,' Pa answered, but Uncle George insisted. 'Won't have it any other way. Mother would be disappointed if you didn't sit at her table,' indicating his wife who was rockin' on the porch shellin' beans.

" 'That young man needs a good meal to keep from being stunted,' she called. 'We'll be lookin' for you shortly after noon.'

"Pa couldn't say no to that, so we went on to take care of business. Th' man Pa went to see lived way up in th' woods, I forget his name. We drove our wagon to th' end of th' road an' walked near two miles down a slim trail t' git there.

71

"We came out o' th' woods into th' man's yard, and he called from th' porch, 'Come on in an' set a spell. Mighty warm today, have a drink.' He motioned toward th' end of th' porch where two buckets sat on a shelf. A gourd dipper hung on a porch post an' I hesitated, not knowin' which of those buckets t' dip from.

" 'Bucket on th' left is 'shine, th' other one is water,' th' old man called. He was watchin' me an' chucklin'.

" 'You keep that dipper out of th' 'shine, son,' Pa said with a grin. That moonshine was as crystal clear as th' water an' I allus regretted not sneakin' a sip.

"We got back to th' Cluttses' shortly after high noon. Now, I'm gonna describe this meal even though I doubt you'll believe any of it."

"Go on, Daylight, I'll believe you," Jones said.

"Th' table was set when we went in an' it was much like other meals I had in those hills, only this one stands out in my mind. Mrs. Clutts must have cooked all mornin'. She had black-eyed peas; butter beans; turnip greens with poke; pickled beets; fried okra; sliced and boiled turnips; radishes, red *and* icicle; crisp, raw carrots; cream sweet peas an' carrots; chicken an' dumplin's; snap beans flavered with bacon grease; an' a lettuce an' cabbage salad with onions, carrots, radishes, cucumbers, an' bacon all chopped fine in it an' vinegar an' oil dressing. There was a big bowl of mashed taters; sliced cucumbers an' purple onions in vinegar; hot cornbread; sliced tomaters; sweet corn on th' cob an' a bowl of creamed corn; a dozen deviled eggs; fried green apples with cinnamon; fresh churned butter; sweet milk, cold as springwater; an' a plate o' fried morrel mushrooms from th' orchard . . ."

"Whe-e-e-ooo." Tom was shakin' his head an' laughin'.

". . . and on th' sideboard there was peach pie, fresh strawberries, shortcake an' whipped cream, sliced cantaloupe, sweet potato pie, an' a *p*-can pie."

"You mean p*kahn* pie," put in a damnyankee.

"Down there, we called it *p*-can," I said. There followed a spirited discussion on th' correct pronouncing an' opinions were divided generally along that Mason-Dixon line.

"That was *some* meal you described there, Daylight, you shore you didn't bunch two or three meals together?" Pres asked.

"I'm sure, 'cause for over an hour, I ate some of all of it. Ever' time a spot cleared on my plate, somethin' else was put there, not that a growin' boy of twelve or fourteen would refuse any of it. I ate all of it, includin' *two* ears of corn, but had to taper off on desserts an' only et strawberry shortcake. Mrs. Clutts sent me off with a slice of *p*-can pie, though, an' 'long about midafternoon we ate it t' tide us over 'til supper."

"Seein's how you eat now, Daylight, I can believe that," chuckled Rip.

"I suppose they have both passed on by now, an' I hope when we sit down with th' Lord for that supper he talked about that Mrs. Clutts is th' cook!"

"I seen dinners like thet whur I growed up in south Missoury," one of th' Rafter boys said, "but I allus had t' eat at second table an' there weren't all thet variety left over by then."

"Yeah, that second table weren't always best," another put in. "I wus near-bout growed afore I knowed fried chickens hed laigs! Pa allus told th' parson, 'Now dig in, preacher, if yuh don't mind takin' food frum th' kids!' "

"Never saw a preacher thet minded," someone muttered.

"I don't know about you boys, but after that meal, I feel like turnin' in an' sleepin' it off," Pres allowed.

We stayed there three more days b'fore that river went down enough t' cross, but th' next mornin' a tradin' outfit come up that had food an' they took pity on us. Pres allowed we could kill one o' th' drag fer meat an' we done pretty good after that.

There wern't any big rivers t' cross after th' Canadian til we got to Dry Cimarron an' it wasn't too bad. By th' time we got to th' Arkansas, it had gone down enough t' be crossable. Those steers shore fattened some along an' we only lost three steers on th' way, but by th' time we got t' Dodge, we had picked up some mavericks and our final count was two-thousand-four head. I don't think that buyer even noticed that two of those "steers" was heifers!

CHAPTER 8
LOST IN THE BASIN

"I haven't told you 'bout th' time we found a preacher lost in the basin." Zenas was standing at the edge of the porch, hands in pockets, looking out over the heat waves rising from the floor of the Tularosa Basin. It was comfortable sitting in the shade of the porch high on the mountainside where it was much cooler than down on the flats.

"When th' range was open down th' Sacramento Valley, cows would follow th' grass up and down th' valley as seasons dictated. They wintered in th' basin where it was much warmer than up in th' mountains an' forage was not covered with snow. In springtime, grass greened on th' basin first, then it would slowly green at higher elevations an' die out in th' flats. It didn't take much herdin' t' git cows up th' valleys an' keep them in green grass. Th' most work was in springtime when cattle were mixed with other outfits an' scattered all over th' basin. We had to round 'em up an' git them headed up th' right valley. Outfits from all around th' basin would get together an' chouse out all th' cattle an' separate th' herds. On th' average, they didn't wander too far, but occasionally we'd have a cow or two as far north as th' Malpais. Mostly, they stayed close along Sacramento River and out west of that a ways.

"Sanchez cows mixed with Rafter JD cows an' we pretty much let them stay mixed through most of th' summer season since our cows wintered mostly around Sanchez range. Come summer an' that whole range was green, we would push those cows as high up th' valley as th' Rafter range went, then let them scatter an' graze. As fall came on, cooler weather would push them down th' valley an' finally out

75

*on th' flats below Sanchez's spread. We just had to be sure some o'
the more stubborn ones didn't get trapped in snow. Come spring, that
whole process would start over in reverse order."*

It was early in my time with th' outfit. We were out on th' flats
'til June roundin' up cows an' sendin' them upriver. That winter
had been wetter than average an' cows had been harder t' round
up 'cause water was so plentiful. That year th' Sacramento River
flowed further out into th' desert than I have ever seen it. By th'
time water holes were just muddy spots, those cows began thinkin' they should mosey on upstream to water an' they became
easier t' handle.

I remember Leapin' Lon swearin' at them then sayin', "I
swear those cows must think I work for them 'stead of the
brand, they's so independent." He popped th' nearest one with
his rope to hurry her on. She turned and stared at him a moment before ambling on.

"She wus tryin' t' d'cide whether t' go for water or have a
chunk of yore hide," Jones grinned.

"Mess with me any, ol' gal, an' you jist might find yoreself on
th' business end of a fork," Leapin' said.

We were dry camped out a ways from th' river, nighthawk
makin' a water run ever' day or so. This was to be our last night
here, then we would move on upriver, pushin'cattle into th' valley where they would be much easier t' handle. Some of our
boys had already eaten supper an' had held what they had
rounded up that day until we drove our few in, then we drove
them on across th' Sanchez spread before dark. Cookie refused
t' move in th' dark, so we were to break camp early in th'
mornin' and help him catch up with th' herd. In daylight about
th' only hazard he could git into was deep sand, so we would
have it pretty easy if he didn't let those mules get him stuck.

Ridin' into camp, we found a surprizin' visitor. It was th'

Methodist Episcopal circuit preacher. I ain't forgot his name, but I won't mention it, for his people still live around here and I don't want to embarrass them by tellin' this tale. He was sittin' in th' shade with th' water bucket atween his knees sippin' from th' dipper. Covered with alkali dust, his face was burned red an' eyes swolen. His horse didn't look much better, covered with dust and lookin' awful fagged out.

"Well, hello, preacher, what brings you so far down this way?" Jones called.

"Nothing but God's design," he smiled back, "it certainly isn't where I intended to be!"

"He just r-r-ride in from thee br-r-rush," Manuel said, wiping flour on his apron. "Say he pas me by but 'cept for my seenging."

"Yes, if he hadn't been singing, I would have walked on by and not seen him," the preacher said.

Lon caught my eye an' nodded toward that droopin' horse. I took his reins an' led him around to th' water barrels. He shore was beat an' I had a time keepin' him from founderin' on water. While he sipped th' little I gave him, I slipped th' saddle from his back an' rubbed him down some with his blanket dipped in water. When he lifted his head, I washed his face and the matted dust from his eyes. He seemed grateful and after a few minutes I gave him some more water. All th' while, men on th' other side o' th' wagon was talkin'.

"Where yuh been, Preacher?" Jones asked.

"I preached at Las Cruces Sunday and planned to cross the basin to La Luz with the mail carrier Monday, but when I got to San Augustin Pass, he hadn't showed up. After waiting a while, I decided to mosey along slow-like and he would catch up with me. I rode all day and he never came. He must have got delayed for some reason. When night came, I decided to keep on riding in the cool to save the horse, but we strayed from the trail somewhere and by morning we were both lost. At sunup, I decided to head straight for the mountains and we've been all day getting here."

"Yore still a good ride from th' mountains an' I don't think you would hev found water when you got there," Lon put in.

"I walked all afternoon trying to save the horse and if it hadn't been for Manuel's singing, I guess we would still be walking."

"First good thing I've heard come from Manuel's singing," Jones chuckled. He dodged a chip thrown by Manuel.

"Many good theengs have come from my seenging, cowboy, but tin ears don't heer eet well!"

I thought a moment or two; two days without water and a fagged-out horse. "You're a good twenty-five or thirty miles south of La Luz, Preacher," I said.

He smiled. "I don't guess I'll make it in time to preach the Wednesday night service with my horse in the shape he's in."

"You might make it with a fresh horse an' a hard day's ride tomorrow. We would lend you a horse, but they have gone on ahead and we don't have one t' spare," Leapin' said. "Maybe you could preach that sermon to th' camp tomorrer night when we catches up to 'em."

"That may just be what the Lord had in mind when we went astray." The preacher brightened some.

Just then, Manuel called supper and we all set to fillin' our plates. We had just settled down for th' business of eatin' when Preacher said, "Gentlemen"—now there's a word rarely applied to cowboys—"Gentlemen, please allow me to bless this meal."

There was a lot of shufflin' for the "gentlemen" t' stand an' not spill food or drink. Manuel crossed himself and we tried t' figure how t' remove our hats. Preacher prayed somethin' like this: "Lord, I thank Thee for this food you so bountifully have provided. Bless the hands that prepared it and for his voice singing in this wilderness. Most of all, Lord, I thank you for the water you have refreshed us with. May its fountains never run dry! Amen."

Manuel said, "Ameen!" as he crossed himself again and gave us a triumphant look as if to say, "There, what do you theenk of my seenging now? I deedn't heer *your* hands an' voice blessed!"

The meal over, we lit pipes and settled back to watch th' sun set and relax a few minutes b'fore bedtime. With cows and cavyyard gone, there would be no watches tonight and all would get a rare full night's sleep.

"Well, Preacher, now that your ordeal is over, do you think you will stray far from the waterin' trough agin?" Jones asked.

He thought a moment before answering, "Oh, I imagine I will, I'm just like any other man, straying here and there. The Psalms say, 'As the hart pants for water, so my soul longs for Thee, O God,' implying that maybe the Psalmist had strayed from the Lord enough to miss Him. It's the same way with a lot of things, it's the fatigue that makes a man enjoy his rest as we are here, the hunger that makes him enjoy his food, and the thirst that makes him enjoy the water."

Lon drew on his pipe a couple of times, "Yore right there, Preacher, life *would* be dull if we hed it easy *all* of the time."

"It's like a newborn calf," the preacher continued. "He doesn't learn anything if you pick him up to walk the first time, but if he works to stand the first time, he's much more likely to make it. The struggle makes him strong. Getting up after you are knocked down prepares you to succeed somewhere on down the line."

"Well said, Preacher, an' now it is time fer me t' enjoy some hard-earned sleep, 'cause I been deprived o' it all roundup!" Jones said, tapping out his pipe. In a few moments he had rolled out his bed and was soon sleeping.

"I guess he don't subscribe to Rip's theory o' storin' up sleep in th' winter," I said.

"Wouldn't work for him, anyway, he don't b'lieve in sleepin' on his own time," Lon chuckled. "Preacher, I'll share my bedroll with you for the night. Gits kind of cold out here 'long about midnight."

"Thank you," the preacher said and we were all soon sleeping under that beautiful canopy of stars.

Manuel wus up earlier than usual, anticipatin' a long drive and busy day cookin' at th' end of it. We had horses saddled an' waitin' by th' time coffee was hot an' ate breakfast while Manuel noisily broke camp. His mules fought th' harness some, bein' lazy after their long rest, but we whispered sweet things in their ears an' got them hitched by th' time Manuel was seated on th' spring seat rarin' t' go. I tied Preacher's horse to th' tailgate and he sat with Manuel in th' wagon.

"Think I'll hang 'round th' wagon an' listen to Manuel cuss those mules in Mex. Wonder if Parson'll know what he's sayin'," Jones grinned.

"We'll know soon's he hits th' first sand hole." No sooner than I said that than th' right front wheel hit a boulder, wrenchin' th' wheels around almost bustin' th' tongue an' throwin' Manuel and Preacher off th' wagon seat. In an' instant, th' air turned Mexican blue as Manuel talked to the mules.

Preacher righted himself and resettled his hat on his head, "Those must be Spanish mules, Manuel."

"Sí, Meester Parson, they unnerstand thee Eenglish but leesen better to thee mother tongue."

Jones was siezed with a fit of coughing and I had to check on the parson's horse to make sure he was still secured. Lon trotted ahead a few yards lookin' for other obstacles. It took a few minutes for us to regain control and I dared not look either of th' two in the eye for some time.

"Don't guess he knows Mex," Jones whispered as he rode by.

Th' rest o' the day passed with Manuel speakin' Mexican to his mules an' American to th' parson. Some of the things he said were hilarious an' we were in stitches all day.

When Manuel stopped for a short noonin', Lon an' Jones rode on ahead spreadin' word that Parson would preach at th' cow camp that night. In those days, hearin' a preachin' was a big deal an' folks would come from miles around to meet an' sing an' hear th' Word spoken even if they weren't church-goin' people. We knew there would be a good crowd there. Even th' mostly Catholic Mexican Americans would come to listen an' be a part of the gatherin'—an' some o' them couldn't understand half of what was said.

We pushed hard t' git to th' campground as quick as possible. The boys had picked a spot up on a bare knoll that had plenty of open space for a gatherin' an' plenty of brush around it for shade for th' horses.

Quick as he got the word, Bob Green, our foreman, had a calf butchered an' big fire goin' before Manuel arrived. It didn't take long for him to get his spit set up an' we helped him load meat on it. Nighthawk an' I were set to turnin' th' spit while Manuel set t' cookin' enough for a big gathering.

Someone came up with a couple of hay wagons an' they took th' beds off an' set them on blocks t' serve as a table and pulpit stage for th' parson. Some of the boys drove our herd on up th' valley so they wouldn't interfere with th' doin's in any way an' by late afternoon, all was ready for a preachin'. Folks began t' gather from most every direction and by time t' start, there must have been fifty to seventy-five people gathered. Th' whole outfit from one ranch showed up. We was some put out they had time t' spruce up an' we were still dusty an' dirty.

I don't know how they done it on such short notice, but near every woman brought a pie or some other dish.

Preacher set meetin' time early enough t' finish an' let people eat an' those that had to git headed home b'fore dark. Folks who lived farther away would spend th' night. When time come, he stood before th' pulpit an' called the people t' worship. Women spread blankets an' seated themselves an' kids on them an' th' men squatted or sat in a ring b'hind them. He led us in four or five hymns we "sang lustily," as he called it. Th' custom in those days was that th' Holy Pulpit was to be occupied only for th' purpose of preachin' an' so it was that when Parson was ready to speak, he climbed up on his makeshift pulpit and takin' up his big black-bound Bible began his sermon. He started slow an' worked up to a reg'lar stem-winder of a sermon about sin an' salvation and th' crowd thoroughly appreciated it. Some was disappointed he only preached about forty-five minutes, but he explained that he reserved full sermons for Sundays and made the weekday sermons shorter in consideration of the du-ties an' demands of th' work week. When th' sermon was over, we passed a hat for an offerin' an' Parson said grace for th' meal.

Th' Holy Pulpit was added to the other table and they both fairly overflowed with food. Manuel an' th' ladies had made a reg'lar feast with beans an' roast, ribs in a firey sauce, an' son-of-a-gun stew. "Ever'thing but horns, hooves, an' holler," as someone said, an' gallons of coffee, not to mention all those pies and desserts. Everyone was filled proper, even th' kids. Families began driftin' away towards homes so as not to be on th' road too much after dark but th' vaqueros lingered visitin' an' catchin' up on th' latest news from around th' basin.

Finally, it was slap-up dark an' quiet settled over the camp. First watch had gone out to th' herd, their only task to keep cattle from backtrackin' to th' desert. We didn't care if they scattered in th' valley so long as they were pointed uphill where greener grass was.

"That was a mighty fine sermon, Preacher," Bob said as he

shook his hand. "Folks at La Luz missed a treat, but folks around here shore got one."

"Thank you, Bob, I suppose that was as the Lord meant it to be or that horse and I wouldn't have gotten lost in the wilderness like that. It did seem that the people were very receptive to the Word. I will try to get down here more often in the future. I know you are busy with the drive, but can I have a word with all the men before I leave in the morning?"

"I'll see that they are all at breakfast an' you can speak to them then," Bob replied.

With that, he set watches for th' night an' we turned in wonderin' what th' parson had to say. Just after daylight, th' Old Man rode in from th' ranch an' he an' Preacher had a little confab b'fore breakfast was called.

"Now Jim, I know you have been around here long enough t' know that cowboy language is full o' profanity on th' whole," Zenas said, *"but I have refrained from speakin' in that tongue in order to make what I say readable without mothers, teachers, and preachers condemnin' th' whole thing as unfit for tender ears. Only in a place or two where it seemed appropriate to th' occasion have I quoted cuss word an' all. I used to be as bad at cussin' as any of those boys, but marryin' an' raising kids an' grandkids, I found that it wasn't necessary to use that kind o' language on the gentler race.*

"Cows an' cowboys seem to require cussin' just to get th' word over to them. We once had an English visitor at th' ranch an' no one could understand him until he learned to sprinkle his talk with 'x-pletives.' Even now a cowboy would have a hard time understandin' such language as 'pass th' salt' unless you inserted a word or two describin' *salt or th' person addressed. I'm not condemnin' or con-donin' th' cussin', just statin' facts as they are. I say this as a preliminary explanation for Parson's talk that mornin', as you shall soon see."*

When th' last night watch came in for breakfast, day herdin' was delayed in order for us all to hear th' preacher. He stood up an' spoke quite earnestly about the necessity of living a life worthy of emulation, pointin' out how important it was to set a good example b'fore th' community. He noted that since cowboyin' an' roundups was strickly men business an' women was not around, it was easy to git into th' habit of swearin' an' usin' language that couldn't be used in polite company, meanin' by that mostly where ladies was present.

"I have a feeling that is the reason so many of you are shy around the ladies," he said. "You're afraid your tongue might slip into using the language of the range and embarrass yourself."

He wasn't far from wrong there.

"You must remember that what you practice is what you become. If you consistently use profanity, you will eventually become a profane person that people are uncomfortable around and you would be uncomfortable in polite company," he continued. "I'm glad Mr. Dearing rode in this morning and I have made a proposal to him which he has gladly accepted. It now remains to be seen if you will accept the challenge I give you.

"The challenge is this: Will you make a solemn covenant with me and Mr. Dearing and before God that from this moment on, you will let Mr. Dearing do all the swearing for this outfit?"

Now, that hit like a bomb. You could have heard a pin drop in th' White Sands thirty miles away. I've always heard the term "cuss like a sailor," but if sailors could out-cuss a cowboy, they would be doin' *some*. Thinkin' about it an' lookin' around that crowd, I knew I had heard swearin' in seven languages, not countin' English.

"Parson, do you mean swearin' in American?" Rip asked hopefully.

"Swearing is swearing in any language, be it English, Spanish, or Apache," he replied.

With that, Manuel's eyes rolled heavenward and he ducked b'hind th' wagon. In a minute, we heard the dishes softly rattling in the wreck pan. It happened that Elfuego Sanchez and Mecio were in that crowd an' Effie spoke up.

"Padre, I am owner of thee Sanchez r-r-ranch down the r-r-r-river, but I am weeling to let Meester Bill do *all* the swearing for the Sanchez r-r-ranch if it please heem!"

Well, that broke the ice, an' we all began to discuss among ourselves th' pros an' cons o' Parson's proposal.

"I know I use swearin' a lot workin' cows, but what else can I *say?*" Wayback asked.

"That would take away half my vo-cab-u-lary." Leapin' was always using big words where he could.

"There you go already using profanity," Wayback said straight-faced.

"Taint profanity, Wayback, jest a big word," Lon shot back.

"I would hate to have my mother know I use some o' th' words I've been usin'," I said. "I guess it wouldn't be too hard t' quit now rather than ten years from now."

"Us old-timers would have it a lot harder," Bob agreed, "but I'm willin t' try ef the rest of you are."

"Twon't do no good 'lessen we all does it." Jones spoke for th' first time. After a few moments, he said "Well the plan has merit. I'm in if th' rest o' you are."

Lookin' around, no one was objectin', so Bob spoke up as foreman o' th' bunch. "Looks like you got a deal, Parson, we're all willin' t' take the oath."

"No oath required, Bob. The Lord said, 'Do not swear, but

let what you say be Yes or No,' but we can make a covenant together."

And that's just what we did; from that time on th' only swearin' t' be done in our outfit was to be done by the Boss— an' that shore did make a heap o' problems for th' rest of us.

The good parson seemed moved by what we had done and smiled broadly as he saddled up an' we said our "goodbyes." The Boss had offered him a fresher horse, but he 'lowed ol' dobbin had been with him some time and knew th' circuits pretty well—except that across th' basin—that he would just keep on ridin' him. The trip north along th' base o' th' mountains was pretty plain an' there was plenty of water, so we didn't worry about Parson an' horse strayin' afar. A wave of th' hand an' he was off, leavin' us with our day's work an' a new language t' learn.

"Let's git those . . . cows t' th' home range, boys," Bob called. "Manuel, we'll stop at th' ranch tonight, so you kin git . . . on up th' trail with them . . . mules. Better provision up for a couple of days beyond that we'll have to chouse those . . . cows all th' way to the top er they'll never go on their own . . . selves."

We all grinned at th' effort he had to make *not* to say certain words, but none of us dared offer any help lest we stumble. This was gonna be harder than we thought.

Manuel nodded, "Sí, Señor Bob, I weel have supper in thee bunkhouse wheen you arrive." Then in Spanish, he said, "Git up you damned ol' mules, we're goin' home an' don't pull any damned shenanigans on me or I'm liable to shoot your ass . . ."

He was interrupted by laughter and shouts from th' rest of us.

"Not in *any* language, Manuel!"

"We heard that, now yore in trouble!"

"Better 'pologize t' th' Boss, Manuel."

"Either that or we start callin' you Boss."

Manuel had his hands so full of controlin' those mules, he could barely cross himself an' roll apologetic eyes at th' Boss as he rumbled out of camp and we roared with laughter.

Now, don't think we took our commitment lightly; we didn't for two reasons. One, in those days a man's word was as good as bond; and two, we all knew what the preacher had said about cursin' was right an' we needed to show more restraint in our language.

"I got a feelin' we're gonna need you t' ride 'long with us some 'til we git used t' this new way o' talkin, Boss," Bob grinned.

"Wish I could, boys," he chuckled, "but th' Austin boys are comin' over to th' ranch an' I've got to be there by noon t' meet 'em. You'll just have t' keep notes on what needs t' be said an' we'll talk over them later."

"Oooh, man, this is gonna be a lo-ong day," moaned Way-back Tom. "I'se feelin' peak-ed a'ready!"

"Mount up, boys, th' sooner we start, th' sooner we finish," Bob called.

There was th' usual antics of horses as we mounted and they shook out their kinks.

"Hold, there you son-of-a—" Lon caught himself just in time.

Th' rest of us was pretty tight-lipped, afeered somethin' would slip out. We got lined out an' headed for th' herd at a trot. A vaquero knows what t' do t' move cows an' we were soon gatherin' up that herd an' headin' them out up th' valley without Bob havin' t' say a single word. The sun peekin' over th' Sacramento peaks found us in good trail formation and well on our way.

We had th' time t' let them noon quite awhile an' got them to th' ranch just at sunset. Manuel rang th' bell b'fore we had our horses unsaddled an' we had t' hurry t' git to th' table afore he yelled at us fer bein' late. Bill Austin was sittin' at th' table when we walked in fer supper. He preferred our table manners t' those in th' big house. After supper we sat on the ramada smokin' an' restin' up.

"Hear you boys took th' parson's oath t' ab-stain frum cussin'," he said.

"Tell yuh what," Rip said, "it's a good thing that parson didn't say anything 'bout *thinkin'* er I'd be in a whole heap o' trouble."

"Yeh, my . . . horse kept lookin' back t' see who was sittin' on 'im," Jones said. "He couldn't unnerstan' anythin' I 'us sayin' 'til he learned t' read my mind, then he wus ok."

"Parson didn' say anythin' about horses not cussin', so I lets mine do th' talkin'," Wayback Tom said. "We got 'long purty good 'cept fer whin I needed t' tell him somethin'. Th' secon' time I talked to him without no cussin', he stopped dead still an' gave me a long look. I hed to talk real . . . kind t' him t' keep th' . . . him frum thowin' me off!"

"This here's gonna be a long . . . pull ef we's to keep thet commitment," Leapin' Lon allowed.

"I'm shore glad Preacher didn' wander inta *our* camp with that idee in his head," Bill said.

"I didn't know much cussin' afore I started runnin' . . . cows, reckon th' two just goes t'gether," I said.

"I think yore right, Daylight, it ain't nat'ral t' say anything 'bout a . . . cow or to one 'ithout cussin'," Rip said.

"That goes twice for the . . . mules, Señor Reep." Manuel was standin' in th' door wipin' his hands on his apron, "I had one h . . . ard time geeting them . . . here, an' they was laughin' at mee most of thee . . . way. I theenk I hire a . . . 'Pache boy to r-r-ride with me an' talk to them for me." That was quite a concession for a Mexican American to say about an Apache, seein' how much they loved each other.

"Say, there's a idee," Jones perked up. "We can hire out our cussin' an' ever'thin' will be ok with th' preacher."

"Ain't 'nough money in this whole . . . outfit t' hire someone fer thet. He'd hev t' be on duty twenty-four hours a day jist t' keep up with any . . . two o' us," Bob said.

"I wrote down all the things I wanted Boss t' say, til I ran out o' paper," I said, "then I jest throwed it away, ain't no good if you cain't say it on th' occasion o' needin' to."

"I 'spects it's gonna be a lot harder t' work proper 'thout cussin' ridin' 'long, s'pose the Boss'd give us a raise, Bob?" Lon asked.

Bob put that in his pipe an' smoked it a minit or two. "Noo, I don' s'pose he 'ould, Leapin'," he puffed, "but he might cut yore . . . pay ef yuh didn' keep up yore end."

Leapin' groaned. "Might hev known, give a man more work an' cut his . . . pay! Didn't I love this . . . work so much, I swear I find some . . . saloon t' hire on to t' swamp out."

"Job's too technic'l fer you, better stick t' the. . . . cowboyin'," Jones chuckled.

". . . lot you knows 'bout saloon keepin'," Lon flared. "Alls you know is how t' kiss the . . . table tops an' floor!"

"Time fer me t' hit the hay afore you two goes t' slingin' fists or lead over the finer pints of saloon keepin'." Bob stood up an' tapped out his pipe. "Ain't slept in a . . . bunk in six weeks, an' I don' want t' hear any . . . snorin' nuther. Bill, you can have my bunk an' I'll climb up on top."

That broke up th' confab 'cept for Jones an' Leapin' joshin' each other about how t' sweep out a saloon.

I sat awhile until lights went out in th' bunkhouse an' th' big house an' went down to th' tank an' washed my clothes an' myself. Them pants was gittin' awful thin in th' backsides, too. They dried on th' back of a chair by th' fire overnight an' was ready to go by time t' I got up. We slept a little later than usual since there was no hurry t' get those cows up th' valley. I heard

Bill get up 'bout sunrise an' soon he an' Charlie rode out of th' yard.

Manuel's holler brought us out an' after breakfast we got busy. Those cussed mules thought their work was over when they got to th' corral an' we had a time convincin' them t' git hitched up agin so soon. I think Rip whispered things in their ears t' git them goin'.

"T'aint fair whisperin', either, Rip," I said kind of low.

"Yuh want t' git these . . . mules hitched up, don't you?"

"Yeah, but Mr. Dearing is right up there at th' house, he could be helpin' us."

Rip just laughed, "Th' Old Man cain't be ever'where, Daylight."

Somehow, Manuel got th' wagon out of th' yard. We didn't wait 'round t' see, bein' we had to gather an' move cows handicapped as we were.

We were gone three days, one more than we expected because those cows were gettin' pretty uncooperative about movin' to th' top of th' valley. Manuel was hard-pressed t' keep us in chow, but by tightenin' our belts a might, we made it. After noonin' on th' third day, he hitched up an' headed for th' ranch, havin' t' hold back those mules considerable.

We took our time goin' back, lookin' th' range over an' cleanin' out a couple o' water holes. It was near dark when we came across our chuck wagon 'bout a half mile from th' house. It had th' front truck gone an' was sittin' on its nose all forlorn-like. It didn't take much t' see that those mules hed run away with Manuel an' we hurried on to th' house t' see what damage had been done.

The front wheels with th' doubletree an' a piece of tongue was layin' not far from th' corral. From there to th' corral was a trail of broken harness and hardware, th' last debris bein th' front end of th' tongue.

"Wowwee," Tom whispered. Th' Old Man was sittin' on th' porch o' th' bunkhouse when we walked up.

"Supper's gonna be a little late, boys," he said. "Manuel's kinda skint up an' the wife's cookin' fer us up to the house. Wash up an' we'll all go up when she calls."

As we washed up, he told us what happened. "The parson told me when we met the other day that he didn't expect us to keep his commitment permanent as a matter of reality an' common sense, but he did want us t' think about th' language we used an' tone it down some.

"I was sittin' in the big room doin' my books when I heard them comin' into the yard draggin' wheels an' Manuel tangled up in the reins draggin' b'hind. By the time I got out there, he had got them stopped an' began unhookin' them from the truck. He was cussin' those mules in two or three languages—it must have been three, 'cause I heard words I'd never heard b'fore. I reached back an' closed the door so the wife wouldn't hear.

"It seemed that Manuel had things under control, so I sat down on the porch an' watched. That cursin' continued the whole time he was unhitchin' things an' I thought two or three times he was goin' to abuse them, but he never did beyond throwin' dirt an' rocks at them as he ran 'em off. He started limpin' toward the bunkhouse an' I pretended to be readin' papers I had in my hand. When he got closer, I called to him.

" 'Manuel, did I just hear someone swearing down by th' corral?' "

"Sí, Señor, I theenk you deed."

"Do you know who it was?"

"Sí, Señor, eet was me, I theenk."

"Don't you remember the covenant we entered into with th' parson the other day, that *I* should do all the swearin' for the outfit?"

"Sí, sí, Señor Deering," said Manuel, "but those mules, they don' unnerstan' weethout thee swearing and you were not therrre to do eet and eet had to bee done *r-r-right theen*!"

"Boys, I think by that, it's time I should release you from the covenant!"

CHAPTER 9
THE FORT DODGE CATTLE DRIVE
1874–75

It wasn't until a few years before Bob Green moved to Arizona and bought a spread there that Zenas had a year-round job at the Rafter JD. Until then he didn't have a job from some time in November until March of the next year. Sometimes he used this time to visit back east or ramble as funds provided or he took on various jobs to tide himself over until the spring roundups started.

In th' winter of 1873, a buyer for the Army passed through th' country lookin' for beef cattle. He told John Dearing that Fort Dodge had received orders t' buy three thousand head at two cents above market value by th' fall of '74. So it was that instead of drivin' cattle out of th' basin into th' Sacramento Valley, th' Rafter JD, C–B, an' Sanchez outfits built up a beef herd of a thousand head. The herd was made up of four hundred each from Rafter an' C-B, and Sanchez threw in two hundred.

Preston Dycus from th' C–B was trail boss with Bill Austin, Tom Short, and Boog Sowell as cowhands. Bill went along t' handle sale negotiations as well as acting as a cowhand. I have t' say that he fit well, not interfering with Preston even though he was part owner of th' C-B. He was a fine hand and held up his end an' then some despite bein' some older than th' rest of us.

The Boss sent me, Enoch Hunsucker and Lon Sims to represent th' Rafter outfit. They sent Manuel and th' Rafter chuck wagon and Tomas Ortiz from th' west side of th' Organs as wrangler. Mecio Sanchez came as a hand representing his dad's interests.

In addition to the cattle, we had six mules for th' wagon and forty head of horses. That outfit could have handled a herd of twenty-five-hundred head or more easily, but because of th' nature of th' drive and th' unsettled Indian situation, th' bosses thought it best to over-man th' drive. It turned out to be a good thing.

The plan was t' drift th' herd north letting them fatten up on th' way and reach Fort Dodge some time in late July or early August. We left th' rodeo on th' 24th of May to th' tune of curses from those left to work th' home range. They didn't know Bill was gonna hire some hands in Tularosa and send them to th' roundup.

It was really hard work t' get that herd out of th' basin and into unfamiliar territory where they would stick together. The whole time in th' basin, day and night, we had t' guard agin runaways. Cookie and th' wrangler got more sleep than us hands which is just th' opposite from normal trailin'. Not to say that *anyone* on a trail drive got any excess sleep.

By th' time we got past Little Black Peak in the Malpaís, th' whole outfit was dead on their feet and our horses were 'bout done in. We bedded that herd on th' north side of Coyote Canyon just south of where Cooper is now. They were still restless and hungry from bein' pushed so hard.

At supper, Preston said, "I think that by driving th' herd hard one more day, we can get far enough from their home range that they'll settle down some. We'll push 'em to just southeast of Gallinas Peak, then take a couple days t' let them graze and rest up."

"Yuh mind ef we'uns . . . rest up a little then too?" Ol' Van asked between sips of coffee. "I don't need eny rest," Boog said. "I've taught my hosses t' herd while I sleep an' only wake me up when they need me. I got plenty o' rest an' relaxation."

"In that case, yuh kin hev my watch t'night as well as yore own an' I'll git some sleep," C-B Tom said. We called him Shorty even though he was just above six feet.

"He just thinks he's got his horses trained," I said. "I passed them on watch last night an' they *both* were asleep, that horse just walkin' on."

"Is it just es dang'rous t' wake up a sleep-walkin' horse es a man?" Leapin' Lon asked.

"I had a sleep-walkin' horse down in Texas once," Bill said. "Walked us off th' bank into th' Pecos one night an' we had t' swim all th' way back t' Horsehead Crossing t' git out! Musta been five miles or more. I traded him to a feller named Nat Straw on th' Chisom ranch for a buckskin." He took a long sip from his cup and continued, "Turned out Nat got rid of *his* horse 'cause he was a sleepwalker an' dumped him in th' Pecos once. I passed through there goin' back t' Texas an' met Nat by chance on th' range.

" 'How'd yuh like that buckskin?' he asked.

" 'Fine,' I says, 'so long as you don't use him as a night horse an' stay away from bluffs an' gullies.'

" 'Yeah,' he says, 'on'y one o' us kin sleep at a time, I guess.'

"We allowed we came out even tradin' sleepwalker for sleepwalker."

We did push th' herd one more day, but Manuel stopped short of our intended ground when Preston found good grass and water south of Gallinas Peak. That herd spread out th' next day and grazed contentedly just as if they knew what we had planned. We needed only a couple of us at a time t' watch them and th' rest of us got some good sleep.

"Wonder if Rip is right about bankin' up sleep fer later," Boog mused.

"Be quiet, I'm two days into last week catchin' up an' yore

disturbin' me," I said.

"By th' way, Zee," Shorty said from underneath his sombrero, "I would appreciate it if you took a bath tonight. I'm tired o' detourin' aroun' you upwind, my horses don't need that extra work."

"*Every*one weel geet thee bath tonight or there bee no breakfast een thee morning." Manuel shook his spoon at us. "An that includes coffee," he added.

"Awww . . ."

"Don' you buck up agin mee, I mean it! Tomas is busy an' you need to bring in more chips for thee fire too." And that was that. When Cookie lays down th' law all obey, even th' Trail Boss.

I guess it didn't matter if we had been further away from Apache country, we would have just traded tribes not th' problems they gave us. They could and did watch us without being seen and they were quick to take advantage of any laxness on our part. We had t' be on guard all th' time.

The first night of our layover was quiet. I guess it gave th' watchers time t' gather their friends, for that second night, no one got any sleep. It began just after our herd was gathered an' bedded at dark. Two Indians had crawled up to th' herd under wolfskins, their smell and movement makin' our steers nervous. Those Indians stood up on the far side of th' herd. Leapin' had seen th' stir and was ridin' around there just as those two jumped up yelling an' waving their pelts. Lon's horse didn't need urging, he broke into a gallop an' Lon steered him near enough to one of th' Indians that he could lash him with his quirt. It wrapped around that fellow's neck an' jerked him off his feet, nearly pulling Lon out of his saddle.

I was on t'other side of the herd riding my Nightbird an' they stampeded right into us. Before I knew it, I was ahead of th' run an' headed straight for camp. I could see destruction coming and tried my hardest t' turn them. Almost at th' last minute, they swerved and barely missed th' wagon. Horses and riders were scattering everywhere.

I had used up my ammunition turning th' leaders from camp and all I could do was yell and wave my soogan at them. All of a sudden a rider crossed in front of me and fired a shot in front of th' lead steer. He veered away from the flash an' we were soon able t' turn him. With help from others as they rode up, we soon had them in a mill and they slowly settled down.

"Spread 'em out, boys, until they cool a little and we'll bed them right here," Preston called from somewhere across th' herd. We walked through that herd, mostly scared t' death they might start up agin an' grind us to a pulp, but they were winded and didn't show run. It's amazing how much heat can be generated by a herd of cattle and get them hot. It's like an oven. The coolness o' th' night and a little breeze helped but before I was out of th' herd, every stitch on me was soaked an' Nightbird was soaked, foamy an' panting.

Turned out it was Shorty that had turned th' leader an' I called to him low, "I gotta get this horse t' water, Shorty, afore he falls out on me."

"Go ahead, Zee, we can handle this bunch. I 'magine I'll be close b'hind you with this cayuse. We're both soaked too."

My poor horse was still panting when I passed another rider on th' way to water. It was Preston. "Good work turning th' herd from camp, Zee, don't let that hoss get too much water at first." He rode on and it wasn't long before Shorty came up b'hind me. We walked our horses slow an' they calmed. By th' time we got t' water they had cooled a bit an' we let them drink a little.

Th' last time I had been that thirsty was when we had that scrape in th' basin when it was Injuns foulin' th' water. I drank

and drank and got madder and madder. When I had my fill, I
sat down and reloaded.

"Goin' huntin', Zee?"

"Damned right I am, Tom, an' I'm lookin' for th' two-legged
kind!" I gritted. I was so mad, my hands were shaking.

"Let me git another drink an' I'll go with yuh."

I watered Nightbird again an' led him away from th' tank. I
stripped th' saddle off an' rubbed him down with th' blanket.

Somehow, Tomas had kept th' cavyyard out of th' fray an'
together an' he drove them up to th' tank. "Tomas, catch out
me a horse and one for Zee, we're gonna go huntin'," Shorty
called. In a few minutes he rode up with a spare out of my
bunch th' boys called Sniffer for th' way he gave little snorts an'
sniffs when he was rode. "Sorry, Zee, this is thee first one I
come to."

" 'S all right, Tomas, he needs ridin' an' who knows he just
might be a night horse."

"I weel have you a horse soon, Mr. Shorty." And he rode off.

It was Tom's cutting horse that he caught and that turned
out good, for he was th' most rested in his bunch. There was a
fire goin' at camp an' we rode by t' see how things were. Manuel
was cleaning up where th' cattle had run through th' fire scattering pots an' ovens everywhere. He held up th' crushed coffee
pot, th' handle swingin' loose, "Coffee's gone. They broke my
sourdough jar an' I can't find all thee pots."

"May not until daylight, either," I said. "Tell Pres me an'
Shorty are goin' huntin', be back in th' mornin'."

"A deer would bee goood, but if you don't geet one, maybe
you geet antelope just as well."

"Th' critters we're huntin' don't cook good, too tough an'
stringy," Shorty said.

"You bee after thee two-legged kind? Bring heem back alive
an' I show you how to cook heem nice an' slow!"

"We jist might!" I said as I turned and followed Shorty.

We rode back to th' first bed ground and around on th' east side found a wolfskin where one of the Indians had dropped it. Th' horses shied from it and Shorty held my horse while I got down and lit a match. There was a place where one had fallen an' th' shod tracks nearby told a lot.

"Looks like Lon got one of 'em, there's drag marks where someone picked him up an' carried him off down to th' gully. They must have hidden their horses there."

"Should hev been a whole passel of them waitin' t' cut out a few head or get th' cavyyard. I didn't see or hear of them, did you?"

"No, wonder what happened to them." I remounted an' started down th' Indians' trail. My horse lowered his head to th' ground, sniffed an' snorted. He shore didn't like what he smelled. We hadn't gone a hundred and fifty yards until that horse stopped an' stretched out his neck sniffin' like he was a dog pointing a critter. We could just make something laying there an' Shorty rode up an' struck a match. It was an Indian, his head at such an angle that we knew his neck was broken.

"There's a red groove 'round his neck, bet Leapin' quirted him." Tom's match burned out and we moved on, my horse takin' th' lead, givin' little snorts from time to time.

"I'd swear that horse o' yours is sniffin' th' trail, Zee."

"Mebbe he's part hound."

"Give him his head an' let's see where he leads us."

"Already done that, Shorty."

We rode on, not sayin' much just letting that horse take us wherever he was going. In bushes, he gave a lot of snorts and fished around. A match or two showed us that several horses had been standing here for some time. Their tracks led up th' hill toward th' herd bed, then came back at a run goin' away. I pointed th' horse's head to their trail an' he resumed his trailing.

Down th' gully a ways, th' scrape of hooves told us that we were on solid rock, but he never wavered or changed his pace. Down to th' junction with another drain and up that drain to th' flats we went. The Drinkin Gou'd, as Wayback Tom called th' Big Dipper, was indicatin' it was near four o'clock when we noted a lighter sky in th' east. Another half hour an' we could just make out th' trail we were following. We figgered there were at least ten riders an' as th' light increased noted that one horse was shod.

They had run while we had had to walk and by now had a lead we could never eliminate even if we rode hard all day. Suddenly Sniffer stopped and turned sharply to th' right following one set of tracks that headed for a gully paralleling our trail. He wanted t' go down into th' gully, but I could see tracks plain from on top an' we walked along th' rim.

"Looky there!" Shorty said, and I looked up an' saw a body layin' at th' top of th' gully. I had been riding with my rifle across my knees and now I crooked it in my arm. A knicker told us there was a horse somewhere in th' brush below an' we drew away from th' rim so that we couldn't be seen from the bottom.

Shorty dismounted and crept up to th' dead Injun. "Looks like 'Pache."

"Peek over th' rim an' see what you can," I whispered.

"They's a pony tied in th' bresh, but if somebody's down there, he's layin' down."

"Don't think a 'Pache would use one of his dead friends for trap bait, do you?"

"Not likely, Zee, but you never know, th' 'Pache Kid would, but he don't run in bunches like this. Mescaleros hate him anyway."

"You boys don't go claimin' my Injun pony, I earned him!"

someone called from behind.

I whirled, bringin' my rifle up while th' thought ran through my head that I was dead anyway but maybe I could get off a shot first.

There sat Leapin' Lon not fifty yards away grinning at us. Tom had th' same look on his face that I felt, pullin' some greenhorn blunder like letting someone get that close to us unknown in open land.

"Where you been, Lon?" I asked, lowerin' my gun.

"Oh, just out chasin' half th' whole Apache tribe back to th' reservation, what you fellers been up to?"

"We're out huntin' A-paches, but all's we found were dead," I said.

"They were alive when I found 'em," he grinned. "Been chasin' after more of 'em, but they mostly got away. Didn't want t' git too far along so that they could see it was only one man chasin' 'em. They might hev turned back on me."

"A one-man posse, huh?" Shorty sniffed.

"More'n enough if'n things 'er right."

"Like a dark night?"

"Th' darker th' better, Zee."

"We had just about given up chasin' them, they got too much of a jump on us. I learned why you call this hoss Sniffer."

"Best trackin' hoss I ever saw," Leapin' grinned. "We was all waitin' 'til you made th' discovery. What say I go down an' git my pony an' ride him, this hoss is 'bout done in."

"Go ahead, Lon, we'll just mosey along 'til you find a way out."

He started lopin' an' hoppin' down th' gully, "Turn that buck over an' look at his back," he called as he went. When we turned him over, his back was covered with stripes and welts, some of them bloody. There must have been a dozen of them.

"Whewee," Shorty blew, "musta caught him runnin' for his horse."

"Don't you know that must of hurt his pride as much as his back!"

"Yeah, most as much t' influence him t' try t' ambush his tormenter afore it got light enough for his buddies t' see that back!"

"Don't look like it worked, poor feller," I said, but I didn't have much sympathy for him.

We turned and rode up th' ridge, Lon coming out of the gully when he could. Now we b'gan t' worry about th' rest of the crew an' what Preston would say to us for runnin' off like that.

"Don't worry much about that," Leapin' said, "he prob'ly unnerstands hot-headed kids wantin' t' git th' ones that hev tried t' kill 'em."

"We didn't leave 'til th' herd was calmed down," I said.

"Ennyway, it was me an' Zee that turned that herd. We was in th' most danger an' did th' most work. We *earned* a right t' chase 'em."

"By th' way," I asked, "where were you in th' run?"

"We-e-el I was runnin' off a army o' Injuns that were jest waitin' t' cut out some cows an' th' cavyyard an' mebbe kill a few White Eyes."

"That one-man army agin?" Shorty asked.

"Why, shore, them Injuns knowed there wasn't *any* white man fool enough t' charge their army alone. They knew they was forty or more right ahind me an' I pressed them so hard they didn't have time t' look back an' find th' truth."

"If you had been th' least bit timid, that race would have turned around an' you would have been th' leader—for a little while at least!" I said.

"Yore right there! Me an' that horse both was sweatin' that

out pretty good, but he stayed right with 'em. I shore need t' find him water, he's pretty fagged out."

We soon got to a tank an' both of them drank long an' deep.

"Save th' dregs fer us, Lon," I called.

"Come hep yo'self, boys!"

We rode on after our drink, Lon's long legs lookin' like they would drag th' ground on that little pony.

"Best mountain horse you ever rode," he said, "too bad th' 'Paches treat them as bad as they do. They'll ride a good horse t' death, then eat him afore goin' on."

"I shore am fagged out," Shorty said, "lost all that sleep I caught up on yesterday an' I bet Preston ain't gonna let me an' Zee loll 'round camp an' catch up tonight."

"Been up near twenty-four an' I'll bet there's twelve more t' go," I moaned.

"Take yore duty as she comes, boys, ain't none o' us had an abundance o' rest, damn those Injuns," Leapin' grinned.

Chapter 10
No Rest for the Wicked

Late that evening we cut our herd's trail before we got back to th' old camp an' followed it to Ancho Gulch where th' bottom is wide an' there's a little stream on both sides of th' valley. It was a good place to camp an' a good place t' defend if and when Injuns came back. Th' sides were too steep for a cow t' climb leavin' th' only place t' run th' bottoms. Th' hills pinched those two streams together a little further down, makin' a good place for one man t' defend agin any invaders.

That left th' upper end as our weakest point. There was a long rope across that upper end stretched about chest high to a horse, tied to some stout trees on both sides. Bill, Boog, and Ol' Van was spread out along it watchin'.

"Where you boys been?" Boog called as we passed. "We give yuh up fer lost an' Preston's already hired a couple o' boys t' take yore place."

"If they's anything like you, he should of hired four jist t' make up for us!" Lon shot back.

"Hope Boss ain't too mad," Shorty muttered.

"Pres *do* get mad, but he's had all day t' git over it. Maybe he won't be so hard on us." Lon didn't seem too worried about it.

Preston was just ridin' up to th' wagon from th' north as we rode in from th' south. He gave his horse to Tomas who threw his saddle on a fresher horse while we ate. We had our plates full an' were eating when he came to th' fire. He spoke, grabbed a plate, and we ate in silence. All three of us had a second plate and cup of coffee.

When our dishes were in th' pan, Preston spoke up. It went something like this, only he used a lot more words I won't say an' some I never heard of b'fore. Zenas chuckled.

"What did you fellers think, runnin' off like that when th' herd needed attention? You surely didn't think you could take on th' whole tribe, did you?"

"I was on th' side those Injuns hit an' I got one of them then," Lon said. "Knowin' th' rest of them was prob'bly b'hind, I charged th' bresh yellin' an' shootin' an' shore 'nuf I flushed a dozen er more out an' they panicked an' ran."

"A one-man army, Lon?"

"Seemed they didn't know no better an' I was afraid t' let up otherwise, so I jest kep' atter 'em. I chased them to near daylight, hollerin' an' shootin'. Quit afore it got light enough fer them t' see how big this army was."

Pres turned to me an' Shorty. "An' you two came *an' changed horses* an' follered him?"

"We didn't know Lon was atter 'em," Shorty said, "er we wouldn't hev. We only knowed he was on that side o' th' herd an' we hadn't seen him since."

"He could have been hurt or somethin' an' we went t' see about him," I added—not exactly what happened—but it sounded good an' I didn't want Pres t' shoot us or string us up first tree we came to.

"We found th' Injun with a broke neck an' then we found tracks o' th' tribe with Lon's horse's tracks in them an' thought he might have been caught, so we kept on goin' after 'em." Shorty's worried look sure looked genuine.

"We caught up to him after daylight at a place he had killed another buck, then we rode back," I added.

Pres seemed a little mollified by that, so he chewed on us a little more, then said, "You saw those boys at th' upper end, I want you two t' ride herd t'night an' Lon you can go down to th' gap an' guard. Don't any of yuh leave 'til someone comes out an' relieves you an' if I catch you asleep, I'll shoot you on th' spot!"

We didn't say anything, just changed out horses an' went. Lon was getting more ammunition from th' wagon when we left an' Pres was lopin' up th' valley to th' rope.

"Won't shoot us on th' spot, it'd spook this herd," Shorty mumbled as we rode out.

"Slittin' your throat might be quieter, but I think I'd rather be shot," I said.

"Zee, you got any t'baccy, I'm gonna hafta rub somethin' in my eyes t' keep 'em open."

"Got a pinch left. I'll split it with yuh."

He took his pinch an' started around th' herd one way an' I went t'other. We bedded th' herd an' I don't know how long we rode. I used up my tobacco an' if it hadn't been for Nightbird stayin in th' circle, I don't know where I'da gone. When Mecio rode out t' replace me, I just rode up th' bank 'til it got too steep, unsaddled an' picketed my horse, an' laid down on th' saddle blanket an' slept. When th' sun came up and th' horse got restless I turned him loose and covered my face an' slept on. Th' sun was straight up when Ol' Van kicked my boots.

"Git up, Zee, Pres wants t' talk to us at the wagon. Chow's gonna be on soon. Nightbird came to the cavyyard an' Tomas sent you a horse t' ride back in on."

I saddled up an' followed Van to camp. That Tomas may have been th' best wrangler we ever had. Don't think he wrangled mor'n a couple o' times b'fore they made him a hand—and he was a good one there too.

At dinner, Preston told us he didn't feel safe this close to th' reservation and he planned on us leavin' early in th' morning an' drivin' a couple of days b'fore we took another rest stop.

Other than a few skinned-up legs and broken horns, our herd came through in pretty good shape. It just remained t' keep them out of trouble an' get them fattened up for market.

I guarded that rope barrier all afternoon an' Boog and I tied cans with gravels in them along th' ropes. That way, one or two could guard in th' night an' we could get more rest. We put one man on night watch since th' herd was confined and we all got some much-needed sleep.

Most of our bedrolls had been trampled near to death in th' runaway an' were balled up in a muddy mess in th' wagon. We salvaged what we could an' slept on them until we got to water where they could be washed. Some of Manuel's cookware had been kicked a hundred yards away. Anything less than cast iron was beaten to a pulp and one of th' Dutch ovens was cracked an' useless. We had make-do grub until we got t' Fort Sumner an' Manuel could restock.

Lucien Maxwell had bought the old fort in 1871 and with a caravan of some thirty families moved there. Jesus Silva was his ranch foreman and he lent several men t' help us ford th' Pecos and bed th' herd northeast of town. We took a couple of days to restock and wash in th' river. Mr. Maxwell was about town some and we met him. He was an interesting man, popular with his people and easy to meet. He was not very tall and his dress was careless. He most likely had a cigar in his mouth sometimes lit and often not. It seemed he had a pallor about him an' folks said he wasn't well. Th' night before we left, he and Silva rode out and ate supper with us. He seemed to thoroughly enjoy camp and left as second watch rode out to th' herd.

He died in July, 1875 and they buried him in a little plot by th' fort. It was in his son Pete's room that Garrett shot Billy the Kid in '81. It seems to me th' greatest insult that they buried Billy, O'Folliard, and Charlie Bowdre in that same plot with

Mr. Maxwell. They deserved t' be in some Boot Hill, not resting with honest folks. But then I guess th' Good Lord won't have any trouble sortin' 'em out. Now, I'm told more people come to see Billy's grave than the Maxwell grave. How soon the great and mighty fade from memory!

From Fort Sumner we went due north to Alamogordo Creek, th' easiest climb up to th' caprock. Even then it was a steep climb and we rested a day before moving on toward Tucumcari Mesa.

Except for th' breaks of th' Canadian River, goin' was pretty smooth. The drive to Tramperos Creek south of Rabbit Ear wasn't too bad. We found pools in th' dry creeks an' tanks enough t' get by on. Tramperos was runnin' an we laid over there a day. From there on creeks came pretty regular. Even Dry Cimarron had a little trickle in it. Crossin' that river was something, with steep bluffs on both sides. We went down an arroyo on th' south side and had t' go up th' river to Carrizo Creek between Black and Middle mesas. Then we had to cut sharp northeast to Two Buttes.

Preston rode ahead an' found out from someone that th' railroad had gotten into Colorado. That was along about th' first of August an' we were running a little behind schedule. Bill an' Preston got their heads together an' decided it would be quicker to ship th' herd on in to Fort Dodge. Bill rode ahead to make arrangements and we turned north. The pens at Granada were right on th' east end of town. We were on th' south side of th' Arkansas River an' lookin' north I could see where th' Santa Fe Trail ran. It was sure a funny feelin' seein' all that development where just a few years ago I was drivin' cattle an' chasin' buffalo away and there wasn't a house between Bent's Fort and Council Grove.

We held th' herd south of town while Preston and Bill

palavered with th' railroad. We could see th' whole length of Granada's only street an' it wasn't far along it 'til you were out on th' prairie agin.

"What's that sign say on that place in th' middle there, Zee?" Van asked. "Seems I can make out some o' th' letters, -A-L-O-O- an' sompin' else."

"Why, don' yuh know whut that is?" Leapin' asked. "That's th' Aloo Millinery and Haberdashery fer wimmin. You don't want t' go there less'n you need a dress or hat."

"Go on, Lon, yuh knows yore wrong es rain, I kin see they's sompin' afore that A an' after th' last O," Van was scornful.

"I know you think that says SALOON," Boog said, "but I got bad news fer yuh, Van, th' place's caught Prohibition Fever from Kansas an' this town's done gone dry!"

"Yore lyin', yore lyin', yore lyin', Boog Sowell, an' I knows it! I'm gonna go up there right now an' git me a big beer an' chase it down with a tall glass o' rotgut whiskey an' you kin put on a dress an' hat with dead birds on it if yuh please!"

He started his horse north when I called, "What you gonna pay for those drinks with, Van, cow chips?"

Van took off his hat an' ran his fingers through his hair. "I'll point t' this here herd an' tell 'em I brought it in an' they'll give me credit, that's what *they'll* do!"

"They'll take one look at your scraggly hair an' beard an' raggedy clothes an' hand you the broom an' tell you t' sweep out an' empty the spittoons an' they'll give you a finger o' gin, *that's* what they'll do!" Lon crowed.

Van throwed his hat on th' ground. "Well, dangit, when's that Preston gonna give me my wages an' let me git human agin?"

"He's gotta go to the bank first," Lon said.

Van came back, too disgusted t' say more. We augered an' spit a whole hour b'fore Preston came back with four vaqueros.

"These boys are workin' for the railroad and are gonna hold

the herd and cavyyard 'til our train comes in. Bill's makin' last arrangements with the railroad and if you come up to the bank with me, I'll pay you up. Horses is too cheap up here to sell, so after a day or two we'll head back south with 'em. Today's Tuesday (which was a revelation to us), I'll need you to help load cattle, then you can have a couple o'days t' see the sights. Our cars are expected t' be here in the morning and we will start loadin' them right away. Zenas and Tom, Bill wants you t' go with him to the fort, so check in with him."

He said all that while he held our attention, knowin' he'd be talking to th' wind when he paid us off. We all rode up to th' bank an' sat outside waitin' on him. It took some time, but when he came out he handed an' envelope to each of us.

"These are drafts drawn on th' ranch an' th' teller said that he would be glad t' cash them for you, paper or silver. Now, don't spend it all in one place, in fact, don't spend it all," he advised as we pushed past him an' hustled into th' bank.

Th' teller was waitin' with a pile of gold an' silver on one hand an' paper on t'other. "All our stores take paper here good as silver," he said hopefully, but we all wanted hard stuff. One by one, we jingled out an' rode down th' dusty street. I was first to th' second barber's chair b'side Lon an' we got sheared, shaved, an' shampooed while th' other boys sat an' fidgeted. We took a bath in th' back room and headed over to th' general store where we bought new clothes an' discarded our old rags.

Zenas opened a cigar box he had beside his chair and pulled out a yellow slip of paper. "I still have the receipt from that store," he said as he handed it to me. There in the neat handwriting of some clerk was a list of the items Zenas had bought on that day.

LEE AND REYNOLDS CO.
GRANADA, COLO.

Date: *Aug 4, 1874*

Item:

1 Black Sateen Shirt $1.17
1 Teamster's Double Breasted Blue Twill Shirt .96
1 Pr. Silk Finished Underwear .81
2 Pr. Black Cotton Socks .42
2 Pr. Levi Straus Denim Bibless Overalls $2.00 Ea. 4.00
1 Orange Grain Leather Belt .21
1 Box of 100 Shells, 44-40 1.46
Total $9.03

"Them prices for sure wouldn't hold for today, would they?" His usual grin and chuckle wasn't there. "Those were th' first bibless overalls I owned an' I sure did like 'em. They only came in one length an' th' clerk showed us how t' roll 'em up in wide cuffs. Some o' that other stuff like th' sateen shirt an' th' silk finished underwear was just frivolous, but I enjoyed them for a little while, just th' same."

Ol' Van and Boog were crossing th' road as Lon and I in our sateen shirts an' bibless overalls left th' store an' I hollered at them, "See you at th' millinary!"

"Make sure they got a big stock o' 'feathers,' " Boog grinned and dodged out of Van's reach.

Jack Callahan had bought th' saloon in '73 from an End-of-the-Tracks follower when th' so-called "Hell's City" moved on to th' current end of tracks. He had been partners with Billy Dixon huntin' buffalo in northwest Kansas 'til he got tired of it an' quit. That was th' first time I heard of Billy, and I was to get more acquainted with him in th' next few months.

The boys straggled in with brown faces and white cheeks and

necks where their hair had covered them and we had a drink or two.

"Let us go geet supper at thee ho-tel," Mecio suggested.

"No need t' leave your chairs, gentlemen, the hotel delivers," Jack said. He opened a side door at the end of the bar and called, "Metta, you got some customers in here."

In a few moments a young woman came through th' door. She was somewhere in her twenties, I guessed, had her hair up in a bun and wore an apron. Her hands were clean and red from washing dishes and she had a pleasant smile.

"I have a blue-plate special of smashed potatoes, black-eyed peas, roasting ears, and beef or buffalo steaks with oysters on the side. The bread is hot and butter's fresh."

We all placed our orders and we heard her givin' them to th' kitchen help. Almost immediately she returned with flatware, a large loaf of bread, and a bowl of butter.

"This should tide you over until the food comes. If you need more bread, just holler."

Now loaf bread ain't biscuits nor cornbread, but serve it hot with butter an' a feller will just about founder on it and that's exactly what we proceeded t' attempt. That loaf disappeared in no time with seven boys around that table butterin' and eatin' chunks of bread until it was *gone*.

Jack had watched with amusement and called, "More bread!" through th' open door. Soon a smiling Miss Metta appeared with another loaf an' eyed th' fast-diminishing butter. "More butter on the way."

"Now, boys, this is th' cat's meow," Shorty said, "Supper in a bar an' a purty girl t' serve it!"

Steamin' plates were soon set before us an' Jack brought us six mugs of beer and one sasparilla for Tomas. He looked perturbed and we all laughed. Tomas was small and looked younger than he really was. At sixteen, he did a man's work an'

Jack brought him a mug of beer, much to his satisfaction.

"Sasparilla's on th' house, cowboy," he said.

Nothin' was heard around that table but th' clink of flatware on dishes and an' occasional hum of satisfaction. Van was first t' push back his empty plate. "Best meal in a lo-o-ong time!" he declared.

Soon all were finished and Metta appeared with a whole pie with a tall meringue topping. "Fresh lemon pie straight from the oven," she said as she served each plate with a slice.

"Lady, I'd pay a dollar just for a piece of pie," I said.

"M-m-m-m, mee also," Mecio added.

"Well you get the whole meal for six bits," Metta replied.

When she came back t' get dishes, there was a dollar on each polished plate an' th' boys had proceeded t' try t' drink Jack Callahan out of business. Tomas and Shorty tapered off early and I didn't drink any. We went out t' look th' town over. It didn't take long. Mecio caught up with us at th' edge of town an' we went to a Mexican cantina and had tamales before riding out to camp. Th' other boys never showed up.

Sleepin' 'til sunup was a luxury. Manuel didn't cook breakfast, just made coffee an' shooed us off. He took th' wagon to town to reprovision and we rode with him. It was a revelation to feed him breakfast at th' hotel. I think that was th' first time he had hominy grits, for he ordered two bowls. We peeked in at th' saloon, but it was quiet as a tomb. Charlie was fixin' up an' putterin' around.

"Haven't seen your boys since they left at sunup," he said, "shape they was in, they couldn't hev gotten far. Bar's closed 'til I get some sleep."

Manuel hurried to th' mercantile and Shorty and I went down to th' tracks t' find Bill Austin. He was leanin' on a fence talking to a man in railroad uniform.

"Howdy, boys, you look chipper this morning," he called.

"Couldn't be nothing else bein' still on duty, so t' speak," Shorty muttered under his breath. He shore wanted t' stay an' celebrate. I, for one, was glad I hadn't, considerin' th' shape they must have been at th' moment, not that I would have imbibed with them. Never could see th' fun in drunkenness an' its aftereffects.

"This is Henry Shell, he'll be conductor on our train," Bill said.

"Howdy, boys," Henry said, "the cars should be in here soon and we will load up and have them at the fort by morning."

"Can't be," Shorty said, "Jack Callahan said it was one hundred twenty miles from here."

The conductor smiled, "Trains go twenty-five to thirty miles an hour, young fellow, shouldn't take more than five hours to get there."

"Only thing we ever seen goin' that fast was wind an' some tenderfoot leavin' th' vicinity of a mad cow," I said.

"Well you'll be goin' that fast with the steers," Bill said. "We are gonna go with them an' Henry's gonna show you boys how t' become cowpokes."

"What's a cowpoke?" I asked.

"You'll know soon enough, it isn't complicated."

Henry's smile told me this was something I could probably live without. He seemed nice enough and he told us a lot about th' operation of railroads. His accent was strange to us and we understood when he told us he was from Illinois.

"Where are the rest o' the boys?" Bill asked.

"We left them at th' saloon last night an' they weren't there when we looked in a while ago," I said.

"Think you can go find 'em? It may take some time for them t' get into shape t' handle cattle."

"Huh! They won't be in that good a shape 'til they cross th' Canadian," Shorty allowed.

Bill laughed, "You are probably right there, Shorty, but we can't load those cows without them. Go bring what's left of them here if you can find 'em."

"Shape Jack said they was in, they couldn't have gotten far," I said.

We rode back down th' street.

"They wouldn't be in th' hotel, would they?" I asked.

"Not likely. Let's look b'hind th' saloon."

They weren't there an' th' saloon was still quiet an' empty.

"Bet I know where they are," I said and we rode north toward th' river.

We saw horses first, haphazardly tied here and there, with only one or two ground-tied. Lon's horse was a hundred yards or so off to th' side an' when Shorty rode out to retrieve him, he found Lon under a button willow bush sound asleep. The rest were scattered around under bushes sleeping. The only responses we got were groans an' curses when we tried t' wake them.

"What're we gonna do, Zee? They won't git up."

"Bet they would if we had a fight an' one o' us got shot."

"Bet they would too, what we gonna fight over?"

"I want t' get 'em up," I said louder.

"Naw, let 'em lay."

"I am not gonna do all th' work loadin' them cows while these hunks lay here sleepin'!" I raised my voice again.

"I say leave 'em be an' you'll do just that!" Shorty yelled back.

"No, I won't," I shouted and kicked a rotten stump with a thump . . . it made a satisfying thump like I had hit a body.

"Don't you dare kick that man again, *leave him be!*"

"No, I won't! Git up you lazy good for nothing!" An' I kicked th' stump twice.

"Do it agin, Zee, do it agin an' I'll shoot you dead right

here." Shorty was screaming.

"You're not gonna shoot anybody, yore a coward," I yelled and kicked th' stump again.

Boom! Boom! went Tom's gun and I answered, *Boom, boom, boom!* Heads were poppin' up. I was in th' act of fallin' dead when Boog shot at me. Lon had come up gun in hand and leveled it at Shorty who also dove for dirt. Mecio yelled, "He's hit, Shorty's hit!" He ran to where I lay laughin'.

"Zenas is hit!" he shouted.

Lon sat elbows on knees, holdin' his head with both hands. "If he ain't dead, Mecio, I'll kill 'im for you, I'll kill 'em both," he groaned.

"What a dirty trick," Boog said and lay back with a groan.

"What's goin' on?" Ol' Van asked. He had slept through the whole thing.

"We gotta go load cows," Shorty said, "git up an' git with it!"

All that got was groans from three prone bodies.

"Come on, Boog, a little dunk in th' river'll cure what ails yuh." Shorty was tuggin' at him tryin' t' get him t' stand. I helped get him up an' we walked him to th' river an' threw him in. Water wasn't deep, but bein' this close to th' mountains it was still cold and Boog came up sputterin'. "C-c-cold!"

Lon came staggerin' to th' river an' fell down an' drank an' drank.

"Drink enough an' you'll be drunk again," I said.

"Never got sober," he muttered.

Van had only rolled over when th' noise stopped and we carried him to th' river. Swingin' him by his feet an' arms, we counted one—two—three and threw him in. He just sank and we were just starting t'jump in an' grab him when he came up choking an' yellin', "Help! Help! I'm drownin'!" over and over.

"Stand up, Van!" we kept yellin'.

He finally comprehended and stood up. Th' water was just

over waist deep. Suddenly he was very energized. "Who threw me in?" he yelled plowin' to th' bank.

Shorty shrugged, "Wasn't us."

He stopped and rubbed his chin, puzzled, "Musta been, yore all dry."

"We just rode up, Van, it couldn't have been us," I said.

Van looked around and tried to gather his mind. "Who could it ha' been?" He shook his head as if to clear it and groaned. Forgetting his anger, he sat down holding his head. Water streamed from his dungarees, turning his socks blue. There was a rim of blue dyed water in th' sand around his behind. Elbows on knees and holdin' his head in his hands he began muttering, "I'm bleedin' blue on my socks—bleedin' blue? That's not blood, there ain't no sich thing as blue blood."

"It's them blue pants runnin', Van," Shorty said.

"Oh, no, it'll ruin my underwear!" He jerked down his pants, but it was too late, th' dye had already stained his new long-handles a lovely shade of blue.

"How's come that there denim runs like a scoured calf but th' clothes it stains won't wash out?" Shorty wondered.

"I don't know," I said, "but ain't we glad those pants are blue instead o' red. It'd be mighty embarassin' for Ol' Van t' spend th' winter in pink bloomers."

We heard a whistle and Tomas said, "Thee train, she bee coming." It rolled through th' station, steam and smoke pourin' and bell ringing, and disappeared down th' track. Somewhere it turned around, came back, and stopped and a man jumped off an' moved a big switch by th' tracks. He signaled th' engine an' th' train slowly pulled up to th' cattle pens on a side track. We had seen empty cars an' didn't need anyone t' tell us t' round up th' herd an' drive it toward th' tracks. There were only two loading chutes an' pens so we split into two teams an' went to work.

When thirty head were in the pen, we opened th' chute an' hazed them into th' car. Most of the time, once they got started th' whole crowd pushed in, but some bunches were stubborn about it an' had to be driven in, sometimes one at a time. When two cars were loaded, th' train moved up and when two empties were in place, another sixty head were penned and ready to load. There were thirty-three cars, so we loaded thirty-one head in th' last ten cars. By late afternoon, th' last steer was loaded.

Bill called us over and gave us our orders. "Preston an' th' rest of you are gonna stay here until me an' Zee an' Shorty get back. We will deliver th' cattle and be back in a couple of days and then we will head home. Stay out of trouble, most disagreements around here get settled with lead."

CHAPTER 11
COWPOKES AND TRAINS

Henry Shell was waitin' by th' end car when we walked up. He had two long poles polished and black from long use and as soon as we got near said, "Now I'm going to show you boys how to be cowpokes." He was grinnin'. He turned and walked swiftly to the front of th' cattle cars. "Sometimes a steer will get down or just lay down and if he doesn't get up, the other cows will trample him. Every time we stop, it will be your job to see that all the animals are standing in every car. If you find one down, use these prods to get him up. You might have to make room so he can stand. I can assure you that any cow left laying down will be in bad shape or dead by the time we get to Dodge."

He must have told others how to be cowpokes and knew that cowboys would not like it and he was right. Still, we were going on our first train ride and that helped our attitude. I "cowpoked" other times because it was a way for me to see some of th' country an' get paid for it. We also got free train tickets home when we took a load of cattle to market.

We proceeded to inspect each car, Shorty on one side an' me on t'other. Only one steer was down and we made short work of gettin' him up. Henry was waitin' at th' last car, a red one called the caboose. When we had stowed our prods and got on, he signaled th' engine an' hopped on.

I found a seat on benches linin' both sides of the car. There was a lot of train equipment stored an' stacked here and there. A little potbellied stove was in one end for cold weather. There was a little cupola in th' roof where Henry sat most of th' time, watchin' th' train. He said sometimes a wheel bearing would freeze up an' make what he called a hot box. It would send out sparks and cause trouble. Th' train would have t' stop and deal with it somehow.

The engine gave a long whistle, belched steam and smoke, and started moving. We could hear and feel th' jerk when each car took up slack and with a last big jerk, the train began t' move. The three of us held on and watched th' scenery as we gathered speed.

"I'm shore glad this bronc finally quit buckin' an' broke in two," I called to Shorty.

"Me too!" he shouted over the noise.

Henry had a big grin on his face. He was enjoying watching our reactions to our first train ride. Th' train slowed some and Shorty looked out a window.

"Looky there, Zee, we're crossin' th' river on a bridge! Shore beats pushin' that herd across some ford, don't it?"

"Did you ever think you would see cows ridin' a train?" Bill asked.

The train began to pick up speed again and was soon moving along at a good clip. "How fast er we going now, Henry?" Bill asked.

"Let me see," he said and pulled out a big pocket watch. He opened th' cover and looked out th' window. When we passed a white post with a number on it, he looked at his watch. After a time we passed another post and Henry noted th' time passed. He figured on a piece of paper for a minute and said, "We did twenty-seven miles per hour in that mile." Figuring a little more, he said, "If we maintain that speed, we'll get into Fort Dodge in about four hours and fifteen minutes. That would be about 1 a.m. We will have at least one stop for water and poking the cows up, so I imagine we would get there some time after 2."

"Them cows won't need waterin' 'til we get there," Shorty said.

"No, but the engine will," Henry grinned.

I stuck my head out of the window and felt th' wind. There was a lot of smoke and cinders. Shorty was sitting across from me and I yelled, "Feel that twenty-seven mile an' hour breeze!" He forgot t' remove his sombrero an' if it hadn't been for his barboquejo, he'd have lost it. Henry laughed and climbed up in th' cupola to watch. I watched out th' windows 'til it was too dark t' see anything, then stretched out on that bench and was rocked to sleep.

Some time later, th' train slowed and stopped and Henry yelled "cowpokes" from th' back door. We jumped up and checked th' cars. Only one or two cows were down an' they got up all right. They were bawlin' some, but seemed t' be takin' their ride in stride.

A man they called fireman was walkin' down th' tracks with a big long spouted can checkin' wheel bearings. Instead of using tar for lubrication like we did on wagons, he was squirtin' oil in th' bearing boxes. There was a water tank on stilts beside the tracks and a long spout was pouring water into a tank in th' car b'hind th' engine.

Soon we were on th' move agin an' next thing I knew we were slowing down for our final stop. There was a row of lit-up buildings off to th' side. Henry said it was Buffalo City. About five more miles and we pulled into a side track for Fort Dodge. The dock was piled high with all kinds of crates and boxes and there were armed guards patrolling. We checked th' cattle one last time and spread our bedrolls out in a quiet spot an' slept.

The train whistle gave a little toot and I near jumped out of my skin. It was building up steam and we hurried to th' caboose. "We're moving up to the chutes to unload the cows," Henry said as we climbed on. The train eased up th' siding and stopped again. We hopped off and hustled up to th' front. There were only two chutes again and a soldier with pad and pencil was standing by each. As we opened the doors and shooed cows out, they counted heads. When the last car was emptied, th' soldiers got together and totaled up. "We got nine-hundred-ninety-five head," a corporal told the officer who was standing talking to Bill.

"Can't be," Bill said, "We loaded one-thousand head."

"Let me see your figures, Corporal," th' officer said. He was a lieutenant, assistant quartermaster, I found out later, a right nice feller. He looked down the list and added up th' figures, then took the other paper and checked it out.

"Looks like the figures are right, Mr. Austin." He handed them to Bill, who looked at them a moment, then handed it back to th' officer.

"Lieutenant, we trailed one-thousand head near five-hundred miles, loaded one-thousand head on that train last night an' unless you can prove otherwise, they's one-thousand head in that pen," he said. He wasn't mad—yet but he was headed in that direction.

"I can only pay you for actual head count . . ." th' lieutenant began.

"Can you show me how five cows got off that train anywhere but in this pen?"

"No, sir . . ." The soldier's voice trailed off and he looked at the figures again.

I peeked over his shoulder at the papers. Each one had a row of thirty all the way down th' page until th' last cars, then only one of the sheets had thirty-one for its last five cars.

"I see where the mistake is, Bill," I said, "the last ten cars had thirty-one head apiece and one of those lists only shows thirty for his last five cars."

"Well, I'll be, you're right, Zee!" Then to the officer he

explained, "We only had thirty-three cars, so we had t' add one extra to the last ten cars to get them all loaded. Your counter missed that."

Now, I'll allow that five head of cattle are not all that important, but I felt just like Bill. We had herded those rannies all that way and by jingles, we should get paid for 'em.

"I know I counted thirty-three cars when I walked up," th' lieutenant said. "Thirty times thirty-three is nine-hundred-ninety so there would be ten left over . . ." He glared at the two counters who shifted from foot to foot uneasily. "I'll take your word for it, Mr. Austin, let's go up and get the quartermaster to cut you a draft." To the two soldiers, he said, "You two wait right here, I'm not through with you."

Shorty grinned and I had t' turn away for a minute. We sat around for a time and soon the two bosses came back. Both of them looked mad.

"That blankety-blank major won't pay for more than what's on th' tally sheets. We're gonna hafta recount th' whole herd," Bill spat.

Well, I can tell you that got some hats dusted. Another half day or more countin' cows! More I thought about it, th' madder I got. One man careless about his work and all of us would have to make up for it. The lieutenant took his men aside and talked to them. His face was red and he shook his finger under their noses, especially at the man who must have been the one to goof up. When he returned, he said, "Fortunately, the cattle are still in the holding pen and we can count them as they come out of the gate to the pasture."

There wasn't anything t' do but recount. The thing I hated about it was that we didn't have any horses. As we walked toward th' gate, I approached Bill.

"Too bad we can't just count th' last five cars that feller was supposed to count."

"Yeah, Zee, it's too bad."

"Them was my five cars he miscounted," Shorty said. "I think I can point out every cow that was in those cars."

Right there is where th' devil entered th' three of us an' we b'came possessed.

Bill looked at him sharp-like. "If you're gonna do that, Shorty, you only have t' know th' last cow out of each car, 'cause that's th' one missed."

"By dang you're right, Bill, an' I *know* I can do that!"

The funny thing is that any cowboy handling cattle can very accurately identify them by their markings, and quite likely, any one of us paying attention could have identified at least four out of th' five cows in question. When we got to th' gate, Bill pulled th' lieutenant aside and they had an intense discussion for a few minutes. Shorty spent th' time lookin th' cows over.

Bill called us over and the lieutenant asked Shorty, "Do you believe you can identify the five uncounted cows?"

"I been lookin' them over an' I have found four o' them already," Shorty said.

"You're sure?"

"For certain, sir." I thought he was gonna salute for a second.

"That certainly would save a lot of trouble for us." The lieutenant nodded as if making up his mind. "All right, mister, show me those cows."

They walked over to the fence an' Shorty began pointing out th' steers. "That brindle over there is one of them, and that one with th' turned-down left horn over there is another. I saw th' third one over in that corner, but he's moved—ahhh there he is by th' chute. Must be wantin' t' git back on th' train . . . Let's see, that's three, now where's that dun with th' stripe down his back . . . yeah, there he is, see him over there?"

The soldier stretched up and saw the one Shorty described. "That's number four, now can you find that last one?"

"I kno-o-o-w wha-a-a-t he looks like," Shorty said slowly, "he's sorta brindle, but with a lot o' orange in his coat an' his tail is bobbed a little."

Now, I knew he was lyin', b'cause that was a Rafter JD she-cow we cut out of th' herd just before we put them on th' trail. She must have had a calf in th' crowd, for we had t' chase her out two or three times. I looked at Bill and he winked. We looked and looked and couldn't find "him."

"If they would only stir around, he'd show up," I said, "I know th' one you're talking about."

"I could send one of my men in an' stir them up a little," th' officer said. I had a good idea which one he was thinking of.

"No, you can't do that!" I think all three of us said it at once.

"Those cows don't know a man afoot an' they would kill him as sure as the sun rises," Bill added.

Well, th' upshot of it all is that we never did find that cow and had t' agree to a count of nine-hundred-ninety-nine cows. I will say this, those were th' fattest longhorns I had seen in a while. They had really filled out on th' trip up.

"Put them in that pasture an' they won't stay that way long," Bill said aside. "That grass is eaten down to dirt already."

The lieutenant was giving instructions to his men and when he finished came to where we were standing.

"The next train west isn't due until 4. How about if I meet you at the quartermaster's office a little after 3:30? That should give him time enough to draw the draft before you catch the train." He might have added that it would take about that long t' recount one-thousand cows, but he didn't.

"Good enough for me," Bill said. "We have plenty of time to get a bite t' eat and look around a little."

After the officer left, Shorty said, "I hope you didn't object to th' way I did that, Bill. We got back four head an' that there major quartermaster might have been suspicious if we had an even thousand."

"I knew what you were doing soon's you described th' fifth cow an' I agreed with your plan," Bill said. "At least we didn't have to go through that count agin. Now let's go get a bite to eat, I'm buyin!"

CHAPTER 12
THE RED RIVER WAR

I got involved in th' Red River War that fall of 1874 sorta by accident an' sorta on purpose, not by any great desire t' fight Indians. I knew many Cheyennes from my Purgatory days an' had no desire t' lock horns with 'em.

Dinner on Bill suited us just fine and we found th' sutler's store and ate crackers and sardines on th' front step. The fort was really bustling and it looked like something big was goin' on. Bein' around Fort Union some, I knew things here were not ordinary army activity. We walked down toward th' depot and were looking at all the supplies stacked there when our friend the lieutenant came by.

"Looks like something big is in th' works, sir," I said.

"You bet there is, we have to get all this stuff down to Camp Supply in Indian Territory and fast and I'm short of freight drivers."

"Looks like you got all kinds of soldiers here," Bill said.

"We use civilian drivers so the soldiers can do the job they were signed on to do, that is protect the public and fight."

I nudged Shorty, "So you need civilian drivers for your freight wagons?"

"Sure do, the Army is paying forty dollars a month and found for good drivers—and I'm not sure we would even require *good* ones at this point."

I looked at Bill and he said, "We're through for th' year, Zee, all that's left is to get back home and pay th' boys off. We won't have anything else to do until spring and I'm sure John has th' same idea for you Rafter boys."

"It would be good if I had something t' do through th' winter," I said, "What do you think, Shorty?"

"I'm game if th' lieutenant ain't too particular about my drivin' experience."

"One trip down the trail should be enough to break you in," he said. "If you want to try it, come on up to the office and I will sign you up."

"You have my blessing, Shorty," Bill said, "Durned if I'm not tempted t' join you if I could."

So it was that Tom Short and I became drivers in th' employ of the US Army, August 6, 1874. The lieutenant signed us up and took us down to th' wagon yard and turned us over to th' wagon master. Imagine our surprise when we found out it was none other than Jack Callahan! He gave a big laugh when he saw us, "How are you doin', boys?"

"Jes fine, Jack," Shorty said, "What're yuh doin' here?"

"Wellsir a fellow come along an' offered me a deal for my saloon I couldn't refuse an' I sold it to him. He's waitin' for a shipment of booze to restock th' place after you boys left," he laughed. "Took th' train in here this morning an' th' Army made me wagon master. I been lookin' for drivers under every rock an' here comes th' lieutenant with you two. Any o' th' rest of th' outfit comin'?"

"Not that we know of, they seem intent on goin' back south," I said.

"Just my luck. General Miles comes blowin' in here mad t' chase Injuns an' stirs everything up. Ever' time I hire drivers, he goes an' hires 'em away for scouts. I hire Billy Dixon an' Bat Masterson t' drive an' next thing I know, they're ridin' away with some Army outfit headin' back to Adobe Walls. I got two-hundred-fifty wagons t' haul an' two-hundred-thirty-seven drivers. If I don't get 'em all, some Army boys is gonna hafta drive."

He showed us our wagons an' where we were t' be—near th' tail end—and introduced us to a few drivers who would be close to us, then hurried off t' recruit more drivers. One of the men we met was L. G. Gainer, an old hand, having made several trips up an' down Military Road. He was glad t' tell us about th' work.

"It takes eight to ten days to make the trip one way— dependin' on weather an' Injuns. If'n you're not freezin' t' death, you're fryin' in your own juices all th' while yore scalp has that crawly feelin an' you wear yore eyes out lookin fer Injuns. Otherwise, it's jist a little Sunday drive—if'n yore mules ain't too wild er stubborn."

Our harness was piled on th' seat and enough rations stored under th' seat for th' trip. There was room left for our bedrolls an' we could store our rifles there, too. L.G. cautioned us to be sure we had plenty of ammunition and always keep our arms near and ready. We slept under our wagons and were up very early th' morning of the 7th of August. Our mules were brought to us and Shorty and I hooked them up to our wagons. Both teams were old hands and had obviously worked together for some time, for each found his place without prompting and we had little trouble getting them in harness.

The Army had crossed th' river the night before and waited on us. General Miles and his staff rode out from th' fort and crossed ahead of th' train. All left for us was to wait our turn to cross and being at th' end of two-hundred-fifty wagons, it was some time before our turn came. Shorty slapped reins and as soon as he was on his way, I fell in behind him. The river was stirred and muddy and th' bottom cut up considerable, but my team made it easy enough and we were soon out on th' prairie. Th' wagons lined up four abreast and I was last one on th' right of my line, Shorty being next to me on th' inside. We were only a few feet apart and had t' guard agin getting too close an' tangling up.

As we passed th' Army, a foot soldier fell in step with us on each side and th' cavalry spread out along our line of march. 'Way out on each side we could see flankers scoutin'. It wasn't too soon for such precautions, either. There had been several attacks up and down th' trail. Even Buffalo City, now named Dodge City, had been attacked in June and a few days later th' mail escort was attacked just south of th' fort. The Army had killed six warriors in that battle and at least one soldier got a scalp.

Everyone was still buzzing about th' attack on Adobe Walls and we heard many tales about it, more than a few of them pure fiction. If they were all to be believed, there were at least five hundred hunters there (all wagon drivers, now) and they killed at least a thousand Injuns with only four white deaths. It wasn't until later in the year that I heard the true story from Bat Masterson and Billy Dixon. I'll have more t' say about that when th' time comes.

Traveling Army wagon-train style was mighty easy. Rest stops were longer and a day's travel shorter than they had been on th' Santa Fe. Our trail was swarming with soldiers patrolling. They had little forts along th' way and th' third day we nooned at one on Upper Bear Creek. It was a miniature fort made out of banked-up dirt and burlap sacks filled with sand. Th' soldiers had done a bang-up job and seemed quite comfortable in their fort. Most of th' time it was near empty with troops patrolling up and down th' trail. The soldiers called these little forts "redoubts" and there was another one on th' east bank of Bear Creek called Soldiers' Graves for two troopers who were murdered there.

There was one at th' Cimarron called Deep Hole and imagine

our surprise when we saw a white woman there! She was th' wife of th' lieutenant in charge an' they say she had fixed up a right nice room for herself. Still, I questioned th' wisdom of exposing a woman to such dangers, not to mention a rough lifestyle. Later on when I was married, I was educated as to th' wills an' whims of women, wives in particular, an' maybe I understood then just how that woman got there with her husband.

Camp Supply was at th' junction of Wolf Creek and Beaver River. Below there, it was called North Canadian or Dry Fork of the Canadian. The Army had built a picket fort, but it wasn't much and not half th' troops there could be housed in it. Instead th' bulk of that camp was a tent city. Supplies were piled everywhere.

It sure looked like th' Army meant business about corralling wild Indians, "wild" meaning th' ones who refused to live on reservations. Actually there were many of th' wild variety that frequented reservations t' stock up on food, guns, and ammunition so they could go out again and kill settlers and hunters. The so-called Reservation Indian had a regular business runnin' supplies out to th' different rebel camps, keeping them well supplied. So on one hand th' US Government was providing supplies to Indians so they could continue with their killing and on th' other hand, sending troops out to get killed fighting Indians. It made everyone furious.

After our wagons were unloaded, Jack Callahan showed us where t' park them an' where t' take our mules. They were in good shape and I could see why th' trip had been so leisure-like, for those mules could be turned right around and make th' trip north.

"You can bet a lot of mules would volunteer t' be Army mules if they knew how pampered they would be!" I observed.

"They would have t' temper that with th' thought that they

may git an arrow in their rump or run off an' made a Kiowa feast," Shorty replied.

General Miles sure stirred things up. Th' second day there, half our train was sent scootin' back up th' road for more supplies and we were told t' get ready t' follow them. Almost as soon as that word came down, we were told t' hitch up an' drive over to th' quartermaster to be loaded.

"Word is they are gonna send us right out into Indian country an' start a new supply camp for winter campaigns," Shorty told me.

And that's just what they did. We drove southwest up Wolf Creek, then south across th' Canadian to th' Upper Washita where th' Army chose a place for their supply camp. Th' next weeks we were on th' road (if you could call it that) constantly hauling supplies from Supply to the new cantonment. The Army kept good care of their mules, but they sure neglected their drivers. We were about worn out.

General Miles wasted no time sending out patrols all through th' plains and they did good work chasing Indians until they decided that reservation life wasn't near so bad as being harassed by th' Army. Even then there were holdouts and th' general was determined to remove them all, even though there was sentiment among the troops that their job was done and th' comforts of Fort Dodge were mighty appealing after a couple months in th' rain and wind and cold.

We didn't have a chance t' get warmer clothes except at Camp Supply and they were in high demand. I made do with a good buffalo robe I bought from a soldier who had a surplus. Wrapped in it up to my tied-down hat with only eyes and nose exposed, I could get by. My boots were stuffed full of socks and wrapped in several layers of burlap bags. Gloves were the hardest things t' keep, for we wore them out often and it was a constant search for more.

Unknown to us there was an event far to th' north in Kansas that changed th' whole complexion of that war. A family by th' name of Germaine (*It was a common error that the family was called Germaine, their proper name was German. J.D.*) traveling along Smoky Hill Trail was attacked by Cheyennes led by Medicine Water on September 11, 1874.

The parents and three children were murdered and four girls were taken captive. After a day or two of fleeing south, the band split, two older girls going on with Medicine Water and the two younger girls with another band. Somewhere out on the Llano, the band was spooked by something and the two little girls were left afoot in the middle of a huge herd of buffalo scattered over th' plain. Not long after, they were picked up by Grey Beard's band and kept as slaves. Shorty and I managed t' stay together most of th' time we drove and th' first of November we drove into the Washita camp and were commandeered for a supply train for a sweep on th' plains. Our troop was commanded by Lieutenant Frank Baldwin with Billy Dixon and William Schmalsle as scouts. We were given twenty-four wagons and I was made wagon master. The lieutenant was ordered to go to th' Prairie Dog Town fork of Red River and then sweep east back to th' Washita camp.

In early November a norther blew in an' we had a regular blizzard on our hands. There was nothing to do but circle the wagons and wait out th' storm. Dixon had been out in Palo Duro Canyon and had discovered a camp of two or three tipis, but th' Indians were warned and fled to th' Llano. I don't know how he did it, but he found us after dark. It was a miserable night and early next morning we lit out for Sweetwater with twenty-three empty wagons, one being lost when we crossed a ravine. It just fell apart going down a slope, ending up in the bottom in several pieces.

November 7th we camped on McClellan Creek when Masterson rode in from th' Washita camp with a message for Lieutenant Baldwin about an' Indian camp near where we were. Well before dawn, scouts were sent out in all directions to try to find a trail to follow to th' Indian camp.

We had just gathered around Lieutenant Baldwin t' get our orders for th' day when Bill Schmalsle came galloping into camp from th' north.

"There's a big Indian camp over that ridge, not a mile from here!" he shouted. "I saw Grey Beard's tipi and there must be a hundred tipis with him!"

"Lieutenant Overton, report to me here with your troop!" Baldwin called. "Wagon master, are your wagons ready to roll?"

"Yessir," I answered.

"Good, bring them up, columns of four, fastest wagons in front and get the canvases off. Lieutenant Bailey, put two men in each wagon with all their weapons and ammunition. Overton, put half your troop on one side of the wagons and I'll lead the other half on the other side. Here's what we are going to do; we will ride into the village at full speed, the cavalry ahead of the wagons. I want continuous fire at any target of opportunity from the wagons. Wagons run straight through the village as fast as you can go. We're outnumbered at least five to one and I'm hoping for complete surprise."

"It's less than half a mile from th' divide down to th' village," Schmalsle said. "Just enough t' get up a good head of steam!" He rode up and peeked over at th' camp. When he rode back, he was shaking his head, "Their fires are going, but there's not a soul outside. They still don't know we are here!"

"Good, let's hope it stays that way," Baldwin said. "Bugler, ride with me when I tell you, sound the charge and keep it up over and over. Are you ready, men?"

We nodded and th' column proceeded up to th' ridge. I was

right of Shorty and as we climbed, I had one of my troops tie a fifty-foot rope to th' back of our wagon and toss th' other end to Shorty's boys and they tied it to their wagon. L.G. Gainer was to my left and when he saw what we were doing, he did th' same with th' wagon to his left.

"When we get to th' village, spread out to th' left and Shorty and I will go right," I said just so he could hear me. He nodded and we climbed at a quicker pace. I slipped down between my seat and th' front endboard. If those troopers were gonna be shooting over my head, I wasn't gonna give them too much of a target. The other drivers did th' same thing and th' soldiers knelt and propped their guns on the seat backs and sides. Now all we had to worry about was one of them shooting a mule!

There were only two columns of wagons over the crest of th' ridge when Lieutenant Baldwin's bugler sounded charge and we whipped those mules up. As we charged down th' hill, our four wagons gradually broke into two columns of two. Shorty spread to near th' end of our rope and we lined up so each would go down th' space on either side of a row of tipis. They toppled like dominoes and more than one Indian was mowed down by those ropes. We drove all th' way through that village from south to north and just outside, th' infantry dismounted and continued back through th' ruins on foot. The cavalry was to th' west pursuing fleeing Indians. It was a complete rout, one hundred troops chasing away five hundred warriors with hardly a loss or injury.

Those mules were winded from their run and we rested them some. Then we turned them and rode slowly back through th' village. Not an Indian was standing and those still lying about were not moving. There was a sudden flurry of activity among th' men around one tipi and I drove up there. Billy Dixon was holding a bundle in a blanket and when I got close, I saw that it was a small child. He kept saying, "You are safe now, you are safe now," while tears were streaming down his cheeks. All the men standing around were affected. Lieutenant Bailey was holding another child.

They were filthy black and their eyes were wide and staring. The skin on them was tight against their bones. They were starved, beaten, naked, and cold. It was hard to believe anyone could be that thin and live. There were burn places around their eyes where cedar splinters had been driven and set on fire. Their fingernails were black and bloody where splinters had been driven under them.

Someone handed them some jerky and they ate ravenously. It was touching to see how those men responded to th' children. Everyone wanted to help them in some way. Soon my wagon was piled high with robes and blankets. Th' canvas was stretched back over th' bows and fastened down securely. As if that wasn't enough, a second canvas was stretched and tied just as securely. Clean shirts appeared and th' girls were clothed. I saw at least six pairs of socks handed to Billy and Lieutenant Bailey and all of them went on the children's feet. Soon a fire in one of the ruins was going and someone was cooking a broth for them.

There wasn't a dry eye anywhere in that crowd of hardened men and no one was ashamed. As the shock of their discovery wore off, tears turned to anger, especially when th' girls kept asking for their sisters and we realized that there were more white captives on th' plains.

"By all the saints in heaven, I'll shoot th' first man who suggests we go to Dodge before those two girls are found," an Irish trooper shouted.

"Hear, hear" and "Amen" sounded all around us. It was right then and there that Baldwin's command resolved to pursue that war to th' end, winter or no and as news of the girls spread through th' Army, that same sentiment prevailed.

By some coincidence, General Davidson's troop was near

and his cavalry rode after Baldwin. Not long after, General Miles rode in with his force and he took over with his usual vigor. Doctor Peter Waters was given responsibility for the girls, Billy Dixon was charged to provide protection for them, and I volunteered and was ordered to drive them wherever the doctor wanted.

Soon, other fires were burning with lodgepole fuel and th' doctor and his aide bathed th' girls in a tipi. The girls came out, warm and sleepy, their skin rubbed pink and their hair washed and deloused. Soon they were packed away, with enough warmed rocks to make the wagon groan under their load. Billy and I accepted each one as the troops brought them to us and we kept the aide busy throwing cooled rocks out th' front and taking warm ones in th' back.

General Miles made camp right there and Doc Waters and his aide made beds for themselves in either end of th' wagon, th' girls safely packed between them. Billy and I slept under th' wagon and there must have been fifty soldiers doing voluntary guard duty around our wagon that night.

The doctor decided that th' girls should be taken back to th' Washita camp where there was more variety in the food. A scout was sent all the way back to Supply to get a list of things the doctor required and by th' time we drove in to th' Washita, he was back from Supply. Along with Doc's things, he brought a gallon of fresh milk.

A more devoted bunch of men to their mission than those troops escorting us could not have been found. When word of our approach reached camp, men rode and walked out to meet us and our path was lined with cheering men. The same thing happened at Supply where the lines stretched more than a mile along both sides of th' road. When Doctor Waters determined that the girls were strong enough to travel, we took them to the train at Dodge and they went to Leavenworth where Mrs. Miles took them in and cared for them. Later, I understand that General Miles became their guardian and he saw to it that th' girls were well cared for and educated.

At Camp Supply someone had painted "The Germaine Chariot" on both sides of my wagon and it stayed there until the old thing finally fell apart. At Fort Dodge I was put in th' trains carrying freight to Camp Supply and that was my occupation for th' rest of that winter. It was *some* cold time, I can tell you, there were three blizzards that caused a lot of trouble and times between blizzards weren't much better.

Th' middle of March, Shorty showed up at Supply and we drove our empty wagons to Dodge, collected our pay, and caught a train to End of Tracks. We rode in to th' roundup camp just as they started south from th' Malpaís and got in on most of that rodeo. It must have been somewhere in June before I thawed out and it was years before anyone heard me or Tom Short complain about hot weather. That may have been th' most unique and memorable experience of my life. For sure it was th' most exciting winter job I ever had.

CHAPTER 13
PERIPHERAL VISION

"I'll tell you about a happenin' that occurred to me back when I wus workin' cows," Zenas said as he settled in his chair one afternoon. He was quiet for a moment, looking out over the basin and gathering his thoughts. "Sometimes things happen that no one can explain, sometimes they are coincidence, an' sometimes you cain't tell. This thing that occurred may have been that coincidence or it may have not, I'll leave it to you t' decide."

Late in the fall of '75 after a good frost or two and ticks had died off, John Dearing sent me an' Enoch Hunsucker down below th' border to pick up a herd of one hundred fifty black yearlings he had bought in hopes of improvin' his herd. We each took two workhorses and a packhorse for our bedroll and vittles an' struck out for El Paso del Norte by way of Las Cruces an' down the river. There was no hurry an' we took our time, checkin' out waterin' holes b'tween Las Cruces an' El Paso. Mexican women occupied th' cantinas same as men an' they were sure entertainin'—'specially if you showed some silver, which we were careful to do.

This Enoch Hunsucker was quite a character. We called him Ol' Van, 'cause he would introduce himself as "Enoch Hunsucker from Van Buren County, Arkansas," one of th' few men on th' range at that time using his real name. He was short and skinny as a split rail, but hard as iron an' when his fuse was lit, you kin be sure it was a short one! We got in so many scrapes

139

that one of th' cantinas shut its doors th' night we come back through with th' cows.

Th' ranch we was goin' to was on Rio Casas Grandes just north of Laguna de Guzman, Mexico. We made a leisurely trip of it seein' th' sights along th' way an' we got there in ten days. This was a huge spread with thousands of head of cattle and as many horses runnin' an open range. Th' owner, Don something, lived in a big hacienda an' didn't attend to everyday workin's of th' ranch. His majordomo was a very capable cow man named Elfego Martinez. He had the yearlings penned up in a big pasture. He gave us two of their finest cow horses t' ride an' we spent a few days looking th' country over an' restin' our horses for th' trip home. Martinez claimed that these "Black Cattle," as he called them, were descended from Coronado's herd, which he had gathered in 1540. They in turn came from a stock imported from Santo Domingo by a man named Villalobos, or something like that. They were well muscled and neatly limbed—and very agile. Th' Mexicans used them mostly for hide, tallow, an' bullfightin'. In color, they was mostly black with a lobo stripe reaching from head to tail an' bein' white, yeller, or brown, but mostly it was sorta a lighter shade of black. Their face was covered with shaggy hair with a brownish tinge, an' they had lines of lighter hair that circled eyes and mouth. They had shorter horns than longhorn that curved a little inward an' down. Their shiny black hooves were neater an' sharper than the longhorns'. We could identify them by their tracks, they was so different.

They were th' strangest cattle I have ever handled. The vaqueros on th' ranch warned us to steer clear of range cattle as they were very aggressive. It didn't take us long t' find that out, either. We was lookin' over a bunch of them when a big ol' bull charged out of th' brush right at us. Our horses knew more what to do than we did, mine turning so fast he almost unseated me an' before we knew it, we were flyin' over th' plain, that bull right on our heels. He must have chased us a half mile afore givin' up, then he stood on a little hump an' bellered at us til we were out of hearin' range. When we last looked back, he was still standin' there, king o' his domain.

On another day we was watchin a herd—from afar—when a pack of wolves came creeping out of th' brush after a meal of calf meat. Instead of runnin', as you would expect, th' calves gathered in a knot an' their mammies made a circle 'round them, horns out. Those wolves circled and circled, but couldn't git any advantage. One strayed too close an' a cow charged him, impaled him on her horns an' tossed him over her head. Before th' carcass could bounce once, another cow pounced on it with both front feet an' stomped it into th' ground. Then both cows joined th' circle again.

After that, th' wolves decided there was better huntin' somewhere's else. Me an' Ol' Van just stared slack-jawed.

"Man-o-live," he whispered, "did ya ever see th' like in a longhorn?"

Now we had both seen a mammy longhorn protectin' her calf from predators, but they was mostly left to theirselves by other cattle. Sometimes a bull or childless cow would lend a hand, but it was rare.

It had been agreed that the ranch would help drive our herd back at least as far as the Rio Grande and further if necessary, so Martinez sent four vaqueros with us on the back trail with the instructions that two were to return to the rancho at El Paso and the other two would continue on with us to th' ranch.

Apaches an' Comanches were bad to raid at this time and these mostly Indian vaqueros came fully armed and loaded. We pushed the herd hard the first two days t' get them out of the notion to stampede for home at th' first opportunity. We was convinced after a day or two that a hundred and fifty black cattle yearlin's was as much work to herd as fifteen hundred longhorns. Those vaqueros was th' best cowmen we had seen.

Now, all of us was used to livin' with an Injun threat an' we were not ones to be spooky about it, but I noticed that Ol' Van would sometimes turn his head sudden-like as if he had caught something moving out of th' corner of his eye. One night sitting by th' fire, he turned his head an' one of the vaqueros asked, "What deed you see, Señor Van?"

"Oh I guess it was nothin'," he replied. "I thought I saw someone passing by out of th' corner of my eye."

The vaqueros exchanged glances and the speaker asked, "What deed thees person look lak, Señor?"

"I jus' seen a shadow o' somthin' white movin' by, thet's all," Van replied a little impatiently. "It wus prob'ly jus' my imagination or a rabbit or somethin'."

That put me on alert and I noticed that Van would look to one side or th' other two or three times a day as though something was there or movin' about at th' edge of his vision. Nothing more was said about it, but I know th' vaqueros were watching Ol' Van too. One day Juan and I were ridin' together beside the herd an' he suddenly asked me, "Señor Zee, do you know what is thees theeng Señor Van is seeing?"

"No, I don't," I replied, "what do you suppose it is?"

Juan didn't answer. After we had ridden awhile, he replied, "There ees a beelief among my people that wheen you approach thee eend of life you can see thee Death Angel coming. Some time hee's dressed in white, sometimes hee's all black. First he passes you by thee corner of your eyes, going to get others, some say. One time you weel see heem coming straight to you an' thees is the time you go weeth heem. Wee beelief thees Death Angel is what Señor Van is seeing," he concluded.

When he said this, hair on the back of my neck stood up. Now I'm not superstitious, but Indian blood in me knows that we sometimes live and move in a world different from white folks, an' can see an' hear th' spirit world, like Geronimo had a vision of his camp a hundred and twenty miles away being attacked an' predictin' th' future, so I didn't take Juan's revelation lightly. Ol' Van kept seein' things move, but nothing more was said about it.

At night, we put a double guard on the herd an' camped close with our night horses saddled an' staked by our bedrolls. By th' time we could see th' green belt of th' Rio Grande, the herd was well trail broke. At El Paso, we penned up th' herd in a pasture an' treated th' Mexicans to a night on th' town, mostly in th' saloons that didn't know us from our first visit. They had a great time an' by th' time we were ready t' go midafternoon th' next day, they could ride without seein' double. We said adios to the two vaqueros returning to th' ranch and drove the herd north on th' River Trail.

By now, those yearlin's was broke to trail like veterans an' we moved them slow to let them graze an' fatten some before that long haul across th' basin. Our method of herdin' was to have one cowboy leadin', one on each flank, an' one on drag. We rotated around th' herd, each takin' one day at each position. We didn't tarry at Las Cruces, but bypassed town an' cut th' San Augustine trail on th' northeast side. Night caught us about halfway between Las Cruces and Organ Tank.

We let th' herd graze late next mornin' since it was only five miles to Organ an' th' grass would be grazed down around th' tank. It was our plan to water and move on over th' pass for th' night. They would have a downhill run to th' basin an' by gittin' an early start an' pushin' hard, we could git cross th' basin to th' river at Elephant Butte by midnight. If it was cows we were drivin', we would have made it a two-day run, but yearlin's ain't got th' capacity as cows does an' needs waterin' more often.

Things went as planned, th' herd tanked up on water an' we

143

eased them over th' pass far enough that th' rest of that trail was a smooth run. We were up early and had a big breakfast. Th' herd was lined out an' movin' an hour before sunup and we got a good jump on th' day. Juan was lead rider and I showed him the mountain we was headed for. I had right flank, Van had drag, and our other vaquero named Lupe was on left flank.

Th' sun was still castin' long shadows when a coyote jumped up and ran straight through th' middle of th' herd! I thought for a minute we had two stampedes on our hands, but do you know those two bunches of yearlin' calves formed two protective circles, heads out! It was some minutes afore dust settled enough so we could see each other. As it turned out, Van was alone with th' hind circle and th' two vaqueros and I had th' lead circle. These yearlin's had circled by instinct, but bein' young an' inexperienced, they didn't know quite what t' do next. I signaled for Van to haze his herd up to us, but every time he approached them or tried to wave them on, th' circle just got tighter.

It was eerie, not a sound was made, but both herds continued to stand guard. Van tried everything to git his calves moving but gentle talkin', yellin', and wavin' didn't work. Juan slipped into th' brush an' down a wash to circle back to help and I saw Van unlimber his yeller slicker from his saddle pack. He rode toward th' circle wavin' it and calling, when of a sudden a larger than average bull calf charged him. He wheeled, but before he could git out of th' way, that bull broadsided the horse and they went down in a pile an' cloud of dust! Th' bull turned and headed for th' circle, head an' tail high.

He didn't do no serious harm to th' horse, havin' button horns, and I saw him scramble up, empty saddled, trot off a couple of hundred yards, an' turn to face th' cows. It was hard to see where Van was across the two circles. His head didn't pop up anywhere and I couldn't tell if th' horse had dragged him off or if he was still near th' herd. In a few moments, Juan eased up on th' southwest side of th' circle an' I saw him start toward th' back of th' herd, then stop. He sat there still as a statue for several minutes and I near died of frustration, thinkin' Van might be layin' out there hurt an' Juan not doin' anything about it. I left Lupe with circle number one and slipped into th' wash Juan had taken. As I eased out of th' brush near Juan, I could see Van layin' on th' ground where they had fallen. He was very still and his left leg lay at an unnatural angle.

"Move verry slow, Meester Zee," Juan called in a low voice. "Ol' Van, he too close to thee cows an' ever' time he move, thee cows they geet ready to charge. We can no geet closer or they will charge us an' might hurt Meester Van bad."

It seemed we waited there hours, Ol' Van lyin' in th' dust and heat, an' us sittin' still tryin' not to stir up those cows any. Juan watched the circle intently and those cows just as intently watched for anything that moved. Over th' heads o' th' cows, I saw t'other circle relax and scatter some, grazing an' sometimes looking our way.

Finally, Juan relaxed a little and sighed softly, "Now, Señor, we can move some. I will ease back down thee wash an' go around to the far side of thees circle an' mayhap geet them moving. Eef I can, theen you can rescue Señor Van."

He slowly backed his horse toward th' wash and, in a moment, turned and disappeared. When he reappeared on th' other side of th' herd, he gave the shrill whistle they used to get the herd moving in the mornings, and like one animal, the circle turned toward him and began to move away. I sat still, the sweat runnin' down my face an' back, lettin' distance grow between Ol' Van and that herd.

Slowly, I dismounted and ground-tyin' my horse, I eased over to Van. He opened his eyes when I touched him and grinned at me. His face seemed as pale as th' white sands he was layin' on. I wiped dust an' dirt from his lips an' gave him a drink from my canteen.

"Think I broke my leg, Daylight," he said through his clamped teeth.

"Shore 'nough, Van." I tried to be calm, but it didn't come out right. For the first time, I looked at his leg and almost got sick.

His bone was stickin' through his pants leg just above his boot and there was a lot of blood soaked into th' sand.

Lupe rode up. "Juan say I be best doctair an' seend me back to help, Señor," he said, dismounting. Looking at the leg, he sucked in his breath and his dark skin turned a few shades paler. "We weel have to get that leg straight, Señor Van, an' that weel hurt some beeg."

"Go 'head, Lupe, an' see if you can make me holler." Van grinned but we could see he was in a lot of pain already.

"Lupe, would it be better if we held the leg still an' moved Van's body to line things up?" I asked.

"It might be, Meester Zee," he replied.

I laid out Van's slicker in line with his leg and where we could lay him on it, then with a lot of coaxing and positioning things just right and with a soaked rag between Van's teeth, I squatted an' put my arms up to my elbows under his arms. Slowly and steadily while Lupe held the lower leg still, I stood enough to clear Van's body from th' ground an' swung him over to th' slicker. Just as carefully, I let him down. With a sigh, he passed out. When Lupe saw that he was out, he quickly straightened the leg, with one hand under Van's knee. When he did, blood poured out of the boot. It must have been full. Lupe gave a little cry of dismay and I could only stare at the half-coagulated blood pooling on the slicker.

Quickly, Lupe cut away the boot with what must have been the sharpest knife in the Territory. Slitting Van's pants leg, he exposed the leg from knee to toe. The leg below the break was white as could be.

"No blood," Lupe muttered.

The jagged end of that bone had retreated inside a ragged tear in his skin and only a trickle of blood came out. We quickly bound up th' wound to stop th' flow, then sat back to assess what our next move should be.

"I theenk he lose too much blood, Señor Zee," Lupe said quietly. "Maybe we can geet heem back to Las Cruces, but eet no look good."

I stood up and looked around. We had only gone about eight miles from our camp. Looking back, I could see Sugarloaf Peak and the hollow just north of it where Aguirre Springs was. We could hold the herd there a few days if the grass hadn't been eaten up. It would take most of a day to ride to Las Cruces and back with help.

I signaled Lupe to come back and he loose-herded the cows back a ways, then came on alone.

"Do you see the tallest peak yonder?" I asked the vaqueros. "That's Sugarloaf, just north of there in that hollow is Aguirre Springs. There's plenty of water for th' herd an' I hope no one has eaten up all th' grass around it. If I can git Van to that spring, can you git th' herd there?" They both nodded. "Ok," I said, "lets find something for a splint an' I'll carry Van there ahead of you, then go on to Las Cruces for help."

It took us a while searchin' th' washes to find sticks straight and good enough to serve as splints. We ripped up a blanket for padding an' bandages and fastened th' splint in place. Using a rag tied around Van's ankle, we pulled th' leg portions apart until the pain was lessened. I determined to leave th' bones apart until I got Van settled at th' springs. As gently as possible, we put Van in th' saddle of his horse, then Lupe boosted me up behind th' saddle. When I was ready to go, Juan handed me his canteen.

"Thees one is full, Señor, an' he weel need much water. Lupe has a full cantina an' we weel git along weeth eet."

Here was a man in th' middle of a desert giving away his water for a fellow hurt cowhand. I'll never forget their generosity, though it was typical vaquero generosity for one in trouble.

Taking the reins of my horse, we started off across th' basin toward Aguirre Springs. Van was very weak an' I had to hold him in th' saddle. He helped some with his good foot in th' stirrup. Before I had gone a hundred yards, I saw that th' broken leg was givin' too much pain for him to go on like that. I called to Juan and he hurried over to us.

"What ees, Señor?" he asked.

"Can you tie Van's bad leg down so's it don't flop around?" I asked.

"Si, Señor, Wee weel tie it to the stirrup straps," he said.

Having done that and ridden a few steps, Van said that it was a lot better and we continued our journey. Still, Van was in a lot of pain. He rode with his head down an' I think he slept or passed out a lot. The sun was nearing noon an' th' heat building fast. Every half hour or so, I gave Van a drink and it seemed to help some, but I noticed he didn't sweat as much as I did, an' I wasn't drinkin' water. He finished my canteen and I wondered if Juan's would last him until we got to th' springs. Looking back, I could see dust from our herd a couple of miles back. I couldn't change horses by myself, couldn't walk an' hold Van in th' saddle, so Van's cayuse had to carry us all the way to th' springs.

It was weary, hot, slow travel pickin' out th' smoothest route. We had to detour around washes normal travelers would have easily crossed. By th' time we got to th' springs, that second canteen was dry by three-quarters of an hour, an' me an' that horse was played out. I had some time figurin' out how to git Ol' Van off th' horse, but I finally tied th' horse close, untied Van's leg, an' swung his good leg over th' saddle. When he got his right foot in th' left stirrup, I hurried around and eased him to th' ground. He was too weak to stand, so I got him seated under one of those cottonwoods that once grew around th' springs an' laid him out as comfortable as possible.

Juan and Lupe were pushin' th' herd right along. They looked like they were only a half hour or so behind. I filled their canteens as I was thinkin' how to git to Las Cruces th' quickest way. North to San Augustine Pass was too far out of th' way, but if I took straight up this draw, I could go through th' pass between Baylor Mountain and The Needles and have a straight shot to Las Cruces.

I left one canteen with Van an' giving my horse a quick drink, I mounted and headed up th' wash. It was rough goin' an' I walked much of th' way t' ease th' horse's work an' save him for a run across th' flats. Th' downhill side of th' pass wasn't so steep and rocky. We made good time an' when we hit th' flat, that horse was ready to move on. I pointed him straight for Las Cruces, some twenty miles away, an' gave him his head. Some time between three and four o'clock, I came upon a little Mexican jacal. There were a couple of horses in the corral and when I told the man my predicament, he loaned me a fresh horse. I left my horse there and planned to pick him up on th' way back. There was a trail from there to town an' I made better time, getting there about six o'clock.

It took me a few minutes t' find Doctor Hardy. When I told him what had happened, he said, "I've got a baby to deliver any time now, and the Baker kids all have th' measles, can't you bring him in, if it's just a broken leg?"

"He's in too bad shape t' move, Doc, th' bone was stickin' out of his leg an' he bled a lot layin' there. When we took his boot off, it was full of blood," I replied.

When he heard that, Doc gave me a straight look an' started askin' a bunch of questions, like "Where was th' break? How long did he lay there? How old is he? What kind of shape was he in before he fell?" an' it seemed a dozen more like that. Meanwhile, he started gatherin' up his gear an' stowin' it in his bag.

"Sam, go hook up Bob to the buggy and git a move on it!" he called through th' doorway.

I saw a barefoot boy hop off the porch an' run for th' barn. Meantime, Doc was gathering bottles of medicine and calling instructions to his wife, who was in th' kitchen,

"Send Sam over to the Holmes and tell them to send for Nita should the baby start comin'. Then have him take this bottle of pills to Mrs. Baker for the kids when they have fever. She's to give them one pill every four hours so long as the fever lasts. I'm going to Aguirre Springs and should be back by sundown tomorrow."

She had come to th' door as Doc talked an' stood there wipin' her hands on her apron tail. "All right, dear, do you have your kit in the buggy? You'll need extra cover up there." Turnin' to me, she said, "Make sure he eats something while he's there, young man. He gets so busy doctoring he forgets to take care of himself. I'm half a mind to send one of the girls with him to take care of him!"

"We have a bunch of riding to do, Mary, and I won't have time to watch after one of those girls," the doc replied.

Mrs. Hardy sniffed and gave me a wink. "You'll have to take care of him, young man, he's like a hound on th' scent when he gets to doctorin'," she said.

We rode his buggy through th' dark to the jacal. Doc unhitched and threw his saddle over Bob while I changed back to mine.

"I had my horses trained to pull and to ride when th' road gave out," he explained.

I gave th' Mexican American a dollar and we headed for th' pass. It seemed that cow pony of mine knew th' way better'n me, so I give him his head an' he took us right up to th' pass. Th' moon had risen over the Sacramentos an' gave welcome light to our path down th' mountain. Still, we had to walk several times.

Juan an' Lupe had a big fire goin' an' we saw it from a long ways off. They came out to meet us, each takin' a horse as we walked on into camp. Doc went right to Van, who was layin' just like I had left him.

"He no eat, Señor Zee, but dr-r-rink much agua, sleep much of time, but thee pain wakes heem," Lupe said.

"You go help Doc, Lupe, an' I'll git me some chow an' rest," I replied.

Juan unsaddled the horses an' led them down to drink.

"Be sure and stake my horse good an' secure," Doc Hardy called, "he'll stray off and head for home sure, if you don't."

I poured two cups of coffee and took Doc one. He took a big swallow and blew to cool his mouth, "Takes me awhile every time to get used to camp coffee," he said, then he turned back to Van.

Someone had left an old lantern hangin' from a limb, an' Lupe lit it for Doc. I looked at Van for the first time an' almost didn't recognize him. His face was drawn and his eyes were dark and sunken. The rest of his complexion was as white as ashes. I got swimmy-headed and almost had to sit down right there. When I had fought through th' feelin' I turned back to th' fire an' sat down. Juan came back from the horses an' sat near me.

"I no theenk eet good for Meester Van, Señor," he whispered, his voice kind of shaky. "Me neither, Juan," I whispered back. I got up an' walked out toward th' basin and sat on a rock, where no one could see me wipin' my eyes.

That Tularosa Basin is most pretty under a moon and that night it may have been at its best. Way to th' north her sands glowed white, while nearby flats were almost purple with splashes of silver light reflectin' off bare spots. Th' high yodel of a coyote floated up to me like an echo, sweet an' low. I've drawn a lot of solace from observin' her moods an' beauty. That night she almost seemed to speak to me, and I felt a lot more at ease when I went back to camp. Doc was sittin' by our fire drinkin' coffee. There was a plate of frijoles sitting untouched beside him. I smiled to myself when I thought of Mrs. Hardy's words, but I knew how Doc felt. I couldn't eat either.

"It doesn't look good, Zenas," he said after a moment. "I think he has lost too much blood to pull through. I'm surprised he has lasted this long. I gave him morphine to ease the pain, but I won't touch his leg unless he gets better."

Juan rode out to see about th' cattle. They were bedded down and quiet after a long day's travel. We left them to their own devices, knowing they wouldn't stray until sunup and they started grazing.

I dozed off a little, and I jumped when Doc scraped his boots getting up to see about Van. I got up and followed him. Ol' Van's eyes were open and he tried to grin at us when we walked up.

"See you found a doc somewheres, Daylight." His voice was high and weak.

"Yeah, I done it," I replied trying to be light, "he's a horse doctor, I thought he would be best for you."

Van smiled and closed his eyes. Doc held his wrist to check his pulse. He laid his ear on Van's chest listenin' to his heartbeat. When he sat back, he shook his head a little.

Van looked up again and said, "I feel better, Doc, th' pain's almost gone. D'yuh think I could sit up some?"

"Sure, Van, let's fix you a prop and you can sit up some, but not much and not for long," Doc replied. I hustled around and got one of th' saddles for a back rest. We padded it with a blanket, then Doc an' Lupe raised Van's shoulders while Juan an' I put th' saddle in place. Van's eyes were closed tight, but he opened them after a minute or two an' looked out over th' basin.

"Someone's comin'," he said.

"Where?" someone asked.

"Way out there toward th' Jarillas, someone dark on th' sands," he replied, then he sighed and closed his eyes. Doc pulled out his watch and looked at it, then wrote something down in his notebook.

Van slept for about an hour, then awoke with a start, though no sound had been made. I was sittin' on one side of him and Doc Hardy had made himself comfortable on th' other side. He had seemed asleep sitting there with his chin on his chest, but he looked up when Van moved.

"Hurtin'," Van whispered almost to himself.

Doc crushed a pill and poured it into a cup of water. "Drink this, Van." He put it to Van's lips and turned it up so he drank it all.

Van closed his eyes. "Looks like he's makin' good time, wonder why he's walkin'?" he said more to himself than to anyone. Slowly, his face relaxed as morphine took effect and he rested. Doc checked th' time an' wrote in his book.

Th' moon was almost straight overhead when I woke again. Th' doctor was just returning from th' fire with a steaming cup.

"He's still resting well," he said, "didn't stir a bit when I got up."

"But I knew when you got up, Doc." Van's eyes were still closed. "That coffee sure smells good."

"Do you want some, Van?" I asked. Doc looked at his watch and shook his head "no."

"I don't think, so, Daylight." His eyes never opened. "He must have walked twenty miles since I looked last . . ." then he drifted off again.

I swear I never saw his eyes open and I was watching him closely. I stared at th' basin as hard as I could, but for all my searching, I couldn't see anything move. I know my eyes were as sharp as Van's. In fact, I had often seen things before him, but there just wasn't anything on that desert that I could see— still or movin'.

There were little streaks of gray reachin' up from behind th' Sacramentos and th' moon had dropped down between th' peaks of th' Organs when Van woke up again. He looked straight at me an' said in a clear voice, "Write Mom an' tell her what happened." Then he turned his head back toward the basin. "Well, there you are, you sure made good time, I never saw anyone walk that far that fast."

His eyes were bright and clear and he was looking steady at something high up at his feet. After a few seconds, he said, "Go with you? Sure, where we goin'?" Closin' his eyes and layin' his head back, he said, "I got to git my boots on . . ." Then he smiled. It seemed a mist rose from him.

I don't know if I shook myself or if I shuddered, but when I looked at Van, I knew he was gone. Doc said softly as he wrote in his little book, "6:28 a.m., October 19, 1875." He looked at me very intently and th' only thing he ever said about it was, "I've seen them go like that a half-dozen times."

Lupe and Juan were standing bareheaded behind Van's bed with faces sad and pale. I reached up and turned off th' lantern. It was quiet for a minute or two, then a mockingbird sang from th' brush above th' springs.

"Well, boys, I got to get back to town," Doc said, "be my luck

Mrs. Holmes has had her baby an' the Baker kids will need watching all night tonight."

He was all business and bustle. From a folder in his bag, he pulled out a form paper and quickly filled it out. "Take this with you and record it at the courthouse first chance you get. You can mail it in care of the county clerk if you want." It was Van's death certificate.

Lupe loped off to get his horse and Juan handed Doc a tin of steaming frijoles and a cup of coffee. The doctor ate quickly, standing. "You'd best better lay him out straight and roll him in his blanket soon," he said when he finished eating. "He'll be getting stiff." Taking out his little book, he quickly wrote something down, tore the page out, and handed it to me. "You might want to keep this," he said, and I've kept it til this day. I paid Doc out of our travel money. He said it was too much, but I made him keep it.

I sent Lupe back to the jacal with Doc Hardy and told him to hire th' man there if he wanted to help us drive cattle to th' home ranch. I didn't know how fast rigor mortis set in, but I wasted no time in layin' Van out. I crossed his arms over his chest and went through his pockets, putting everything in a flour sack. We left th' splints on his leg. When I was done, we folded th' blanket over him from both sides and tied it with rope.

Scouting around, Juan found a good place for the grave at the head of a little wash beside a large boulder. The banks were steep and with a little digging we hollowed out a place. It was all we could do to carry Van up th' hill to the grave, but we finally made it. We laid him gently in th' bottom of th' hole. Juan was about my age and it was his first burial without a lot of people helping. We was both used to death, but always before there had been others that took care of things. This time, we were in charge. It was th' hardest thing I had ever done up to that time to cover that body. After we had gotten it covered good, we caved in the banks over him an' covered th' grave with large stones. Th' last thing we did was to roll th' boulder over at the head of th' grave. Taking an old knife, I scratched and carved th' headstone:

ENOCH HUNSUCKER
OLD VAN
Died Oct. 19, 1875

It was near noon before we got to look at th' herd. They had scattered some, but we rounded them up pretty easy. Juan's movin'-out call brought them together might near as good as hazin' them in. We moved them around th' base of th' mountain towards Dripping Springs so as to save th' grass around Aguirre.

That long afternoon sure weighed heavy on us. Juan was quiet an' that suited me fine. I thought a lot about what he had said about the Death Angel and what Van had said he could see and we couldn't. Then Doc Hardy had said he'd seen it a half-dozen times. It all made me think a whole lot.

The shadows was creepin' 'way out on th' desert and we were headin' th' yearlin's back to Aguirre when Lupe showed up. There was another rider with him and when we got near enough I could tell it was a young boy about thirteen or fourteen years old, ridin' a horse I had seen at th' jacal.

Lupe waved cheerfully as he rode up, "Señor Ortiz could not come, but he seent hees son Tomas to help us. He say Tomas as good vaquero as he is."

Tomas smiled, and removing his sombrero gave a little bow. "I try ver-r-ry harrd to please you, Meester Zee, I have herd cows, but never have I beeen on thee trail drive."

"I'll bet you do just fine, Tomas," I replied. "How about you an' me bringin' these calves on in while Juan an' Lupe ride on

and cook us up some chow?" Lupe nodded and I saw him give
Juan the eye and they moved off together. After about a hundred
yards, they broke into a lope an' soon disappeared around th'
foot of th' mountain.

Tomas had already moved to th' off-side rear of th' herd an'
was gently moving them along. By th' time we got back to camp,
I knew he could handle cattle. He was very interested in these
cows, having never seen their kind before. I told him a lot of
what I knew about them an' he asked a lot of questions that
made me feel good about havin' him along. We watched them
bed down and then turned for camp. The coffee was hot an'
Lupe had fried up a pan of salt pork and was busy cookin' a big
pan of scrambled eggs he must have brought from th' Ortiz
farm.

Juan and Lupe were both very cheerful around th' camp an' I
began to suspect I knew th' reason. After supper, I told them
my plan to start very early again in th' morning and try crossin'
th' basin in one hop. Tomas rolled up in his saddle blanket right
after supper and I knew that wouldn't be adequate for th' night,
so I gave him Ol' Van's bedroll. When he was plumb asleep, I
turned to the two jollies and said, "Ok, where's th' jug, or have
you two yahoos drunk it all up a'ready?"

They both grinned and Lupe went to his bedroll and pulled
out a half bottle of mescal. "Weeth Señor Ortiz's compliments,
Meester Zee, he thought we should have some comfort because
of our trials."

He began to pull out th' cork and I stopped him. "Hold on a
minute, Lupe." I picked up four cups and led th' way to Ol'
Van's grave.

"I never drink without my friends," I says as we poured four
cups full. I set Van's cup on top of th' boulder. We hunkered
down around th' grave an' sipped on our drinks. Now, mescal's
right powerful as you know, but when yore tired an' you've been

a month on th' trail without a drink, it's a *mighty* powerful drink to start out with. By th' time we were lookin' at th' bottoms of our cups, we had lost all gloom of th' day. We had 'bout told all th' stories on Van we knew, an' it was full dark. I poured Van's cup over the boulder, ignoring th' sigh from th' two vaqueros. "There you are, Ol' Pal Van, yore last drink, now you sleep well."

Zenas was quiet for a minute, his chin on his chest. "I'm 'bout told out today, Jim, come on back tomorry an' I'll finish my tale about crossin' th' basin with those Black Cows an' th' 'Pache we run into." I nodded, still scratching out my last notes. It was a long drive back and forth, but I wouldn't miss the rest of this story for anything, especially when he mentioned Indians.

CHAPTER 14
KEEN SIGHTED
IN THE TULAROSA

I was a little early getting there the next afternoon and Zenas was just finishing lunch. I entertained myself walking around the place and inspecting his garden he had been working. When he came out, he was back to his usual cheerful mood, having put the memory of yesterday's tale behind him. "I'll bet you're anxious t' hear about our encounter with 'Paches in th' basin, aren't you?" He grinned.

Well, if it hadn't been for th' light of th' fire, we would have missed camp that night comin' back from Ol' Van's grave. I don't remember crawlin' into my roll, but I woke up there next mornin'. Th' moon had come an' gone and it was still very dark. Th' fire had been stoked up an' by its light I could see that Tomas's bed was rolled up. Juan was stirrin' around th' food and Lupe was just stirrin'. Pulling on my boots, I looked up as our horses came walking in with Tomas riding behind.

"Thee leetle cows are fine, Señor Zee, they are just beginning to stir," he said with his big grin. I saddled up my horse and Juan's while he cooked, and we had a quick bite before packin' up an' headin' out. Just before we packed it all up, I diluted th' two fingers of mescal left in th' bottle an' gave th' two vaqueros each a sip. They looked grateful and with a nod, we were off.

Tomas took drag without a word being said. It was Lupe's turn t' lead an' I was on th' right flank. That bunch of little cows gathered up at Lupe's call, an' fell right in behind him like always. We pushed them hard and by sunup, we were as far out in th' basin as we had been two days ago. I kept my eye out for that blessed coyote, but he didn't show this time and we passed on some distance south of where Van had fallen. We were not halfway across by noon, but th' herd was ready for their customary noon rest, so we eased up an' let them graze on what little was there. I got out th' coffee pot as Juan built a fire an' we all had a cup. Not much was said with three headaches in th' crowd.

Now I've seen longhorn cows go days without water, I've seen them walk fifteen miles to graze and then a couple days later walk fifteen miles back to water, but I never seen what those yearlin's did. We moved on an' by sundown had walked them near twenty miles. It was still a good five or six miles to th' well, an' the cows were gittin' restless. Ever once in a while, one would bawl out, especially those in th' drag an' I thought they might be sufferin' for water. Just about th' time it got full dark, that herd started milling. We couldn't stop the mill, an' gradually, they all lay down an' wus quiet. They had bedded theirselves down for th' night! I couldn't believe it. Juan an' Lupe just grinned at me.

"Theese little ones just lak their mamas, no travel at night," Lupe said.

"They no need agua like you theenk, Señor Zee," Juan grinned. "We make camp, now, no?" he asked.

I could only nod. "May as well, boys, pick a spot an' Tomas an' I will watch 'em til you call supper."

We circled th' herd and it was just like any other night with them. They paid us no mind and settled right down for a long nap. After a while, a call came from camp an' we headed for chow. We could smell coffee an' I was surprised at how hungry I was. Tomas being still growing was hungrier than any of us and didn't waste any time diggin' in. We were all amused when he went back to th' pot for a third helping.

Apaches still considered this their land an' there was lots of traffic from th' Mescalero Reservation to th' ones still living wild along th' Gila an' on th' reservations in Arizona. They was always causin' mischief an' I got more an' more cautious as we neared th' mountains. I set watches for th' night, giving Tomas first watch, since some of us would most likely be awake through most of it. I gave him Ol' Van's gun an' showed him how to shoot it, with instructions to fire if trouble appeared. Juan and Lupe could take care of themselves, but Tomas was too young and inexperienced to take risks with. I determined to risk stampeding th' herd rather than to git him hurt. All was quiet and nothing happened during th' night. I had last watch and th' herd was just stirring when Lupe rode out to relieve me so I could change horses and eat. We had camp just about packed up when I heard Lupe whistle th' herd up.

We had been movin' an hour or two, when of a sudden an Apache rose up from a wash and ran straight at th' herd waving a blanket an' yelling. Instead of stampeding, the cows formed their protective circle—and it was the quickest an' tightest I had ever seen. Th' Injun reined up for a moment—you could see th' surprise on his face from across the herd. I spurred my mount an' headed around toward him as fast as I could, keeping out of range of those cows. Seein' me comin' from one direction an' Juan from the other side, th' Apache suddenly spurred his horse—directly at the herd! Instead of breaking, the cows stood fast an' two bulls charged th' Indian's pony from either side; the one getting there first hit th' pony on th' shoulder. He spun around from that blow just in time to take a broadside from th' other bull an' go down in a cloud of dust, th' Injun leaping free.

Now, th' first bull saw a second target appear from th' dust and took after the Indian. Running as fast as he could, the Apache was rapidly losing ground when Juan galloped down on him, and yelling, gave him an arm to grab as he passed. The Indian grabbed and swung up behind Juan in one motion, as they left th' bull behind. The pony had recovered his feet and was making tracks north as fast as he could. Heads high, and snorting, the bulls watched th' retreats and returned to th' circle satisfied.

Juan was running toward me with the Indian behind him trying his best to unseat him. I drew my gun and yelled, but the Indian didn't stop struggling until he heard my gun cock. I was riding knee to knee with him by then and he made to jump off when I called in Spanish, "Hold on or th' cows'll git you!" That calmed him some, though his eyes were still wide and he was shaking. By then, Juan and I were laughing and Lupe and Tomas rode up grinning and laughing.

The bewildered Apache looked around at us with a puzzled look, then grinned broadly. "Those some mad cows," he said in pretty good English.

"You bet, Injun," I said regaining some control. "You almost got your ticket to the Spirit World! These black cows don't take scarin' like longhorns. If they'd been growed, you might have a horn stickin' through your belly right now." He was a young man, about twenty, I would guess, and I was more concerned right then about other Indians lurking around. Hoping he was a Mescalero where I was known, I said, "My name is Zenas, who are you?" in his language.

"I am Nah-kah-yen—Keen Sighted—son of Nah-tanh." He seemed relieved to know who I was as it was known that I had Indian blood and had been honest and fair with the tribe. "He has spoken of you."

I knew Nah-tanh well, we had crossed horns a time or two, but we were mostly on friendly terms, trading horses and hunting in the hills together. This was not Nah-tanh's blood son, but he was being trained by Nah-tanh after the Apache way. Probably he was Nah-tanh's nephew.

"Your father is a good man," I replied. "Where are your

companions?" I asked, making a show of looking around.

"I am alone except for my wife. She hides in the arroyo," he said, pointing toward the wash he had climbed out of. "We are returning from the Gila where we visited her people."

"Were you hungry enough to eat a black cow?" I asked, pointing to the herd.

"Sí, we have no meat since day before yesterday. My wife is with child and she is very hungry all the time. We have had no meat," he repeated.

"We will water at the well at Elephant Mountain and camp at Monte Carlo Gap tonight. If you will come there, I will have meat and will loan you a horse to ride to Elk-Silver because of my regard for your father." Reaching in my pocket, I brought out the jerky I kept for munching on and handed it to him, "This ain't much, but maybe it will do 'til tonight."

Keen Sighted nodded, "I will come, friend Zee, because of my father's regard for you."

I nodded and he slipped lighty to the ground, then in Spanish for my vaqueros, I said, "Travel well, my friend, we will see you tonight at Monte Carlo."

To me, Zenas said, "You are saying, 'You could have given him a horse then,' and that is right, but I wanted to see how trustworthy and truthful he was. An honest man will keep his word and if he kept his word, I knew I could trust him with a horse."

Our trail to th' well and then north to th' gap was about twelve miles. Keen Sighted could walk directly there and th' distance would be less than ten miles, a leisurely walk for an Indian, even one with child. My three vaqueros looked at me wide-eyed.

"You would ask an Apache to our camp, Señor? He will slit our throats!" Juan said.

"No, Juan, this is a Mescalero and I know his father well. If he is truthful, I will loan him a horse and he will be on his way without doing us harm."

"Even so, I weell sleep lightly tonight," Lupe vowed, his eyes big.

Tomas nodded agreement. "I shall keep Señor Van's gun in my hand all night!"

The trip to the well was uneventful—that is, after we got our cows out of that defensive circle. They sure had a mind of their own, telling us when t' sleep an' when to walk. I had some time with th' man at th' well. I won't mention his name 'cause some of his folks still live around here. When I rode up ahead of th' herd, he hollered from th' jacal, "Water's fifteen cents a head for horses an' ten cents a head for cows." I could see he was hidin' behind th' long barrel of a double-barreled shootin' gun an' th' well was within his range.

"Must have had some experience sellin' water," I called back, carefully gaugin' th' range of that scattergun an' stayin' out of it.

"You damn right, an' I got me a good enforcer," he hollered.

"I'm Zenas Meeker from th' Rafter JD over on th' Sacramento. I need t' water a hundred and fifty head of yearlin's an' my horses, put that gun down an' come on out an' talk, I won't do you no harm."

"Turn yore horse an' let me see th' brand . . . it's Rafter JD all right, but how do I know it ain't stole? I'll come out, but Bessie's comin' with me."

"Ain't you man enough to get someone t' hold Bessie an' you come out an' talk?" I was gittin' a little agitated. Th' head disappeared, but Bessie's snout stayed. There was some talkin' goin' on in th' house, then th' door opened a crack an' th' man's head said, "I'm comin'."

I got a glimpse of a skirt and a bare foot and Bessie's muzzle wavered a bit, then was hoisted up to point straight at me. I could see one eye sighted down that barrel. T' tell th' truth, I'd a whole lot rather a man or boy be holdin' that scattergun than a woman. Th' man stepped out an' I nearly laughed. His shirt was a tatter to match his pants, cut off shin high an' he was barefoot—th' dirtiest feet I ever saw. He walked straight to me an' I was afraid t' make any sudden moves, cause Bessie was pointed straight at his back. If I'd sneezed, he'd probably got both loads. When he got near, I calculated he was out of lethal range of ol' Bessie and I got down off my horse and loosened his cinch. He wandered over to the half-filled water trough and began to drink.

"That'll be fifteen cents," the settler said.

"I'll pay you with th' rest." I was a little put out. We squatted in th' shade of a mesquite an' I rolled me a smoke. Ol' Bess's muzzle follered us. Th' settler looked hungrily an' I tossed him my sack an' paper. He quickly rolled one an' we sat back to smoke. I took my time, enjoyin' my smoke.

"What were those prices agin?"

"Ten cents a cow an' fifteen cents a horse," he repeated firmly.

I took a long draw an' squinted at th' mountains. "Think I could make Wildy's Well by sundown. Water's mostly free there if you draw yore own." I was talkin' as mostly to myself.

The settler shifted his feet, "That's near twenty-five mile from here, you sure those cows could make it after crossin' th' basin?"

"I calculate it's about fifteen miles," I said as I stood an' stomped out th' cigarette butt. "Yep." I made as though I had made up my mind.

Th' settler looked disappointed, I'm not sure it was at th' prospect of losin' a sale or th' cigarette butt. Bessie's muzzle, th' eyeball, an' th' skirt disappeared and th' door slammed.

"I could go seven an' a half on th' cows . . ." he said, more as to himself than to me.

"Would yuh go ten on th' horses?" I asked, tightening the cinch on my horse.

"For all th' others, but that un'll still be fifteen." His chin stuck out a little stubbornly.

"Wel-l-l-l, I'll think on it some," I said, kickin' dirt an' scratchin' for the fifteen cents.

"That still seems awful high for yearlin's . . . aw, go ahead an' start drawin' an' I'll send in a few head at a time." He eyed that well an' I could tell he wasn't relishin' any work involved. It was gittin' on toward midmornin' an' that sun was hot.

"Tell you what," I said as if suddenly havin' an idea. "*I'll* draw water for th' herd for five cents a head an' seven an' a half for th' horses."

He hesitated.

"I'll buy one of those fat nanny goats for a dollar . . . *and* throw in tobacco an' makin's," I offered.

"Wel-l-l-l . . . ok," he said reluctantly.

"It's a deal?" I offered my hand.

He took it a little hesitantly, glancing at the jacal. "Deal."

"We'll start right away," I said.

I drew the trough full, filled my canteen, and returned to the herd. Tomas and I cut out ten head and hazed them in. The trough was almost empty when the cows and Tomas's horse were satisfied. I took them north a ways and let them graze a little while Tomas filled the trough; then he rode out with his ten after they were watered and I returned to th' dry herd in time t' see Juan an' Lupe haze our remaining horses in. Lupe came back and we waited for th' horses to finish. Juan had to draw more water to satisfy those horses. He whistled when th' trough was full and Lupe pushed his ten in. It took us over three hours to water th' whole herd and water was gettin' low and stirred up in the well by th' time they was all done.

The settler stayed under that mesquite th' whole time, counting heads and notching his counting stick.

"I counted 150 cows at five cent, nine horses at seven and a half cent, and one horse at fifteen cents," he said as I walked up. "Th' cows was $7.50, th' horses was sixty-seven and a half cents, and with th' fifteen-cent horse came to a total of $8.32 and a half, which I rounded to $8.33."

I gave him $8.35 an' he made a big show of not havin' two cents to his name. I evened things out by lettin' my horse drink again, and the settler was sauntering towards his shanty when I left th' yard, goat in tow. I hadn't gone far when I heard pandemonium break at th' mansion.

"You let them have that water at half price? You lop-eared idiot, I'll git t'other half out'n yore hide, of all the sorry, no good . . ." and so on and on until I rode out of earshot, which was some farther than I had expected.

The boys had drifted th' herd northeastward around th' base of th' Jarillas toward the gap. You should've seen th' grins on those Mexicans' faces when I rode up with that goat. They shore love goat meat. We made camp early on th' east side of th' pass where shadows made it cooler. In a flash, that goat was killed, bled an' skinned, and cut up for cookin'. We had gathered fire wood along, and Tomas was busy digging a fire pit while the other two butchered. It wasn't long 'fore the pit was half full of coals an' just right for roastin' goat meat. Frijoles, coffee, and meat were coming along together when Juan looked up and said, "There they are, Señor."

They stood at the edge of th' brush watching. I had just scanned the area where they appeared and seen nothing, then like smoke they appeared, the woman a few paces behind her husband. I rose and signed "welcome" to them and they came on in. Keen's wife was not much more than a girl, probably no more than fifteen or sixteen years old, and it surprised me that she was so large with child. Apache custom is that the mother-to-be stays with her family until the child is delivered and well enough to travel, but this couple had apparently broken with custom for some reason and were going to his people before the birth. She looked hungrily at the food and I signed for her to sit down. Lupe was already dishing up a plate and when it was full, he handed it to the girl. She looked questioningly at her husband and he said something to her in their language I didn't understand. She nodded and began to eat hurridly. Tomas approached and offered her a cup of water, which she took with a little bow. All our attention was on her for a few minutes and we forgot about eating. Juan cut off another large chunk of meat and gave it to her.

While she finished eating, I got out my pipe and lit it. Taking a few puffs, I passed it to Keen Sighted who solemnly puffed a few times before returning it. "Did you travel well today, Nah-kah-yen?"

"Yes, it was well. I am on the track of my horse. He must be heading to the home range. Too bad he didn't take us." He smiled a little.

I smiled too, but not for the same reason since most likely he was riding and the wife was doing the walking. Not that an Indian that could walk fifty miles a day, desert or mountain, would mind walking ten or fifteen miles in a day.

"I will give you two horses for the rest of your trip if you will not eat my black cows," I smiled.

Keen Sighted smiled too, "That will not be necessary, Zenas, one horse for my wife to ride and I can lead it so it will be gentle for her."

This was a real surprise; for an Apache warrior to walk while his wife, even with child, rode. I nodded and was quiet for a moment.

"You are a good husband, Nah-kah-yen, I wish you health

and many children."

Birdsong (for that was her name, I learned) was finishing her meal and looked questioningly at her husband. He nodded and said a few words in their language. As quickly as she could in her condition, she rose, refilled the plate, and pouring coffee into the cup, brought the food to Keen Sighted. When I started to rise, she motioned for me to stay and hurriedly filled another plate and gave it to me. Taking my cup, she refilled it with coffee. The others were stirring toward the fire and she said in very good Spanish, "Please be seated, Señors, I will serve you."

They began to protest, but she quickly had three plates filling them and they saw that protesting was futile. We ate in silence, as was the vaquero custom, Birdsong seeing that our cups were always full. When we finished, she took the dishes and scrubbed them clean with sand and grass. Stacking them by the fire, she sat down at her husband's feet.

"I must be going," said the young warrior. "I wish to be to Wildy's Well tonight and Dog Canyon tomorrow. When my horse returns to the meadows, my people will be alarmed and look for us."

"That is good, Nah-kah-yen," I said in Spanish, "but before you go, there is another who must be fed."

Birdsong caught her breath and looked around. They knew how many of us there were and she could not have missed anyone. I dished out another modest portion of food, and turning, presented it to the girl.

"This is for the Little One, my sister," I smiled.

Her hand flew to her mouth and her eyes widened in realization of my little joke. "Aie," she exclaimed as she took the plate. Keen Sighted chuckled at her and handed her his remaining coffee. She ate while we fashioned a simple blanket saddle and caught up my most gentle horse. Juan handed Birdsong a sack of food.

"Tell your people about the Black Cattle, Keen, and that the Rafter JD has them to breed all their cows to behave the same. Before long, they may be chasing us for a change, but they must avoid Rafter Black Cows or any that have black on them. You can bring my horse down to me if I haven't visited you and gotten him. Give my regards to your father and travel well, my friend."

"And you travel safely, Zenas. I will tell of the Black Cows, but I do not think they will believe me." He chuckled as he helped his wife onto the horse. "Perhaps I will bring them to the Sacramento to learn by seeing for themselves."

Taking the reins, he struck out straight for Wildy's Well. After watching them for a while, I turned to the three standing near,

"I'll bet Wildy never knows some of his water is missing, don't you?"

"Sí, Señor Zee, they seemed good Indians, but I weel sleep better tonight in some other place!" Lupe declared.

"Wee also, Meester Zee," chimed Juan and Tomas.

There was nothing to do but break camp and move on while daylight remained. The boys pushed the herd along until I had to call a halt. I think they would have gone all night if the cows had cooperated. I never mentioned the fact that we were leaving a trail a blind man could follow—in the dark. This portion of the trip was across the flattest land of any we had traveled. There wasn't any change until we hit the breaks at the foot of Otero Mesa, which was out of our intended pathway, so I had the Mexicans turn the herd in a large circle about a mile in diameter until we had circled around to within a quarter mile of our own trail. With the herd bedded down, we would not be visible and the vaqueros could keep an eye on our back trail. *I* had no intention to lose sleep worryin' if some Injun was goin' to slit my eyelids an' stake me to an anthill.

The night passed quietly with no incidents. I took first watch, since I was sure the others wouldn't sleep and I could rest peacefully. It was the best night's sleep I got on th' whole trip. Except for hearing that coffee pot rattle occasionally, there were no disturbances. I awoke early and refreshed, to th' company of three bleary-eyed and grumpy vaqueros sitting glumly around a dying fire. They seemed almost disappointed nothing had happened, but considering all th' depredations Apaches had visited upon their people, I was pleased they had behaved as well as they did. Had it not been for me, there would have been dead Indians festering in th' desert.

After a quick breakfast, we headed the yearlings as straight for Culp Canyon as we could, skirting the breaks. Those boys from th' ranch must have been watchin' from th' pass, for as we turned for th' canyon, Tom, Leapin' Lon, and Rip rode out to meet us with a whoop and a holler. Instantly, it seemed, those cows were in their circle, watching this new threat riding down on them. The boys froze for a minute and Tomas, who was riding point, eased out of range of the cows and around to where Juan and I sat on the right flank.

"Are thees our freends, Señor Zee?" he asked.

I grinned and nodded, "Let's see how they react to these blacks."

Juan grinned and Lupe, hearing from across that silent herd, grinned. He sat very still. We could see th' boys conferrin' about th' situation, but they were out of hearing an' we weren't about t' holler at them. Presently, the confab was over an' they started walkin' toward us. Even their horses was payin' attention, their ears pricked forward. Lon was in th' lead an' when he got in th' danger zone, th' herd on that side snorted and raised their heads a little. It was just like a ripple around that circle, th' rest comin' to attention, still looking outward from their positions. A few more steps, and a young bull suddenly separated from the circle and charged Lon. Lon's horse first turned to face the bull, then sensing the determination, whirled and raced away, the bull on his heels. Rip and Tom had stopped when the bull charged and now they beat a hasty retreat also, their horses needing no prompting. It was an education seeing how those cow ponies reacted, not being used to such behavior. The bull chased Lon a good quarter mile, then stopped and watched th' retreating horse and rider, his head and tail held high. When he was sure th' challenger was leaving, he gave a bawl and trotted back to his place. I could see Tom's mouth working, but couldn't hear a word he said. As quietly as I could, I turned tail to th' circle and walked away. When I was a safe distance from those cows, I turned towards th' boys. Seeing my actions, they also backed away and circled to meet me. Tom sat where he had stopped, not interested in getting any closer.

"Holy crow, Daylight, whut kinda creature is thet?" Lon almost whispered as he rode up close. "Is them cows or devils?"

"They are called Black Cattle, Lon, an' they's somethin' diff'rent," I replied. "It'll take some gittin used to t' herd these cows."

"If'n that's whut they does when danger comes, it'll be a pleasure t' drive a herd of *them* to Dodge. Imagine a trip up th' trail with no stampedes, them longhorn days is numbered!" Rip exclaimed.

"Say, whur's Ol' Van?" asked Rip, suddenly realizing he wasn't with us. I guess my face must have showed, 'cause they both got real quiet.

"Van's horse fell on him and broke his leg. He died at Aguirre Springs."

It was all I could say. Even though they had a hundred questions that needed answerin', they let it lie until I could talk about it more. Around the fire an' over th' next few days, I told them th' events of Van's death.

After a few moments, Lon asked, "How do ya git these critters movin' agin, Daylight?"

"Well, yuh don't jist go hazin 'em," I replied, "Juan knows a trick."

I waved to Juan to start them up an' he rode around to th' trail an' gave his "let's go" whistle. Those yearlings fell into line and followed him up that trail jist like it was an everyday thing. Th' boys jist stared slack-jawed.

"Well I'll be . . ." Lon murmured.

"Black cows that don't stampede an' come whin ya whistle!" Rip said in wonder. "Many more of *them* an' we won't be needed. Boss could jist hire a couple of school kids t' take them up th' trail! Do they brand theirselves, too?" he asked.

Lon fell into place on th' left flank behind Tomas, an' Rip fell in behind me on th' right. Th' cows paid them no more mind. I kept glancin' back t' see how they was doin'. They sure rode a wide flank, not knowin' those cows an' not wantin' t' antagonize them none. Way back behind th' herd, Tom rode drag *behind* Lupe, that's how he got th' name "Wayback."

That dry tank about two thirds of the way up th' canyon used to be full most of th' time, fed by a spring that has since dried up. We pulled in there an' camped. The three hands had brought a packhorse loaded with supplies an' had cached them at th' tank. With our herd bedded down an' quiet, we proceeded to have a good feed. Me an' my Mexican vaqueros opened an' ate a can of peaches each for our dessert.

When I had finished th' last drop of syrup, Rip said, "Tell us what happened to Ol' Van, if yuh would, Zenas."

It wus th' first time I ever told th' whole story an' th' hardest time I had tellin' of it. Juan, Lupe, and Tomas helped me some and our listeners sat as quiet and still as ever I seen them. In the end, Tomas told about our toastin' at th' grave. It was th' first time we knew that he had follered us up there an' watched. He told it in an amusing way even admitting he had taken a nip

or two from the bottle himself. That sorta relieved our sad an'
solemn mood and we spent th' rest of th' evenin' tellin about
antics an' scrapes Ol' Van got into and sometimes out of. I
guess you could call it a wake without a body. We turned in
early, anticipatin' reachin' th' ranch next day. It got pretty chilly
that night and you could tell there was a weather change comin'.
Hopefully, we would git home before it turned bad.

We got an early start an' it was a downhill run from th' pass.
We rode in to th' ranch midafternoon an' put our herd into the
small pasture near th' ranch house. Mr. Dearing was proud to
see us an' commented on th' fine shape of th' cattle. They
seemed content to graze an' drink at their leisure and explore
all four corners of th' pasture.

I told Bob Green an' Mr. Dearing about our trip an' how
Van died. I drew out a map showing where his grave was so's it
wouldn't be lost. I told Bob what a good hand Tomas turned
out to be an' that he might consider askin' him t' come back to
work in th' spring. It pleased me to hear Mr. Dearing tell Bob
to draw full wages for all three of the vaqueros from the time we
left El Paso. They more than earned it.

We found an address for Ol' Van's home in Arkansas in his
things and after a few days I felt like I could write his family
without too much difficulty. We gathered his things up with his
death certificate in a package and mailed it to Diamond,
Arkansas in th' southwest corner of Van Buren County. Mr.
Dearing wrote a check for his wages an' his horses an' sent it by
letter along with our condolences. A couple months later we got
a letter to let us know that th' package and letter had arrived
and thanking us for all that we had done.

Most of what I had learned about Black Cattle, the rest of th'
hands had to learn by experience, since they didn't believe me.

I greatly enjoyed watchin' their education an' let 'em know it. Wolves an' coyotes got a education, too. We found more than one stomped into th' ground and we never knew of a Black Cow losing a calf to them.

All cows have a wonderful sense of smell—can smell water ten miles off if'n they's very thirsty. Some'll auger they can see things that far, but I'm convinced it's their sense of smell. Well these blacks could smell things a reg'lar cow can't. Les an' I was out one day an' found a mama black with calf back in th' brush.

"Now, whut's thet cow doin' out here away frum th' rest?" Les asked. It *was* unusual fer a black, they usually stayed in a bunch, even whin calvin'.

"Been here awhile," I said, "thet calf's near a yearlin'."

"Guess we better mark him if we can."

That proved a job. Whin we approached them, mama backed up to a cut bank an' assumed her customary defensive position. We laughed whin that calf came out b'side her an' pawed th' ground like he was nine hunnert pounds an' full growed. By splittin' up an' some good ropin', we got mama b'tween us an' I threw her so Les could git her legs tied. She lay there bawlin t' beat ninety.

Les shook off my rope an' I took th' calf on. We had a tussle. He wasn't hard t' rope, but whut t' do with him after that wus a problem. Ever time I threw him, he would be up afore I could git to him t' tie him off. Finally, Les came t' help an' we got 'im down.

"You start us a fire, Daylight, I'll jest sit here with my gun in hand case one of them devils breaks loose."

It didn't take me long t' gather wood an' start that fire, I can tell you. Th' whole time I wus on th' ground, hair on th' back o' my neck was standin' up an' my back felt like it did walkin' through a cemetery late at night. I throwed that iron in th' fire an' didn't rest 'til my feet was in stirrups.

"Yuh kin breathe, now," Les laughed.

I rolled a smoke an' said, "As my granny used t' say, you can go t' hell an' sizzle! Let's see how you breathe while yore fixin' thet calf!"

"Bein boss o' this yere outfit, it's my job t' oversee th' doin's, *not* do common labor. Thet burnin' an' cuttin's yore job."

"Not sure I 'members how, think you could dem-on-strate once more? I don't have nuances of th' art quite down."

"The best way fer you t' learn is t' *do* while I sits up here an' directs while overlookin' th' hull operation. I'm a better shot if'n one o' those critters gits loose or if daddy cow shows up."

"Let's flip for th' priviledges," I said. Th' upstart of it all wus that I lost th' argyment *an'* th' coin flip—an' I done th' flippin'!

Thet iron got hot mighty quick, almost like it was skeered too. I made short work o' brandin' an' notchin' his ear but cuttin' was messy as my knife was dull an' I got pretty bloody. That steer was *some* mad. He chased me to my horse an' plum out o' sight. All Les had t' do was let mama loose an' she passed up destroyin' him t' catch up with her baby. Les hoorawed me th' whole trip back to th' wagon an' got no end of enjoyment telling 'bout my gittin' run off by a mere calf. I was so bloody I had t' change clothes. Manuel wouldn't let them on th' wagon.

"Theese feelthy rags, they draws thee flies something awful, Daylight!" he said an' he threw them out of camp.

I got them an' threw them up on a boulder, intendin' t' wash them when we got t' water. After we had heard Les's story th' fifth time—an' it got bigger with ev'ry telling—we turned in.

It wus jest after midnight, best we could tell, when our horses spooked an' there wus th' worst bawlin', stompin', an' snortin' you ever heard comin' from just outside of camp. We was all up in a second, thinkin' there must be a stampede, th' herd was up an' listening but stayed quiet an' we could hear Rip an' Wayback singin' as they rode herd. Th' noise continued fer some time an' no one could git their horse settled enough t' go see. We could hear th' commotion fadin' an' finally th' horses agreed t' go see whut th' fuss wus about. 'Way out on th' prairie, we saw two cows movin' off up th' valley an' that was all we found.

At breakfast, Rip asked, "Whut th' devil were you waddies thinking makin' all that noise last night? You *wanted* t' stampede that herd?"

"Yeah," Wayback put in, "we hed t' ride double an' sing 'Sweet an' Low' jist t' keep 'em on th' ground. I swear!" He shook his head in disgust.

"We wusn't makin' any noise, you sprung-legged spavined rannies," Lon shot back. "Thet noise wus none o' our doin'."

"We would hev swore . . . you two wus up t' something . . . if'n we hadn't heard your caterwallin' down by th' herd," Jones said b'tween sips o' coffee. "Wouldn't be s'prised if you *did* hev something t' do with it."

Just then th' cavyyard came up an' we all got busy catchin' up mounts. Nighthawk wus grinnin' big as a possum an' called across th' ropes, "Better check on yore duds b'fore goin' out, Daylight."

I could see they weren't on th' boulder, so I rode over t' see where they had blown off to. Th' ground was tore up like it had been plowed an' disked an' there wasn't a sign of my clothes. I thought I saw my shirt a ways away, but when I rode up, it was only a scrap, then I saw another scrap stomped in th' dirt. A little further on was a ripped-up leg o' my overalls. We followed a trail of plowed ground an' scraps of those clothes for a full quarter mile, then th' plowin' stopped an' we could see tracks of a cow an' calf walkin' on.

"Ain't thet a willie fer yore whiskers!" Lon said. "Whut d' yuh suppose thet's all about?"

"Must be some kind o' devil cow," Jones mused.

"That wus a new pair o' overalls." I was mad. "I'm gonna find that cow an' nail her hide t' th' barn!"

"Not if'n it's got a Rafter brand, you won't er I'd nail *yore* hide to th' barn." Bob wus grinnin', but I knew he would do it.

"Let's see whut those devils look like." Jones trotted on.

"We can work this end of th' range today an' still git th' job done," Bob allowed, so we all rode along those tracks.

They led right back where Les an' I had branded that calf and we saw th' two o' them disappearin' into th' brush as we rode up. Tracks told th' story plain. Those two cows had come back to that fire an' stomped and scattered it all over, then they had followed our trail all th' way to camp. More than half of that way was in pitch black, so we knowed they didn't follow our tracks.

"Must hev been trackin by scent," Jones said.

"Bet you keep that knife sharp frum now on, Daylight," Lon laughed.

"*I'll bet* yore proud you didn't wear them clothes all night." Wayback was shakin' his head.

Zenas sat thinking for a minute, then smiled, "One other thing needs tellin' afore this story ends":

There was some disturbance in the small pasture one night a couple months later, an' next mornin' we rode out t' see if everything was ok. One young bull had nubbin horns growin' an' impaled on one of 'em was a leather leggin'. He seemed proud of it an' shook it at ever'one who came around. They was no way of catchin' him to remove th' leggin' so long as they were all together, so we jist let him keep his trophy. He acquired th' name "Apache Black" an' grew to be a magnificant bull, king of his range. A few days later, I found my horse I had lent Keen Sighted in the horse pasture an' I knew he had th' same trouble I had explainin' Black Cattle. After that, the Rafter JD never lost a cow with black on it to a 'Pache banquet.

I saw Nah-kah-yen a few years later on a hunt up between Mayhill an' Elk-Silver. He had a fine-lookin' son with him, told me his name was Nah-Tanh Zee.

Chapter 15
The Jackson Theory of Devolution

"What'chya think of Darwin's Theory of Evolution?" Zenas asked as we settled in for another tale. I hesitated and he smiled, "Don't worry, there's no right or wrong answer to that. I know it has stirred up a storm of controversy, especially since those an-thro-pol-ogists have been diggin' up bones an' makin' fantastical animals out of 'em. This isn't the first time this question has pestered th' minds of folks around here. I'm gonna tell you about it happenin' once afore an' th' sermon that came from it."

Years ago when I was a young buck workin' for th' Rafter, there came a couple of scientists into this country lookin' for fossils an' such. They was some young fellers from some big university back east an' they contracted with th' Boss t' look for bones on his land. Bein' they were so green, Mr. Dearing wouldn't let them loose alone an' had one or t'other of us tag along with them t' keep them out of trouble. Well, none of us liked it much for they were as obnoxious as they were ignorant of th' finer points o' livin in a real world. They were continually gittin' into trouble of one kind or another an' we had a time keeping them alive an' in one piece.

Well, these boys got to spoutin' off about evolution an' how it put th' lie to th' Bible an' all. It was plumb upsettin' to folks an' by th' time of our brush arbor meetin' in late summer afore fall roundup, folks was fit to be tied. Our Methodist Episcopal circuit rider was a middle-aged man named Martillis Jackson, who had been a vaquero over around Deming and Silver City an' as such had been endowed with considerable common sense. We ranch people especially enjoyed his preachin' b'cause he spoke our language. His meetin's was always well attended by ranchers an' cowhands 'cause we could enjoy his sermons almost as much as those good eats an' pretty girls.

That year we put th' arbor down on th' Sacramento a couple o' miles upriver from where Pinetop is b'cause there was plenty of water still there an' most folks round here preferred baptism by dunkin'. This also meant that folks had to camp, which wasn't new to any one of us. In fact, we rather enjoyed it.

Word had got out that Preacher was goin t' address th' evolution controversy and that encouraged an even larger attendance than usual. We allus had a good singin' b'fore every sermon an' my how those folks could sing! Mrs. Jeanie Austin brought her pump organ down from th' ranch, a good thing for our meetin' but not good for that organ in th' end. Miss Olive Holmes came with folks from Las Cruces to play. She was always popular with us boys, partly b'cause she could play so well an' partly b'cause we liked t' glimpse her ankles when she pumped th' organ. When th' old folks wasn't around, she would play us some popular songs of th' day. We sang about an' hour that first night b'fore Preacher got up t' preach.

There was always some announcements t' be made b'fore th' sermon an' as was th' custom back then, Preacher Jackson stood in front of th' pulpit t' make them. The pulpit was reserved for speakin' th' Word, all other talk was done outside th' Holy Desk, as it was called.

When he was through with mundane announcements, he said, "I have heard a lot of talk about this evolution controversy on my circuit this time and I have prepared a sermon in response to it. Some time this week I will give that sermon in the evening service." This caused a stir, there were a lot of nodding heads and a few "amens."

"I don't know yet which night that will be," he continued, "it depends on how the meeting goes." He turned to stand b'hind th' Holy Desk an' as he went, there was an excited murmur run through th' crowd. It got deathly quiet except for a baby in th' back squallin' out as Preacher opened his big black-bound Bible, and proceeded to give a stem-winder of a sermon. Back then, if a preacher spoke for less than an hour, it wasn't called a sermon, but you can bet this first night he gave a *sermon*. In fact, it was a good sermon and a half, then th' invitation was another half hour. He sure knew how t' get a gospel meetin' off on a good foot!

They was a lot of speculation about what Parson Jackson would say about evolution the next couple of days, but he kept mum about it, not a hint from him. 'Course, bein' a cow man we knew he would be aginst that theory, but how he would attack it was another question.

"I'll bet he'll chunk th' whole idée," said Leapin' Lon Sims.

Bob Green rubbed his chin like he allus did when he was thinking. "Cain't say it's *all* wrong, Leapin'; look how the horses adapted to their new conditions when they went back to the wild."

"But that's just nat'ral," Les put in, "if we was turned loose in the desert, we'd learn purty quick how to eat cactus an' mesquite beans afore we starved."

"Just what I mean, Les, we would *e*-volve from beef eaters t' bean eaters, and purty quick, too!" Bob replied.

"You ain't sidin' with them perfessers what says th' Bible ain't true are yuh, Bob?" Tom looked perplexed.

"No, not at all, Tom, but it's possible that *some* o' what they're sayin' might be true. Like they say, it's an' ill wind that blows *no* good."

"I think you're right about that, Bob," Gene Little said, "them academic boys tend t' run ahead of practical applications a lot an' git theirselves in over their heads."

"They shore murkied th' water whin that Durham bull chased them into th' creek!" Wayback Tom laughed.

"That may be where they proved th' kin o' man an' monkey, the way they skinned up those mesquite trees," Leapin' laughed.

"Trees warn't th' only things skint up, those boys looked like th' bad end o' a cat fight when they finally come down," Tom was chuckling.

"How long was they up there?" I asked.

" 'Bout two hours, I'd guess."

"Two hours!"

"Yeah, I'd guess that at least, they kept hollerin' for me t' run him off, but I p'tended thet I was afeared o' him an' ever time I made a run at him, he chased me off, so I let him stay. He musta stayed on th' prod from about 4 'til sundown."

"Sun don't set 'til 8, Tom, that's *four* hours!" put in Rip, who was allus a stickler for accuracy.

"Mayant hev been," mused Wayback, while th' rest of us enjoyed a laugh. "It was th' first time in two days I got t' relax some, knowin' those two wasn't up t' something harmful, stupid, er dangerous."

"That shore wus a long time fer ol Durham t' hang around," I said.

"He'd o' gone sooner ef I hadn't tole those boys t' whack him with a stick ever once in a while."

"You kept him mad at them?" Gene Little asked between laughs.

"Well I tole 'em an' *tole* 'em *not* t' git down off their hosses whin that bull was around, but they wouldn't listen . . . es usual," Wayback fussed.

By now, we were all laughin' at th' vision o' what Tom hed put those two perfessers through.

"How'd they git down, Tom?" Les asked.

"We-e-l-l-l they fin'ly d'cided whackin' him with sticks wus no good an' tried bein' still. After an hour or so, that bull lost int'rest an' wandered off a ways. I p'tended t' attack him an' he chased me over th' hill where I sent him off t' find some sweet heifer. I *tole* those guys not to git down til I said it was safe an' durn if they didn't mind me, so I cotched up their hosses an' run them under their trees an' tole them t' climb down on 'em an' not t' ever git off'n them less'n I said so. You know, I never had any more trouble with thet agin while I was nursemaidin' 'em."

"They told me about it th' next week when I was watchin' them," said Les, wiping away tears, "an' I near busted keeping my face straight. I had t' make up some excuse 'bout ridin out t' check cows so's I could laugh. I laughed so hard my hoss turned around t' see ef I was ok. I told him about it an' he got t' laughin' so hard I hed t' git down an' walk!"

"Did you hear whut th' 'Paches did to them?" Bob asked.

That brought more chuckles from those that knowed, but o' course some hadn't heard, so Bob told th' story. "They had hired a couple o' Mescaleros t' guide them an' keep camp. After a few days o' putting up with 'em, they let them know they had given 'em Injun names. O' course, they were mighty curious about that an' got the 'Paches t' tell them what the names were. They were awful proud an' b'gan callin' each other by them an' telling ever-one about it. We still haven't found out who told them their names meant 'Great White Horse's Ass' and 'Little White Horse's Ass,' but when we do, that man's gonna git one good chappin'!"

"I hear they're planning on comin' out next summer an' bringin' more help with them," I said.

"Shore hopes th' new ones is of a higher caliber o' intelligence than them two!" Tom said, shaking his head. "I'd rather sweep out saloons than watch herd over mor'n one or two o' them critters!"

We could all agree with that. Well, sir, you could just about know Parson kept us in suspense about that sermon right up until Thursday night, when at th' end of th' service he announced that he would be speakin' on the subject o' evolution on Saturday evening. That put th' qui-etus on our plans t' slip off t' town Saturday afternoon, 'cause no one wanted t' miss that!

Crowds Saturday night an' Sundays allus run biggest 'cause those not able t' git away for th' whole week was sure t' show up for Sunday services. It was when a lot of townspeople got their chance t' come out an' even some churches in town would cancel Sunday services so's th' congregations could attend.

There was no small amount of anticipation about that Saturday night service an' folks b'gan gatherin' early. Singin' was extra good an' I thought we would never git to that sermon, but finally time came for Parson to step b'hind th' Holy Desk an' a pin drop would have made an awful noise in that arbor. From th' beginning, it was an unusual sermon b'cause he didn't even open his Bible, just laid it on th' desk and there was a stir about that.

Then Zenas began quoting the parson and it was a few moments before I realized that he had memorized the whole sermon word for word! In the end, he had to repeat it twice so I could get every word right just as he told it.

"I know a lot of you have been anticipating hearing me speak on the theory of evolution and I have set aside tonight to do that. It will be shorter than usual because there's only so much you can say about the subject. I apologize for the brevity, but I promise to make it up to you with tomorrow's sermon." And with that said he launched into his talk.

"There's a lot being said today about a man named Charles Darwin and his theory of evolution. His writings have been shouted from the rooftops by some of those in the scientific community and condemned as originating in the nether parts of hell by those of the pulpit. Now, I consider myself a man of the pulpit, though my pulpits tend to be more of the tailgate or brush arbor variety than under a steepled roof. It may be that some day when there are towns and a settled population, I may have a regular pulpit, but for now I must go where the people are.

"I was raised wild and lived wild for some years, even fell so low as to cowboy some before I received the Call. This put me at a disadvantage when compared to the regular members of my profession, for though I am no longer wild, I retained my natural curiosity about things and thus it was that when I first got the opportunity, *I bought Mr. Darwin's book.* Furthermore, against the warnings of my fellow clergy, *I read it,* every word.

"Mr. Darwin proposes some very interesting theories and I think most of them hold water, but just like all theories, when they hit the light of day, this one needs some refining. Already there is much discussion, and many alternatives and refinements have been proposed by layman, clergy, and scientist. As I am apparently one of the few of the cloth that has stooped to read this book, I feel it is time for me to weigh in on the topic.

"First of all we need to know as much as possible who Mr. Darwin is. He is a scientist of the first order. He has contributed much to the world of science. On his now famous worldwide tour, he met up with some islands in the southeast Pacific with some very unique wildlife, and ruminating on the things he found there and elsewhere, he came up with his famous theory. By studying these unique animals in their habitat, he has determined that organisms evolve in response to the things that influence them in their surroundings. I cannot disagree with that. In fact, I have observed that very phenomenon in action.

"Using Mr. Darwin's theories as a foundation, the scientific world has deduced that all life has originated from one source. In the world of reasoning, that thought process is called 'taking an idea to its logical extreme.' Out here, we would call it *what-iffin'*. Usually, logical extremes and what-ifs carry an idea too far from the realm of possibility or reality, and I think that has been the case with the subject we study today. Now, I agree with the idea that all life came from one source, but my source stops at Creator God. Beyond that, things get dark and murky. For instance, the idea that all life evolved from one organism 'way back when' disagrees with Scripture where it says that God created the various plants, each bearing seed *according to its own kind,* and that He then created the living creatures *according to their kinds. According to their kind* means that apples have apple tree seed, that oaks have acorns that make oak trees, and horses have colts and cows have calves. It's only when man got to messing with that premise that we got mules. That's as far as my what-iffin' will let me go.

"Not to say that the reality of the logical extreme cannot go back farther, I just don't care and it wouldn't bother me if it does. I hold to one truth that is presented in the first four words of Genesis: *In the beginning God . . .* In those four words, God wound the clock of time, set it ticking, and began the creation process. I don't care how He did it, I don't care when He did it, I just know *He did it.* Here's an interesting idea: What if when God set that clock, he set another one that ran backwards to it? Try taking that to its logical extreme!

"But I've wandered off the trail. It's been proposed and some would demand that we believe that man has descended from the apes, but looking at the ape of today and man of today, I would say that man is in the ascendant from where the ape is. You have to admit that we have gone much, much farther than merely adapting and adjusting to the things around us that would influence us. Our environment didn't need us to read and write to survive. It didn't require that we build ships and trains to move us. No, we did that on our own independent of the forces of nature.

"In other words, the family of man, on the whole, is smarter and better than the ape family. In fact, we have dominion over the ape and all other creation, just as God said we would in Genesis 1:26.

"It has been my observation that all things tend to fall apart, that more often than not, organization and orderliness tend to just plain go to pieces. For instance, take a herd of cattle on the trail. Those cows have organized themselves into a regular society with the lead steers in front, and each steer in his assigned place behind, even to the drag. It's the same way day after day, but let something unexpected happen like a sneeze or a flash of lightning and all that organization breaks into a thousand four-legged pieces running in a hundred directions. A simplified example, I know, but the point is that order and organization are the temporary states in life and disorganization and chaos are the rule.

"So how is it then that wild and disorganized apedom can evolve into organized and rational mankind? Not likely, I say.

"If, as Mr. Darwin says, we respond and adjust to forces in our environment, why didn't the forces that made man out of ape force all apes to adjust? If the forces were not uniform or universal, where was the necessity to become man? That man evolved over the eons cannot be denied, but he evolved from his own seed, not some others'.

"Just the same, the similarities between man and ape cannot be ignored, but I think the proponents of the ape-to-man theory have it backwards if cross specie evolution did occur. I think it more likely that any evolution that may have occurred was in the form of man-to-ape in keeping with the organization-to-chaos rule.

" 'And just how could this happen?' you ask. Again, I refer you to Scripture: In the first chapter of Romans, Paul talks about the wickedness of men and three times he uses the phrase, God *gave them up*—to lusts of their hearts, to dishonorable passions, to a base mind and to improper conduct. In other words, because they acted like base animals, He *gave them up*. Is it too much of a stretch to suggest that because God *gave them up* for acting like an animal, they eventually *turned into* an animal, namely, apes and monkeys? Why not? We marvel that the ape looks and sometimes acts so much like humans, maybe, just maybe his ancestors once were.

"One could argue that if they could go from human to ape, the reverse could also be true. Possibly, but we have never seen either happen and it would go against the convention that all things tend toward chaos. I propose that my theory of *de*-volution holds as much water if not more merit than *ev*-olution!

"Another idea has been built on the premise that we have ascended from apes and that is that mankind is not native to the Americas because there is no evidence that there ever were apes in the New World. Obviously, if the original theory is false, all succeeding theories built on it collapse. Here again, I would like to pose another idea for consideration: Before the white man brought the Word to this land, the Indian, whose blood in greater or lesser proportions flows through the veins of most of us here, lived in primal innocence. As the Apostle Paul said, where there was no law, there was no sin. Therefore, there was no fall and no Indian was *given up* to descend into the ape world. Hence, no apes live in the New World. I like that idea, don't you? I believe we will eventually find that man has been here as long as he has been in any other part of the world.

"And there you have it, my friends, the Jackson theory of de-

189

volution! Take it or leave it as you wish, but this you should hold on to: *In the beginning,* God *created the heavens and the earth!*"

With that, he was finished an' stepped down from th' podium. We were some surprised, for he hadn't raised his voice or gestured or nothin' an' we thought that he had only given us th' introduction when he quit! When th' crowd realized there was going to be no invitation an' the service was ended, someone in th' back yelled out, "Amen, Preacher, Amen" an' gave a whoop that let loose th' whole crowd hollerin' an' shoutin'. We gathered around him shakin' his hand an' clappin him on th' back 'til Miss Olive b'gan playin' a hymn on th' organ an' we settled down an' sang with gusto for another half hour b'fore mothers started hustling little ones off t' bed an' th' meetin' broke up. That talk wouldn't have qualified for a full sermon, only lasting twenty minutes or so, but it was th' talk o' th' basin for years t' come.

Zenas twisted around in his chair and looked me directly in the eye, one eyebrow cocked. "Now, lest people who read this jump to the conclusion that those folks was just a bunch of country bumpkins, let me say right here that they were not. They knew th' tongue-in-cheek manner in which that sermon was presented and they were educated enough t' know that message was given to point out weaknesses of th' theory in a lighthearted way without insultin' th' believers of it. These people were of the soil and by that I mean that they were mostly all well acquainted with nature and they knew that the wonderful way it was knitted together was not a random or haphazard thing."

We hashed that sermon over an' over, so much so that instead of sittin' around reciting cans that winter, we worked until we had reproduced th' whole sermon word for word. It filled many a long evenin' in th' line shacks of several outfits, workin' t' recite it right an' we had contests and arguments over who could do it best with just th' right inflections Preacher used. They was a dozen fellers could give it perfect and whenever cowboys gathered someone was sure to recite it. I've seen fellers argue by th' hour over some little line or inflection or where t' put a comma or dash.

This is what Zenas told me about "reciting cans":

Most vaqueros of old days didn't have much if any formal education, and we mostly taught ourselves t' read an' write. Spendin' a winter in a line shack was *some* burdensome if you didn't have somethin' t' read. Usually, it was one book an' by spring a feller might have read it four or five times 'til he was sick an' tired of it, or he had memorized most all of it. If you were lucky, you might get an old squatter's cabin where th' Missus had papered their walls with newspapers an' you could read walls all winter. If not, you'd git so hungry for new material you would start reading labels on cans, then you'd start memorizin' them. By spring, you might know th' total contents of a dozen can labels, then when you got together with the boys you would have contests t' see who could recite certain labels th' best. We'd bet on th' contest or there'd be fines for missing a word or punctuation.

Sometimes in camp, th' Old Woman would set a certain can by th' fire an' th' contest would start. We'd recite in unison, each man listening for his neighbor t' misstep an' callin' out fines.

Take for instance, this sentence from that coffee can: *We custom-roast our original blend to bring out its peak flavor and aroma, giving you the rich, beautifully balanced flavor that you expect in your cup.* We would recite it this way: *We custom hyphen roast our original blend to bring out its peak flavor and aroma comma giving you the rich comma beautifully balanced flavor that you expect in your cup period.* Th' tricky parts is punctuation. If you recited like reading a brand, using "bar" for hyphen or "dot" for period, there was a fine for each infraction.

Old Bull Durham cigarette tobacco used t' have coupons on th' bags you could save up an' order books with. They was mostly th' classics like Shakespeare or such an' th' outfit would git together an' order from what we had collected. Every line shack had at least one or two books. Sometimes when we could, we would ride over to th' next shack an' trade books.

Gene Rhodes would read while breakin' or ridin' a horse. Someone found him one day sittin on a horse's head reading while th' horse calmed down enough t' break. Another time he rode up to a neighbor's house readin' an' sat there until he finished th' book, then he put it away an' rode off without ever gettin' down an' visitin'. They's a lot of quotes an' references to th' classics in his stories that he gleaned from those old tobacco books.

All in all, I would say that a cowhand was educated as much as any feller from th' city. Difference bein' that we learned from those coupon books an' gathered an awful lot of plain common sense from our work. A feller livin' in th' city didn't have much *country* common sense exposure in his environment, everything being tamed down and routine like. It's when you run into things unforeseen an' unknown that you learn t' git along in this world.

CHAPTER 16
OF HONEY AND THE BEE

Lest you become confused, dear reader, I must explain that Zenas is about to skip back in time and tell stories of happenings before he joined the Rafter JD. These are stories the vaqueros told him around campfires and in line shacks when the snow was deep and they were tired of reading.

When th' Austin-Dearing outfit moved into this country they drove a wagon with a matched pair of mules. They were out of th' same mare an' so alike they say it was hard t' tell 'em apart. The first one they named Honey and when the second one came along two years later, they had a heck of a time figuring out what to call him. Finally, they just gave up and called him Bee.

Those two mules were inseparable; where you found one, the other was sure t' be nearby. They were both gentle-broke by a man in th' community and they could be ridden or worked as a team. It turned out that pullin' a wagon or a buggy was their favorite task. It seemed that they relished th' challenge of pulling a load and drivin' them was a dream. Bill Austin said he could hitch them up an' tell them to go to town and they would go straight there without a gee or haw all day.

They were five and seven years old when they crossed th' Pecos at Horsehead Crossing and two days later Bee died in th' night. The boys never knew for sure, but they suspected alkali water of th' river kilt him. They found Honey standin' over th' carcass, head down an' mournin'. When they tried t' hitch him up with another mule, he flat rebelled, fightin' an' kickin' man, mule, an' wagon. Finally they had to turn him out to th' cavyyard and hitch up another team. That night when they brought th' cavyyard in, Honey wasn't with them. Their horse wrangler was an experienced hand and he swore that Honey was there at th' noonin' an' he never knew when that mule left.

They figgered they knew where he was an' John Dearing saddled up his night horse and rode alone twenty miles back in that Comanche-infested country t' get his mule. That's how much they thought of him. Sure enough, he found Honey standing over his dead partner. John saddled th' mule and rode him back, making it by noon th' next day. Honey spent th' next few days tied to a tailgate 'til they figgered he was out of any notion to turn back. After that, he turned in an' stayed with th' cavyyard.

Honey was good for ridin', but there was no way he would team up with another mule to work, so they didn't attempt t' do much with him 'til they was settled on their new range. On a trip to El Paso, Bill Austin bought a mule that matched up with Honey pretty good an' he brought him home an' turned him in th' horse pasture. After a few days, they caught up Honey an' that new mule an' put them in th' corral together. Things went pretty smooth an' it seemed that they was gittin' along pretty good—*until* they tried t' hitch 'em together, then it was th' same old fight. Peace was only restored when they were back in th' corral.

Word got around that the outfit had a mule they couldn't team up and one day a Mexican American rode into th' yard and asked for Bill.

"Meester Austin," he said, "my name is Ponciano Esquival, I hear you have a pr-robleem weeth one of thee mules."

"Shore do," Bill said and they ambled down to th' corral as

Bill told Ponciano th' story of Honey and Bee.

Ponciano watched the mules awhile, then went into the corral an' caught up Honey. After giving him a thorough looking over an' movin' him around some, he said to Bill, "I beleeve I can train these two to be a team if I had them for a while."

"Well, he ain't no good t' us like he is, what do you propose t' do an' how much will it cost us?"

"My grandfather and father were famous horse trainers among my people and they have taught me thee secrets of training thee ani-mals. I have spent most of my time along thee Santa Fe Trail working weeth mules and I have developed a particular skeel weeth them. Eef you weel let me have theese two mules for one month, I can break them to harness together, but I must take them away, for my methods are secret."

Bill rubbed his chin. "I don't know about that, not knowin' you an' all. Who have you worked for around here?"

"No one, Señor, I am new in thee country, but I have letters from others who have used my services."

With that he pulled out a sheaf of letters and handed them to Mr. Bill. All of them were highly complimentary of Ponciano, saying his methods were gentle and results were excellent. The signatures were impressive, Ceran St. Vrain, F.X. Aubry (though he was dead by then), George Bent, and others.

"I've heard of these fellers, but have you trained any mules for folks around here?"

Ponci, for that is what we came to call him, dug at the dirt with his toe. "No, Señor Austin, you would be thee first one I work for in thees area. I have tir-red of the work on thee trail an' wish to locate my family here near our families."

Bill thought a minute. "I tell yuh what, Ponciano, I need that mule workin' mighty bad, but I cain't let him offen th' place. What if we gave you a place off by itself an' let you train them there?"

Ponci grinned, "That would bee ver-ry good, Meester Austin! I would bee weeling to work for twenty dollars a month an', how you say, found?"

One thing I can say about Bill Austin is that he was a *good* judge of character, both human and animal, an' he saw something in Ponci that he liked. I think he also guessed that Ponci didn't have any secret place he could train his mules an' so offered him one of our line shacks. They shook hands an' th' deal was set.

"Come back in five days an' we will have things set up for you," Bill said.

"Sí, Señor, I weel be back early on Thursday."

We spent th' next days gittin' th' corral at th' line shack rebuilt. It was up th' river an' off to itself where Ponci could work his secret magic on those mules. Manuel stocked th' shanty with food, especially things Mexicans relished in their diet.

By Wednesday evening all was ready. Th' boys was mighty curious about this mule trainer an' there was more than th' usual number of them still hangin' around when Ponciano Esquival and more rode into our yard, for Ponci had brought his entire family of wife an' about a dozen kids ranging from fourteen years on down. It was quite a parade, with Ponci riding in front on his fine horse an' his wife behind on a big rangy mule, a babe in arms and another cherub bouncing along in front of her. They must have had all their household goods piled on that donkey being driven by a half-dozen barefoot boys. Th' fourteen-year-old was a girl in th' blossom o' womanhood an' every vaquero took special notice.

Ponci rode up to where Bill an' Gene Little were standin', removed his sombrero, and gave a little bow. "I have come to work, Señor Bill."

"Very good, Ponci, this is my foreman, Gene Little, he will

have one o' the boys show you th' line shack. The mules are already in th' corral up there. We have only stocked food for one man, though."

"Oh, we weel not need thee food, Señor, my wife, Susano, has brought food enough for our stay and thee boys weel catch rabbits and such for our meat."

"Good." Bill was relieved. "Just the same, you go ahead and use what is there, that was our agreement."

"Thank you, Señor, we will go now." He turned and followed Leapin', who had mounted up and was waiting.

The boys watched th' parade pass on with amusement. "Did you see thet gal?" someone asked as they disbursed for their assigned chores.

"Now, how do yuh think we coulda missed *her*," said his companion, slapping th' back of his head an' dislodging his sombrero.

That line shack got more than usual traffic in th' next few weeks. Th' boys'd "just happen" t' drop by an' see if Ponci needed anything. Mostly, they came around mealtime, for Susano and her daughter, Yesenia, were excellent cooks. They had industriously spruced up that old shanty until it was a clean an' comfortable home. Meanwhile, Ponci worked on the two mules. At times he was frustrated with all that traffic comin' an' goin' an' Charlie had to warn th' boys t' slow up on their visits so Ponci could work.

At the end o' four weeks, Ponci, with one of his many sons sitting beside, drove into th' yard one evening on a wagon pulled by Honey an' that other mule, circled, an' pulled up in front o' th' bunkhouse. They could tell that Honey was doin' his job, but wasn't likin' it very much. He was mighty skittish an' kept eyein' his partner. Th' boys havin' finished supper were all sittin' around th' bunkhouse porch watchin' a sunset an' chewin' th' fat. When they saw those mules, they were *some* surprised, but bein' savvy, no one moved or made any noise. Gene Little leaned on one of the posts as Ponci drove up.

"Señor Leetle, I have thee mules brroken to pull some, but they need more worrk to bee just rright."

"I can see that, Ponci, how much more work do they need?"

"I theenk two more weeks would geet them ok and four more would make them verry good."

"Well, Mr. Bill told me b'fore he left to give you more time if you needed it an' it looked like you was makin' progress. It's for sure you're makin' progress, so go ahead an' take another month. It'd be nice if they got to where my granny could drive 'em."

"Oh, I theenk that bee too much for theese two!" Ponci shuddered and th' boys grinned.

Gene carefully stepped down from th' porch an' walked to Honey's head, talkin' soft to him. Honey was nervous 'til he recognized Gene an' calmed some, but he kept rollin' his eyes at his mate. "I think some blinders would help Honey, do you?"

"Sí, Señor, I have thought thee same theeng."

"Rip, go get th' two bridles with blinders on 'em an' put them in th' back of th' wagon for Ponci."

Rip nodded an' rolled off th' end o' th' porch goin' 'round b'hind th' bunkhouse t' keep from spookin' Honey.

"This other mule seems calm enough," Gene said, rubbin' his nose—th' mule's nose, that is.

"Sí, he is thee calming one. Wee call heem Serenio." Later, that was shortened to "Sary" an' sometimes strangers wondered why they had a he-mule with a girl's name.

Gene stepped back up on th' porch. "Anything else you need, Ponci?"

"Eef we could have some flour and cornmeal for my found, eet would bee good," he replied apologetically. "Susano didn't plan on staying longer."

"Probably didn't plan on feedin' half th' dern outfit, either!" Gene replied, looking around as people ducked their heads. "I'll get Manuel t' bring you another month of supplies up tomorrow."

"Gracias, Señor!"

Just then, Rip came up b'hind th' wagon an' laid bridles in th' back, makin' some noise that made Honey's ears slick back.

"Uh-oh!" said Gene as Honey danced. "Let 'em go Ponci, adios."

"Onda mules, adios, amigos!" he called as they bolted out of th' yard. His boy rolled backward off th' bench, arms an' legs thrashin'. They left with a rattle and a run and Ponci let them go, keeping a guiding hand on th' reins.

Th' boys sprang off th' porch watchin' them go. "Well, did yuh ever think you would see that!" Lon laughed, slappin' his leg with his hat.

"He's shore got Honey working at it," another said.

"Wasn't worth shootin' afore," a onetime victim of Honey's insanity muttered.

"And all that without a mark on 'em! That Ponci is *some* trainer!" Rip said.

"Manuel," Gene called, "git vittles t'gether for Ponci an' run them up to him t'morrow an' go heavy on flour an' cornmeal. Send those kids some o' those extry cans o' peaches an' tell Ponci t' see if he can git Honey t' stand still while loadin' th' wagon!"

Ponci was busy th' next few weeks polishin' up th' team an' by th' third week, they were doin' very well. All three bosses rode up an' saw a demonstration of what had been accomplished. They were impressed and praised Ponci for his work. Th' end of th' month came and Ponci drove into our yard one morning with a wagon bed full of kids and all their belongin's, donkey and horse trailin' b'hind. "I have fineeshed my work, Señor Beell, an' now wee weell move on to our new home at La Luz," he beamed. Honey and Sary stood quietly while the kids all bailed out of th' wagon, chattering and laughing.

Bill shook his head. "I never expected t' see that again!"

"Hee is ready to work, but there are still some things to bee ironed out," Ponci said. "I have trained heem in Spanish an' to talk to heem in the Angleesh makes him theenk of hees friend Bee an' he geets opset. Eef you have much trouble weeth heem, I will come back an' work more weeth heem for free."

"That sounds fair, Ponci." An' Bill Austin wrote him out a check with a generous bonus for his work. Mr. Austin sent Rip with th' wagon to take the Esquival clan to La Luz.

"There an' back without a single hitch!" Rip bragged.

Ponciano went on to be a successful trainer an' lived many years at La Luz. Some vaquero lassoed Yesenia a couple of years later an' together they raised a passel of kids.

Chapter 17
The Organ Babatism

"Now," Zenas said, "I have told you all that, to tell you this."

Honey and Sary made a good team an' worked for the ranch a good many years, but occasionally Honey would walk under th' moon, especially if someone forgot an' gave commands in English. Then, he would likely run away or do something else stupid. Sary had t' put up with it an' go along with Honey's antics or git hurt. In fact, th' old boy learned to bolt as quickly as Honey did when he heard a command in English.

They made a showy pair and the boys liked t' use them when they were out an' about in th' public eye. Like when they hauled that organ down to th' brush arbor meeting that time. Things went well, with Gene drivin' them down an' the boys had a good time showin' off the team, givin' kids an' girls rides up an' down River Road.

The last thing on the arbor meeting agenda was baptism; that ordinarily occurred th' morning after th' last preaching. Preacher waded out in th' river where it was deep enough to immerse for those who wanted it and th' ones who wanted sprinkling had t' wade out to him too. It was a solumn occasion and th' crowd of witnesses was very quiet. One at a time th' candidates waded into th' river. As one man waded out to where Preacher Jackson stood, a little tyke looked up at his mother and asked in a loud voice, "Is Papa gonna git babatised, Ma?"

Preacher smiled and answered, "That's right, young man, yore papa's gettin' babatised."

Th' outfits left for home after th' baptizing was over, leavin' Rip an' Gene t' haul th' organ back. When th' partners had split th' range, Les an' Lon had gone with Mr. Dearing an' Rip stayed with th' Austins.

Les an' Lon stayed around to help out b'fore headin' back to th' Rafter. They had just loaded th' organ an' tied it down when along came that bootlegger that lived up at High Rolls. Temptation was too great even after a week of meetin' an' th' boys bought his last quart of 'shine. It didn't amount to much split four ways, but suspicion is that Rip got th' lion's share.

After shootin' th' breeze awhile an' lettin' th' 'shine soak in good, Gene said, "Rip, why don't you drive th' wagon first an' I'll spell you in a while?"

" 'S fine with me," Rip muttered, an' he climbed up an' settled on to th' spring seat. Shaking their reins, t' wake up dozing mules, he called, "Giddyup!" Honey's ears perked up, then laid back on his head. Too late, Rip yelled, "Onda! Onda!" but Honey had seen th' moon an' away he went down River Road, patient Sary keeping pace and Rip sawin' on th' reins.

When it looked like he wasn't gonna stop for a *while*, Rip steered into shallow water, hopin' to slow th' runaway some so Honey would calm down. Water got up to th' mules' bellies an' they had just about stopped when the right front wheel hit a big rock, broke th' front axle, and dumped th' wagon.

Rip an' the organ got bapbatised.

The others weren't far b'hind an' when they rode up, Rip was just sittin' up sputterin' an' coughin'. The organ lay on its back slowly bubbling away as it sank further into th' water. Fortunately, those mules hadn't gotten tangled or fallen, but th' tongue had twisted th' traces so that they couldn't move.

Three horses waded into th' river, three ropes grabbed th'

dry side wagon wheels, an' they pulled it upright. Th' organ was still in place, th' quilts wrapped around it drainin' water. Still, th' bed was awash an' it took some time t' get th' remains out on th' bank.

Rip started for th' bank, tripped over a rock, an' fell face first into th' river again. 'Stead of gittin' up, he just sat up with his elbows on his knees an' his head in his hands. It didn't take long for a crowd t' gather helping an' offerin' advice. There were lots of cries of dismay from th' ladies an' one young miss sweet on Rip waded out into that river an' sat down b'side him, dress and all. She talked to him a long time while he just sat there shakin' his head.

They unwrapped soggy blankets an' set th' organ on th' ground, where water continued t' drain out of th' poor thing.

"Boys, she's ruined," one of the men said. There was a murmur from th' crowd an' a few women dabbed their eyes.

"You don't think we can dry 'er out an' she'd come back?" Leapin' asked.

Our organ expert shook his head, "Nope, you'd have t' take 'er all apart an' dry every piece an' even then she'd probably rust. That veneer will come loose, curl up an' turn black, an' th' other wood will probably warp an' turn. Nope, boys, she's ruined for sure," he concluded.

More murmurs came from th' crowd an' they slowly began t' leave, castin' sympathetic glances at two forlorn figures still sittin' in th' river.

The family of th' young miss drove up an' called. After a moment, she stood up, stooped an' kissed our fallen hero's head, an' waded back to th' shore, water streamin' from her long skirts. Gathering up her shoes, she plopped down on th' tailgate an' th' wagon moved off, leaving a trail of water as far as it could be seen.

Th' boys got busy riggin' up a skid for that broken wheel an' loadin' th' organ remains into th' wagon. Finally, Rip got up an' waded ashore. He looked at th' organ an' sadly shook his head.

"Well, boys, I guess that's the end of my C-B days."

"Wasn't your fault, Rip," Gene said, "it's that damned mule's fault!"

Rip shook his head, "Nope, Honey didn't say 'giddyup!' "

"But you can't take *all* the blame," Les argued.

"Maybe not . . . maybe so, but one thing's for sure, I cain't look Miss Jeanie in the eyes an' say I'm sorry, that just won't be enough. Gene, I'm quittin'. I gotta make some money an' pay back the damage I done an' I cain't do it on cowhand wages."

"You don't need t' quit, we'll all pitch in an' help pay for a new organ."

Rip shook his head. "The whole outfit could pitch in six months' pay an' not have enough t' pay fer it. B'sides, I couldn't stand t' see Miss Jeanie cry when she sees that organ. Bill's holdin' three months' pay o' mine, tell him t' give it to Miss Jeanie an' I'll make the rest good soon's I can." He sat down an' pulled off his boots, dumpin' water out an' tying soggy boots across his saddle. "Gene, you got some paper an' a pencil, I want t' write Miss Jeanie a note."

Gene tore a sheet out of th' back of his tally book an' Rip composed a short note to Miss Jeanie. "Take this to her an' tell her I'm sorry fer th' mess I made." He mounted up, an' with a wave, started down th' river road. We could hear him singin' low an' sad. His voice faded as the road dipped into a gulley, then we heard him faintly when he topped th' far bank. Then he was gone.

Gene an' th' boys had th' job o' haulin' that soggy organ home in that broken wagon. Leapin' Lon d'cided t' help Gene git home an' Les headed to th' Rafter JD t' let them know what happened an' where Lon had gone.

When they limped into th' yard, broken wagon and soggy

organ layin' flat in th' bed, Charlie Austin walked out on th' porch an' asked, "What happened?"

Gene rode over where Honey couldn't hear an' said, "Rip said 'giddyup.' "

Charlie got awful mad. "That sorry mule, I'm gonna git rid of him, I'm gonna grind him up an' make mincemeat outta him, I'm gonna tan his hide an' nail it to th' barn, I'm gonna . . ." Words failed him an' he jist stood there getting madder an' madder. "I'm gonna git rid of that Honey," but he never did.

Miss Jeanie was sad about th' organ, but she didn't cry 'til she read Rip's note. No one knew what it said an' no one asked. Bill said she kept th' note in her Bible an' looked at it ever once in a while.

The organ sat on th' veranda for a long time, slowly fallin' apart. One o' th' boys tried pumpin' her a couple of times, but all she did was gurgle and Charlie finally had it taken down to th' gulley. The boys did save th' mirror off it an' put it up in th' bunkhouse where Miss Jeanie couldn't see it.

Ever once in a while th' two outfits got news about Rip. Someone saw him down in Juarez runnin' a faro game, then he was seen in th' same business in El Paso an' Las Cruces.

About a year an' a half later, a freight wagon all th' way from El Paso pulled into th' C-B yard late one evenin' with a big crate addressed to Mrs. Jeanie Austin. She was mystified as to what it was an' suspicioned that Charlie had gotten her something. They set it on th' porch an' th' boys uncrated th' finest-looking pump organ you could ever see. It was after th' crate was opened that th' freight driver handed her an envelope.

A note inside read:

Dear Miss Jeanie:
Here is an organ to replace the one Honey and I ruined.
                              Your Humble Servant,
                                Joseph Van Winkle

Well that took the cake. Those C-B boys gave a yell an'
throwed their hats in the air an' danced a jig right there in th'
yard. Miss Jeanie was laughin' an' cryin' all at th' same time.
She ran into th' house an' came back with some music an' sat
right there on th' porch an' played that organ 'til th' sun went
down.

In early spring that year, Rip showed up at th' Rafter an' the
Boss hired him. Asked why he didn't go back to the C-B, he
said, "I still have trouble thinkin' about facin' Charlie an' Miss
Jeanie an' I want t' be where I can keep an eye on Les an' Lon,
maybe keep them outta trouble some. B'sides that, I shore don't
want t' be where I have t' talk t' mules in a foreign language!"

*We had been talking about the cattle business and ranching in the
basin and I had asked Zenas to tell me more about the basics of
working cattle, especially in the arid basin. He said he would think
on it and when I returned one afternoon, he was ready to talk about
it.*

Just like any other operation in th' outdoors, ranchin' is dictated
by an' revolves around th' seasons. In less watered places its
more important than others. When I first came into th' basin,
grass grew thick an' lush. I guess it had taken thousands of
years t' adapt to its environs, but adapt it did. Lookin' at it
summer an' winter, you would declare it was dead, but let spring
or summer showers come an' that grass would green up fine.
Just remember when you look out over this basin that brown
ain't dead, young man.

Well, ranchers fell right in on that grass, knowin' cattle could live off it year-round without havin t' cut hay. It wasn't but a few years til th' range was overgrazed an' native grasses almost killed out. That's when this country turned into real desert. I tell you, it ain't near like it was when I first saw it, and man an' his cattle are th' culprits that changed it!

I've already talked a little about how we ranched, but it wouldn't hurt t' go over it again. Winters are relatively mild in th' basin, so about late September or October, we would push cows out of th' hills onto th' plain t' winter. O'course th' same thing was happenin' on every range that ringed th' basin. We generally got some rains an' snows through late winter an' as it warmed, grass greened an' cows started fattenin' up.

We had spring roundup in May usually—hopefully after th' last bad weather an' when th' grasses in th' valleys were greenin' up. It was a chore gatherin' an' sortin' out brands, brandin' an' countin' 'em, an' sendin steers t' market. Th' hardest part was convincing those waddies that they needed t' leave th' basin an' head up th' valleys when they were hock deep in green grass where they were. Once they were convinced that it was ok t' move out, it wasn't hard to keep track of them.

In th' mountains, spring is greatly influenced by elevation, things greenin' up at th' lower elevations first, but as green moved up th' mountains so did cattle, following until they came up aginst timber or bluff that stopped their progress. Then after a few weeks, th' seasons reversed and cattle were pushed back down th' mountain by frost and lack of forage until they spilled out on th' basin for th' winter.

Ridin' herd was easy enough through th' year. All we had t' do was make sure they had water, keep strange cattle out, an' make sure our cows stayed on their range, which meant some o' those wild ones had t' be run back down from th' ridges or they would roam plumb over th' mountain into someone else's range.

You can see how changes of season influenced our work. It

was all comfortable and predictable, almost to th' point of bein' boring. Th' thing we looked forward to most was spring roundup when th' boys who didn't winter over on th' ranch came back an' we got t' visit with all th' other outfits around. It was hard work, but a fun time too.

It was several years b'fore I worked up to a year-round job an' I would generally have t' find other work durin' winter months. Lots of times I would use that time t' visit back home or ramble around seein' things that interested me but I *never* rode that grub line, not once!

Chapter 18
Possibil-ities

The worst roundup I remember was th' spring of 1876. Th' ranchers d'cided t' hold their roundup early b'cause that winter had been unusually dry an' th' basin was picked near clean. Trouble was th' rains came all in a bunch after th' gather had started an' we did th' roundup in mud instead of dust. Believe me, dust is much to be preferred over mud at a roundup! If we got t' work a whole day, we would have t' change horses three times instead of th' customary twice.

By th' time we turned our second mud-covered bronc loose an' saddled the third, we were so wet and covered with mud it was hard to tell who was who—got so we welcomed a hard rain so's we could wash off. It wasn't unusual on th' range that our dirty pants could stand by theirselves, but that's th' only time I saw shirt, vest, an' coat stand up alone. If it didn't rain in th' night, most of th' dried mud would crumble off when we put our clothes on next morning. Ever'thing took on a dull brown or red color of th' dirt we worked in, never washed out as long as I had those clothes, either.

I had in my string a horse I hated t' ride. He was about th' most skittish horse I ever saw. Once he bucked me off an' ran away when a butterfly flew up under his nose. Mostly I avoided riding him an' Bob was always after me for that. My string was about wore out with th' mud until I was forced to saddle up this jughead one afternoon. He did fairly well until someone scared up a jackrabbit an' it run b'tween his legs. That done it.

Now, I wasn't a slouch at ridin', I've done my share of bronc bustin', but don't let any cowboy tell you he ain't never been throwed 'cause if you ride, yer gonna fall! The only cowboy I ever believed when he said that was th' drugstore variety an' then he wasn't including bar stools in his count.

Even with me on th' lookout for his antics, he got th' best of me an' it wasn't long until I lost a stirrup. He felt th' thing flap aginst his side an' his next jump was sideways an' I lost my seat. My other boot was deep in th' stirrup an' wouldn't kick free, so there I was bein' dragged through brush an' cactus, getting kicked every third jump an' gen'rally gittin' beat t' pieces. If Preston Dycus hadn't shot th' horse, he would have killed me—darn near did anyway. His last act on earth was t' fall on my leg an' break it.

I don't remember much o' that ride, but I heard that bone in my leg pop an' that brought me to in a world of hurt. By th' time they got to me, I had put five .44s into that horse's hide an' was still pullin' th' trigger. They had t' *lift* that horse off my leg to keep it in one piece an' I near bled t' death afore they got it stopped. I was a real mess. What part of my backsides that still had hide on was full o' needles an' thorns. Th' back o' my head was all lumpy from hittin' rocks. I had broken ribs an' my foot that stayed in th' stirrup was broken across th' top. When they started t' cut my boot off, th' foot was so swollen it just popped out.

'Course, I didn't know all this until they told me later. They laid me in th' wagon an' Lon drove me to Doctor Hutto's at Tularosa. Even in my state of unconsciousness I could tell every bump he rode over, even though he drove carefully an' made it as smooth as he could.

When we got to Doc's, I was so stove up that they laid me on a door t' carry me into th' house. There were no hospitals in those days and Doc Hutto had a room set up for serious cases.

Th' first thing they done was lay me out on a table an' cut off all my clothes and Eusebio Flores set to work cleanin' me up. Doc gave me a shot of morphine an' I dreamed sweet dreams while he set my leg an' sewed it up. He couldn't put it in a cast because th' bone had stuck through my hide an' he needed t' keep it open, so I had splints tied to my leg.

Eusebio kept th' thorns an' needles an' they half filled a quart jar. He even dug out a gravel or two. Doc didn't even try t' count broken ribs, he just taped my chest up good and tight so I had t' breathe with my stomach. It eased th' pain there quite a bit, but there were plenty of painful places elsewhere t' keep my attention.

What t' do with me after that was a problem. I couldn't lay on my skinned-up backsides, I couldn't lay on my stomach because of my ribs, but my broken leg needed traction an' my broken foot couldn't be touched. My right leg and ribs were th' broken ones an' they finally determined t' lay me about three-quarters on my left side so my back was clear an' my leg scotched up with pillows an' tractioned to th' foot of th' bed. By bending my left leg I could stick that foot over th' edge of th' bed where nothing but covers touched it. If I stayed in that position an' Doc kept morphine in me, I could tolerate things fairly well. And there I lay for three weeks. Every once in a while they would turn me as much as possible so's I wouldn't get bed sores, but it was a trial, believe me.

On th' third day, th' surgeon came down from Fort Stanton an' examined my foot. He poked an' felt around on it an' set a couple of bones, then they wrapped it good and tight to a board. He told me he thought all th' bones had gone back into place an' it would be best t' just leave them alone until they healed. If some were not set, they would have to be repaired by surgery. I guess they all set for I never had surgery and my foot works near as well as it did b'fore th' runaway. I can feel little knots on some bones where they knit back, but they don't bother me.

They had a time keeping my back from getting infected. Eusebio watched it closely an' bathed it religiously with alcohol an' peroxide—sometimes I thought just t' see me squirm. He was studying under Doc t' be a doctor himself and after a few years he came back from th' east a full-fledged doctor. Made a good one too.

Ever since th' Civil War, women had been interested in nursing an' there was a big movement on t' see that it happened. Doc had a young lady in th' community determined t' become a nurse. She pestered him into letting her assist him at no cost. He reluctantly agreed, but drew th' line where he felt things were too rough for a lady t' see. He did let her treat me and I had t' admit her touch was much more gentle than Eusebio's after I got used to it, her bein' female and all. She was one of those rare redheaded Spanish women. Her ancestors were of true Spanish descent and had recently (in th' past fifty years or so) arrived on this continent.

I never got so sick o' layin' in one place in my life an' I guess Doc Hutto figgered if I felt good enough t' gripe about it, I was good enough t' sit up, so toward th' end of th' third week he an' Eusebio sat me up on th' side of th' bed. I was weak as a kitten and never had such mixed feelings. One part of me felt good about sitting up and another part really wanted t' lay my head back down on that pillow. It was a nice warm day and they got me in a wheelchair an' rolled me out on th' patio where I could take in some sun an' look out over the basin. Far to th' south below White Sands I could see a column of dust an' I knew where th' roundup was. It was good t' see they were in dust instead of that cursed mud.

The sun felt good an' pretty soon that redheaded nurse brought me out a glass of lemonade. Since they didn't have any other patients at th' moment, she sat an' talked to me a while until that sun got th' best of me an' I dozed off. I woke under a warm blanket just in time t' see ol' Sol drop b'hind th' San Andres and those golden rays shoot up across th' sky. Eusebio brought out a tray of food an' I fed myself sitting up for th' first time. After that, I sat on th' patio almost every afternoon and even got to where I could wheel myself around in that chair an' get into th' shade when I got too warm.

It was getting toward the end of four weeks since my wreck an' I hadn't had a bath. I was getting so ripe I could barely stand myself an' sponge baths were not doing much good. Eusebio had been gone several days on some errand and I heard Doc augering with that redheaded nurse over something one morning. Finally I heard him say, "Fine, young lady if you think it should be done today, you do it yourself!" Then all got quiet.

After a few minutes I heard someone working rather furiously on th' patio, then th' nurse came into my room from there. I could tell she was worked up over something, probably over their argument, I thought. Her lips were compressed an' her jaw was set. By that I knew not to say a thing. When a woman gets that look about her its best to *lay low*. She didn't say anything, just got th' wheelchair and rolled it to th' bed for me to get into.

When she rolled me to th' door, I saw that she had hung sheets around th' outside and there was a stool draped with a towel and a large tub of steaming water on th' patio. It began t' dawn on me what that argument had been about an' I opened my mouth to protest an' she said, "Shut up and get on that stool!"

Somehow, I stood up on th' heel of my broken foot and she moved th' wheelchair away and put th' stool in its place. Just before I sat down, she reached under my nightshirt an' jerked my shorts down.

"Sit!"

When she came around in front, her jaw was still set, but her face was as crimson as her hair, clear down to her dress collar. She pulled those shorts off my legs an' handed me another towel. "Cover yourself."

Then she pulled my shirt over my head an' threw it in th' corner with th' shorts. There I sat naked except for a splint on my leg, my chest taped up and a towel wrapped around my middle. I squirmed an' held on to it for dear life. Th' breeze told me it didn't quite cover all my backsides an' I couldn't get *it* covered without exposin' other things that was more vital t' *keep* covered.

She reached for th' top piece of tape on my ribs an' I braced myself. Zip! Off it came and th' rest followed close b'hind. That jaw was still set like iron an' there was fire in her eyes. I was afraid to make a sound. Very carefully, she removed th' wrapping from my foot and placed it in th' tub. That water was *hot* but it felt good at th' same time. She studied th' splint an' for a minute I thought it was coming off too, but she let it stay. She took a dipper and poured hot water over my head, then washed my hair. That warm water sure felt good running down on my shoulders and back. It was muddy and gritty.

Now, she got a washcloth and a bar of soap and sudsed it real good. A whisp of hair fell over her eye and she brushed it aside an' looked me straight in th' eyes. "Now, I'm *going* to give you a bath. I'm gonna start at the top and go down as far as possible, then I'm gonna start at your feet and go *up* as far as possible . . ." She hesitated a moment, took a deep shaky breath, and I will swear that her face got redder. ". . . then . . . *you're* gonna wash the possibles!"

I couldn't help but grin at that and it broke th' ice. She grinned and said, "Hush!" With that, she began to wash me down to my waist. My but it felt good an' I didn't think anything about a beautiful woman doing it, it just felt good. I was a little nervous and began to talk as she worked. She was nervous too, but determined to get her job done. She scrubbed an' we talked on.

That water cooled fast an' by th' time she had finished rinsing me, I was shiverin' cold. Doc Hutto appeared an' I guess he was eatin' a little humble pie. "You did good, Maria," was all he said. He had a couple of blankets warmed in th' oven an' a clean nightshirt. I got th' shirt over my head an' Doc had me lock my hands behind his head an' he lifted me up. While I stood, th' nurse wrapped a blanket around my shoulders and wheeled th' chair behind me. As soon as I was seated, she wrapped th' other blanket around my legs.

"There," she said, "how do you feel now?" There was a glint of triumph in her eyes, a hint of red on her neck, and her cheeks were very rosy.

"It feels fine, thank you very much."

I was a little embarrassed and suddenly very, very sleepy. I don't remember much after that except that a pillow was put behind my head and I was vaguely aware that there was bustling around me cleaning th' patio off. I was warm and cozy and floated off into a deep sleep. I awoke with a midafternoon sun shining in my eyes. There was a steaming cup of coffee on th' table by my elbow. It wasn't cowboy hot or cowboy strong, but it tasted good and warmed all th' way down. I heard th' door squeak behind me an' Doc came out with a tray of food. "Are you awake enough to eat?"

"You bet, Doc." I was hungrier than I had been since I got hurt.

He settled into another chair while I ate. "Well, how did you like your bath?"

"It was great, I feel like a new person."

Doc chuckled, "Is that b'cause of th' *bath* or th' *bather*?"

I didn't say anything, but I thought it would have felt just as good if a monkey had done it. Funny, but when you're in th' shape I was in, modesty an' attractions of th' fairer sex just aren't as important as during normal times, though th' touch of feminine hands was much more comfortin' than Doc's or Eusebio's. I don't know, but I would guess that it reminds us of our mother's care. I was sure glad she had th' nerve and determination t' do what she did.

"That young lady has *grit* and first thing tomorrow, I'm gonna hire her. With a little training she will make a good nurse and I need help!"

Now, knowin' Doc Hutto as we did around there, that was high praise an' I felt good that he had recognized th' young lady's potential. It also put me t' thinkin an' I recognized that she *was* a cut above average and th' man that won her affection was gonna be fortunate indeed. Not that I thought I had a chance, but I determined to try—as soon as I was on my feet again. To make any attempt at that after today might make her victory seem cheap and spoil what she had accomplished.

"How is it that she came here t' work for you without a half-dozen grannies chaperonin' her, Doc?"

"Mainly b'cause she don't have no grannies or mammy t' guard over her. She was raised by her father alone an' never got burdened by that old world culture—grew up free so to speak, though she certainly was taught t' be a lady in all other respects. Educated, too. Sure a cut 'way above any run-of-th-mill plaza girl. Her pa only agreed t' let her try this nursing business because th' Missus would be around t' see that everything was proper. They have struck it off good an' my wife is teachin' her t' cook.

"I had Ma watch her bathin' you an' she told me she learned a new meanin' for th' word *possibles*!" His shoulders shook in mirth an' I had t' grin too. It still hurt to laugh or breathe deep.

We watched Ol' Sol go down b'hind th' mountains and listened to night creatures come out, then Doc heaved himself up an' said, "Time t' get you ready for bed, young man. I saw your back when you were getting a bath an' I think it might be well enough for you to lay on it some, what do you think?"

"I would like t' try, Doc, there were only a few places tender t' touch an' I think spread on a mattress, they wouldn't bother me."

Just then th' screen door squeaked an' Maria came out with Mrs. Hutto close behind.

"I see our patient is awake and clean," she said, "smells better too!" She took my tray and hurried back into th' house.

"I brought tape and wrapping for his foot, Doctor," Miss Maria said. "I thought it would be easier to fix him up while he is sitting."

"Good," Doc nodded, "but let's get him inside where it's warmer. You light lamps while I wheel this busted broncho in."

When I was rolled in, they set to work. First, th' nurse opened my shirt and washed my ribs gently. It hurt, but I didn't flinch. Tape had scalded my skin and someone had applied some kind of salve on it while I slept. I guess it was nurse Maria, but I never knew when it happened. Meantime, Doc was preparing th' foot board. When she was finished washing me, he showed her how to wrap th' foot and let her do most of it, coaching her along.

"We're going to let him lay on his back tonight, so we want the board to stick beyond his toes a little to keep the covers off his foot and let his heel rest on the bed."

When they were finished there, he showed her how to apply tape to my ribs.

"Now this is uncomfortable for the patient, but necessary to get them tight so he will heal properly, so don't be squeamish about hurting him, it's the result that is important."

He was talking to her as though I wasn't there and I could see she was very pleased at his change in attitude. While she was applyin' the tape, he talked. "This man is very lucky one of those ribs didn't cave in and perforate a lung. If it had, it would have really been serious. Normally with fractured ribs we would wrap the tape all around his body, but th' wounds on his back made that impossible in this case, so we had to use tape partway and hope for the best."

We heard a rig rattle into th' yard an' Doc stood up. "Sounds like your father is here, let's get our patient in bed and I'll go out and speak to him while you finish up here. Be here at seven in th' morning an' we'll see how our patient fared."

He showed her how t' help me stand and get on th' bed without undue pain an' trouble, then left th' room. I could tell she was very pleased.

"Looks like you found yourself a job!" I whispered.

It made her smile and blush with pleasure an' she tucked me in and left th' room in such a hurry she forgot to trim th' lamps.

A moment later, Mrs. Hutto tiptoed in an' put out th' lights. "I told that man she would make a good nurse, guess she made a believer out of him today," she whispered. "Don't you mention she forgot the lamps, now."

I think she may have been as pleased as Miss Maria and as I thought more, I guessed a nurse would take some burden off Doc's wife too, for now he wouldn't be calling her away from her work to help him with some patient.

That was th' first night I slept well since my fall and when Doc and nurse came in next morning, my back had stuck to th' shirt in only a couple of places. Doc had her help me into th' chair an' showed her how to apply salve an' medicine to my back. From then on, I was her patient with Doc only checkin' on me every day or two. Eusebio began makin' house calls with

Doc an' nurse Maria minded th' office with help from Mrs. Hutto.

"He may let me help in a birthing soon," she told me one day, and I guess her progress was rapid after that.

I can say this, she took good care of me and I was a little spoiled when Doc gave me a pair of crutches an' told me t' git out of that bed an' go somewheres an' heal. When I left th' house, there sat Manuel on th' supply wagon, all loaded an' ready t' head for th' ranch.

"Meester Bob has some broncs hee wants you to break for heem, Zee. Doc says you're up for eet!" he grinned.

Th' Boss was kind enough t' let me hang around th' barn an' clean things an' do little chores for him th' rest of that summer and he kept me on through th' winter. By spring I was as near good as new as I was gonna be. I had paid off all my bills an' I began courting that nurse serious-like. To my surprise, she let me an' I've been courtin' her near fifty years, now. She nursed for old Doc Hutto 'til he died an' I guess she has helped treat half th' people in th' basin one time or another. When we moved down here an' ranched, she delivered babies in this neck of th' county. Half th' girls an' one boy are named Sophia or Maria after her, he chuckled. That boy'll sure grow up tough, won't he?

"Zenas Leonard, that tale gets longer by the telling." She had stepped out on the porch and laid a hand on his shoulder. He patted it softly and grinned, "And I ain't told th' half of it yet!"

"And you better not, either, you scamp!"

CHAPTER 19
WILL CASTLEBERRY:
GUIDE, GAMBLER & GUNMAN

The Guide

"Some things I can verify as Gospel truth, but they's some I can't an' this is one of those. Rip told us about his adventures th' two years he was gone and this is one o' th' more probable ones he told. Other tales would come under th' heading o' fairy tales or outright fabrications!"

After he left th' boys that day, he wandered down th' river trail an' Buck, his horse, carried him halfway down Culp Canyon trail b'fore he came to his senses an' realized where he was. "Well, ol' hoss, I reckon you knows where you're a-goin', so be on yore way an' I'll jist tag along." He gave Buck his head just t' see where he would go an' when he got to th' mouth o' th' canyon, he turned north toward Dog Canyon. There, he drank his fill in th' spring branch, then looked back at Rip as if t' say, "Are you gonna sit there all night or are you gonna get down an' give me a rest?"

"All right, you lazy plug, if you ain't up t' night ridin', I guess we can rest here, but we ain't gonna stay right here or you might find yoreself with a 'Pache owner come sunup."

They rode on north a ways, Buck going reluctantly. Off in th' brush they found a little opening with some grass an' Rip took off th' saddle an' picketed the horse. He didn't worry about Apache thieves for Buck hated them passionately and would raise a fuss if any neared. Rip's bedroll was well on its way to

220

th' ranch so he spread the saddle blanket an' lay down for a night of restlessness. If he dozed off, he would hear himself tell those mules "giddyup" an' wake with a start, or he would hear th' crack of th' wagon wheel and splash, dumping him into th' water. He always woke up before he got soaked. Either way, he didn't sleep much. He gave up tryin t' sleep long b'fore daylight an' lay watchin' th' Big Dipper swing around th' North Star 'til it b'gan t' fade.

Breakfast was th' same as supper—nothing—an' Buck had grazed all grass in his picket, so he saddled up and they were on their way. To his surprise, Buck turned left an' got another drink b'fore continuing his trip north. The horse's behavior was a puzzle and amused Rip. Just at noon, they rode into La Luz an' Buck went straight to th' hitchin' rack at th' first saloon.

"Good boy!" Rip laughed as he got down.

He had a little money in his pocket, enough for a lukewarm beer and a plate of tamales smothered in green chili, which he took at th' bar.

"Anything goin' on?" he asked as Barkeep gathered up dishes an' poured another beer.

"Just some pilgrims looking t' cross th' Jornada to Las Cruces an' afraid t' go by theirselves. No one else interested in takin' th' trip an' they been layin' around here for three days," he said as he shoved dishes through th' window to th' kitchen.

"Think they'd hire a guide?"

"Been looking to, but no takers. They should be in here soon an' you can ask."

Rip lingered over his beer an' after a few minutes three men came into th' bar. They were dandies of th' eastern variety, buttoned vests, coats even in this hot weather and plug hats. Their polished shoes had lost their shine to dust.

Without a word, Barkeep set up two beers and a glass of whiskey and th' men took up their offerings. Whiskey drinker was a short stoutly built man who sipped his drink sparingly while his two companions tilted their glasses until they touched th' brims of their hats and drank deeply.

"Never thought I could enjoy lukewarm beer," one of them said as he sat down his half-empty glass.

"One surely dries out in this desert," the other beer drinker said in a strange accent.

Must be one of those Britishers, Rip thought.

"I say, young man," th' Brit said as he turned to Rip, "do you know anyone bound for the Las Cruces?"

"Not this time o' year, I don't."

"Is there *ever* a good time to go to Las Cruces from here?" th' tall beer drinker asked.

He was so tall, th' short one would have fit under his extended arm and not touched it. They were an amusing bunch, Too Short, Too Tall, and The Brit.

"We have crossed the entire country to get there and we *must* be there by Monday next," The Brit said.

"We would pay someone well to guide us there," Too Short said. He took a sip and grimaced. "Damned rotgut," he muttered.

Barkeep gave a small smile an' refilled th' shot glass. Rip noticed it was from a different bottle. Too Short swirled it a moment or two and took a sip. He sat the glass down firmly, his face turned dark red, and he grasped his throat choking and coughing and gasping for breath. His companions slapped him on the back several times and he gradually regained his composure.

"Wha . . . wha . . . t . . . wa . . . s . . . 'at?" he rasped in a whisper, wiping tears from his eyes with a dingy handkerchief.

Barkeep looked at the bottle in his hand and feigned surprise. "Oh my gosh!" he said, "I picked up the wrong bottle! I'm very sorry!"

"I . . . say . . . again . . . *What . . . was that?*" still in a hoarse whisper.

"Here, wash that out with a drink of the good stuff." He tossed out the shot glass contents, set up a new glass, and poured a generous portion from the original bottle. Pushing it toward Too Short, he said, "This is on the house, sir."

The little man took it cautiously; he wet his lips with it and tasted with his tongue. "Better," he said, "much better," and he took another small sip. Setting his glass down, he asked for the third time, firmly, "What was that other stuff?" His voice was coming back.

Barkeep studied th' bottle's label carefully and set it on the back counter, "Rotgut."

Too Tall hid his face in his glass and The Brit got choked on his drink. Rip chuckled.

As if nothing had intervened in the conversation, Too Short turned to Rip and asked, "Do you know this Jornada?"

"Grew up on it, practically."

"Will you take us to Las Cruces?"

"Be best t' wait until fall."

He didn't mention that th' mail carrier made th' trip three or four times a week. Obviously, no one else had either.

"We *must* be there by Monday next," The Brit repeated.

Rip wondered what "Monday next" was. *Must be some English holiday,* he thought.

"I hate goin' out there in th' middle o' summer," Rip said, "it's hot and dry an' dangerous."

"We'll pay you well," Too Tall said—for the second time. They had been here before.

"See here, young man, we will pay you twice 'well' if you will get us there by Monday next!" The Brit said firmly as if Rip could not refuse th' offer.

"Just how much is 'twice well'?"

"It's fift . . ."

"Twenty-five dollars." Too Short's voice rose over Too Tall's.

Rip rubbed his chin, "That's just 'well' out here, 'twice well' would be fifty."

"Too much . . ."

"We would pay thirty," The Brit interrupted.

"Fifty's the reasonable . . ."

"Oh for Pete's sake!" Too Short interjected. "We'll pay you twenty dollars each if we could stop this infernal dickering and get on with it! That's sixty dollars, silver, twenty in advance, what do you say now?"

"Wel-l-l . . ."

"Toot yer horn if ya don't sell a clam, feller!" Too Short drove a hard bargain.

"I'll do it, but I don't cotton to it," Rip said.

Barkeep pursed his lips. *Whee-oow, you're gonna take these greenhorns direct across those sands near sixty miles in one ridin'?*

Rip glanced his way with th' slightest shake of his head.

"Good! When do we start?" Brit asked.

"Starts coolin' off 'bout 4. We could start about 5 and travel in the cool of the night. Might get t' Aguirre Springs by noon tomorrow, Las Cruces by morning next."

Barkeep smiled as he studiously polished a glass.

"We'll load the buggy and be here at 5 sharp," Too Tall said.

"Won't get five miles in a buggy in that sand, you'll have t' ride horses."

"Horses! But we have luggage," Brit exclaimed.

"Best not t' take luggage, you'd probably leave it in the basin sommer's, the road's scattered with abandoned gear. We'll have t' travel light if we make it." Rip was tiring of all this talk. *Maybe sixty dollars ain't enough*, he thought. "How much would your luggage weigh?"

Too Tall thought. "Two-fifty, maybe three-hundred pounds."

"That's way too much. If you can cut that to maybe seventy-five pounds total we could carry that on a packhorse."

"What if we had two packhorses?"

"We have t' carry water for the horses an' the less horses the better it will be. Cut your load to bare essentials. I will provide a packhorse and water kegs if you pay me half now and half at th' end of the trip."

"Very good." The Brit slapped th' bar. "We have a deal!" He handed Rip thirty dollars.

"Better make it here by 4:30 so I can load," Rip said, turning toward th' door. "We have a lot to do."

They all started for th' door and Barkeep called out, "Your tab, gentlemen!"

Too Short tossed him six bits an' called, "Keep th' change," as if ten cents was a big tip.

The barkeeper shook his head and muttered, "Wish I was a mouse on that packhorse, it would be some ride!"

The trio did some feverish work, trading horses and buggy for three riding horses and cutting their luggage to seventy-five pounds. It was done with much fuss and bother to th' amusement of all witnesses. In th' end they left several crates at th' hotel to be picked up later.

Meantime, Rip bought a nice-looking mule at the livery, a blanket from th' mercantile, and a couple of small kegs from th' saloon. Filled with water, they would fit nicely on each side of the pack. Nothing remained to do but wait for 4:30, which he did in th' saloon, Buck and mule resting in the shade of a big cottonwood.

The barkeeper cleaned his glasses and smiled to himself

A little before 4:30 Buck wandered out to th' stock an' began loading water kegs. He was just tying off th' second keg when our travelers showed up. Each had a carpetbag slung from th' saddle horn. Too Tall's was bulging and heavy but the other two were light, probably containing clothing only.

"We have cut our luggage to the bare minimum," Too Tall said apologetically. "This bag has the items we absolutely must have."

"All right," Rip grunted as he lifted the bag. He laid it between th' kegs noting a muffled clink and th' locked clasp. He carefully checked horses and equipment, making small adjustments.

"Everything looks good, now let's fill our canteens and get goin'," he said at last.

"Canteens? When you have two kegs of water?" The Brit exclaimed.

"That's water for our horses. You will need a full canteen for yourself," Rip replied. "Watered horses'll git you outta the desert alive. All the water in those kegs won't git you out alive if you have t' walk. The mercantile has one- and two-gallon canteens. I never went into the basin without one, an' the bigger the better." He could have added that he gave most of his water to his horse on those trips, but didn't.

It was just a short walk to th' store and they were soon back, Too Tall and The Brit carrying two-gallon canteens while Too Short sported two one-gallons. "Ran out of the big ones," he explained.

"Be sure they are full and wet the outsides good, it'll keep the water cool that way," Rip instructed. On their return, he said, "If you have arms, be sure they are loaded and handy. You never know when they will be needed out there."

Too Short and The Brit pulled weapons from their pockets and checked them. Rip noted that Too Short's gun was small, a large caliber revolver with a short barrel. *Not meant for long-range targets,* he thought. Brit's gun was some larger, but of small caliber, probably a .32. He handled it competently, then stored it in his coat pocket. Too Tall had mounted and patted a bulge on his hip. "She's *always* ready to go," he said with a smile.

"Horses watered and ready to go?" Rip asked. At their affirmative nods, he turned and mounted up. "Time t' go!"

He followed the trio, noting closely their riding abilities. The Brit rode straight up and rather stiff in th' saddle. It was obvious Too Tall was used to riding, but Too Short bounced along, his stirrups a little too long.

They were pleased and excited to be on th' move at last and bantered back and forth as they rode. Too Short dropped back and rode beside Rip, askin' a hundred questions about th' country and such. After a silence not long enough for Rip's comfort, Too Short said, "It's awkward not knowing names and such and this quaint custom out here of not giving names is bothersome to us. My name is Ben Smith—now I know names like 'Smith' and 'Jones' are reserved for those who don't wish for their real names to be known, but my name *really is* Smith, born and bred."

Indicating Too Tall, he said, "His name is Rufe Thompson, a more believable name, I suppose, and the other gentleman is from England and is James Towery."

"James *Percival* Towery," The Brit corrected from ahead. "You may call me Percy."

There followed a long silence puzzling to Rip until he realized with a start they were waitin' for him to put a name on himself. He stammered an' apology, "Sorry . . . my name is Castleberry, but folks just call me Will."

"Well, Will Castleberry, I'm glad to meet you!" Ben Smith grinned and extended his hand. His grip was firm.

At th' edge of th' basin, Will called a halt and they gathered around him. "From here on, I want you t' follow my instructions to th' letter, jot, and tittle. I will lead, with th' mule behind me, he being th' most important member o' this train. Next, will be you, Ben, then Percy." He put Rufe last since he obviously had th' largest gun and more riding experience. "About dark, I will tie us all together so someone doesn't stray in th' dark. We will travel all night and into th' forenoon with only a couple of breaks. If you or your horse need t' stop, sing out, otherwise, we travel quiet so's we don't attract attention t' ourselves." Turning to Ben Smith, he said, "Your stirrups are about two inches too long. Take them up or you'll have a sore-backed horse halfway across and end up walkin' a good portion of th' way."

"Told you so," Rufe said.

When stirrups were adjusted and th' man mounted, Rip said, "Now ease th' load on your horse by using your knees an' legs. That bouncin' along will wear th' horse out. Better *you* be a little sore than him out here."

The other two men grinned, but didn't say anything. Smith clamped his jaw and nodded. He had heard th' sermon before.

"Now take a good long drink before we start. It's better to take long drinks than to just sip water along, you'll use less water and get along better. No alcohol as we cross the basin."

That said, Will turned south down th' trail along th' foothills. They reached a fork in th' trails about 8:30 and Will called a halt. "After we rest a little, I will tie us together and we'll start across."

They rested a bit, then walked a mile or so, taking th' dimmer trail for Point of Sands. Will tied his rope to his saddle horn, then to each of the other three saddles. He fastened th' mule with a separate rope. *Better to lose pilgrims than t' lose this mule,* he thought grimly.

"Try to keep the line slack so you won't be pullin' us around." To Rufe, he said, "Keep an eye on the back trail an' let us know if someone shows. Those that travel this trail in summer do so at night t' avoid th' heat, so they mostly will be friendly but it would be good t' be alert anyway." Rufe nodded. Will was confident this man had traveled much in wild places and he was glad.

It took a few minutes for the horses t' get th' pace set just so. Constant jerking of th' rope was more uncomfortable to them than to riders. The mule took advantage of his mobility and walked beside Buck, nuzzling him occasionally. "Yore a right friendly thing," Will said, "must have been someone's pet."

To this, th' mule seemed t' nod yes.

"Well! 'Pet' seems to suit him just fine," Ben chuckled.

Talk and banter faded with daylight an' by th' time it was full dark, all talk had ceased. Buck was familiar with th' trail, but Will stayed alert, navigating by th' silhouettes of western hills and stars. Soon hills faded into black and stars were his only guides—that and Buck's senses. He knew Point of Sands by a small change in direction Buck made as their trail turned toward Antelope Hill—forty-five miles of trail straight as an arrow. Will set their new course by th' stars and gave Buck the reins. An occasional tug on th' tether rope told him Ben Smith was makin' sure Will and company were still there. A rising quarter moon shed more light and as it rose, they could make out the trail until it disappeared into th' distance.

It was near midnight when Percy called for a halt. Will found an open spot and turned off th' trail a hundred feet or more and they dismounted, Ben and Percy stiffly, but Will noted that Rufe seemed more at ease. The man promptly walked back to th' trail and stood watching for a few minutes.

It was after midnight judging by th' stars. The horses had been on th' trail about eight hours and it was time to water them. Fillin' his sombrero alternately from each of th' kegs, he watered horses, saving th' last for the mule Pet.

"Not much water for them, is it?" Percy asked.

" 'Bout a gallon, I guess. They don't need much an' I ain't got a ten-gallon hat." Will grinned, his teeth showing white in th' moonlight.

They rested awhile and walked until Will called, "Mount up," then rode on. The horses were refreshed and they didn't stop until the sky was streaked with light.

They were just north of due west from Black Brushy Mountain.

"Twenty-one or -two miles to the springs," Will announced. "We should be there b'fore noon."

As th' sun rose, shadows of th' San Andres retreated across th' basin and their backs warmed. Soon heat waves rose and they were hot. Will was glad his sombrero cast a big shadow, those plug hats didn't give much shade.

There was a lot of pulling from canteens and they were getting light, a worrisome thing to greenhorns. The horses had rims of white salt where their sweat had dried. Little was said. The trail joined a larger trail from Monte Carlo Gap and they followed it toward th' pass.

"Where does that trail go?" asked Ben.

"It goes to Monte Carlo Pass. That's the trail we normally take from La Luz, but it's about a day longer than the one we took."

They reached the foot of th' pass and turned to Aguirre Springs just as th' sun reached its zenith. Their horses sensed water and picked up their pace. Soon they were unsaddled, watered, rubbed down, and rolling contentedly in th' dust. The men watched from the shade and ate their lunches, which for Will consisted of a can of tomatoes and a can of peaches. With horses tethered on what sparse grass existed so near th' spring, they settled down for a nap to await sundown.

The heat seemed to bother Percy and Ben, but Rufe followed Will's lead and stretched out on th' ground, his face covered with that silly little hat, and napped. Ben and Percy were a ways off sitting an' talking earnestly.

Maybe by Monday next I'll know what these three are up to, Will thought. *Not that I'm all that interested.* He drifted off to sleep, lulled by th' lazy drone of bees hurryin' from one bloom to th' next.

The Organs were casting their shadows over th' springs when they rode out. All seemed refreshed, but Ben Smith was very sore from his ride, though he said little about it. The sun was still an hour high when they reached th' top of San Augustin Pass. They paused to rest and take in th' view. To the east, th' Tularosa Basin was slowly turning from orange to red to deep purple. Those White Sands still shimmered and Will pointed out th' pencil-thin trail they had followed from Point of Sands. Though they professed seeing it, he suspected Rufe was th' only one who really did. A few yards west and they stopped again to view th' land ahead. Will pointed out Las Cruces, " 'Bout fifteen miles from here. We should be there by nine, ten o'clock," he guessed.

"Well, let's go," Ben said, flippin' th' reins, "my ars' an' legs won't last much longer."

"Looks like it's mostly downhill, Ben, yore horse will be thankful for that!" Rufe called as he followed.

James Percival Towery sat another moment, gazing at th' vista. "What beautiful forsaken country," he whispered as to himself.

Will agreed with the beautiful part, but experience told him th' country was far from forsaken, especially in the valley of th' Rio Grande. Almost reluctantly, they moved down the mountain, following the fast-diminishing form of Ben Smith.

It was 9:30 and they were taking their traditional drinks in a cantina just at the edge of town. Will had ordered Ben a bottle of tequila and his eyes opened wide at the first sip. "What is this?"

"Beats rotgut a mile, don't it?"

"For sure!" he replied, then he spied the worm in th' bottle, "Is it poisoned?"

"One's in ever' bottle." Will offered no other explanation.

"Well I'll be . . . Lord Percy, you have to try this!" He called for two more glasses and poured a drink for each of his companions. They sat and sipped and commented on the qualities of their drink.

A little into his fourth, Ben had taken on a rosy glow and his aches of th' past days were forgotten. "Fine, fine," he muttered, swirling th' remnants in the bottle.

"If that little worm needs liquid to survive, he's soon going to die," Rufe observed.

"Pray tell, what *do* you do with th' worm?" Lord Percy asked.

"Some eats 'em, but not me," Will replied.

"We sh-hould buy another bottle an' tran . . . transh . . . move th' poor feller so he won't die," Ben slurred.

"I for one am willing to let him have the dregs and transfer a *new* worm to the old bottle," Percy observed.

Rufe laughed, "Takes some getting used to, but it doesn't seem t' hurt the drink."

"Some say it isn't as good without a worm," Will said.

He noticed Rufe only drank sparingly and stayed alert to goings-on around him. *Must be his job t' guard th' others,* Will thought. He was a little nervous himself, thinking one of his acquaintances would appear and call him by his old name. He stood up and said, "Well, I must push off. It's been a pleasure meeting you men and I'm glad you got here b'fore Monday next."

"Here here, man, don' run off sho shoon," Ben said, "It's early an' w-e got 'nother worm comin'."

"Gotta go."

Percy stood and proffered his hand. "You have done us a great service, Will, and we are grateful. This balance we owe you was well earned." There were two twenty-dollar gold pieces in his hand.

"I thank you," Will grinned. *Two months' pay for two days' work ain't bad,* he thought.

"My man, it was all earned and welcome to it."

"Thank you, it's been a pleasure." Will tipped his hat, more for the purpose of pulling it down lower over his eyes than for a salute. "I wish you well, mebbe we'll meet agin." He glanced back at th' door and Ben was shakily pouring another round from a new bottle. Rufe was watching him and gave a little nod.

I'd hate t' be ol' Ben in the mornin', forgot t' mention the hangover's worser with that stuff. Will stepped into the night an' gave a sigh of relief.

He stood at th' rail a minute scratchin' Pet's ears an' thinkin'. All his business had been taken care of, he was paid and Buck and Pet were rested. "Bet you think you're gonna sleep in a nice corral t'night, but yore wrong about that, boys. We're movin on an' right now!" With that he mounted and turned their heads south out of town.

San Pablo was quiet when he rode through, even th' cantina was dark and still. Their hoofbeats echoed from adobe walls and they were soon past th' last house. In another hour, Will turned down to th' river and watered th' animals. Hobbled and picketed to willow bushes, they seemed content and Will laid down under a bush and slept to th' tune of rippling water.

Coffee, crackers, and sardines served as a fine breakfast and as th' sun rose, they were headed for th' ford to San Miguel. Without a moment's hesitation, they took th' road less traveled to Mesquite instead. *What a difference a little water makes in this country,* Will thought as he rode past green gardens and dark green fields of peppers, melons, and corn. *If th' basin had water, I bet it'd be just as green.*

Pet trotted ahead to th' end of his rope an' as it sagged he stepped into th' field and jerked off a leaf from a cornstalk. Munching contentedly, he resumed his journey without so much as a tug on th' tether.

"Learned that trick quick, boy, been here afore?" Will grinned. He let th' horse set his own pace and they reached Mesquite midmorning and Vado just before noon.

He bought a couple of melons from a woman who had a dozen kids running around th' yard and moved on down to a large cottonwood by th' river. There were several young boys swimming and he had one of them sink his sack of melons to th' bottom of th' river to cool. He idly watched them play while he ate his lunch. They were burned almost black where their skin was naturally exposed to th' sun, th' contrast between that and th' portions of their bodies normally covered was stark. He noticed that among th' younger boys there were no tan lines. Being deeply tanned all over attested to th' fact that they rarely wore *any* clothes. Young as they were, they swam as proficiently as the older boys. *Musta been born in the water,* Will thought. *Most of 'em are hardly weaned.*

Leaning back on his saddle and pulling his sombrero over his eyes he drifted off to th' music of boys laughing and calling. His siesta was interrupted by silence and he raised his hat to find himself surrounded by naked boys, one holding th' dripping melon bag. "We go now, Señor, here is your melon."

"Melons," Will corrected, sitting up. "I cain't hardly eat both of them, how 'bout you boys helping me?"

They replied with a chorus of "sí's" and melons were soon sliced and distributed. They squatted on their heels eating hearts out of crescent slices and spitting seed. Toddlers stood about eating contentedly, juice and seed dripping from their chins and running down their rounded bellies.

A sow with her brood poked her head through th' bushes having smelled melons and they tossed their rinds to her as they finished. Rind tossing graduated into a rind fight and soon there was melon rind flying in all directions, mama sow and pigs running from one to th' other and gobbling pieces up.

Ammunition depleted, the boys returned to th' river to wash off melon, sand, and an occasional spot of blood. One toddler made to go home without bathing and was caught by an older boy and tossed into th' river howling in protest. The older boy turned to dress but found himself covered with sand and sticky juice from th' toddler and returned to th' river, playfully dunking th' still protesting toddler.

Will's entertainment was soon dressed and dispersed, and quiet again settled over th' scene. "Well, boys, party's over, guess we should move on," he said as he saddled Buck. He heard a suppressed giggle and turned to see a bevy of young girls approaching for their turn at the water, more toddlers, female this time, with no tan lines.

"Just leaving, Señoritas," he said in the native tongue. "You can have it all to yourselves."

As he rode off he could hear splashing and laughter. He bypassed Berino taking th' river road instead and passed th' afternoon at a leisurely pace, sleeping again that night to gentle murmurings of th' Rio Grande.

This leisurely pace of his served t' heal hurts suffered at that cursed organ babatism, but Will was constantly reminded of his intention to replace the organ.

"We can't do that on cowboy wages," he told his companions as they rode along, "got t' think o' somethin' that'll pay lots an' fast."

Buck nodded as if he agreed and Pet snatched a green ear of

corn and chewed thoughtfully. As they rode into a village—that shall remain unnamed in our story—th' need for a thirst quencher struck our late guide and he stopped at th' cantina.

CHAPTER 20
WILL CASTLEBERRY:
GUIDE, GAMBLER & GUNMAN

The Gambler

Just as he ducked under th' ramada, a flying sombrero whizzed by his nose, followed by its owner, who narrowly missed a head-on collision with our friend. Close behind came a man in a dirty apron waving in his hands a shotgun commonly carried by stage guards. Will quickly stepped to the side, and tripped over a chair. As he fell, his gun came up, but th' gunman ignored him, instead hurling invectives and curses in at least three languages at the fleeing man.

Just as the runaway reached his sombrero, the shotgun came up and with deliberate aim the gunman let loose both barrels. Will winced and closed his eyes, not wanting to see the gore that was sure to be.

For a second everything was still—deathly still. Will heard th' shotgun click and when he looked, the gunman was retrieving shells from a pocket beneath his apron and stuffing two into the breeches. He slammed the barrels closed and resumed his tirade.

From th' street came shrill pleadings. "Please, por favor, Señor, do not shoot again, please, please." Th' pleas rapidly faded as distance between shooter and victim increased at a record pace.

Will, who was watching the shooter over th' sights of his .44, chanced a glance at th' street. There, lying in th' dust, riddled and smoking, lay th' mortal remains of a sombrero while its former owner disappeared around th' corner of an adobe house down th' street. Halfway to that corner a sandal lay in th' dust.

Still cursing, th' gunman turned to look at Will and stared down that gaping muzzle of the .44, "No, no, Señor, I am not mad at you, please remove the gun," the excited man pleaded, repeating the request in two more languages for good measure.

Will lowered his gun, "Yore shore death on sombreros!" he grunted. "What'd he do, try t' rob yuh?"

"Sí, hee rob me by letting hees freen break thee farrro bank las night! Come, I weel geeve you cold beer to quench your thirst an' tequila to settle your nerves."

He hurried through th' door as Will righted himself and dusted off. Still jabbering, th' gunman turned barkeeper set a mug of beer on the rough boards serving as the counter, and reached for the familiar bottle with the worm and poured two shots, tossing one off himself. The shotgun had returned to its usual spot beneath th' backboard.

"Now I have no faro game for tonight an' these ees payday for thee men. They will want to play an' I have no game!"

Will set the half-empty mug down. The beer was freezing cold and he had a pain just behind his eyes. "How did you get that so cold?"

"I geet ice from El Paso. Many come for my coldest beer in thee vallee."

"No doubt," Will muttered, rubbing his forehead. "Say, I'm a fair faro dealer, maybe we could work out a deal."

"You not cheat Pablo an' wee weel maybe work out a deel." He glowered as he spoke.

Will was sure he didn't want to disappoint Pablo. "No problem there, I don't know enough 'bout the game t' cheat anyone, 'specially when he has a shotgun."

Pablo smiled. "Mebbe I show you a trick or two. You can use?"

"Maybe. Mostly I played t' try an' figger out how the dealer cheated me, but I never caught a one of 'em. Too slow, I guess."

The faro table sat against th' wall opposite th' bar. It had a large space cleared around it for customers, even some chairs for those inclined to sit. Will noted there was no window or door nearby, the presence of which has saved many a dealer from harm. But as he sat in th' dealer's chair, he noted a shelf under th' edge of th' green-felt cloth. It was just right for a gun and hand to fit in. *Got an equalizer,* he thought. The board was worn, th' run of spades glued to it were scratched and faded from long use, and th' trey was missing entirely. He found it on the floor and returned it to its spot on th' board.

Pablo rummaged b'hind th' bar and brought out th' deck and chips. "Chips are two bits and pot limit ees ten pesos," he said, blithely mixing th' two monetary systems.

"No big spenders, huh?"

"Not beeg, but many players," Pablo smiled. "You weel bee thee busy man!"

The deck of cards was almost as bad as the board cards, bent, faded, an' frayed. "Got a new deck?" Will asked needlessly.

"Thees only deck een town, mebbe I geet new one next time I go to El Paso," Pablo yawned.

"Don't get there very often, do you?"

"Thee cards are two years old, steel goood."

Will marveled. Two years of nightly use and still goin'! The cards were in good shape for their age! They were so bent and swelled they overflowed th' dealing box. Spreading th' deck face up, he counted. They were all there except that the four of hearts had been replaced with a joker from th' same deck with th' numeral four and crude red hearts drawn on th' face. It showed th' same wear as th' rest, front and back.

Guess it'll have t' do, Will thought. "I'll give her a try, Pablo, but don't expect any high earnings from tonight's game."

"Sí, I weel make up at thee bar, mebbe. We weel have a game for thee fun of eet."

Will put Buck and Pet in a corral behind th' cantina, stretched out in th' shade, and dozed off. Near sunset he roused, threw his gear on th' low roof, and sauntered into th' cantina for a bite of supper. Tamales smothered in that green chili with another cold beer served well and he was ready for work.

It was after sunset when the first of th' night's crowd began arriving. Their eyes lighted up when they saw that their faro game was on in spite of th' exit of that last dealer. Will heard several comments about "El Gringo dealer" and Pablo had t' explain over and over that this was only a temporary job until he could find another dealer. Th' crowd seemed reluctant t' play with a stranger, but lure of th' cards was too strong and they eventually overcame their distrust and approached. Pablo sent over a case keeper and th' punters gradually began t' play. Will pretended to know only rudimentary Spanish, though he was proficient in the language. He got great amusement from their comments and had t' concentrate not t' show that he knew what they were saying.

Legend has it that the term "Greengro" originated from an unpopular Anglo merchant who had a store on the border. He habitually hummed and sang Green Grow the Lilacs, *thus earning the uncomplimentary nickname, shortened in use to "Gringo." (JD)*

A few women, their chores done, wandered in and gathered around a table in th' corner eyeing El Gringo over their beers. Two or three even bought chips and bet half-heartedly. Interest in th' game was lagging and Pablo behind th' bar looked worried. Will knew something would have to be done to liven up th' game so he began a string of commentary on th' game, making up funny names for players and commenting on their play. Th' crowd listened quietly, then began t' warm to his chatter, and betting became brisk, if for nothing else but to hear El Gringo chatter.

Before they realized it, the hour had changed from late to early and the crowd gradually thinned. Pablo was pleased with th' results and as he closed up asked, "You weel come back tomorrow?"

"Right now, all I want is some shut-eye. I can stay over another night, I guess."

Five minutes later, Will was rolled up in his blanket by th' back of the building asleep.

That second night was busier than th' first. It was unusual, Pablo said, for payday had always been the big night before. Will greeted repeaters with their adopted names, all of which were more or less complimentary. New punters came expecting to receive nicknames and Will obliged with some help from th' old hands. There was much levity and th' game proceeded briskly late into th' night.

Pablo prevailed upon Will to stay out th' week and he agreed for a cut of th' profits. Attendance stayed high and there were times more people were playing or watching th' game than were at th' bar. Will was amazed he hadn't lost th' bank and had actually made money.

Pablo hired a girl t' pass through th' crowd taking orders. By closing time Saturday night, his moneybag was so full it wouldn't jingle.

"Señor Weel, I would like verry much ef you would be thee new dealer for me."

Will had been giving it some thought and it seemed to him that this would be a good way to earn money quickly enough to replace th' organ.

"Tell you what, Pablo, if everything is satisfactory, I'll buy out the bank when I can and run my own game. I'll pay you a percentage of the profit as rent an' such."

There followed a discussion of terms of employment that carried over into Sunday afternoon. Pablo wanted twenty-five percent of th' take. Will countered he would give twenty-five percent if Pablo gave him fifteen percent of th' bar proceeds, which was entirely too much t' ask and Pablo said so. They finally agreed that Pablo would get a tithe of th' gains down to two dollars per night minimum. Will liked th' case keeper and hired him to continue working. He was sharp and kept a close eye on th' game, a real help when bets were coming hot and heavy.

By the end of th' next week, Will had bought th' bank an' was working on his own. Business settled into a steady pace and went well. An order to El Paso brought him six decks of cards and he refurbished the faro board and put one of th' fresh decks t' work. It was a surprise to Will that he had been there a month and had a fair amount toward paying for a new organ.

Once in a while there was some excitement, as when someone was making a run or th' dealer cleaned up. Will ran an honest game, which gave punters an almost even chance.

Word got around about th' game and there were unsavory visitors from time to time, but Will kept his eye on them and one would-be robber was stopped cold, finding himself in a crossfire between a .44 and a double-barreled shotgun. His precipitous departure through th' front window hardly caused a ripple in business—after customers returned from their various hiding places, that is. Pablo grinned and set up drinks on th' house and business continued as usual.

It got too usual and Will was aware of a nagging restlessness. Buck was restless and Pet got fat. One night when things were quiet, Will feigned boredom and traded places with his case keeper. From his new vantage point, he gained new inspiration for commentary and jokes. The case keeper played nervously at first but slowly gained confidence in himself. By end of th' night, he was doing well and th' crowd had a good time.

Now, the case keeper grew ambitious and more and more often he was th' dealer. Will encouraged him to talk to his punters and was pleased to find that th' man had a wry sense of humor that kept the crowd smilin' and makin' bets. A germ of an idea sprouted in Will's mind and one morning he had a long talk with Pablo. By siesta time, Pablo had agreed t' let th' case keeper become dealer if Will maintained control of th' bank and ran th' game at least twice a month, preferably on paydays and holidays. It didn't take long for Will and the case keeper t' work out a deal between themselves about how their partnership would work, and Will was a (mostly) free man. Still, he had to make money and faro seemed t' be th' answer so from th' partial deck he made another board, pasting down clubs.

Buck danced with joy as they rode north out of th' village. At a crossroads, they took th' road to La Union and nooned at th' river crossing. Both animals relished grazing on th' roadside and drinking from a flowing stream while Will dozed in the shade.

It was dusk when they rode up th' street of La Union. Just as Will remembered, there were two cantinas, one on each end of th' street. The one on the east end of town was th' most lively, being handiest for those coming up from th' river valley, while th' west end languished away on th' dry side of town. There was already a crowd at th' east end cantina as he passed. By contrast, th' west end of th' street was near dead, only a few people from nearby houses visiting and catching th' latest gossip before bedtime—and bedtime came early on this end of town. By nine o'clock Will was th' only customer in the place and Barkeep b'gan closing down.

"Not much goin' on t'night, was there?" Will asked.

"Not much goes on here *any* night," the man said with a smile.

Will was surprised that the man, obviously Spanish, spoke perfect American. "It might be livelier if you had a Faro table."

"They all starve out, not many gamblers on this end of town," the barkeeper said as he wiped the bar for the last time.

"Do you mind if I set up my table here? I'll pay you ten percent of th' take."

"Ten percent of zero isn't much," he said with a grin.

"Well, how about a flat fee of a dollar a night?"

"That's a more sure thing around here," he laughed. "I'll take it. Where would you like t' set up?"

Will had already selected the space between th' side patio door and a low window as th' best place for a table.

"That's where all of them want," Barkeep laughed. "The last dealer announced th' bank was busted as he went through the door—or was it th' window? I forget."

So the deal was set; Will paid th' first night in advance and next afternoon late, he set up his table. *No need for a case keeper for a night or two,* he thought.

Soon th' regular crowd began wanderin' in. They eyed th' faro table and dealer and went to th' bar for their drinks, found a table, and sat. No one offered t' play. There soon were about a dozen men in th' room an' still no takers on faro.

Will waited until th' first round of drinks was about gone, then called out, "A free drink for anyone who places a bet on th' table, Señors." It was quiet for a moment or two, then a man at th' nearest table tossed a coin to Will. "On dos."

"Name your drink, amigo. Any more bets, gentlemen, two bits minimum?"

"Two bits on thee trey," called a man from th' bar. He moved over to place his bet. Soon there were a half-dozen punters, all with their new drinks in hand, and Will began play.

From th' corner of his eye, he saw two women enter and seat themselves at a table with their drinks. They declined Barkeep's offer of a free drink to play, contented to watch th' men and talk. Another woman or two came in and sat at the table with the others. After a while as they rose to leave, Will called out, "Señoritas, tomorrow night will be ladies' night from 7 to 8. I will buy a drink for any señorita who plays during that hour."

They smiled shyly and chattered to themselves as they left. The seed was sown an' Will hoped he would have enough to cover th' expense sure to come.

First thing he did when he set up the next night was t' pay his rent. That became his first order of business every night he was there. He made sure never to be in arrears or ahead with th' payment. Th' cantina owner was Spanish American with th' unlikely name of Jasper Roberson. He had been raised in th' family of an Army officer after he had been found in his dead mother's arms, victim of a 'Pache raid, hence th' name Jasper. It was strange t' hear him speak Spanish with an accent.

Seven o'clock came an' went without a sign of señoritas. Play was slow and desultory, th' few men not showing great interest in th' game. Will was beginning t' think he had lost out on his bid to attract ladies. Then near 7:30, several women came in a bunch. They stood shyly by th' door looking at Will. One of the ladies pushed her way through from th' back and approached th' faro board. From under her shawl, she produced a two-bit piece and laid it on th' ten. That seemed to break th' ice and th' rest crowded around placing their bets. Play began and Will's lively chatter soon wiped out their shyness and th' señoritas laughed and joined in th' fun.

Other women trickled in and joined th' group until there were more than a dozen crowded around his table. Each first time bettor got a token good for one drink at th' bar. Will noticed several women slipping coins to others who apparently had no money, but he didn't say anything. Several bet more than once and play continued lively until th' last lady placed her bet and got a token. Then, almost as one, th' group headed for th' bar where Jasper was swamped with orders. Will grinned and counted his tokens left. He had bought fifteen drinks and lost a few dollars in th' process. *An investment in future earnin's, I hope,* he thought.

There were more than th' usual crowd there, men coming in t' see how their women fared and soon th' lure of cards drew them to th' game. By th' end of th' evening—about 9:30—he had almost broken even for th' night. Jasper was pleased for he had taken in quite a bit more than th' fifteen drinks Will had bought. "Word must have gotten around that you were here," he said, "there were a couple of men here from the east side of town."

"More, th' merrier," Will said as he folded his gear up and stowed it behind th' bar. "See you tomorrow." Lights were all out by th' time he reached th' door. "Shore git t' bed early 'round here," he called.

By end of that first week, Will had hired a case keeper. In th' third week, Jasper hired a second barkeeper and ordered more supplies a month ahead of time. Business continued good and only fell off when Will had to return to his original game. Even though he was making money, it was slow because of th' low bets. At this pace, it would be a long time before he had enough to buy an organ.

The only place he knew of higher stakes was in mining camps, so it was that he decided to head for Colorado and th' gold fields. It wasn't hard t' find a buyer for his business, th' faro dealer of th' east side of town got it an' Will's old case keeper bought his first game. By midsummer he was headed up th' river road, aimin' for Colorado, his pockets jingling.

It was a leisurely trip with stops along th' way. He stayed a few days in Albuquerque picking up a few pointers here and there by playing faro and observing th' play of others. Sunrise one morning found him topping th' pass in Tijeras Canyon on the Turquoise Trail to Santa Fe. This was a busy time for th' trail, having several mining towns and settlements along its pathway. La Madera was slowly fading after its bloom, but Golden, Madrid, and Los Cerrillos were booming.

By th' time he had witnessed gaming at Golden, thoughts of Colorado had left his mind. Action was heavy enough and stakes high enough that he would make th' kind of money he needed. If he set up shop in town it would have to be on th' street, for there were no vacancies for faro games in any saloon or hotel. Even brothels had games so it was that he passed on to Madrid, but th' coal mining town was dusty and dirty—not a healthy place for one used to fresh air and sunshine. He shook dust from his clothes as he left town and breathed fresh air again.

If Golden and Madrid were promising, Los Cerrillos was paradise. In addition to turquoise mines, there were gold, silver, and lead mines, all going big—and no coal dust!

No one knows when turquoise mining began. It was going long before th' Spaniards came in the early 1500s. Fortunately, they were looking for gold and bypassed turquoise. Not finding gold that was there, they moved on.

When Will came to town, there were three hotels in addition to th' Wortley. There were more saloons than there were houses in La Madera and they were never closed. Even Simoni Merchantile was open more than it was closed and th' Clear Light Opera House hosted some of th' biggest names of th' times.

To a vaquero like Will, it looked like pandemonium but he could see possibilities of big things here. It didn't take him long t' see that his bank was far too small for these operations, where stakes started high and went up. If he was t' start business here, he would have t' step up his game *and* his bank. Th' third saloon he hit that night had a dealer looking at his forty-eighth hour without sleep since his partner had walked out and he was desperate. It took little persuasion for Will to take th' dealer's seat. It was a great deal for him, he got a goodly share of th' profits and operated on someone else's bank.

His first "shift" lasted twenty-four hours and he was getting concerned when his banker showed up with his case keeper. They were both looking refreshed and bright.

"Thanks for spelling me," he said. "I couldn't have lasted another hour without risking losing th' whole bank."

"No problem," said Will, yawning.

"My name's Sam Ruple. Most people call me Rupe," he said as he took his seat behind th' table and continued th' game that had been going nonstop since who knows when. How 'bout us takin' twelve-hour shifts at this thing, think you could handle that?"

"Shore could."

"You can keep Ernie there for your case keeper. Tom an' I been working together so long we almost know what th' other is thinking."

"That will be fine," Will said.

The case keeper Ernie had showed up a couple of hours after Will started running th' game and relieved case keeper Tom. He had stayed with him for th' rest of th' time. A smallish teenager, he was very fair skinned from spending so much time indoors. He watched th' game with an eagle eye and several times had saved Will from making a mistake with a voice so soft that punters hardly heard what he said. Will was pleased with his work.

So it was that Will found himself with a steady job. He and Rupe worked out a deal where Will got a percentage of his profits and could gradually buy into th' business until he owned half—which meant that he provided half of th' bank. There were good shifts and bad shifts but overall they made good money. Will was stacking it up pretty good and he eventually had enough money t' buy an organ.

It required a trip to Santa Fe to order th' organ. He arranged with St. Vrain and Company to purchase and deliver th' instrument. Now that took some doin', considerin' that th' organ had t' be ordered from Boston, shipped to Freeport, Missouri, loaded on a wagon, and shipped to Santa Fe on th' trail. Then someone had to take it all the way down to th' ranch. By some miracle it got there without a scratch and you know th' rest.

Chapter 21
Will Castleberry: Guide, Gambler & Gunman

The Gunman

It was a year after Will ordered th' organ before it was delivered and he was hesitant t' leave until he knew it had been safely delivered. Even after he knew that, he stayed on, making good money with an idea that he could get enough t' buy a little spread somewhere and raise cattle. He and Ernie became close friends and worked well together at th' table. Still, he remained a mystery to Will. The boy disappeared after work and Will didn't even know where he stayed, except that he lived with kinfolk somewhere south of town.

The boy was soft-spoken and quiet and got a lot of teasing about his soft features and fair skin. Some of th' miners would take a disliking to this "sissified" boy and try to manhandle him, but he carried a butcher knife and more than one miner got his ribs scratched before he got th' message t' leave th' boy alone. For th' most part Will stayed out of confrontations, letting th' boy handle them on his own. Only a time or two did he have to step in and have an over-aggressive customer removed.

Of course, th' town was pretty rough and there was a usual amount of trouble daily. I forget th' name of th' saloon (might have been Bucket of Blood, ever' camp had one), but it kept tight rein on misbehavers. Even so, from time to time trouble would break out regardless of th' vigilance. Everyone wore a gun and it was necessary. Will and Rupe had a peg in th' wall behind them where they hung their gunbelt for all to see. To all appearances, they were unarmed, but in a slot under th' table was a Colt .44 ready for immediate action. Fortunately, neither one had to resort to it in th' time Will was there.

In every mining camp there are those who think they can run roughshod over anyone and everyone. By process of elimination and conquest, th' title of chief bully shakes down to one or two men. In Cerrillos at th' time Will was there, it had come down to one man by the name of Hunt. Everyone knew when he came to town. As he got into his cups making his rounds of th' saloons, he got louder and meaner, leaving a trail of broken furniture and noses behind him. His specialty was bullying gamblers and most of th' gamers left by th' back door as he came in th' front. It frustrated him no end that he could not find a one in town. Only Rupe and Will stood up to him.

When Hunt came to town, both dealers stayed on duty, one behind th' table and th' other by th' bar. More than once he was buffaloed while in th' midst of bullying th' dealer. Strange to say, he never caught on to what was happening to him, for by th' time he got to th' Bucket of Blood, he was so drunk he could hardly stand. He would wake up in th' alley where he had slept it off and attribute his aching head and lump to his night of debauchery. He would more or less quietly take a hair of th' hound that bit him and leave for his mine, not to reappear until next payday.

Someone must have clued him in about Will and Rupe, for th' last time he came into town he started his rounds at the Bucket. Straight to th' bar he went and when th' barkeeper poured his third drink, Hunt grabbed th' bottle from his hand and turned to th' faro table where Will was wondering how long it would be before th' bully left and he could resume play, for all his punters had sudden needs to be somewhere else. Rupe had yet to appear but Will met th' man calmly. "Want t' place a bet, Hunt?"

"Yeah," Hunt growled, "I'm bettin on th' duce." And he laid a pile of silver on th' card.

"Anyone else want to play?" Will's call met with silence.

"Looks like I'm th' only one," Hunt sneered. "Play!"

At that moment, Rupe walked through th' door and sauntered to th' bar. A whispered word from th' barkeeper warned him that Hunt was not yet drunk. He turned with both elbows on th' bar and watched. Will looked up and shook his head slightly.

"I said play," Hunt yelled, slamming his fist on th' table. He was stone sober.

"I'll match Hunt's bet and put it on th' ten," Rupe said as he laid silver on his choice.

Will shuffled and put the deck in the dealing box, then drew. The soda card was queen of hearts, banker's card was th' ace of spades, and player's card was three of spades.

"Ha, I won!" Hunt exclaimed.

"He bet on the duce," Ernie said, though the remark was unnecessary.

"You keep out of this, you little girl!" Hunt snarled and backhanded the boy so hard he slammed against th' wall and slid to th' floor. In th' moment of silence that followed, th' sound of a gun cocking filled the room. There was a general shuffling as people sought refuge.

"That wasn't necessary, Hunt," Will said staring him straight in the eyes.

Neither man looked away. Rupe backed away a step or two, keeping out of the line of fire but close enough to get in on the action if needed.

"Oh, th' coward has a hidy gun," Hunt sneered. "Bring it out an' let's see what you can do with it."

"Don't have to," Will smiled. "It's pointing right at your cojones an' I'm wondering if they'll ring if I shoot them. *Don't move!*" he demanded.

Fortunately Hunt was sober and could think straight for once and realized his danger. A drunker Hunt would have sprung into action and most likely gained th' advantage.

"Now," Will continued, "drop your weapons, gun and knives and all."

"Not on your li . . ." Hunt began, only to be cut off by th' unmistakable sound of Barkeep's double barrels of buckshot being cocked behind him. He whirled around.

"Maybe you better do it, Hunt," Rupe said.

Th' scattergun was waist high and aimed square at his chest. There was a scramble as onlookers beyond Hunt got out of th' new line of fire. Hunt froze for a moment, looking from one to th' other, weighing his options.

"Got you in a crossfire, Hunt, whatcha gonna do?" Will said softly. Ernie groaned and moved behind him.

"When this is over, I'm gonna kill th' lot of yuh." Hunt's eyes blazed. His captors didn't blink.

"Lay down your weapons—*now!*" Th' muzzle of his shotgun rose slightly.

Reluctantly, the big man laid his gun on th' table, along with his belt knife.

"Now take your boots off," Will directed.

Hunt glared, but th' muzzle of that .44 was now in plain sight held in a steady hand. He sat on th' floor and as his right boot came off, another knife fell out.

"Thought so," Will grunted, rising. "Watch him, Rupe."

He gathered up th' weapons and placed them on th' bar.

"Put these out of reach, if you would, Charlie."

Uncocking his gun, he laid it in th' pile. Turning, he began unbuttoning his shirt. "You're a pretty good fighter, Hunt, and I'm pretty good myself. You may eat my lunch, but while you do, I'm gonna get a sandwich or two."

There was a general shuffling and scraping of chairs and tables being moved and like magic a large space was cleared of obstacles, encircled by a ring of faces eager to see a good fight. Already two or three tinhorn gamblers were taking bets. Odds were heavy in Hunt's favor. Will pulled off his boots and stood up only to be met with a huge fist in th' middle of his chest that knocked him into th' crowd. Hands caught him and shoved him back into th' ring. There were shouts of "Go git 'im, boy."

Will had just enough control of his rush t' dodge as Hunt flew at him. As he crashed to th' floor, his feet flew out and tripped the big man. Before he could rise, Will landed hard astraddle his back, slamming his body into th' floor and knocking th' breath out of him. Gripping both ears, he slammed Hunt's face into th' floor three times before th' big man could resist.

With a roar he rose, tossing Will off like a fly. Will landed on his feet and as Hunt whirled he turned straight into Will's fist to th' jaw. It stunned him just long enough for Will t' get one-two-three blows to th' gut before another haymaker sent him flying. Hunt rushed in for th' finish, but as he leaped, Will kicked both feet into his gut and his momentum sent him flying over Will and into th' crowd. Eager hands returned him to th' ring.

There was little finesse to Hunt's fight; he had always depended on his brute strength, which seldom failed him. Will, on th' other hand, was thirty pounds lighter and two inches shorter and had to depend on his ability to avoid damage to survive. They circled warily until a boot came out from th' crowd and shoved Will in th' back. "Foul!" cried th' crowd and th' offender was quickly subdued by several well-placed blows from partisans. He crept to th' back of th' crowd to lick his wounds.

Meantime, his kick had propelled Will into Hunt's reach and he took full advantage, landing several blows to Will's head and body. Somehow Will avoided his grip and backed away. Seeing his advantage, Hunt rushed in and head-butted Will in th' throat. His teeth snapped shut with a crack heard all over th' room. Will bit off th' end of his tongue. The taste of blood filled him with rage and even as he fell, his hands found Hunt's ears and forced his head down as Will's knee flew into his face. They landed in a pile with Hunt on top. A stout chair leg rolled out of th' crowd and Hunt grabbed it. His first blow struck Will beside th' head and he was just conscious enough t' dodge th' second blow before his body went limp.

Th' big end of the club shattered and flew into th' crowd leaving Hunt holding a jagged stub. Wiping blood from his eyes, th' big man rose to his knees, cursing at th' prone body before him.

"Now you sorry piece of trash I'm gonna finish you once and for all."

Grasping th' remnants of his club with both hands, he rose to his full height to drive those jagged splinters into th' inert body beneath him.

Just as he reached his highest, with club held dagger-like in both hands high above his head, four shots rang out—bang-bang-bang-bang—so fast the sound of th' first shot seemed not to have died out before the last shot sounded. Hunt was driven back by force of th' bullets, his eyes wide in surprise. He fell straight back, his arms still extended over his head, ending with his head on th' floor an' his legs beneath him in a grotesque position. The room was filled with smoke, confusion, and panic as men flew for doors and windows.

There against the wall where Hunt had knocked him lay Ernie, Will's smoking gun still in his outstretched hands. He had literally shot between th' legs of a spectator standing in front of him to hit his target.

Shakily, th' boy rose, his face welted by th' print of four

fingers, his left eye swelling shut. "Got him," he whispered.

"You sure did, boy," Charlie the barkeeper said from where he had risen from behind th' bar.

Rupe carefully uncocked the shotgun and laid it on th' bar. "Couldn't use th' damned thing in this crowd!" he muttered.

Ernie walked over to where Will lay, still unconscious. "Here's your gun back, Will, thanks for th' use." He lay th' gun on Will's chest. "Better be getting on home."

"Wait, boy," Charlie called coming around the end of th' bar, "here's th' hidy gun. I put another shell in it so's you'll have six. You will most likely need it afore you get out of town. Hunt had friends."

"That's right, Hunt had friends an' we're gonna send ya t' hell after him!" It was the man who kicked Will into th' ring and three others stood by him at th' back door, guns drawn. Ernie whirled to face them, gun rising to meet his second hand.

Charlie reached th' shotgun and Rupe was left in th' middle. All he could do was dive for th' floor and grapple for his holster gun. Even as he pulled it, four rapid shots rang out amidst three or four ragged shots coming from Hunt's friends. There was th' sound of breaking glass behind th' bar.

There was a pause an' Rupe watched four bodies crumple to th' floor at th' back door. Two more shots rang out from th' kid and the lights went out. All was still except for soft feet padding toward th' back door and fading away down th' alley.

"You ok, Charlie?"

"Yeah," he grunted, "I got a light."

Rupe lay still on th' floor while a match flared and a candle slowly rose above th' bar. There was noise of a crowd in th' street calling out questions no one answered. Rupe blinked, picked up one of th' fallen lanterns, and Charlie lit it with another match in both his hands to steady his shaking.

"Stand back!" came an authoritative voice from th' street.

"Make way, move away from that door! Bill, stay here and don't let anyone in 'cept Doc if he gits here."

It was the town marshal and his deputy coming lately on th' scene. "One o' Hunt's buddies told me he was beatin' up a tin-horn at th' other end of town or I'da been here much sooner," he said. "I'll nail that feller's hide to th' jailhouse wall." He stopped in the middle of th' room and looked carefully around. "Hunt's dead, what about this other feller here?" he asked, indicating Will.

"Don't know, Marshal, I'll check." Rupe knelt over Will. "He's still breathing, just got knocked out, I guess."

"Looks like you got a scratch and lost yore mirror—agin, Charlie," the marshal said.

Rupe looked for th' first time and noted blood soaking Charlie's sleeve and the broken mirror behind.

"What's this we have here?" th' marshal called from th' back of th' room.

"That's th' last of Hunt's friends, I hope," Charlie called as Rupe tied up his arm. "It's just a scratch, Charlie," he said.

The four lay as they had fallen, all dead.

"Marshal, Justice Martin's here, do ya want t' see him?"

"Yeah, tell him t' grab his witnesses an' come in for an inquest. Tell Doc he's not needed if he shows up. These men are all dead."

"What about th' man that *ain't* dead, Marshal, think he might need a doctor?" Rupe asked testily.

The crowd around windows and doors had hushed when their talking started, now there was a buzz as th' news spread. In a few minutes th' justice and four other men entered.

"Step around th' wall, men, don't move a thing," th' marshal called.

They stared at Hunt. Rigor was setting in and his arms and head had risen from th' floor. It was as if he were coming alive and rising t' strike.

"Doc's here," Deputy Bill called as a tall slim man pushed his way in.

"Don't need you, Doc, ever'one's dead here," Marshal called.

"A lot you'd know about that," Doc snorted. He knelt over Will. "This man's not as dead as you pronounced and he needs attention."

"I knowed *he* wasn't," Marshal rejoined.

Doc stepped to th' door. "You four there, yeah you, come in here. Take that door down and lay it by this man." Carefully, two men helped Doc roll Will on his side as the other two gently pushed the door against his back. They rolled Will back on to the door and after getting him centered, carried him over to Doc's office. His wife, who was a competent nurse, took over while the doctor continued his examination.

"You seen enough of this body, Martin?" he called, indicating Hunt's mortal remains.

"We got to lay him out afore he freezes thataway and we can't get him in a box."

"We seen enough," Martin called.

Two more onlookers were enlisted in aiding Doc to lay Hunt out straight. Best they could do was to pull his legs out from under his body until he lay with his knees still bent and his toes just touching th' floor.

"Quickest rigor mortis I ever saw," Doc muttered.

He examined the other four and determined they were indeed dead. Justice Martin formally convened an inquest while Doc laid out and examined the bodies. Charlie and Rupe sat by the bar answering questions while the marshal stood beside them. Charlie had a stiff drink to steady his nerves.

"Don't you dare get drunk, Charlie!" Doc said sternly.

The glass rattled as Charlie tried to set it down without spilling.

"Doctor, can you tell us how these men died?" Justice Martin asked.

"Can't tell you *how*, but I can tell you what killed them," Doc retorted,

"Take them in order of their demise, if you will," the justice said.

"Hunt died first," Rupe called and Doc knelt and cut away his shirt.

"Not much blood here," he reported.

Then he leaned back on his heels and gave a low whistle. Witnesses and committee crowded around. There on Hunt's bare chest just below his left nipple were four holes, two overlapping each other! The marshal pulled a silver dollar out of his pocket and laid it over th' wounds. Not a hole showed.

"Some shooting," he said.

"Ernie did that laying on th' floor over there, his head propped up on th' wall and shootin' between th' legs of some man standing between him and Hunt," Rupe explained.

This was met with some disbelief and there followed a long discussion with Rupe and Charlie explaining every moment they remembered. It wasn't until someone lay on th' floor like Ernie, others playing th' part of Hunt and th' spraddle-legged onlooker and Doc establishing that the wounds had a slightly upward trajectory, that the committee began to believe them.

They turned their attention to the other bodies, Doc examining each in turn. Number one victim on the left had a neat hole in th' middle of his forehead, a big exit wound in the back of his head, th' bullet impacting the wall. Number two died from a shot to his heart. Number three had a hole in his forehead and number four a shot in his throat that had severed his spinal cord in his neck.

Charlie and Rupe's testimony that all of this shooting was done by one person using two guns was met with disbelief. It wasn't until all guns in th' room had been examined, and th' evidence determined that no other guns present except Will's had been fired an' that four shells and one live round remained in th' gun, that th' men began to reluctantly believe th' two witnesses.

Examination of th' room accounted for every shot, including two in th' floor and one in th' mirror that th' four had fired as they were dying. There were several other bullet holes in th' wall, but Charlie and others had been careful to write th' date they were made and th' name of the shooter if known.

No one had ever seen such a demonstration of marksmanship as this and there are those that remain skeptical to this day. Although several had witnessed th' killing of Hunt, only Charlie and Rupe had witnessed th' second shooting. They had many a heated argument over th' matter until finally both refused to talk about it. It remains in their minds th' greatest demonstration of shooting they had ever seen, made all th' more unbelievable by th' fact that a boy of fifteen or so had done it.

It took some time to establish the identities of all th' victims but it was done at last, well after sunup. The inquest determined that Hunt's killing was justified in that he was in th' act of killing another. Th' four were killed in self-defense and therefore no charges were to be made.

The marshal was not present when the verdict was read, having left with his deputy to find Ernie, which was never done. No one knew so much as his last name, and no one in a wide circle of th' town claimed kith or kin to th' boy. He was never seen again.

Will lay unconscious for nearly thirty-six hours. When he awoke, he could only see through slits in his swollen eyes. His head and neck hurt so much he couldn't move and he continually had th' taste of blood in his mouth. His teeth ached and when he tried to feel around with his tongue, it hurt. He tasted blood. When he next awoke, th' room was dark except for a candle flickering somewhere. *Why don't they have a lantern?* Will thought. *Where am I anyway?* He started to turn his head and the pain made him groan.

"Are you awake there, boy?" a man's voice asked.

A cool hand felt his forehead and Will tried to open his eyes wider without success. "Don't exert yourself, I'm Doctor Schull and you are in my office."

Will tried to speak, but it came out as an unintelligible croak.

"I'll bet you are thirsty, here, draw on this."

He felt th' coolness of a glass straw on his lips and drew cold water out of it. There was a taste of lemon and it felt good until he tried to swallow. He choked a little and Doc said, "Don't try to swallow, just let th' water slide down your throat. You've had a hard blow there and it's a wonder your throat didn't swell up and choke you. That blow to your head caused your brain to bruise and I don't want you to raise your head one inch for a few days. If we can keep your brain from swelling, you just might live."

Will remembered with a start—and even that shot pain through his head. "Where's Hunt? Is Ernie ok? How about Rupe and the game?" All of which came out completely garbled and unintelligible.

"Lie still and catch your breath a moment and when you are relaxed, I'll tell you what has happened," Doc said. That cool hand felt his forehead again.

"Here's a cloth for his head," a feminine voice said from far away, it seemed. A cool cloth was laid over his forehead and eyes and he slept.

When he awoke, it was lighter and a spot of sunshine reflecting off water danced on th' ceiling. It made him dizzy and he closed his eyes again. It was this way for several days with Will coming and going, voices drifting into and out of his consciousness. He remembered that glass straw and th' cooling water with that lemony taste, and a couple of times th' straw brought him some warm broth. He felt its warmth through his body and slept. Gradually he was awake more, and more aware of his surroundings. He would lie and listen to th' noises of th' house, Doc treating someone in th' next room, dishes rattling softly from th' kitchen, and soft female voices in conversation.

Something was in his mouth. It was coarse like a thread and he gave it a tug but it didn't give. Carefully he felt with his fingers. There was a knot and it was attached to his tongue—a stitch! No, *two* stitches! Further exploration found th' line of a scar forming along th' front edge of his tongue. Then he remembered he had bitten it off for some reason, but why? For that matter, why was he lying here and why was he hurting? He closed his eyes and tried to remember. There were days lying here, how many? He didn't know. What was before that? Th' game! Rupe, Ernie and Tom the case keepers, Charlie the barkeep, but where were they? In the bucket . . . in the bucket? That doesn't make sense, what were they doing in a bucket? Not a bucket, *the* bucket . . . The Bucket . . . of Blood! That's it, the Bucket of Blood Saloon! But where . . . Madrid . . . no, coal, dirty dust . . . Cerrillos! That's it, they're in the Bucket of Blood in Los Cerrillos!

Then it all came back to him, Hunt, th' fight . . . he could see Hunt over him, a club in his hand and swinging—then rising to swing again. He writhed . . . and in th' fading light, four shots, one on th' other, bang-bang-bang-bang. . . . he slept again, only to awake with a start to th' sound of those shots, . . . bang-bang-bang.

"Are you dreaming, boy? That's good, what were you dreaming about?"

"Bang-bang-bang," Will slurred.

"Did it all come back to you?"

"No . . . those shots . . . all I remember . . . then it was black."

"Well, I'll tell you the rest. Those shots saved your life. They all four went into Hunt's heart in the space of a silver dollar. It was Ernie that did it with your gun. When he fell against the wall your belt fell with him and he shot Hunt just before he was going to kill you with that jagged chair leg."

"It was black, but there were more shots, lots of shots, then it went quiet."

"Those shots were the most remarkable thing I have ever seen," Doc said. "Charlie gave Ernie the hidy gun fully loaded for protection just before four men came after him. That boy killed all four with four shots and never missed a one. I have *never* seen anything like it, and I doubt I ever will again."

"Where's Ernie?"

"No one knows, he just shot out the lights and disappeared, hasn't been seen since."

"Rupe, Tom, Charlie?"

"They're all ok. Rupe and Charlie are still arguing with everyone about what the kid did, hardly anyone believes them, it was so fantastic."

Will thought it over and over th' next few days. Who would have thought Ernie could do that? Doc let him have visitors and Rupe was th' first to come, then Tom and Charlie. Rupe and Charlie filled in some of th' details for him. It was so unbelievable, but Will believed his friends without any doubt. Everyone continued to look for Ernie, but it was useless, he was gone.

Will got better gradually. He threw up the first time he tried to sit up and spent another day on his back, but after that he improved slowly until finally Doc let him go. He still couldn't work and he and Rupe agreed to sell th' game and split th' proceeds. Rupe and Tom headed for Colorado and Will went to Hot Springs at Elephant Butte where he spent what he had left, after paying Doctor Schull, in quiet living and treatments for his head wound. He was warned that another blow to th' head like that would most likely kill him and it was a more cautious and circumspect Will Castleberry that saddled Buck one early spring day and crossed the Jornada. Rip Van Winkle rode through Rhodes Pass and across the basin into La Luz.

"Rip talked a lot about that time away from th' basin and I discovered what his other name was by accident. Not to say that those two names were his only *names," Zenas chuckled. "That fight was th' talk of many a campfire and th' subject of many a hot argument. We used to talk about our gunfighters like we talk about our ball players today, gunfighting being th' most common 'sport' in the west at that time.*

"Will was real sensitive about anyone doubting the legend of Ernie's shooting, and like Rupe and old Charlie, he finally quit talking about it. No one ever saw Ernie though I know Will looked for years. A long time ago, I ran across someone who just might have been Ernie in another name. If I outlive certain people who have sworn me to silence, I maybe will tell you about it." Zenas chuckled at some long kept secret and I wished long life and health for him.

CHAPTER 22
SOME WESTERN PHILOSOPHY

The story of Will Castleberry and Ernie caused Zenas to talk about the times and mindsets of the younger frontier and the people who settled the land. These were his thoughts after he had told me about Will and Ernie.

Times I grew up in were violent and they were exciting at times, but there were also days and months of just plain hard and boring day-to-day work. I was fortunate t' miss out on wars and battles for th' most part, and the ones I was in are best not discussed.

One magazine we got with our tobacco coupons was *Police Gazette*. We got great amusement out of their accounts of gunfights and outlaws in our region. Comparing them to what *really* happened gave us a lot of entertainment and laughs. Those dime novels from th' trains were so exaggerated and distorted that they ceased t' be funny and I quit reading them. Most of what was written there was made up and outright lies. If you believe Ned Buntline, Kit Carson was seven feet tall and had t' have an extra horse just t' haul his scalps around. I heard Kit say that he hadn't killed a dozen Indians in his whole life.

Th' west was settled in several stages, first stage being by adventurers, men who could live without laws an' institutions that maintained order. They lived by their own laws, which were at times and of necessity rather loose. Of course, this crowd included a goodly number of outcasts and fugitives.

Ranchers came in th' second stage. They ran their cattle on open range and owned very little of it at first. They didn't hesitate t' keep th' range they claimed by force if necessary. Still th' absence of organized society made them a law unto themselves at times but their law was more in line with th' settled country they came from. Gradually, that first stage was forced t' conform with them or move on to other frontiers.

Our next set of pioneers was traders and merchants. They settled in towns and served th' gentry o' th' first two stages. Close behind them came farmers, mostly immigrants and dispossessed from th' east. Ranchers gladly accepted this settlement, it being to their advantage t' have towns nearby where they could resupply and where there was a more ready source of labor. By now, remnants of stage one were either conformed, gone to th' wilderness, or hunted as lawbreakers. Good folks gradually won out over bad, but it was th' bad that got all th' attention.

Everything was on a pretty even keel until some meddler back east invented barbed wire, or "bob war" as we called it. It did more t' upset society and nature than anything else. Ranchers and Indians hated th' stuff an' farmers and lawyers loved it.

Charlie Goodnight over in th' Palo Duro built up a herd of pure blooded buffalo, th' only pure blooded ones left now. A bunch of Navajos rode over t' see them one last time and when they got ready to go home, Charlie had t' tell them how b'cause fences confused them. I'm convinced most fence cutting was done by those who resented restrictions on their movements, not b'cause they were intent on breakin' an' stealin'.

When Charlie Goodnight drove his herd into Palo Duro Canyon, he passed th' camp of Dutch Henry and his outlaws one night. Charlie rode right into camp and made a deal with Henry that he would not bother th' gang if th' gang left his riders and cattle alone. Dutch agreed to that and as far as I know both kept their word. Not that Dutch was so honest or that Charlie was crooked. Charlie knew there was no law on th' Llano and that gang could do him much damage. At th' same time, Henry knew that Charlie was a formidable man t' deal with and he didn't need him for an enemy.

Another agreement Mr. Goodnight made was with sheep men. They set boundaries for their ranges and both sides kept them. Even so, Charlie's hands patrolled his border, turning back strays of all species. It's interesting that th' only one to intentionally violate that agreement was a herd belongin' to th' governor of New Mexico Territory, th' representative an' upholder of law.

It's been my experience that few men are all bad and no man is all good. I have to say that very few of th' men I knew were dangerous or bloodthirsty, they were to all appearances common and reasonable people. I only knew one man who would murder for hire and he ended up swinging from a rafter in a barn in Indian Territory. Few were men like John Wesley Hardin and John Selman, who killed and murdered for the pleasure of it.

A man's pride and integrity were his ultimate possessions and to question them was to invite deadly trouble. A lot of feuds started over unkind words we would ignore today. Back then, a man didn't and couldn't afford t' ignore them. That's not to say that men didn't josh and tease, there was a lot of that, but we knew when words were meant and when they were not. It was one thing to josh a friend, but you were careful what you said to or about strangers.

A lot of people think the Civil War ended at Appomattox. It didn't. If anything, it got worse. It was fought in the South and Southwest, most especially in Louisiana and Texas, Arkansas and Kansas, and borderline Missouri. Gradually, order came to those regions, but it came at th' expense of the western states and territories. These were th' places men—both good and bad—came to t' escape violence in their homelands. More often than not, violence came with them or followed soon after.

Cattle on open range were a ready source of income for these men, whether it was rustling unbranded cows or downright stealing of herds, th' distinction being that rustling was not frowned on so much as stealing. The growth of some brands was phenomenal, their cows having t' bear twins and triplets t' account for their increase, but a calf bearing a different brand than his mammy was not condoned. The problem with this phenomenal growth was that neighboring ranches generally had a corresponding drop-off in production. It led t' tension among neighbors and gave meaning t' th' term "ridin' for th' brand."

Cattle drives were another problem for ranchers of all sizes. It is th' tendency of cattle to join a bunch of moving cattle and many a herd has arrived at th' end of a drive with more head than it started out with. When th' Slaughter boys drove through from Texas to Arizona, they picked up cattle by th' dozen an' they didn't bother t' cull 'em out, either! The only one I knew of that stopped th' herd was a little widow woman who *made* John Slaughter give back her milk cow.

It became necessary for ranchers to check herds coming through for cows with their brands. Local cattle associations hired men to cut herds and cull out local brands and cattle without th' road brand of th' drover. This was a hassle for th' drive and resulted in hard feelings all around. It didn't take long for gangs of thieves to get the idea of posing as legitimate representatives of those associations and cutting herds and stealing what cattle they could. A lot of their success depended on which side had th' most firepower or determination. If they were repulsed, they would likely return later and attempt to stampede th' herd and make off with a bunch of steers. It was bad enough that Indians in th' Territory worried them, but a gang of white men was worse.

A lot has been said about hatred between ranchers an' homesteadin' farmers that followed th' trains into cattle country and most of it is untrue. A smart rancher got possession of th' water on his range first off. Homesteadin' dry lands was a passing thing and in fact helped th' rancher for he bought up those homesteads as th' farmers starved out and thus gained deed to property he already had use of. Another good thing about th' homesteader is that he brought his family with him and that included daughters of which there was a definite shortage on th' range. Many a cowhand has courted and won th' hand of a homesteader's daughter. I might add too that more than one soiled dove has become th' respected wife of a prosperous rancher and a pillar of th' community. I guess it could be said that she had fulfilled a need of society in both of her occupations, but most men would keep that thought to themselves.

Guns were an essential part of a western man's makeup. On th' range, they were protection against dangerous critters, some of which could be th' two-legged variety. In reality, th' threat of hot lead made for a level field both "on th' prairie" and in town. That fast draw showdown at high noon in books and movies was sure a revelation to us westerners. I don't know of a single incidence where this was done for real. Most men viewed th' quick draw as a good way t' get your foot or leg shot and if you had t' make a quick draw, you were at a disadvantage right from th' start. It was a foolish man who went into a fight with his gun still in his pocket. If a fight threatened, guns were already drawn and ready for action. Many times th' sound of guns cocking, be it in th' saloon or courtroom or street, sounded like a passel of crickets and usually it was enough t' cool th' hottest heads. Most of th' time it was followed by th' sound of guns uncocking and being reset on empty chambers and life continuing at a calmer pace.

The western man was, as a whole, a superior marksman. He took his accuracy seriously and worked hard to be th' best he could. I have known some men whose accuracy was unbelievable unless witnessed firsthand. Our favorite topic of discussion around th' chuck wagon was about gunmen and their exploits, who was faster than who and could outshoot th' other. We followed them like folks today follow baseball players. From stories I've heard, there must have been a hundred or more witnesses to th' Earp-Clanton fight in Tombstone—and don't think all folks thought those Earps was th' heros o' that fight. When Wyatt avenged his brothers' ambushings it was th' only thing we talked about. First thing fellers in th' line shacks asked a visitor was, "Any news from Tombstone?"

We knew a few men who went up t' fight in th' Johnson County War when big ranchers tried t' wipe out little ones, Tom Horn, Frank Canton, and others. Of course in that fight we were all in agreement for th' little guy.

Will Castleberry was present at what some believe was th' greatest show of marksmanship ever seen. He was teased no end for "sleeping" through it all, but he believed those who witnessed it. One thing that made that incident so unique is that the boy did th' shooting with weapons he was unfamiliar with. Usually, to fire that fast, th' trigger was tied back and th' shooter fired by thumbin' or fannin' th' hammer, but this was done at th' expense of accuracy. Arguments and theories about Ernie's technique have never ceased—or been settled for that matter. I heard tell of almost th' same thing occurring in Dodge City and I've always wondered if it wasn't Ernie did both. The greatest mystery is who he was, how he learned t' shoot like that, an' where he disappeared to.

I've heard that Wyatt Earp has said that he never got off th' first shot in a fight and it's a fact that he was never hit. *His* first shot seldom failed t' settle th' question. Bill Tilghman practiced th' fast draw, but most of his fights he entered with gun already drawn.

The efficient use of six-shooter and rifle was th' great equalizer of th' time. Clay Allison was lame; Little Luke Short probably never had it out with a man his size or smaller; Doc Holliday was weakened by consumption an' probably couldn't have fought his way out of a paper bag, but men paid attention when he was around and armed—and he was armed all th' time. Billy the Kid was a runt of a boy; Pistol Pete over in Oklahoma was cross-eyed but deadly with a pistol. He killed all four men who had murdered his father. For pure grit, I don't think you could beat Jeff Milton, who fought off would-be train robbers after he had been shot with a shotgun.

I heard about an old cowboy who was a night watchman in Oklahoma City. Local kids got t' questioning him about bein' a cowboy and th' thing that made them disbelieve him was when he showed them how he shot his pistol. They knew he wasn't for real when he slowly drew his gun, spread his feet and crouched, holding his gun with both hands, and *sighted* th' gun. One night a robber beat him up and burglarized th' warehouse he was guarding. As th' thief rounded a corner in his car making his getaway, that old cowboy aimed and fired through th' passenger-side rear window and hit th' robber in th' head with one shot. It made him a *real* cowboy hero of a bunch of boys.

Another marksman was Bill Doolin. He stayed up in th' hills on Gene Rhodes's ranch unknown t' Gene. After he shot a plunging killer horse who had thrown Gene an' was about t' stomp him into mush, he stayed at Gene's place. That's another example of good and bad in a fellow. Gene saw good in Bill and appreciated it. So long as Bill stayed on th' good side, he was welcome. On th' other hand, if Bill chose t' stray, he would move on so as to not bring trouble on Gene. He, Bill that is, was killed as he was moving his family from Oklahoma. Gene always believed he had decided t' go straight and was moving to New Mexico t' start over.

Lots of men on th' run hid out in this area an' in th' San Andres Mountains, especially. Rhodes never harbored any of them except maybe Doolin an' no one could fault him for that. We never asked a stranger who he was or where he came from. Most we asked, if that, was, "What would you like to be called?" Or we made up some nickname th' stranger didn't object to. We was big on nicknames: Leapin' Lon, Wayback, Daylight, Ol' Van, an' dozens more.

Did people take the law into their own hands? I guess you could say that, but it was because th' law was remote, crooked, or impotent. Why take a man to th' authorities when they were a hundred fifty-two miles away and when there was a certainty that th' culprit would be turned loose or "escape" to continue his lawless ways before justice was served? Even when tried in court, th' tendency was to turn th' guilty loose or merely give him a slap on the wrist and turn him loose. Juries usually colored their decisions by what they perceived as th' right thing t' do an' not by th' letter of th' law. Too many of today's courts are more interested in practicin' law than justice.

The Lincoln County War was evidence that local governments were not always run by honest folk. Just because a man carried a badge didn't mean he wasn't a crooked thief or killer. That fact only reinforced a cowboy's tendency t' judge a man by what he saw and not by his position or what he was told. Both sides of th' Lincoln County War claimed backing of th' law. In fact, Billy and his gang were deputized at one time, the same time Sheriff Brady was in office. There was no neutral ground in that county. Everyone was forced t' take sides, leave, or suffer th' consequences.

Vigilance committees served when and where law couldn't or

wouldn't. Wasn't there a sheriff named Plummer in Wyoming that ran as rough a gang of cutthroats and killers as ever existed? It was vigilantes that hanged him. What about Mysterious Dave Mather at Dodge or that marshal up there that was robbing banks? What did they do for honest men?

Sometimes thieves, murderers, and robbers were hung when they were caught and justice was served. In many cases it was a matter of survival and if survival of good people depended on elimination of bad people, then you did what you had to do and went on. And you *didn't* talk about it—ever.

There's a passage in th' Law of Moses, Exodus 21, I believe, that talks about an ox that gores. Basically, it says that if an ox gores he becomes a candidate for an immediate barbeque and th' owner is not held responsible. But if th' owner of th' ox does nothing and the ox gores again, then the owner is responsible and is to suffer th' same consequences as th' ox—that is, death, not th' barbeque. Now, do you think that is punishment for th' ox? No, it's t' keep him from goring again, *which he will do.* An owner's responsibility is to see that his ox never gores again. To not do anything shows a callous disregard for th' life and safety of others.

The application to us is this: hanging a murderer is *not* to punish him, but *to prevent him from doing it again,* which he *is* likely to do. I sometimes wonder what will they think when a judge or a lawyer or a jury member stands before the Judgment Seat with the blood of innocent people on their hands because they were too lenient and let a killer kill again. If the guilty continue to kill off innocent people, how can th' innocent survive? You can call hanging or shooting or execution of any kind cruel, but th' murder of innocents is much, much more cruel.

It took a lot of blood, sweat, and tears t' tame this country and it appears we have just about done it. Sometimes it's kind of sad that future generations can't experience th' wilderness as we did, but then, they will live longer and peacefully where most o' those that came before didn't. That has to be good, but I still hate that bob war!

CHAPTER 23
TOM WASHINGTON

"I guess ol' Wayback Tom Washington was th' most interesting man on th' Rafter JD," Zenas said. We were sitting on the front porch in spite of the cold wind coming down the mountain off snow that had fallen higher up the last few days. A glove with the fingertips cut out kept feeling in my hand, but my writing was mighty shaky that day. This would most likely be the last story before winter shut down any more writing on the porch.

We were up on th' mountain chousing down stragglers who didn't let a little snow slow down their grazing. So long as grass stuck out above th' snow, they would stay. Trouble was they tended t' stay too long and got in trouble th' first heavy snow or blizzard come along. We lost a few head like that from time to time and Bob kept after us t' get 'em all down.

"Start out high where th' snow's deep and there ain't no tracks," he'd say as if we was greenhorns without any sense.

"Want us t' git th' ones leavin' tracks too?" Lon drawled.

Bob didn't answer, just eyed him. We laughed and pushed Lon out th' door. It was agravating work, for sure as shootin', some o' those cows insisted on backtrackin' back up th' mountain in snow and we would have t' run 'em out again.

"I ain't gonna keep runnin' them doggies out'n th' snow ever' day," Jones declared. "Today they're gonna go down th' mountain far enough so's they can't git to th' snow in one night."

"They be passin' up some good graze, you do that," Wayback allowed.

"Naw they won't, they'll backtrack an' get it, but they won't get back to snow. Trick is t' figger how far down t' drive them so they don't miss grass an' don't git in snow agin."

"That calls for some deep figgerin'," Rip said, "who you gonna git t' do that for you, Jones?"

"Won't be you, that's for shore. Here, let me put that saddle on afore you git it on backards agin."

Rip slapped his hands away. "I'll saddle my own horse the way I want to, you be sure t' git one o' your gentle ones t'day. I ain't gonna listen you moanin' all day about gittin' throwed."

"Th' only time I ever saw Jones throwed was when Fat Rita throwed him out o' th' cantina last spring," I said.

"She never done it . . ."

"Had him by th' scruff o' his neck an' belt an' he was on his tippy-toes just a flyin'."

"I seen it maself, Zee, an' he was squawkin' lak a settin' hen," Wayback said.

"Shore weren't no rooster crow," Leapin' Lon said.

"You fellers quit jawin' an' get busy or you won't have time t' eat Manuel's lunch an' he'll be mad for a week," Bob called from th' bunkhouse porch.

"Shore don't want t' make Cookie mad," I said as we mounted.

Cold mornin's like that day, horses had t' get their kinks out an' there was a bit of crow hoppin' an' buckin' afore they lined out in a lope. When they were warmed up after a ways, we slowed them to a walk. Sure enough, a goodly number were back in th' snow. Especially th' blacks. Snow had a special attraction for them, coming from hot and dry Mexico where they had never seen it.

Midafternoon, Bob and th' Old Man rode out with two other

men. One of them was a buyer looking for fall feeders and the other was obviously his black "boy."

Wayback's eyes flashed lightning and he fumed. "Don't that nigger know he's been freed? He don't have t' kowtow t' anyone, jis be his own man."

"Maybe he likes it, gets paid good," I said.

"Like hell. He don't git nothin' but hand-me-downs an' crumbs. Look how he's dressed."

Wayback was getting madder and madder and when his hand started restin' on his gun, I distracted him by letting a couple o' those black steers get away and start back up th' mountain on the run. By th' time we had them back, Boss and buyer were far down th' mountain headin' for th' ranch, that black "boy" trailing behind. Wayback stared at them for a long time. Leapin' had t' distract him or I think he would have followed them.

After supper we were sittin' around th' stove, nothing but th' fire lightin' th' room, and I asked Tom, "Which one of them two would you have shot this afternoon?"

Wayback looked sharp at me, then grinned. "Don't know, Zee, might o' shot 'em both, th' buyer for treatin' a man that-away an' th' other for *lettin'* 'im!" He thought a moment, "Maybe I woulda shot th' buyer first t' see what th' 'boy' would do. If he carried on over th' man, I might have shot him too. If he danced a jig an' shouted, I'da let him go."

"Bein' someone's 'boy' might be better than starving," Jones said.

"No it would not!" Wayback's eyes flashed and we were quiet for a minute or two until he cooled off. He grinned and all we could see was his eyes and teeth in th' dark. "I shore git worked up 'bout that, don't I? Guess it's mostly b'cause I know what slavery is about, havin' been there myself."

All was quiet for a moment. Bob knew a story was coming

and threw another stick of wood in th' stove. We listened to th' tick-tick of metal heating up as th' fire caught.

"You all knows I was a sailor once, come 'round th' ho'n an' up th' coast. We sailed to th' Sandwich Islands and bought sugar and such and traded it up an' down th' coast from th' mouth o' th' Columbia t' San Diego. You know I jumped ship an' ended up here, but you don't know what I did afore that." He paused for a long moment, then took a long shaky breath. "Well, I'm gonna tell you!"

It was one o' those moments you always remember for th' stillness of it. Even th' ticking of that stove slowed and faded. I don't think anyone was breathin', I sure wasn't. Back then and especially in New Mexico, no one talked much about their past except to those that already knew it. There were a lot of folks who went by another name in another life and you risked harm askin' personal questions. Name changing was all too common, especially among Texians who felt moved t' leave their state for one reason or another. For Tom Washington to tell his past was extraordinary.

I wuz bawned in Rockin'ham, Richmond County, Nawth Car'lina. Mah Pa was named Jacob an' Mammy was Easter an' my name wuz Josh. We b'longed to John T. Chandler an' all us slaves wuz Chandlers 'cept'n my Granny, Lovey Wall. I had eight bruders an' sistas. We wuz field hans wukin' in de cotton.

I started and looked to see who was talking in that high-pitched singsong voice. It was Wayback using that language of those darkies I had first heard on th' docks at Fort Osage. Tom bowed an' shook his head. For th' first time I noticed he had taken off his hat and his bald spot shone in th' firelight.

Marster John wuz a b-a-a-d man, yassa. He near starved us t' death if he didn' wuk us t' death fust. Ef yous didn' wuk yo quota, yo got da whip. Mah Pappy wuz whupped four times an' us kids got it too, even little Louisa, hardly six year old. They wasn't any holidays, we wukd *all* de time. Weren' 'lowed t' go t' church or meet t' sing an' pray. Ef Marster finds you readin' or writin' ya gets lashes an' sold. Brudder Soloman got sent t' th' salt mines an' brudder Luke looked atter th' sheep.

All we had t' eat, we growed. We's in de fields early an' started wuk soon's we could see an' wuked til slap-up dark. Den we got t' wuk our garden 'cause all we got t' eat we growed. We killed da swamp hogs too, an' Pappy caught rabbits, coons, an' possums for meat. Mammy put possum grease on Pappy's back atter he been whupped.

One day he was wukin', clearin' for a new field, when he seed a rabbit run in da hollow end ob a log. Quick as a wink he stuffed his coat in de hole an' he wuked all day in de cold widout it. Nightime come an' Pappy carried dat log home happy es can be, but when he pulled out his coat de rabbit 'us gone. Somebody hed stoled it. Nights we walked about an' stole what we could eat.

We got one pair o' shoes a year an' when dey was gone we went barefoot. Mah feet would crack open an' bleed in de winter-times.

Miz Emma Chandler wuz nice, but Marster John wuz th' very nick. Dey lived in town an' kep' da wuk mules dere. They weren' many, Marster had plenty o' two-legged black mules. He would take what we had an' 'lowance it back to us. Pappy went to Marster Steven, Marster John's brudder, an' he made Marster John gib our meat back to us.

I don' know how big 'at plantation were er how many slaves run it. Dere wuz two colored overseers, Bob Chandler an' Charles Chandler. Bob overseed da field work an' Charles drove da carriage. He ud brag 'bout de places he been—Laurinburg an' Lumberton. Once he even drove clear t' Wilmington, bragged 'bout seein' da big ships an' sich.

De white folks hired patterollers to guard da roads an' streets agin us colored folks bein' out widout passes. Ef dey caught you, dey beat you afore takin' you t' Marster. Mos' likely you gets 'nudder beatin' fum him. De patterollers wuz white trash an' dey wuz plenty ob dem.

One summer, I chopped cotton wid a new darkie dey called Bammy. He uz 'bout my age an' we ud race t' see who got de end o' de row fust. When no one wuz 'roun', he ud sing dis song:

> When de sun come back
> When de firs' quail call,
> Den de time hes come
> Follow de drinkin' gou'd.
>
> De riva's bank am a very good road,
> De dead trees show de way,
> Lef foot, peg foot goin' on,
> Foller de drinkin' gou'd.
>
> De riva end a-tween two hills,
> Foller de drinkin' gou'd;
> 'Nuther riva on de other side,
> Follers de drinkin' gou'd.
>
> Wha de little riva
> Meet de grea' big un,
> De ole man waits . . .
> Foller de drinkin' gou'd.

Atter ever' verse he'd sing dis chorus:

Foller de drinkin' gou'd,
Foller de drinkin' gou'd;
Fer de ole man say,
Foller de drinkin' gou'd.

One day I ax him, "Bammy, what dat song you sings?"

"Why, don' you know?" he's so s'prised he drap his hoe.

"No I don' know, why don' you tell me?"

"Well, marster, its all 'bout runnin' 'way t' Canady."

"Whar's Canady?"

"It be a country 'way up nawth under th' drinkin' gou'd thet don' have no slaves an' de bounty men cain' git dem dat goes dere, nudder."

"You follers a drinkin' gou'd? Dat gou'd done walkin'?"

"No, no, I d'clair youse de dumbest nigger I ever see. Looky up in de sky in de night an' see a drinkin' gou'd in de stars up nawth. Dat's de way to Canady."

"How you learn dis t'ing?" I axes.

Jus' den Bob he sing out, "Josh, Bammy stop dat jawin' an' git busy wid dem hoes er Ise gonna use dis whip!"

Atter a few moments whin Bob not lookin', I whispers, "I asks *agin,* how you learn dis t'ing?"

"De Peg Leg Joe tol' me."

"Who dat?"

"Peg Leg Joe? He a one-legged white sailor come to Mobile wurking on de plantations as a ca'penter. He talk to de black folks 'bout runnin' 'way t' Canady by follerin' de drinkin' gou'd an' marks he put on dead trees an' things o' a left foot an' a peg right foot. He'd meet you at de big riva an' take you to Canady safe an' free."

"Bammy, nex' time I says it you an' Josh gets five licks!" Bob calls.

Dat ended our jawin' fer a while. Bammy goes t' hummin da

tune an' de wurds keep goin' t'rough my min'. I allus wuz t'inkin 'bout runnin' 'way, but de on'y place I knowed t' go wuz de swamps an' dat mos' es bad es de plantation, what wid de 'skeeters an' fevers an' bounty men chasin' you all de time. I never heard o' dis Canady. When we finish dat row an' walkin to de nex' empty un, I ax Bammy, "How fur?"

"How fur whut?"

"How fur t' Canady?"

"*I* don' know, neber been dere!"

"How fur you t'ink it are?"

"Peg Leg Joe say it many days, say stay by de riva, hide in de canes, don' steal food er anyt'ing er dey know you dere an' send de paddyrollers or bounty men atter you. He say sometime people leaves food an' sich in de canes fer you, but don' 'spect much."

We starts 'nudder row an' Bob, he see our face, dat end any talkin', but I'm a t'inkin' all 'long. Ever' chanct he git, Bammy sing dat song, near drive me crazy so's one day I gits me a new hoein' partner. She be purtier dan dat Bammy too.

De more I t'ink 'bout it, de more I wants t' go t' Canady. Winter come an' it's cold. My bare feets crack an' bleed an' I don' t'ink de nawth country good idea ef its colder dan dis. Comes t' me I don' wan' t' go nawth, I don' wan' t' go t' de swamps, I jis wan' t' go. But where?

Dat Charles, he allus talking big 'bout where he go, Lumberton, Bennetsville, Wilmington. Mebbe I could git t' Wilmington an' git on one o' dem boats dat sails away.

Goin'. All I t'inks 'bout. Comes spring an' de cotton plantin'. Soons we gits de plantin' done, comes de hoein'. I have de same partner I ends wid last year an' she's a sweet t'ing, growin' up an' blossomin' into a real woman. It seem Bob take a special interest in us an' gittin' our quota done. He keep raisin' it til we can' make it, den he whip me good. When he finish, he grab my partner an' starts draggin' her to de woods.

We all knows whut t' come. Soon's he's outta sight, I grabs my hoe an' follers. It's not hard t' find dem, she's hollerin' an' cryin'. Bob's on top o' her rippin' at her clothes an' I breaks th' hoe over his head. He grabs for th' whip, but I beat him to it an' I b'gin whippin' him good. I give him two stripes fer ever' stripe he give Pappy an' when I'm done he one bloody mess, ther's not a rag on him.

Young girl, she gone an' whin I looks, she hoein' by her mammy. All de niggers hoein' jis lak nothin' happen. Bammy go t' singin' dat song out loud an' I knows it meant fer me. I has t' go now er gits kilt, eder by Bob er Marster John.

Quick es a deer, I runs fer de swamps at de edge o' de field. I runs right down th' rows where all de tracks is an' whin I gets to de en', I makes a big leap into de bushes so no one sees my tracks. I looks bak an' dat sweet girl an' her mammy hoein' de row I jis come down, wipin' out all my tracks. Dats de las I evah see ob her . . . still see her hoein' dat row . . .

Tom paused and the track of a tear on his cheek reflected in the light. After a moment, he continued.

Dere I wuz barefoot in de swamp briars an' vines, not a t'ing but my shirt on my back an' dat ol' black snake of a whip in my hans. I runs an' wades fer d' riva, knockin' cottonmout's out'n de way in de water an' copperheds on de high groun'. I near cross de riva not knowin' it till I feel de current pullin'. Ise out o' breath an' sweatin' an' dat black wata she sho feel good, so I's lay in it an' let dat lazy current take me. Don' know how long I floated lak dat, when I comes to myself it be late afternoon an' I ain' put much room atween me an' dat plantation. I gets t' t'inkin 'bout whut Bammy sing; "De riva's bank am a very good road." Ise on a riva dat got no bank, but it am a road, on'y it don' foller de drinkin' gou'd. Still it go to de ocean somewhere an' dat's where Ise aimin' for.

Ob a sudden, I 'members de Charlotte road crossin' ob de riva an' knows dey be watchin' dere fo' me. I crawls under de brush an' sits real still waitin' fo' dahk, on'y Ise 'fraid de snakes be out in de dark an' Ise not wantin' t' meet up wid dem. Near dahk, but 'fore I cain' see no snakes, I grabs a old log an' pushes it out in de wata. I got my hed cobered wid brush an' dat black snake tied roun' de log fer a handle.

I cain' go faster dan de current er de watchas'll know sompin's wrong, so here we are jis floatin' easy down de riva. I hears a little sound an' purty soon a big bullfrog clim's up on de log an' sits. Dey beginning t' sing on de banks an' dat frog he b'gin t' sing too. De bridge come into sight an' I dares not look fer showin' myself. I don' know ef dere's a watcha er not.

I don' t'ink I takes a breaf de whole time I see dat bridge. Atter I passes under, de back o' my neck get all crawly an' I knows someone a-watchin' me, but nothin' happen. Dat frog he keep on a singin', cussin' dose frogs he passin' by an' darin' 'em t' do anyt'ing 'bout it. De trees come back to de edge o' de bank an' arch ova de riva lak a tunnel an' it black es sin in dere. A ways into it I hears dat song bein' hummed soft an' low an' I sees a candle shinin' on de bank an' I knows it's Bammy. I moves ober by de bank an' dere sits Bammy an' sista Louisa cane pole fishin', da candle in a bucket turned on its side so's it on'y shine on de riva. Dat ol' bullfrog jump off kerplash an' when I stan's up, Louisa give a squeak an' drop her pole. She hide b'hind Bammy an' he laughin' at her.

"Hi dere, Josh, when you start growin leaves out'n yo' hed?"

"I fo'got."

Louisa come an' hug me tight, she not want'n t' turn loose. "We t'ot you mite be comin' dis away an' brought you some t'ings," Bammy said. He han' me a poke an' I smelt biled goobers.

"Pappy sent you dis choppin' axe." Louisa han' me a hatchet. It was fresh sharpened. "Mammy sen' you some clothes, too." Dere wuz a lak new shirt an' pants I knowed come off'n de clothes line back o' Marster's wash house. He had a boy jist some bigger'n me an' I knowed someone lef dem on de line after dark jist so's dey could come t' me.

"No one hes missed you yit, dey's all out looking fer Bob an' no one's seed him. Marster's sayin' he don' run 'way, but de paddyrollers is swarmin'. I don' know how you got by dat bridge."

"Is Bob ded?" I asked.

"Not las' time I looked, but he ain' no shape t' move about. He one mess an' da flies done blowed 'im."

"Why you bring Louisa, yo knows dey beat her too, dey catch you!"

"She mak sich a fus me an' Mark has t' bring her er not come, He's bak at der road watchin'. She be safe down here by de riber wid me, dem paddyrollers scairt o' da snakes."

"Patterollers," I corrected. Some niggers jist can' talk right.

"Any ways, dem *paddy* rollers ain' gonna be out long, de voodoo owls am a-singin' an' dey's scairt ob dem. Say, dat Bob's snake yo got dere?"

"Let me hab it an' I'll put dem on Bob's trail, sure."

"I needs it t' hep me git away."

"Den gib me a piece ob it."

I takes de hatchet an' cut off some o' da tails an' gib dem to Bammy.

"That be 'nough, dey'll be huntin' da Fay'ville road for him come mawnin'."

"I got t' be goin'," I said an' dat set Louisa t' bawlin'. She hung on me lak a cocklebur.

"Hush, chile, yo'll hev ever patteroller in th' country down on us. I wants yo t' go back an' take care ob Mammy an' Pappy,

dey be in a mite o' trouble whin de Mars. see's I's gone. Don'
you let dem beat Pappy, hear?"

Louisa nodded. I could see tears drippin' off'n her cheeks an'
her nose wuz runnin' down on her lip. I kissed her an' set her
down by Bammy.

"Take dis bucket an' candle. Dere's a flint an' steel in de
poke. Go down a ways an' make a raft. Yo'll jist hafta go where
dis riva road takes ya. I gots ta go if'n dere's som'in' gonna happen on da Fay'ville road t'night!"

"Ok, Bammy take good care ob Louisa an' don' git into
trouble yosef."

I listen t' dem go an' pick up da bucket. Dey hed lef' da
canes an' I took one an' lef' da udder one fer dem. Wid da
fishin' pole tied under da log an' da bucket tied alongside, I
pushed off an' floated down da riva. Somewheres 'long da
Fay'ville road a pattyroller was gonna git it an' soon dey might
be looking fer his killer—an' dat jis might be me.

Come mawnin', I push in to de bank where I knowed da
woods wuz deep an' curled up on da sand an' slept. Skeeters
kep' wakin' me up an' da sun wuz high when I fin'lly gets up. I
ate a handful ob goobers an' started looking for logs. Dey wuz
on'y two near dere an' I tied dem onter my log. As I floated
down de riva, I pulled more logs out'n de bushes an' soon had
a raft tied t'gether wit dat unraveled black snake whip. I could
sit on it an' stay dry an' wid a long pole keep da raft movin' at a
good pace.

Da on'y place I was scairt ob gettin' caught was where da
road crossed d' riber atween Cheraw an' Wallace, but I got by
an' moved on. Sometime I lose da channel an' hed t' pole
'round an' find it agin, but I didn' feel in no rush knowin' da
news ob my runaway had passed by me an' mebbe da longer I
stayed on da riber da less likely folks ud connect me wid da
Chandler runaway. Fo' sure I hed t' change my name, so I

names myself atter Thomas Jefferson an' George Washington an' b'come Tom Washington.

I neber saw any cricks jine da riber, it jist kep' gittin' bigger an' da cypress swamps wider. On'y place dey got narrow wuz where de fields hed been cleared down close to da water. Da little village o' Pee Dee wuz right on da riber, but I passed in da night an' nobody seed me. Down below where da Little Pee Dee ran into th' Big Pee Dee, dey call da riber Great Pee Dee. It were more open an' I had t' hide daytimes an' move at night. Ob a sudden da wata 'us salty an' I suffered for drinkin' wata. Da riber flowed through a plantation called Brookgreen an' I got some food an' fresh wata from some ob da slaves workin' da fields close to da riber. Dey uz da fust persons I hed talked to, an' dey sho did soun' funny, not lak we talked at Chandler Plantation.

Not long atter dat, da riber opened up into a bay an' I hed t' leave my raft. I wuz on da ocean side so I walked t'rough da piney woods an' brush to da beach. Dere wuz boats 'way out on da wata, but none close 'cep' little fishin' boats that wuz goin' nowheres I wanted t' go, so I walked da beach south knowin' I would find da mouth o' da bay where da Pee Dee flowed into da ocean. Gradually da land come to a point an' I looked 'cross da wide mouth ob da bay. I wuz at a dead end wid nothin' lef' t' do but fish an' watch. On da second mornin' I seed sails o' a big boat comin' down da bay. Dere wuz a breeze comin' off da lan' an' da tide wuz goin out, but I didn' know nothin' 'bout tides den.

Da bay looked t' be 'bout a mile wide dere an' I figgered if da ship come down da middle, I'd have only 'bout a half mile t' swim t' git to it, so judgin' her speed, I times myself so I could be dere ahead o' da boat an' dey would pick me up. I hadn't reckoned on da current bein' so strong an' it pushed me out toward dat ocean. Da ship was veerin 'way from me an' da waves was gittin' bigger an' I had t' swim hard t' git to her. I wuz shore played out when it got to me. Dey was a man in da front t'rowin' out a line wid a weight on it an' callin' out numbers. As da ship passed by, I grabbed da rope an' wrapped it 'round my arm. It jist pulled me along a ways 'til da man seed me an' called for he'p. Dey hauled me up swingin' on my arm an' I t'ought dey'd pull it out by da roots afore I got on da deck. Ise so played out I jis' laid dere a while, dose sailors crowdin' 'roun' me axin' a hun'erd questions.

Soon dis man dressed up come up an' da men back up. "Who are you and what were you doing out in the ocean like that?"

I figgered he wuz da captain ob da ship an' I sits up smart an' says, "I come t' git a job on dis here ship, Marster."

"Well, I'll be damned," said Marster Captain.

"Now I'm gonna stop right here and say that all people know about sailor language and how rough it is. Though Wayback quoted all th' profanity spoken as he remembered it, I will not repeat it here out of respect for our readers and mothers and fathers that might not let their children read it otherwise," Zenas said. It was consistent with his policy about the balance of the stories he told.

Tom paused for a moment and we could hear th' slow tick-tick of th' stove cooling down. Bob stirred and walked to th' door. "Boys, I see by th' drinkin' gou'd that it's past midnight an' if we got t' bed right now, we would barely get four hours' sleep afore Cookie called breakfast. What say we hit th' hay an' let Wayback finish his story tomorrow night?"

There was reluctant general agreement to that and Leapin' Lon kicked Rip's chair. "Wake up an' git t' bed, Wayback's finished fer th' night."

"I ain't asleep an' I heard same as you. Kick my chair agin an' I'll hafta give you some comeuppance yore pa missed."

"My pa never missed a lick at that an' if you think you need to, come on ahead, ol' man."

There weren't five years between, but Lon never missed th' chance t' point out Rip was older. Someone banked th' fire an' I was in bed b'fore he was done. I lay there a few minutes an' thought about th' tale Wayback had told. We grew up at th' same time, but what a difference in our lives! I couldn't imagine bein' born into slavery. It was such a cruel thing and I have never understood the minds of those who practiced it whether it be white men on a plantation or pirates on a river or Mexicans with Indians—or Indians with Mexicans, for that matter.

I drifted off t' dream about slaves and frogs and black water with snakes. Cookie's call came way too early.

"I swear, I been rollin' things 'round in my head all day an' still cain't fathom all that this here Josh Chandler said las' night," Jones said, "What's a 'paddyroller' eney way?"

"Don't you know?" I asked.

"*No* I don't know an' I bet *you* don't either."

"Do too."

"What is it, then?"

I waited til he was near t' bustin an' said, "It's a patterroller!"

Jones's quirt hit my horse's rump, "Go git that steer out'n th' bresh an' earn yore keep, you scaliwag!"

Some of th' boys was from th' south an' knew well what Tom had said, but boys from th' north hadn't been exposed to it and it was just like a foreign language to them. My great-grandpa Sam Meeker grew up near plantations in Carolina an' Tennessee an' knew some about slaves. He said they came over from different parts of Africa an' spoke several different languages. When they talked, they used a blend of their language and English and many times they couldn't talk very well to slaves from other plantations.

He said there were lots of runaways livin' in th' woods and they moved down into Florida an' lived in th' Everglades with th' Seminoles. Some of the Cherokees bought and held slaves and brought them over th' Trail of Tears t' Arkansas and Kansas. They held them until well after th' war, claimin' they were their own nation an' immune t' USA laws. Eventually, it became too expensive t' keep them an' they were freed, some well into th' twentieth century. Then those slaves had t' fight t' be included into th' tribes as freedmen, though they had lived Indian for generations an' some of them couldn't speak English.

Talk was lively all over th' mountainside and at lunch, discussin' what that slave boy had told them and tryin' t' decipher what he had said. Eventually we began t' get it an' by night we thought we could listen and catch on without mulling it around half a day. Chores was done an' supper laid away in record time. It was some warmer and we left th' door open for fresh air. Tom sat next to th' door, leaned back on two chair legs, fanning himself with his hat.

Dishes stopped ratting in th' kitchen an' Manuel appeared at th' door wipin' his hands on his apron, "Señor Bob, who ees thees man Josh thee boys talk of? You hiring thee new man?" Manuel was concerned that he would have another mouth t' feed.

"No, Manuel, they were talking about a man Tom knew a long time ago. I'm not hiring a new man, too close to th' end of th' season fer that. Tom's fixin' t' finish his tale about this Josh, would you like t' listen?"

"Sí!" He disappeared and returned without his apron an' draggin a chair over to th' door propped up opposite Tom.

"One thing I want t' git straight right off," Les said, "what in th' world is a patteroller?"

"An don' say it's a paddyroller!" Jones put in, glaring at me.

"Lawse-a-mercy, patterollers is dem white trash da Marsters

hires dat goes up an' down da roads an' woods lookin' fo' colored folks not 'posed t' bee dere," Josh said. "On'yest da *dumbest* blacks calls dem *paddy*roller!"

The effect on Manuel was electric. He started, looked at Tom, his chair banging down on four legs. He scooted away down th' wall putting as much distance between him an' Tom as he could. "Sacre . . ." and he crossed himself.

" 'S ok, Manuel, Tom's jest purtendin' he's ol' Josh," Rip laughed.

"Paddyrollers . . . patterollers . . . pa-ter-roll-ers . . . pa-trollers! They was *patrolin'* th' roads!" Lon slapped his knee.

"Well, I'll be . . ." Rip's voice trailed off.

"Ise *tole* you plain, right off."

"How did you live in that swamp?" Bob asked.

"Oh I lives we-l-l dere, 'sepin' da blood Ise lost t' da skeeters. I swears I near got tired o' flounder an' catfish an' pan fish. It sho' were good t' git all I wanted t' eat. Ise near fat whin Ise out'n dere. Los' *all* dat fat swimmin' t' dat boat, I tells ya. While Ise layin' on dat deck dryin' out, dat captain he look at me mean an' say, 'You're a runaway, aren't you?'

" 'Naw-w sir, Ise a freedman, comed down here t' fin' mah dear ol' Mammy an' dem bounty men gets atter me an' takes my buggy an' ho'se an' mos' strips off'n all mah clothes. I on'y 'scaped by da skin ob my teeth. I wants t' git plum outta here an' yo' fine ship de fus' t'ing I see goin' away. Ise make a good sailer fo' yo.

" 'By golly, you're a good liar and damned if I won't help you! You can work off your fare helping Cookie down in the galley to start with. If you do good there, I might teach you to sail a boat.'

"A pale man in fancy clothes was watchin' all dis an' he say, 'You're not helping a runaway are you, Captain?' I knowed by his talk he a southern genelman.

" 'If you please, Mr. Sargent, I have the tide and a fair wind and I'm underway. I will not waste my time taking this man back to be whipped or worse. I need another hand an' the Good Lord may have just given him to me!'

"Wid dat de Captain he turn 'way. 'Lars, get that man some clothes and show him the galley. Tell cook he has a helper for the time being.'

"Dis man Lars gib me a han' up an' I takes a step or two an' my laigs cramps up sumpin' awful an' I falls down agin yellin'. Two ob da han's grabs me up an' one on each side heps me walk it off an' soon my legs feels better. Dat Lars, he come bak wid a pair o' duck pants an' a cotton shirt. I puts dem on rat dere an' *flings* dem raggedy clothes ober de side. My pants too big an' I has t' hol' dem up wid one han' all de time til someone han' me a piece of rope I can tie 'em on wid.

"Dey takes me down inter de belly ob dat ship an' to a kitchen, but dey calls it a galley. De cook he glad t' see me an' put me t' wuk rat off—an' I wuk, I tells ya. Dis cook, he an old sailor, talk funny lak a Englishman. His name wuz James Doughty an' he could tell s-o-m-e tales. Claim he some English captain's steward an' got in trouble whin he struck a orficer. They gonna hang him, but de captain let him 'scape in a Spanish harbor an' he swum to a USA ship. Dey take him on an' he 'ventually make his way here, to be a US citizen. He speak ver' proper English an' swear t' make me talk lak dat.

"Rat off he start teachin' me de 'King's English' he calls it. Sound lak a whole new lang'age an' I has trouble wid it. Ever' day he teach me sompin' new an' if'n I don' use it whin I talks, he gives me a whack. I swear I was sore fo' six months." Tom's voice changed from high whiny singsong to a mellow baritone, leaving one dialect behind an' taking up another.

Manuel squirmed uncomfortably.

"Before long I was speaking pure King's English and Mister

Doughty's not hitting me anymore.

"He told me all kinds of tales about his service in the British Navy, said it was the best in the world when he was in it. He was some kind of highfalutin servant to officers like ship's captains and such. His favorite was the last one he served, said that man became a lord admiral or something. They were always getting into scrapes and the captain would get them out.

"We sailed south down the coast and across to Haiti where the southern gentleman got off. I stayed shy of him, afraid he would try to take me back to Carolina and was glad to see him leave. Doughty said he was looking for slaves and *he* was glad to see him go. As soon as I could talk proper, that cook took it upon himself to teach me to read—and he did it with a passion. I sure learned quick, but if I wasn't quick enough I got a rap on the hand with a hickory spoon. He made me read every evening and the other sailors would come and listen when they had the time. We read mostly the Holy Bible and poem books from England. There was a new book written by Poe that he had me read. Some of those stories made me shudder and I didn't like them very much. The sailors loved them and asked for them when they could. I liked reading the Bible and Washington Irving most of all, though that headless horseman gave me chills.

"I told him about being a slave and he said serving in the Navy was not much different. They had press gangs that would take men right off the streets and put them on ships. Sometimes they didn't touch land for three or four years. The only difference between slaves and sailors was that the sailors got paid some.

"About halfway down South America, the captain put me on the deck and I learned to be a sailor. It was sure hot, but as we went further south it got colder and colder. Sometimes the rigging had ice on it and crackled underfoot. They gave us heavy clothes and I got a pair of shoes. It was stormy going around the horn and we were glad when we turned north in the open Pacific.

"Somewhere near the equator, James Doughty died. We buried him at sea and the captain made me the cook."

Tom was quiet for a moment, then said in the voice we were used t' hearing, "I think I've told you most o' th' rest o' my doin's—them's that are safe t' tell," he grinned.

"Señor Tom, hees back," Manuel exclaimed, "hee speak many language."

"Sí, and I knows a le-e-tle Mexican too," Tom chuckled.

"My grandmother and Uncle Jerry always said only those that have been in slavery know the full blessing of freedom," I said.

"I b'lieve they're right, Zee," Tom replied.

"Ya ever wonder what happened t' yore family, Tom?" I asked.

"Ever' day, Daylight, ever' day. I 'spose most of 'em air dead by now, maybe little Louisa's still living, but she's likely taken another name an' got children of her own. Would I go back there? No, I think not. I might have t' shoot that monster Chandler if'n he's still livin'."

Les spoke up, "Tom, I'm a southern boy, but my folks didn't have no truck with slavin'. I had t' leave before they pressed me into the Confederate army, and they was a lot o' folks thinkin' just like me. All southerners were not for seceding or goin' t' war agin their country."

"I joined up when the issues was states' rights, but when Lincoln published the Emancipation Proclamation an' the war became an issue of freedom or slavery, I lit out for the unknown. I seen too much of slavery t' fight t' preserve it," Bob said.

"That's when the Union made you a soldier an' sent you west t' fight Injuns?" Rip asked.

"*That* was some experience," Bob shook his head.

"States' rights weren't much o' a issue t' fight over," Rip

said, "lots o' northerners agreed with the rebels on that, but freeing slaves, *that* got folks up north enthused."

When people started talking' 'bout th' war, it usually got hot sooner or later, even in our bunch, and it was time t' change th' subject. "Bob, I heard th' Navajos're comin t' Mescelero next week t' race horses with th' 'Paches. Any chance the Boss'll let us off t' go see th' fun?" I asked.

"What you want t' go there for, Daylight, you're so tight you won't even bet on 'em," Jones said.

"Purty smart, I say, ef he's takin' tips from you!" Rip drawled.

"You sayin' I don't know good horseflesh?" Jones shot back.

"It ain't that you don't know good horseflesh, Jones, you just don't know *fast* horseflesh!" Tom laughed.

"I s'pose you do, huh?"

"I do ok for myself."

"Daylight, I'll ask Mr. Dearing tomorrow if he thinks we could get off a few days. Maybe we could all go up an' have a look, one last adventure b'fore we shut down for the winter," Bob said. "Do I have t' tuck you boys in ever' night? You don't git t' bed now, the whole bunch o' yuh'll be grouchy all day tomorrow."

"We went to th' races at Mescelero and I won twenty-five dollars from Jones on one race. Wayback was right, Jones didn't know fast horseflesh!" Zenas chuckled. "Tom stayed on with us at th' ranch several years until he got busted in a dust-up with one of those black bulls an' his horse. When he was able t' get around again, he went to Santa Fe an' got a job with th' AT&SF porterin'. Done good enough he finally married and settled down somewhere. I heard he was raisin' horses an' kids by th' dozen."

CHAPTER 24
LA CURANDERO

"James, do you know much about th' Spanish-American culture?"
Zenas asked me one day as I put my foot on the first step of the
porch.

"I know some, having lived around here most of my life," I replied.

"Know anything about curanderos?"

"Aren't they some kind of folk doctor?" I asked. I didn't say "faith
healer," for that held uncomplimentary connotations mostly reserved
for itinerate tent revivalists of questionable character.

"Yes, they're healers in th' community that use folk remedies t'
heal people. They's good ones an' bad ones, th' bad ones not lasting
in th' business long. Good ones are highly regarded and are only
consulted when th' old home remedies aren't working.

"The most famous one I ever heard of was a man named Pedrito
Jaramillo down on th' border in southeast Texas. He was very popular
and traveled up and down the Rio Grande healing people 'In the
name of God' as he would say. He died back in '07 but even now
when th' curanderos have a difficult case, they invoke Don Pedrito's
name with their treatments.

"Sophie has consulted one here a few times and I must say she has
enjoyed good health without much input from our Anglo doctors." He
chuckled, "Old Doc Hutto must o' been spinnin' in his grave!

"I'll tell you about a happenin' Mecio Sanchez had with a curan-
dero years ago."

★　★　★　★　★

You remember me talkin' 'bout Mecio an' his pa, Elfuego, runnin' a ranch on th' Rio Sacramento south o' th' Rafter outfit? They don't live there now, sold out and Mecio bought a little place over on th' Pecos by Artesia. He raises peppers an' has done quite well; says peppers is a lot safer than chousin' half-wild cows. I question th' *half* part o' that, but I guess he's tryin' t' be charitable to th' critters.

At any rate, this happened before he sold out on th' Sacramento an' Elfuego was still living. The old man was always active an' took part in runnin' th' ranch until th' last few years of his life when he spent most o' his time watchin' grandkids. Mecio an' his wife, Carlita, musta had just about one a year there for a while 'til they figgered out what caused them. I'd say they done all right by them, all of 'em turned out good except that youngest boy.

Somewhere 'long about 1900, well, I guess it was '03 t' be exact, th' old man started getting sickly. It got so that he was not able t' get out'n a chair without help an' Mecio d'cided it was time t' consult a doctor.

They made th' trip to Alamogordo and saw a doctor there who examined Elfuego and found nothing wrong with him except old age. As they were leaving th' office, Elfuego asked if they could go to La Luz to visit an' old friend. Mecio and Carlita had shopping t' do so they decided their oldest boy (I misplaced his name) could drive Elfuego to La Luz in th' wagon. Of course, the rest of their covey set up a howl when they saw th' pair driving off and there was a stampede down th' street t' catch up with that wagon. Two o' th' youngest would not have made it had th' wagon not stopped. Th' last mom and dad saw, th' wagon was disappearing in a cloud of dust, arms and legs swinging from every side.

It was one of those very rare moments when Mecio and Carlita were left to themselves and they thoroughly enjoyed the afternoon together. Late afternoon found them standing outside th' merchantile beside their bundles of purchases looking anxiously for the return of their wagon. At last it appeared to their great relief, but when it got close, they realized Elfuego was not in the wagon.

"Lucero (*that* was his name! Zenas said, slapping his knee), where is your grandfather?" Mecio asked.

"He had to stay in La Luz, Papa," a half-dozen voices answered; the following babble from a half-dozen voices told the details of the story, all quite unintelligible. Finally the confusion died as eager hands and curious eyes helped load bundles into the wagon while Lucero explained what had happened to Grandpa.

"Grandpa's friend, Señor Alejandro, took him to a curandero and he will have to stay there a while to be treated."

Mecio nodded slowly, thinkin' to himself, *The cost of some curanderos is high and the results are low.*

"It is all right, Papa," the soft voice of little Juanita, the second born, who was not so little by then, said. "Señor Alejandro says the curandero asks very little and only if Grandpa is cured."

"That is good to hear, dear one," Mecio said. Nita, as she was called, was the image of her mother and Mecio loved her dearly.

The trip home was very eventful, as it always is with such a crowd of children. They stayed that night by th' little stream out of Dog Canyon, the children playing in th' ruins of old Frenchie's orchard, climbing trees and rock walls, chasing lizards and creatures not used to seeing such as these humans. Frenchie's cabin had fallen into ruin and the children avoided it, remembering their father's story of how he had been found shot to death in th' doorway.

They tied their dog to th' wagon so he could warn if there

were intruders and slept peacefully through th' night. Morning found them passing the Lee ranch. No one seemed to be at home and they didn't stop. By th' time th' sun had set, they had reached home, kids still energetic and Mama and Papa worn out.

That same morning, Elfuego had returned to th' curandero to find out what his treatment was to be. The healer had spent th' evening before meditating on th' case and what a proper treatment should be.

The moment he saw him, he said to Elfuego, "There is a large log by the long hole of the Lost River. Every day at sunrise you must go there alone and sit on the log and meditate. Think of your life from as early as you can remember and all the things that have happened up until the present. Mornings stay only one hour, but at sunset you are to sit on that log and meditate. Do not leave until it is quite dark. If you start this evening and do this faithfully for ten days, you will be healed."

So it was that evening found our friend sitting on that log, watching leaves drift down on that long pool of water, th' last pool before sinking into th' sands of th' basin. He had some time reaching into his mind for th' first memories of his youth and he actually had to start at a point he remembered and work backward until his memories faded. It was fascinating to him, th' things he could remember if he put his mind to it and he was surprised when he realized suddenly that it was pitch black.

All th' houses he passed were dark, only dogs fussing at his intrusion. Alejandro had left a candle burning in his room so he was guided to it without disturbing others. He was tired and slept soundly until shaken awake at dawn,

"Time to go, my friend," Alejandro said softly.

His wife handed Elfuego a soft taco filled with meat and chili as he left. The log and peaceful pool were just as he had left them and he settled down, taking up his thoughts where he had left them. He was just getting to th' time his mother had given him his first shirt, really a gown that reached to his knees, when he heard a little cry of dismay behind him.

Turning, he saw a lady near his age standing there, her reboso pulled over her head, one hand holding the hem covering her face to the eyes.

"You must leave," she said, "Don Curandero has told me to sit on that log and it is not proper that you should be here alone with me."

"B-but Don Curandero has prescribed the same for me," Elfuego stuttered, well aware of th' impropriety of the situation.

"Surely you have found the wrong place," she said.

"Perhaps it may be that *you* did not understand." Elfuego was sure he had followed his directions correctly.

"I understood perfectly and this is the place he told me to go."

"I-I don't understand, he knows that it is forbidden," he said, meaning that a man or woman of their culture must not be seen alone with strangers of th' opposite gender.

"Neither do I, but I shall find out now!" She turned to go.

A thought occurred to Elfuego and he called, "Wait!" She turned back to him and he asked, "Is it possible, Señorita, that you are a widow?"

"Yes, I am," she said, indicating with her free hand the black dress, which didn't necessarily indicate widowhood since most ladies her age wore black regardless of their marital status.

"I too am a widower; would it be improper for two such as we are to sit on the ends of this log and obey Don Curandero?"

She hesitated a moment, thinking. Would it seem improper if they were observed each sitting at opposite ends of a twenty-foot log? "I do not know . . ."

"Is there only one long pool and only one log?" he asked

sincerely, not knowing.

"You are not from here?"

"I have been away a long time and this is the only one I remember."

"This is the only long pool."

"Then Don Curandero must have known it would be proper for us to be here at the same time."

"I-I suppose . . ."

"Then I shall take that end of the log and you may sit here where the sun shines and it is warm."

With that, Elfuego strode to the opposite end of the log and sat down. He was returning to his thoughts when, out of the corner of his eye, he saw the lady sit down on th' very extreme end of th' log, her back to him. *Let her be,* he thought.

As it warmed it became uncomfortable for the widow to sit in th' sun in her black clothes and she timidly scooted over into the shade. Soon the hour was up and she was about to rise when she noticed that he had risen to leave. She sat until he had time to get to th' road, then she too rose and left. She followed him up the road and noticed he turned into Alejandro's yard. Her home was further along and she hurried by, not looking right or left.

Evening came and all was quiet when she passed Alejandro's house, but she was dismayed to find that stranger sitting at the long pool. When he saw her, he rose without a word and moved to his end of the log.

Presently, he heard a rustle and saw a glint of light. The lady had a candle lantern and it gleamed on the ground ahead of her as she left. He sat a moment longer until he got to a stopping place in his memories. He had gotten his first pair of pants and th' time he had fallen from th' ridgepole of th' little henhouse and busted his knee was a good place to leave his memories. He had torn his new pants and still carried the scar of that event.

He followed the faint glow of th' lantern until it passed Alejandro's.

Gradually th' two got used to their routine and each other. Eventually they would begin walking together to and from th' pool and they were the talk of that little village. Some thought it was a scandal and others smiled at th' wisdom of Don Curandero. The two had grown up in the village and though they were some years apart, they shared common memories of life back then. Elfuego walked with a new spring in his step and his eyes were bright. Maria Martinez, for that was her name, was cheerful and happy. She even wore a brightly colored reboso to th' river.

The ten days prescribed for Elfuego expired, but still he stayed on, making his daily trips to th' log with Maria. Her time of healing had also expired and she was sure she was fully cured, but she didn't mention it to Elfuego. The last Sunday of each month was th' day the priest from Tularosa said Mass at th' little La Luz chapel. It was there that Elfuego and Maria were wed. It was a simple ceremony after Mass, but word had spread that it was to be and th' celebration that evening was long and joyous, as those events should be.

A vaquero rode into Mecio's yard one day and handed him a note from his father. He would be at Paxton Siding the next Monday morning, would he please meet him with the wagon? Mecio was puzzled, for his father much preferred a horse to being jostled in a wagon. He must be in bad shape not to want his horse. Early Monday morning the son and Nita were at the siding with th' wagon bedded in straw and blankets for th' ailing Father.

They saw smoke from th' engine long before they heard its whistle and even then it came as an echo off the eastern mountains, as though that were th' direction it was coming from. It was unusual that it would pull into the siding and Mecio wondered what it meant. Was his father that ill?

The porter descended and set his little stool before th' passenger car door. A man hopped down and turned to help a lady down th' steps. It was Nita who recognized her grandfather first and she ran to him, throwing her arms around him in a big happy hug. Mecio reached them just in time t' hear his father introduce the strange woman. "Juanita and Mecio, this is my wife, Maria Sanchez."

There was a moment of shocked silence, then Nita said, "Oh, Papa, have you gotten us a grandmother?"

Elfuego and Maria laughed, the lady blushing prettily, "Yes, I have!" he said brightly, giving Maria a hug, which only served to fluster her more.

Mecio bowed low to the lady and said, "I am so glad to meet you, Señorita. Welcome," he stammered.

A boxcar door slid open and porter and conductor were unloading boxes on th' little dock. Elfuego said, "We have brought her things; that is why we needed the wagon."

By the time they had all th' boxes loaded, there was little room in th' wagon. Elfuego insisted on driving and Nita sat between him and Maria chattering happily. Mecio was content to sit on the tailgate and ponder the events taking place. Their chatter and laughter told him that his father was indeed much more his old self, and this made him smile.

They drove into th' ranch late in the afternoon, the horses tired from th' long pull up th' valley. A swarm of children descended on th' wagon, only to stop and stare at th' stranger sitting there. Carlita came to th' door wiping her hands on her apron. When she saw Maria, she quickly turned back and a few moments reappeared without apron and her hair freshly brushed. Elfuego had hopped down and hurried around th' wagon to hand Maria down. He held her longer than necessary, renewing th' blush to her cheeks. Turning to Carlita, he introduced Maria. Carlita caught her breath, then composing herself embraced Maria. "Welcome, Mother, to our home!" she said, though her mind was racing to fathom where in the world they would find room for another in that crowded little house.

Little Nita grabbed Maria's hand and turned her to the children standing shyly and, for a very rare moment, quietly. "This is our new grandmother, Mama Maria," she exclaimed grandly and started naming each child to Maria. "That is Lucero unhitching the horses, he's the oldest—I'm next oldest—this is Tomas, and that is Pedro, Simona, and this is little Diego," she said, patting the toddler's head as he peeked from behind his sister's skirt.

So far, Maria had hardly had room to say a word and she didn't get to for some time as those excited children gathered around her telling her all the important things about their ranch, like where their chickens stayed, the names of th' calf and goats, where th' olla and dipper hung and where each child slept.

Pedro tugged at Maria's hand. "Where are you going to sleep, Mama Maria?" As she opened her mouth to answer, Simona grabbed her arm and cried, "You can sleep with me, Mama, I have the best place to sleep."

At that moment, their mother came to Maria's rescue, "Nita, you and Simona go set the table; Tomas, draw a fresh bucket of water for the house, then water the horses; Pedro help your big brother with the horses."

Elfuego took advantage of these distractions and led Maria to th' side of th' house. There under the cottonwoods was the beginnings of an adobe building. "We were building a room for the boys to sleep in since the house was so full, but now I think we will have to build more so we can live here and you can have your own kitchen."

"Oh, but that might disappoint the boys," Maria exclaimed.

"They sleep outside most of the time anyway, so they would only sleep inside in the worst weather."

"Perhaps they can have this and we could find a suitable place somewhere else."

"We will see." Elfuego patted her hand.

Eventually, the children got th' important things said that a grandmother needed to know and Maria was able to talk. She told of her life in th' village and about the curandero's prescription for her sadness. She and Elfuego told of their meeting and treatments that soon turned into courtship and about their marriage and th' celebration following. Maria had no kin in La Luz but there were many dear friends and Elfuego had become reacquainted with old friends so that they intended t' spend time there as work on th' ranch allowed.

Mecio smiled to himself since the bulk if not all the ranch work had fallen on his shoulders in the past year or two. The thought occurred to him that maybe now Elfuego would take more interest in the ranch. He certainly was a changed man since his visit to the curandero.

We will see, he almost said out loud.

Supper was late and th' family still stayed up past their usual bedtime. Carlita insisted that Maria and Elfuego take their bed.

"Please do," Mecio said. "We still have the bedding in the wagon and Carlita and I will enjoy sleeping under the stars tonight." Other thoughts were stirring at the prospect of a rare night with Carlita alone.

Soon th' house was dark and Carlita was snuggled close. They listened to th' chatter of th' children as they talked among themselves and to Maria and Elfuego. Finally, they heard Maria telling the children a story and all was quiet. Her voice faded away and silence prevailed.

"Do you like her?" Carlita whispered.

"Yes, I think I do, she seems like a very sweet person and the children took to her right away. That's a good sign." He chuckled, "That's the first time I have ever heard of a curandero prescribing a woman to cure an illness. It may be that I'll have to consult him one of these days."

There was a sharp slap on his bare chest. "*I* will cure you and you won't have to consult with any doctors for the treatment!" They both tried—partially successfully—to suppress their laughter; Carlita pulled the cover over their heads and they laughed more.

Eventually, the labors and events of the day overcame and they were just drifting off into sweet sleep when they heard the patter of feet running to th' wagon. The tongue creaked under an unexpected weight and there were grunts and thumps as the creature fell into the wagon bed between th' dash and the seat. With more grunts, he righted himself and a little round head peered over th' back of th' seat, silhouetted by a million stars.

"Mama, are you there?" Diego asked anxiously in a voice louder than necessary.

"No," Mecio said in a deep gruff voice, "I am a big black bear . . ." He didn't finish for th' boy tumbled onto his chest and face.

"Me can't sleep, Mama," th' boy said ignoring his father and struggling to get under th' covers.

"You wipe your feet before you get in this bed," the mama demanded.

There was the sound of feet hastily rubbing on the top of the quilts and Carlita gave a sigh of resignation. Mecio chuckled and received a kick on his shin. All the tumult had covered sounds of another approaching the wagon and suddenly a head peeked over the side.

"Mama, I'm cold, Nita took all the covers."

"Come on down, Simona, and Papa will get you warm."

So four slept in that narrow wagon bed that night, Mecio and

Carlita back to back in th' middle and two wiggling kicking tots on th' outsides. Those two adults arose early in th' predawn, sore of ribs and legs, and left two tots sleeping th' sleep of angels.

In the days that followed, they finished th' bunkhouse and Elfuego and Maria moved in. That fall, Elfuego and Maria rode up to the curandero's house leading a pretty dun colt with white forelegs and blaze. It was ample pay for the curandero, insufficient in th' minds of Elfuego and Maria, but it was th' best they could do.

Maria had found a pretty site above the river where through the winter a three-room house rose and in the spring Maria and Elfuego relinquished the bunkhouse to th' boys for a home of their own. They spent th' rest of their days there and th' family lived in harmony, th' path between those two houses wearing wide and deep.

"Now I've told you that tale to tell you this one," Zenas said.

He looked out over the basin speckled with cloud shadows and sunshine. "There's many a man left his bones layin' out there. Two we know of, a boy of seven or eight and his father. (*This in reference to A. J. Fountain and his son, whose bloodstained buggy was found, but no other trace of them ever found, though some still searched in vain.* [JD]) They shoulda put Pat Garrett's bones there too, though I guess th' cemetery at Las Cruces is fitting. Ol' Van's over there at Aguirre Springs. Ma an' I have our names on a plot at Pinetop, but I would prefer t' be buried right here where folks as come t' visit can look out over that basin. Th' view's never th' same, is it? Always changin'."

After a long pause, he continued, "I've been havin' some pains in my chest lately and Sophie insisted on takin' me to a doctor, only she took me to her curandero instead. Well, he didn't look me over much, just held his hand over my heart a moment, then he looked at Sophie and said, 'La pala y azadon.' That's all. Now we both knew what that meant and right there that man lost money. He didn't treat me and he didn't heal me and for sure I didn't pay him! It upset Sophie some, but I laughed. It ain't a hard diagnosis t' say a ninety-three-year-old man's gonna die."

CHAPTER 25
EPILOGUE

It is sufficient to say that it was several years before the curandero's "shovel and hoe" were required. In the meantime, we sat on his porch and I wrote down his recollections as they appear here. Zenas continued active and healthy, refusing to leave his little place for more comfortable living closer to town and to the doctor.

He died peacefully in his rocker on that front porch, looking out over the basin and its white sands. When Sophia found him, she said there was a smile on his face. She said he had no complaints except for occasional little flashes of white in the corners of his eyes.

Zenas had asked me to write his obituary and keep it so it could be placed in the paper quickly. The morning after he died, I got a call from his oldest son with the news and requesting me to give the obituary to the papers, which I was glad to do. This is the obituary as Zenas wished it written. All I had to do was to fill in the dates and details in italics:

Zenas Leonard Meeker died peacefully *at his home on Culp Mountain September 2, 1940.* He is survived by his wife of *63 years* Sophia Gomez Meeker of the home, one daughter, Amira Bonds of Alamagordo, two sons, Jesse and Samuel of rural Pinetop, ten grandchildren *and two great-grandchildren.*

He was born September 3, 1844 on Osage Creek,

Carroll County, Arkansas, son of Jesse and Amira Dread-fulwater Meeker. He is preceded in death by his mother and father, two brothers John and Jacob, and two sisters, Parlee and Luzina.

Zenas was named after renowned mountain man and benefactor, Zenas Leonard, of Fort Osage, Missouri. He led an eventful life as hunter and trader at Bent's Fort, Fort Union, and old Rayado. He was drover on the Santa Fe Trail for Bent, St Vrain & Co. He was involved in the earliest ranching in the territory working first for William Bent on his Purgatory Ranch in Colorado. For a time, he ran a herd on the range east of Las Vegas. His first work in this area was for pioneer rancher John Dearing on the old Rafter JD on the Sacramento River. For several years he was foreman of the ranch until he purchased a ranch of his own. He has lived on Culp Mountain the last several years where he ran a few head of cattle and enjoyed looking out across the white sands of the basin.

Funeral services will *be graveside at Pinetop Cemetery, Friday, September 5 at 2:00.*

As in the case of one who lives long, he had outlived most of his generation, but there were a few at the service. One of his many grandchildren drove Mecio Sanchez over from the Pecos; Lon Sims came down from Tularosa; a man named Hardy Mc-Ewal, whom Sophia had never met, came over from Las Vegas. He was very gracious, explaining how Zenas had given him his start in business years ago when he was just a lad. He could have added "and had nothing" but that was the common state of nearly everyone in those days.

Little Dee Harkey came over from Roswell, but no one knew what his relationship with Zenas had been. There were a multitude of younger people, friends of the children or kin on Sophia's side of the family. She caught a glimpse of two men standing aside from the crowd. One was Oliver Lee and someone said the other was Gene Rhodes, a man she had heard Zenas talk about, but had never met.

There were letters in the next few days, a card from the Albert Fall family and a nice letter from the widow of Charles Ilfeld from Farmington. There was even a note from Governor George Curry who had been Territorial Governor for a time. All these were a great comfort to Sophie and she kept them in a drawer with her Bible.

The boys bought her a little place in Pinetop and the old place was quiet. One day a car parked by the street and a man got out of the passenger's side door. He was tall and erect, a crop of white curly hair peeked out from under his wide-brimmed hat. It was Tom Washington, old Wayback, come to pay his respects. They sat on the porch and sipped lemonade and Tom told Sophie some of the experiences he had had with Daylight, some Sophie had heard and some she had not.

The Culp Mountain place was taken into the Fort Bliss Reservation and the proceeds helped Sophia remain independent. Publication of this book came after Zenas's passing and a generous portion of the proceeds from those earlier editions kept her comfortable until she passed away in 1947. She rests beside Zenas now.

ABOUT THE AUTHOR

James D. Crownover has been a student of the American westward migration for many years. Upon retirement from an engineering career, he has found time to write about the times. Inside every major event in history are hundreds of smaller events performed by men and women with little notice from the historian. The two-time Spur Award winner is convinced that these unnoticed people and the aggregate of their unnoticed labors are the essence of any great event in history.

These are the people he wants to recognize and write about.

The employees of Five Star Publishing hope you have enjoyed this book.

Our Five Star novels explore little-known chapters from America's history, stories told from unique perspectives that will entertain a broad range of readers.

Other Five Star books are available at your local library, bookstore, all major book distributors, and directly from Five Star/Gale.

Connect with Five Star Publishing

Visit us on Facebook:
https://www.facebook.com/FiveStarCengage

Email:
FiveStar@cengage.com

For information about titles and placing orders:
(800) 223-1244
gale.orders@cengage.com

To share your comments, write to us:
Five Star Publishing
Attn: Publisher
10 Water St., Suite 310
Waterville, ME 04901